Praise for Kem Nunn and THE DOGS OF WINTER

"Nunn has fashioned a darkly layered tale of people who are desperate to make their lives whole again. . . . [His] twisting plot and cliffhanger chapter endings carry the same cadences as an Elmore Leonard detective story. Nunn's strength as a writer comes out in his mood-setting descriptions of the rural North Coast, where, like the weather, the locals' behavior can be fickle to the extreme. With all the evil lurking out there in the dim light of the redwoods and frigid swells of the North Coast, THE DOGS OF WINTER qualifies as a surfing Gothic."

—Terry Rodgers, *The San Diego Union-Tribune*

"If Elmore Leonard and Cormac McCarthy had teamed up to write a surf novel, they might have produced THE DOGS OF WINTER. . . . Nunn does a masterful job of driving this . . . potboiler to its climax. . . . . By the time the sea foam clears, Nunn has added a modern-day adventure sport to the long list of literary confrontations between man and nature—a very twentieth-century version of a struggle once played out in tales of pioneering, exploration, and the harpooning of great white whales."

—Daniel Duane, *The Village Voice*

"Nunn has given us a book that anyone interested in the existential problems and terrors of modern life will want to read. . . . Nunn is a fine writer who knows just the right tricks for fusing physical action with mental turmoil. He also knows how to make a good plot, and he creates a number of credible and fascinating characters out of contemporary California culture."

—Alan Cheuse, *Chicago Tribune*

"Stunning. . . extraordinary . . . compelling, violent, and very American. . . . THE DOGS OF WINTER has enough story to keep a reader on the edge of his seat for days on end. . . . an amazing book."

—Alden Mudge, *BookPage*

"Like all great books, THE DOGS OF WINTER operates on several levels of meaning—along with the page-turning suspense. . . . Nunn trusts the tools of his trade above all else, and THE DOGS OF WINTER is his triumph and our treasure, a mature, ambitious, highly readable masterpiece."

—Jamie Agnew, *Agenda*

"Kem Nunn sets out to explore the consequences of failure, the demands of courage, and the healing powers of penance. That he stocks his tale with bruised heroes who munch Pop-Tarts and watch *Star Trek* makes his success that much more remarkable. This is a serious, richly satisfying novel . . . infused with sad wisdom."

—Steve Friedman, *GQ*

"Terrific. . . . And what a story it is: deftly, beautifully plotted. . . . Nunn has written something truly powerful; to say this book is about surfing is to say *The Sun Also Rises* is about bullfighting. He has made the sport a metaphor for life lived at its edges, at its most intense. This is a fine, strong novel; if there's justice in the world, it will give Nunn the reputation he deserves."

—Anthony Brandt, *Men's Journal*

Also by Kem Nunn

Pomona Queen*
Unassigned Territory
Tapping the Source

*Published by WASHINGTON SQUARE PRESS

KEM NUNN

THE DOGS OF WINTER

WASHINGTON SQUARE PRESS
PUBLISHED BY POCKET BOOKS

New York   London   Toronto   Sydney   Tokyo   Singapore

A Washington Square Press Publication of
POCKET BOOKS, a division of Simon & Schuster Inc.
1230 Avenue of the Americas, New York, NY 10020

Copyright © 1997 by Kem Nunn

Originally published in hardcover in 1997 by Scribner

All rights reserved, including the right to reproduce this book or portions thereof in any form whatsoever. For information address Scribner, 1230 Avenue of the Americas, New York, NY 10020

ISBN: 0-671-79334-9

First Washington Square Press trade paperback printing March 1998

10 9 8 7 6 5 4 3 2 1

WASHINGTON SQUARE PRESS and colophon are registered trademarks of Simon & Schuster Inc.

Cover design by Joe Perez
Cover photo by G. Motil/Westlight

Printed in the U.S.A.

This book is dedicated in memory of my good friend,

Michael Allen Caylor.

Long may he ride.

ACKNOWLEDGMENTS

The author wishes to thank the many people who gave of their time and expertise during the writing of this book. In particular, the author wishes to thank Larry "Da Hog" Mathews of the Northern California Indian Development Council, Steve Hawk and the crew at *Surfer* magazine, John McNaughton, Bill Barich, and Jane Rosenman, my editor of fifteen years.

CONTENTS

THE
DOGS
OF
WINTER

ONE

HEART ATTACKS

1

The first big swell came early that year, a gift before Christmas, wrapped in cloud. In downtown Huntington Beach, in Southern California, Jack Fletcher did what passed for sleep in a rented studio apartment and the phone call woke him. He had been into the beer and muscle relaxants again and it took him several moments to identify the caller. When he did, he recognized the voice as that of Michael Peters, publisher and editor of *Victory at Sea,* the oldest and most successful of the half dozen or so magazines devoted exclusively to the sport of surfing.

There was a considerable amount of background noise on the line and Fletcher concluded the man was calling from the condo the magazine kept near Sunset Point on the North Shore of Oahu where it appeared a party was in progress. It occurred to him as well that it was the call he had been waiting for. The recognition was accompanied by a slight quickening of the pulse.

"Here's the situation," Peters was saying. "The pot is up to twelve hundred dollars. R.J.'s already down six. There's a deuce and a jack of hearts showing. Should he pot it or pass?"

Fletcher righted himself on a lumpy futon. He drew a hand through his hair, then used it to massage the back of his neck. "What?" he asked.

"Come on," Peters told him. "We need a little advice here, Doc. Does he pot it or pass?"

Fletcher found that he could envision the party house quite clearly—the cluttered rooms, the empty beer bottles, the spent roaches, the boards propped in every available corner, the inevitable surfing video going largely unwatched upon some big-screen television, ensuring that whatever else was happening, regardless of the hour, there would always be waves. There would always be girls and golden sand and blue skies filled with light.

Seated in the darkness of his apartment, Fletcher felt himself quite taken by a wave of nostalgia, a kind of sorrow for his fall from grace. There had been good times over there, he thought—twenty seasons of trips to the islands. Twenty years of iron men and holy goofs. In the darkness of his room, he was suddenly more lonesome for their company than he would have thought possible.

"Okay," Fletcher said. "Give it to me one more time. The cards, I mean."

"A deuce and a jack."

"What the hell," Fletcher told him. "Pot it."

He could hear Peters talking to the others. "The doctor says pot it," Peters said. The words were greeted by a chorus of voices, a moment of silence, and finally an explosion of laughter, hoots, and catcalls.

"A deuce," Peters said. "He's down eighteen hundred bucks." The man's voice was full of pleasure.

"By the way," Peters continued, as if this were somehow incidental to the game. "The Bay broke today. Close out sets."

Without really thinking much about it, Fletcher found that he had risen from the futon, that he had begun to pace. It was happening more quickly than he would have imagined. Peters had first contacted him about the trip less than two months ago in mid-September. Neither man had expected anything like this so early in the season.

"I checked the buoy readings for you," Peters continued. "They're just beginning to show. Fifteen feet. Fifteen-second intervals. It should be coming up. I'm putting Jones and Martin on the red-eye to LAX."

Fletcher drew a hand over his face, the three-day stubble. "What time is it?" he asked.

"Ten o'clock."

"Here or there?"

Fletcher could hear Peters sigh, even with the bad connection. "Here," Peters said. "You'll have to figure your end out on your own. The way it stands now, you pick up Jones and Martin at the airport and drive straight through, you should hit it just about right."

"I got you," Fletcher said.

"I hope so," Peters told him. "You should have been on this already."

There was a moment of silence between the two men, and Fletcher could hear once more the din of voices issuing from across the sea. It sounded to him as if he heard someone say, "Just tell the dude not to blow it this time."

He supposed it was Robbie Jones. The boy had been one of the contestants at last year's Pipe Masters event. Lost in the throws of a major hangover, Fletcher had gone into the water only to shoot the finals with a roll of previously exposed film. It had proved his last gig for Peter's magazine, or any other for that matter.

"That was Robbie," Peters said. "He said to tell you not to blow it."

"Maybe he should tell me something else," Fletcher said. A portion of his desire for their company had died on the vine.

"What's that?"

"Maybe he should tell me what flight he's going to be on."

Peters laughed. "Yeah," he said. "I guess cab fare to Heart Attacks would be a bitch."

When Fletcher had the information he required, he returned the cordless to his machine. He set about flipping on lights and pulling on clothes. Dressed, he made up the futon and found his way to the kitchen. Unhappily the place was a litter of soiled dishes and empty bottles. Less than a year ago he'd had a wife to aid him in such matters. Now, in the aftermath of the divorce, his wife was living across town, in the company of his daughter, in the neatly manicured little bungalow Fletcher had purchased more than a decade ago in the last Orange County beach town where such a thing was still possible on something less than a six-figure income. And Fletcher was alone, doing his own dishes in a one-room apartment. A clock above the stove told him it was 3:00 A.M. A cooler man might have used the opportunity to grab another couple hours of sleep. Fletcher was no longer cool. He mixed a protein drink in his blender and used it to wash down a pill.

As a kind addendum to his failed marriage, Fletcher had managed to get himself bent on a sandbar in Mexico, on what should have been a routine session. His back had not been right since. It was a matter of some concern. When the X-rays and MRI failed to turn up anything, his doctor had spoken in vague terms of various arthritic conditions, suggesting that Fletcher see a rheumatologist. Fletcher had declined. Arthritic conditions did not figure into his deal with the universe. He saw instead an acupuncturist where twice a week he lay listening to the taped recordings of whale songs while a dark-eyed beauty rerouted his energy channels. Between visits he relied heavily on pills and beer. That Michael Peters should have called in mid-September, in the midst of such decline, to offer a plum like Drew Harmon and Heart Attacks had come as a bolt from the blue, a thing scarcely to be believed, for each was the stuff of legend.

One was the old lion, the holy ghost of professional surfing. The other was California's premier mysto wave, the last secret spot. They said you had to cross Indian land to get there—a rocky point somewhere south of the Oregon border where Heart Attacks was the name given to an outside reef—capable, on the right swell, of generating rideable waves in excess of thirty feet. There were no roads in. They said you risked your ass just to reach it. If the tide was wrong, or the swell of insufficient power, or not properly aligned with the coast, if there was poor visibility, due to fog or winds or heavy rains, or anything else that might prevent you from actually seeing the wave, you would never know whether you had reached it or not. If, on the other hand, one did find it, one risked one's ass all over again. The reef lay among some of the deepest offshore canyons in the northern Pacific, naked to every hateful thing above and below the water. Nor were the homeboys keen on visitors. At least one photographer Fletcher knew of had been badly beaten. Others had gotten in but come back empty, convinced it was a hoax. Still, the legend remained, kept alive by the occasional murky photograph, the tale told by someone more reliable than the average idiot, someone who claimed to have actually seen that outside reef work its cold, gray magic.

Photographs of the place were understandably rare. The ones Fletcher had seen were of a uniformly poor quality, shot from the hip, on the run, making any real estimation of wave quality difficult if not impossible. A chance for access with someone who knew the ropes would have been any surf photog's dream; that the guide should turn out to be Drew Harmon was so perfect it was almost a joke.

There was a time when you couldn't pick up a surfing magazine and not see Harmon's picture. World champ. Pipe master. One of the first to charge Hawaii's outer reefs. And then he was gone, walked on the whole deal. Some said he had run afoul of the law. Others said he had simply tired of the sport's growing commerciality, the consummate soul surfer gone off to surf big, soulful waves. A decade's worth of rumors floated in his wake. Recent photographs were as rare as those of Heart Attacks.

The last anyone in the surfing community had heard of him was that he had shown up in Costa Rica for a legends event, then pulled out before the contest. That was five years ago and he had not been heard from since. Not until September, when Michael Peters had picked up a phone to find Drew Harmon on the other end. The man was calling from Northern California and he had called to say that Heart Attacks was for real—a world-class big wave hidden among the rocks and fog banks, the recipient of Aleutian swells. He'd been surfing the place for the past two winters and he was ready for pictures. His only stipulation was that Jack Fletcher take them.

Peters had called Fletcher the following day, asking to meet at the Pier restaurant in downtown Huntington Beach. Fletcher's machine had taken the message. "Don't bother to call back," the message had said. "I'm gonna be there anyway. Just meet me in the bar. Five o'clock. I'm sure you can find the bar."

Had things been better, Fletcher might have blown the guy off. As it was, the month of September had found him beset by leering in-laws and moon-faced brides, shooting weddings as far inland as the Pomona Valley, the land of the powder blue tuxedo. He had accordingly, at precisely five o'clock on the following day, made his way to the Pier restaurant overlooking the graffitied boardwalk and polluted waters of his old hometown.

In fact, the meeting had not been especially cordial. Fletcher had found his former employer seated in the glow of a magnificently swollen sun, poised to descend behind the isthmus which bisected the northern quarter of Catalina Island. The scene was framed by the tinted rectangles of glass which formed the bar's western wall, and the room was filled with a dusty orange light.

Peters was a tall, heavily built man, roughly the same age as Fletcher. Both were in their early forties. Peters had lost most of his hair. What was left he wore pulled into a shiny black ponytail just long enough to dangle over the collar of his shirt. Fletcher considered this something of a bullshit hairdo, more appropriate for aging Hollywood types than former big-wave riders. As Peters rose to greet him, however, Fletcher was reminded that a big-wave rider was exactly what the man before him had been, that beneath the rounded edges there was still the man who'd ridden giant Waimea—in the old days, before wave runners, leashes, or helicopter rescues—then gone on to make enough money in the drug trade to buy his way into the good life. He was still, Fletcher supposed, somebody you wouldn't walk to fuck with.

"Dr. Fun," Peters said. He spoke without enthusiasm.

Fletcher seated himself at the bar, facing the beach. No one had called him Dr. Fun in a long time.

Peters sat down next to him. "How are you, Doc?"

"I'm okay."

Peters studied him for a moment. "I hate to tell you this," he said. "But you look like shit."

Fletcher had responded by ordering a drink.

"You still in the movie business?"

"Oh, you know. A snuff flick now and then."

Peters forced a laugh, leading Fletcher to conclude the man was probably a connoisseur. As for Peter's remark, it had been aimed at a recent project of Fletcher's, an off-beat little opus called *The Dogs of Winter*, a phrase generally reserved for big waves generated by winter storms. In Fletcher's movie, the doctor had trailed a pair of metal heads from one wave pool to another across the continental United States. In fact, Fletcher had been rather fond of the film. He'd thought it prophetic and funny, in a bleak sort of way. Others seemed to miss the point entirely, particularly those in the industry. Most, Fletcher believed, were pleased that it had failed, Michael Peters among them.

"Okay," Peters said. He sighed, tapping the bar with an empty bottle, allowing Fletcher to see that he intended to come right to the point. "I didn't get you down here to bullshit with you. I've got something and I need to know if you're up for it. I should add that it's more than you deserve."

"Intriguing."

"Manna from fucking heaven, that's what it is," Peters said. At which point, Peters had told him about Drew Harmon's call.

Fletcher's first impulse was to believe that he was being fucked with in some way. It was too good.

"Don't worry," Peters assured him. "I tried to talk him out of it. I told him you were out of the loop, that you had become a fuck-up, that I had half a dozen guys could do the job."

Fletcher decided the man looked just unhappy enough to be telling him the truth. The knowledge did something to the pit of his stomach, a sensation not to be had in the wedding chapels of Santa Ana.

"Jesus. I'm surprised he even remembers."

"Come on."

"So I shot him in the islands."

"No shit."

Fletcher had smiled then, giving in to the memories. For he had been young and innovative in those days, one of the first to experiment with poles and helmet rigs. He'd backdoored a peak behind Drew Harmon at Rocky Point once. Fifteen years ago, and the shot was still radical.

Peters had looked unhappily toward the beach, where a considerable number of gulls circled in a thickening orange light. "This isn't going to be easy," he said. "You know that. We get the place on the right swell, surfing it is one thing, getting good shots is something else. You get fog up there. You get rain. You get clouds. The light is shit. Harmon knows that too. That's why he asked for you. Radical conditions, a narrow window. You better have somebody who can get the shot. His problem is, he thinks you're still the one."

"What do you think?" Fletcher had asked him.

Peters had given him a hard look. "What I think don't count, Doc. He's the man on this one. But I'll tell you this. You go, we're all going to find out. We're going to find out if you're still the one or not."

And that was how they had left it, until this morning, until the coming of the swell.

Fletcher finished his protein drink. He added the soiled blender to the mess in the sink and went outside. It was the finding out that occupied his mind just now, standing at the side of the garage, searching for the proper key in the moonlight. He had begun to swim again, marking his progress by the number of lifeguard towers he could pass as he slogged along beyond the surfline, but his progress was slow and he had counted on several more weeks of preparation.

As he slid the key into the door, it occurred to him that not long ago he had stood in almost this same spot. His daughter had come for a visit. She'd brought a friend and the girls had played at being fairies, paper wings taped to their backs, clad like gypsies in a funky array of old slips, gaudy belts, and feathers. The friend owned a dog—a small brown-and-white terrier—and as Fletcher stood on the deck, he'd become aware of the children and dog racing around him in dizzying circles, and he had felt himself at the eye of something. In its midst, he had experienced only loss, a sense of dislocation. The feeling was an unnerving one and had haunted him for several days. It suggested, he decided, a continuum from which he was set apart, a failure of purpose.

Fletcher's gear was stowed in the garage, in a metal filing cabinet to which the owner had granted him access. It was gear he had not used in some time. The Gore-Tex stuff bags were dusty and the home of spiders. He brushed them off then wiped them with a towel. He pulled out the old waterproof housing he'd made himself, examining it by the dim overhead light that filled the garage.

The housing was composed of a bright orange plastic, its seams stripped with silver duct tape. It was, by any contemporary standard, too big and too heavy, but it had served him well and he had once made something of a name for himself by losing it at the Pipe on a huge day, then staying outside to dive for it on the reef where eventually he'd found it, lodged in a crevice among the coral. It had been his second winter in the islands, and he had needed the pictures to pay his bills. To have lost the camera would have blown his entire scene. Still, diving for it had been a rash act. It was a big day and beneath the surface there was no way to see what was coming. He could easily have been caught on the reef and stuffed into a crevice himself. But later, people seemed to remember what he had done.

He took out his old Nikon and his 230 mm lens, which was the largest he still owned. They were using 600s from the beaches now, with converters and automatic focus, and the camera did half the work. Fletcher believed a man should find his own focus, should be forced to pull the trigger himself. It was also true he hadn't the money to modernize his act. His, it seems, had gone for such items as doctors' bills, an acrimonious divorce, a failed movie. He supposed he'd had it coming, for his desultory ways. For that failure of perception which had allowed him to conceive of the extended party as a suitable response to life's trials. He had meant no harm. He had failed to compensate, was all.

When he'd laid out what he intended to take, he went back to the apartment. He took his heaviest wet suit from the closet. He took booties and gloves as well, then discovered that he had lost his hood. It was while he was looking for the hood that he found the book, a battered paperback with the ludicrous title: *A Wave Hunter's*

Guide to the Golden State. He'd picked it up years ago, thinking it might be good for a laugh, only to discover its authors had, in fact, worked their way from Oregon to the Mexican border with a thoroughness Fletcher had been compelled to admire. He sat with the book now on his futon, suddenly curious to see if the authors had managed any photographs of something that might pass for a world-class big wave in the northern reaches of the state.

The appropriate section was filled with small black-and-white photographs and Fletcher was treated to a monotonous parade of murky slate gray humps marching over slate gray seas toward slate gray rocks, set before slate gray skies. Disappointed, he turned to the text where, to his sharp delight, he found something of interest—a rumor, even then it seems, but the elements were accounted for.

"In a place where Northern California's most pristine and remote public lands meet with the reservations of the Yurok and Hupa Indians," the authors had written, they had picked up word of a long point capped by grasslands, around which huge waves had been known to wrap, exploding finally upon a deep, natural bay. The place was known to the locals as the Devil's Hoof, and they had gone in search of it.

They had approached from a campground to the north. Access was difficult. Fletcher could imagine them out there, a pair of hippies slogging through creek beds in baggy shorts and huarache sandals, coming at last to the coast only to find themselves nearly trapped upon a huge bolder field without exits.

A medium tide and small surf had permitted a northbound crossing where they had huddled for the night on a sandy beach at the base of steep cliffs. They had awakened to spectacular scenery and a flat ocean but had looked with a surfer's eye upon the configuration of land and sea, permitting their imaginations to run wild with what might have transpired there, had they hit it on another day. For they had indeed seen the grasslands capping an arm of land which formed the northern end of a great bay and around which a northern swell of sufficient size and power might push. "As yet unconfirmed," they admitted. "Definitely unridden and likely to remain so. Too big. Too cold. And too lonely."

"Still," they had crooned, in a riff appropriate to the age, "this is sacred wilderness. The path is treacherous and at times unmake-able. But if one perseveres, the magic of this land will be yours to appreciate. It is a place where native Americans lived in harmony with the land, long before the white men came. It is a land of the Great Spirit—the place where the wilderness meets the sea."

They had concluded with a last item of interest. It had to do with the nearest town, a small, logging community where they had stopped long enough to buy a tire for their bus. The name of the town was Sweet Home. It was the town Peters had named as their destination, the place from which Drew Harmon had made his call.

Fletcher had added the book to his gear and gone back to look-ing for his hood when the phone rang once more.

It was Michael Peters.

"They're off," Peters told him. "I put them on the plane myself."

"That goes without saying," Fletcher said. "You wanted them on the right plane."

"Lighten up," Peters told him. "Make believe you're still Dr. Fun."

"You know what Robbie Jones was doing the last time I saw him? He was head-butting some guy's car."

"I remember that. The Op Pro. The guy was checking out R.J.'s girlfriend, man. What do you want? He's an excitable boy."

"He's a moron. The only guy on the tour any dumber is Sonny Martin."

"You're just sore, 'cause he was needling you about blowing the finals last year. Anyway, I should point out to you that Mr. Jones has gotten religion. He's a new man."

"No."

"Born again."

"Christ, Martin too?"

"Are you kidding?"

"You're doing this to me," Fletcher said. "It's punishment for get-ting the gig."

"Forget it," Peters told him. "These guys are going. Besides, that's not why I called."

There was a moment of silence on the line. It occurred to Fletcher that Peters was probably on his car phone, alone upon that great red plateau of pineapples in the first light of a tropic sunrise.

"You know what they say about this place," Peters said. "It's not just the drop. They say it's got that old magic, the way the Bay had it, in the old days, before they turned it into a theme park."

"Maybe it's all that Indian land," Fletcher suggested. It suddenly felt to him as if some offering of peace was about to descend.

"Maybe so," Peters said. "Harmon's married now. You know that?"

"I hadn't heard. Who's the lucky girl?"

"Don't know. No one does, as near as I can tell. Last I heard the guy was living in Costa Rica. He calls from Northern California. Tells me he's married, that he's gotten himself a chunk of land . . ."

"That was probably how he got the land," Fletcher said. "He found himself an heiress."

"Half his age no doubt."

"With a large trust fund."

The men allowed themselves a moment of laughter.

"I ever tell you about that time in Biarritz? We're camping on the beach for two days, waiting on a swell. Finally we get it. I get up at dawn, look out. There it is, corduroy to the horizon. The sun is out. The wind is offshore. I hear something and I look up. A Mercedes wagon pulls up and stops. Door swings open. Out steps Drew Harmon. Man's wearing shades and an ankle-length fur coat. I can see this blonde sitting in the seat behind him. He's got at least four boards racked to the roof. He pulls one out. Pulls on a wet suit. Walks down. And rips. For about three hours. Never says a word. Just rips. He leaves and the wind turns around, starts blowing on shore. Half an hour later and the place is shit."

In fact, Fletcher had heard the Biarritz tale before. But then surfers did love their stories. Big waves and outlaws. Anybody who could grow old and stay in the life. Drew Harmon was all of those things.

"You remember when I took over the magazine?" Peters asked. "You remember what it looked like then? We changed all of that, Doc. You changed it. All that shit you shot from the water. That was heavy stuff. You set the standard, man. You upped the stakes . . ." The man paused, moved perhaps by his own rhetoric.

"What I'm trying to tell you," Peters said finally, "is that I'm pulling for you on this one. Sonny Martin's nothing new. But R.J. is. He's the real thing. You get Jones and Harmon, passing the torch in mysto California surf . . ." The man paused once more. "You can tell the newlyweds to go fuck themselves."

Fletcher had been off the phone for a full five minutes before it occurred to him that Michael Peters had just made reference to the weddings. He paused at that point in his packing. He looked with some wonder upon the first light. You lost your money. You fucked up your back. In the end, it was hard even to maintain one's front. In the end, they knew. In the end, they had you. He glanced at his watch. He stuffed the last of his gear into his bags and went with it into the alley where he had parked the old Dodge. As he did so, he was just in time to see a pair of egrets as they swept up from the remains of the Bolsa Chica wetlands where once his great-grandfather had come on horseback from Los Angeles to hunt with his friends. The birds passed almost directly above him, wing to wing, sleek prehistoric shadows before a tarnished silver sky.

2

Travis woke early to the sound of distant thunder. Checking his clock, he found it to be 4:00 A.M. He lay awake for some time, his hands clasped behind his head, listening to the waves. He began to think about the meeting of the tribal councils he'd promised to attend upon the coming evening. With the approaching season, tensions were running high on the river.

The federal government had recently divided the fishing rights on the Klamath. The Yuroks had the first twenty miles of the river, which included its mouth. The Hupas had the rest and believed themselves to have been short-changed. Between the commercial fishermen who fished the ocean, the Yuroks at the river's mouth, and the licensed sports fishermen loosed to fish anywhere they pleased, the Hupas' take was drastically reduced. As a consequence, some had been coming downriver anyway, fishing Yurok water. There had been incidents of violence. The government had empowered certain Indians to enforce the boundaries. It made for an ugly situation. Hence the meeting. The bad blood, however, ran deep and went way back and included transgressions, imagined and real, from a time before Travis was even born and thinking about it was enough to keep him awake, in the dark room, with the sound of the waves which might otherwise have put him to sleep.

At length, he got out of bed. He fixed a cup of coffee, dressed and went outside. He found the streets empty and wet with a frail light beginning to gnaw at the edges of the sky.

He crossed the street and walked along a narrow strip of land which skirted the bluff. The ocean thundered beneath him. A chunk of pale moon wandered off above the town of Sweet Home. Beyond the distant pier, he could see the masts of boats marking the harbor and in some interior place could hear their rigging like the mail of ghosts and heard as well the cries of circling gulls, though in point of fact, he could hear neither where he walked along the cliff for the sea was too loud here and even the birds had been driven away by its agitation.

He walked the wet strip of grass, coming in time to a half circle of stone and concrete where a single wind-bent tree held forth against the elements and found that he was not alone with the morning.

There was an old man there, bearded, bundled in a sailor's pea-coat, sporting yellow slickers and a Greek fishing cap, and when Travis caught sight of him, he smiled and went up beside the tree and the corrugated railing upon which the old man leaned.

"What's up, Pop?" Travis asked.

His father regarded him with a sideways glance.

"Waves get you out of bed?" the old man wanted to know.

Travis allowed that they had.

He leaned against the rail and for a moment neither man spoke. They watched the light collecting above the sea. The two sometimes met here. They lived only blocks apart but by some mutually agreed upon arrangement, neither ever dropped in on the other. They spoke on the phone, or met along the trail that skirted the cliff.

"Damn swells will muddy the water," the old man said.

Travis nodded.

His father had come to the town in the forties, at the end of the war. He had logged and fished and worked in the mills. He had married a Hupa woman. She had given him a son and two daughters and died of cancer at a premature age. One of Travis's sisters had died young as well, in a traffic accident. The other lived in San Francisco and neither man had much to do with her. Travis had come back to Sweet Home after college, alive with a sense of purpose. He'd come back married to an Irish Catholic girl he'd met at Berkeley. When that ended, he had married a Hupa woman—which union had gone only the better part of a year. Now he was alone, with two children by different mothers, in a shabby apartment with alimony and child support eating up two-thirds of what he made. To his father, married eighteen years to the same woman and faithful even to her memory, these follies did little to elevate Travis's stature. It wasn't that the old man rode his case. It was a look was all, a word here or there. Each man pretty well knew what the other thought. In point of fact, Travis was rather fond of the old man. As for his part, the old man would have to make do with the cold comfort of feeling superior to his only son. Travis would have had it otherwise, but things were what they were, and he imagined they would live with it.

"Give the fish something to eat," Travis said. He made reference to the debris stirred up by the storm.

"You say," his father said. The effects of weather upon the industry was a matter of debate between them.

The old man was some time in studying the horizon.

"Frank tells me he asked you to dance with them this year."

"He did," Travis said. In fact, he was somewhat nonplussed at having been asked and was unsure what to do about it.

"They want you to bring the beads."

"They do."

The beads had belonged to Travis's grandmother. She had been a shaman of some repute.

"You going to do it?"

"I don't know."

It was a ten-day affair. The Jump Dance. A ritual to make war on evil.

"Why not?"

Travis shrugged. To go would require fasting. A certain purity of thought. "I don't know if I'm up for it or not," he said.

The old man laughed at him.

"Frank seems to think you should do it."

"Frank's a preacher. He's looking for converts."

"Timing might not be so bad. You get them to invite the Yuroks, you go dance with them, you might get them to agree on something."

"I don't think it works that way."

"How does it work?"

"Sometimes I wonder."

The old man spit to the windward. "Lots of stiff-necked bastards, you ask me."

"Who's asking?"

The old man just looked at him.

"Walk up the street," Travis said. "I'll buy you a cup of coffee."

Travis and his father drank their coffee, sitting opposite one another on the brick planters which marked the entrance to the town's single strip-mall. For all the talking they did, they might have been a pair of founding fathers effigiated in stone and set before this mall which was itself a kind of monument, erected upon that wave of enthusiasm which had accompanied the coming of the state correctional facility to Scorpion Bay. The mall was home to a dozen businesses, one of them the office of the Northern California Indian Development Council and Travis's place of employment.

Travis watched as a pair of brothers, Bill and Tom Jenkins, parked in front of Ned's doughnut shop and got out of their truck. They were men Travis had gone to school with and on this morning they were up early, dressed for the river in hip boots and coveralls. Travis raised a hand. The brothers nodded in his direction. He watched them with some degree of melancholy. There was a time when they might have invited him along. A time when he might have accepted. Those days had passed. There was new money in Sweet Home. There were new tensions. There were also old wounds. It was the old wounds in which Travis had come to traffic and his life had grown more solitary in consequence.

He watched as the men left the shop and drove away. They had not gone more than a block before he heard honking. He believed he heard a man's voice as well, a catcall set before the morning. He turned to the sounds.

What he saw there was a woman. She was tall and willowy, and even from the distance at which he first saw her, he knew her to be Kendra Harmon. She was walking toward them along a gray sidewalk still damp from the night's rain, and with the passing of the truck, the crack of her boot heels was all that could be heard. She passed without a word and if she had recognized Travis, which well she might, Travis could not see it, as her eyes were covered by a pair of tiny, wire-rimmed dark glasses. She wore a ball cap as well, a black one, with her hair pulled out the hole in back and the bill pulled low over her face, as if there was someone from whom she was trying to hide.

Travis watched as she entered the mall. He saw her look about for a moment and then go up to the door of his office and peer inside.

"Friend of yours?" the old man asked.

Travis watched with some surprise. He could not imagine what she was doing there. "She's married to that surfer," he said. "The one that rides the big waves up by the Hoof."

"One that got bit."

Travis nodded. He had, on the occasion of Drew's taking possession of his inheritance, dined with them in their shack on the river.

It had been an odd evening, with Drew very much the mountain man in possession of his child bride. Travis had taken another man with him, a Yurok who owned land near the Harmons' and whom, Travis had concluded, it would be good for Drew to meet. What he remembered most about the evening now was Drew's complete disinterest in affairs relating to the reservation, together with what Travis had taken as a profound unhappiness on the part of his wife.

Kendra had been pregnant at the time. She had fixed a dinner of fish and vegetables. Travis had thought her pale and exotic and maybe just a little neurotic. Or, perhaps, he had decided, she was simply lonely in a new place without sunshine. She seemed pleased to have visitors, but soon after supper, Travis and the Yurok had been whisked by Drew to his workroom for a detailed rundown of his interests and inventions. The foremost of these were surfboards and old woods and he had spoken at great length of the Hawaiian Islands where he had been allowed to prowl among the archives of the Bishop Museum, making template drawings of ancient boards found in the caves of Hawaiian kings and which he seemed to believe were possessed of a kind of magic.

Eventually Travis had given up trying to turn the conversation toward matters pertaining to the neighbors with which Drew had surrounded himself. In the end he had gone home wasted on beer and Hawaiian buds, with a headful of Hawaiian magic and the distinct impression that the arrival of Drew and Kendra Harmon would not lead to happiness. Within a week, the girl had miscarried and Drew had been bitten by a shark.

The last he had heard of Kendra was that she had been seen walking deep in the woods at the side of the river in the dead of night. It was a matter of some talk on the reservation. The *kidongwe* roamed at night, his face painted black, armed with a weapon of human bone and sinew. Not something one would want to meet by the river in the hour of his strength—not, at any rate, if one believed in the old tales. But then the old tales were still taken seriously on the reservations. The black magic, in particular, was taken seriously, and it was a matter of some curiosity to Travis that this was so. For once, there had been a healing magic as well, and it puzzled him the black magic was what held sway in the minds of his people.

He watched now as the young woman continued to look into the glass. "I guess I should see what she wants," he said. He stood as he said it.

"You want some free advice?" the old man asked, for he had been watching the girl, and watching his son as well.

Travis just looked at him.

"Stay single. You can't afford another mistake."

Travis thought of responding, then thought better of it. He left the old man seated upon the planter and crossed the mall to his office.

The woman had her back to him but turned abruptly at his approach. She was still pale, he thought, and exotic in some way he found difficult to pin down—the product of a climate other than what the coast of Northern California had to offer. What he had forgotten, or somehow failed to notice, was exactly how attractive she was. The cap and glasses could not hide it. The whiteness of her skin was set in contrast to the black radiance of her hair. He watched as she raised a hand to touch the hollow of her throat with the tips of her fingers. The gesture recalled the impression left by their first meeting. It suggested a degree of excitability, an undercurrent of complications Travis found difficult to resist, though, in fact, he had followed such paths before and always to calamitous endings.

"You're Travis," she told him. "Kendra Harmon."

"I remember."

As if to further accentuate her coloring, she was dressed entirely in black—boots, jeans, and a blouse. Over these she wore a leather jacket several sizes too large. It was an outfit in which she might have passed for some long-legged teenager, though Travis supposed she was in her mid-twenties. "What can I do for you?" he asked.

"I was wondering," she said, "if we might talk."

In recent months, Travis had hired a secretary, a young Hupa woman by the name of Denice. She came in three days a week. Saturday was not one of them. In her absence the office was dark and empty and damp.

As Travis turned on lights, Kendra Harmon seated herself on an old couch beneath a bulletin board. The board was filled to overflowing with various fliers, handbills, and leaflets. The material spoke in elevated tones of everything from night classes in Native American Studies to stints in the armed services.

When he had brightened the place up as much as possible he seated himself on the edge of his desk. He discovered Mrs. Harmon examining the board at her back. She was turned in what Travis found to be a provocative pose—one which accentuated the aquiline profile, the long line of her neck, the faint movement of her pulse.

"Anyone from around here ever go to Kuwait?" she asked.

There was a poster on the board advertising jobs in the Middle East. "Never."

She turned to him. "Not one?"

"Not a single one."

"But it's such a nice poster."

Travis nodded. "Yeah, and it cost me ten bucks."

"That's too bad," she said.

He thought maybe she was joking with him, but if she was, he couldn't see it.

"You probably wonder why I'm here."

Travis shrugged. He noted for the first time that the cap she wore was embroidered above the bill with a silver skull and crossbones. The skull had tiny red dots for eyes and a toothy smile and it was something he had seen before. He had, if he was not mistaken, seen it worn by the previous owner of the trailer in which the Harmons now lived, a local girl recently murdered by an unemployed Hupa fisherman named Marvus Dove. The observation struck him as somewhat unsettling.

"Do you mind if I smoke?" she asked.

Travis handed her an ashtray from his desk.

Mrs. Harmon placed the ashtray near her foot. She took a pack of cigarettes from her jacket then sat with it in her hand. "Amanda left things," she said. "There were boxes in the workroom that came with the trailer." The words issued in a kind of staccato burst, as if she had been harboring them for some time.

Travis nodded. Amanda Jaffey was the name of the girl killed by Marvus Dove, and Travis concluded that he had been right about the cap. He noticed for the first time a tattoo on one of Kendra's fingers—her ring finger on her left hand. This puzzled him, for he thought the tattoo familiar and yet he could not recall having seen it there before.

"No one ever showed up to claim the things," Kendra said. "I wound up going through them. There were some clothes there, stuff I could use." She looked at the unopened pack of cigarettes. "I'd heard that Marvus Dove's family had hired a private detective. I was wondering if this was something he ought to know about."

"Marvus Dove is dead," Travis said at length. "Why would his family hire a detective?"

"I thought you might know. I remembered you had this office. I can't exactly ask around on my own. We're not liked there."

"Who told you they hired a private detective?" It was an absurd notion.

The girl shrugged. "Someone."

"A *wagay*. Not an Indian."

"*Wagays*. That's what you call us?"

"Some do."

"So why not an Indian?"

"Because an Indian wouldn't hire a private cop for a dead Indian. They probably wouldn't hire one for a live Indian."

"What would they hire?"

"A *hee-dee*, maybe. If they hired anybody."

"What's a *hee-dee?*"

Travis smiled. *Hee-dee* was a word he'd heard his father use. He was not sure where it came from. "Someone adept at the black magic," he told her. "If they thought Marvus had been innocent, they might hire a *hee-dee*. See if the medicine man could figure out who did it, put a curse on them."

"I see," she said.

He watched as she shifted her weight on the couch. The sunlight sliced across the floor and fell upon her boots. They were simple black cowboy boots and he wondered if they had belonged to the dead girl as well.

"So what about this *hee-dee?* You think he might want to look through her things?"

Travis placed his hands on his desk top, palms flat on either side of his legs. "I'm sure he would. But then I happen to know that Marvus's boys need a new engine for their boat." He paused, looking for some reaction, though with her eyes hidden behind the ridiculous glasses, he felt himself to be addressing the grinning skull on her cap. "I would hate," he said finally, "to see them throw their money away on false hopes."

"Does this mean that you know who they hired, but you won't tell me?"

He could see that she was quick to anger. Unhappily it did not serve to make her any less attractive.

"Marvus is dead."

"I know that."

"They caught him in Neah Heads with blood on his caulk boots, and he hanged himself in the jail."

The girl was silent.

"What good is it going to do his family to pay for a curse?"

"What if Marvus Dove didn't do it?" the girl asked. "Maybe this person could look at these things. Maybe they would know . . . Maybe they would see things . . ."

The Hupa had a particular word. *Oo-ma-ha*. It was not easily translated. It meant something like "beware," but carried with it a dimension of time. Beware now, here and now, of this place, of this thing. He had grown up with that word. It was considered applicable to the river which was shifting and treacherous, the claimant of many lives. It occurred to him quite suddenly that the presence of Kendra Harmon now called forth that word as well.

"The Doves are poor," Travis said finally. "They should spend their money on the engine."

"I see." She returned the cigarettes to her pocket. The ashtray remained at her feet, unused. "You're an unbeliever then."

Travis laughed. "Let me tell you something," he said. "I believe this. I believe that if I were you, I wouldn't go walking by the river at night." He was finding that he did not want to talk anymore about Marvus Dove. Nor, he decided, much to his chagrin, did he want her to leave. The office would go empty without her.

"Is there some reason why I shouldn't?"

"Some would say it isn't safe."

"Someone says that about everything."

"You might meet your *hee-dee*."

"Why should that bother me, if they're all frauds?"

"Let me put it this way," Travis said. "The point is not so much that they are frauds or not frauds. I mean we're talking about stuff that's been around for hundreds of years. I think there are a few that are truly adept, practitioners of the old arts. Others . . ." He spread his hands as if to dismiss them. "The thing is this. The black art is not a healing art. To even be interested in it requires a certain kind of person." He stopped once more, watching her. "Even if you could know for sure that the Doves had hired such a person. Even if you could find that person, which I doubt you could, you would not be welcomed as a friend."

She exhaled then and it seemed to him as if some spark had gone out of her. "Of course you're right," she said. "It was crazy, wasn't it, a crazy idea . . ."

He smiled. Her sudden vulnerability had taken him off guard. "I can tell you what to do if you ever meet a person like that," he offered.

"A *hee-dee?*"

"They would probably not identify themselves to you in that way."

"And what would I do?"

"You would have to show that your magic is stronger than his."

She seemed to give this a moment's thought.

"Tell me," she asked. "Is it always a him?"

"If you believe the old stories. The *hee-dees* were usually men, although they could change their shapes into bears or wolves. Their opposites were the shamans. Among the Hupa, the shamans were often women."

"Could they change their shapes as well?"

"I don't know."

"So tell me what you do know."

Travis rose and went to a series of bookshelves which lined the wall behind his desk. They were simple shelves, pine slats set upon concrete blocks. It took him a moment to find what he was after— *Indian Legends of the Pacific Northwest,* and Power's *Tribes of California.* The latter was considered something of a classic.

"What I know's in here," he told her.

As she took the books, their fingers touched.

"Thank you," she said. She seemed genuinely pleased. "I will read them and get them back to you."

It was of course what he'd had in mind. "There's no hurry," he told her.

"Someone else might want them."

"The ones that should never do." In fact, he had been here nine years and she was his first borrower.

"Oh," she said. "Well, I'm a fast reader, anyway." She looked at the books. "Have you ever met one?" she asked.

He was momentarily at a loss.

"You said there were a few who were truly adept. I just wondered, have you ever known one?"

"I've met some that thought they were."

"I mean the real thing," she said. "Someone you believed in."

"My grandmother was supposed to have been a shaman," Travis told her. "She died when I was very young, so I never really knew her. When I was a little older, I got to know a friend of hers, a woman by the name of Rose Hudson. If you thought a *hee-dee* had put something on you, Rose Hudson was the kind of person you might go to. She could see if they had or not. If they had, she had the power to do something about it. At least that was what people thought . . . But I would say, if anyone was the real thing, she was. She had a way of looking at you. Used to spook me sometimes."

"Is she still alive?"

"No. She died a couple of years ago."

The girl looked disappointed.

"She lived up the coast. You know the Heads?"

"Fairly well, actually. Drew and I used to go up there when we first moved here. Drew was looking for a spot he'd heard of. I discovered that little river valley. Drew would surf. I would hike along the river. One day I came upon this burned-out trailer and got chased by two pit bulls. I never went back."

Travis laughed at her. "Lucky you didn't get eaten," he said.

"It seems much funnier now."

Travis nodded. "That might've been Rose's place," he said. "There's only been two or three families ever lived up there. Most of 'em crankster gangsters."

"Crankster gangsters?"

"You know. A little meth lab, a little pot field . . ."

"You have names for everybody, don't you?" She gave him an odd little smile then, almost mischievous, the hint of a secret self. "So tell me," she asked. "What do you call yourself?"

Travis was a moment in responding. Unhappily, he was a moment too long. He watched as she tucked the books beneath her arm and made for the mall. Framed by an aluminum door jamb she faced him once more. "Thank you for the books," she said.

He saw her disappear into the fragile winter light. He did this with some regret. The little smile seemed to linger, a ghost of itself, like the cry of a bird one hears in the night.

When he had waited what he thought to be a reasonable amount of time, he closed the office and went outside. The wind had kicked in off the ocean, breaking up the clouds, driving them from the sky.

He found the morning awash in light. He checked the planter to make sure the old man had not stuck around, and found that he had not. In his absence, Travis passed through the town alone, coming finally to the bluffs overlooking the sea.

There were a pair of surfers out at the cove that formed the town's main beach. The waves were windblown and confused and the surfers did not seem to be getting many rides, but he found that the sight of them reminded him of Drew Harmon. Travis understood he was something of a legend, another order of being, apparently, from the boys bobbing in the icy slop of the cove.

The man had not been on the river a week after Travis's visit when there was an incident, somebody using his beach to launch boats. There had been words. Drew had roughed up a couple of men, Hupas come down river to fish Yurok waters. It was a dangerous thing to have done and Travis had spoken to him about it. In the process, he had made a last attempt to educate the man as to the politics of the reservation. But Drew had brushed the incident aside.

"It wasn't much," Harmon had told him. "Guys got out of line. I slapped 'em around a little." At which point he had held up his hands for Travis to see. "I didn't hit 'em. Not with my fists. I just slapped 'em." Of the men in question, one had required hospitalization.

Travis looked once more into the windblown cove where the two rubber-clad figures continued to struggle against the chop. Surely, he thought, there were more sensible places to surf. One would have thought the Harmons might have sold their inheritance and gone back to the islands. Perhaps things would have gone better for them in the sunshine. At which point it occurred to him why Kendra's tattoo had seemed familiar. The murdered girl, Amanda Jaffey, had one just like it. He would have to check with someone to verify this, but he was almost certain of it. The recognition settled upon him as might a cloud. Perhaps what he had taken as a mild neurosis was, in fact, a good deal more. Perhaps she was mad, he thought. He had already concluded something of the same with respect to her husband. Perhaps they were mad together. Maybe that was what they did, in their trailer on the river.

If so, Travis thought, he resented their madness. For it interfered with the things that he had come here to do. He didn't need Drew Harmon slapping around the locals any more than he needed the federal government fucking with the fishing rights on the river, or Kendra Harmon, wandering the woods in a dead girl's clothes, making inquiries about *hee-dees* and private investigators. What he resented most, however, when all was said and done, was that even in light of such premonitions and resentments, he could not quite drive the ivory-skinned Mrs. Harmon from his mind, leading to his final conclusion that perhaps he was as mad as they were. Boredom and isolation had driven him to it, this unhappy positioning of himself between the worlds and he looked once more to the sea and to the north wind which had driven away the clouds. Very soon now and the winds would be out of the north each day, and with them would come the rains. The forests would grow dark along the banks of the river. The big winter swells would turn the cove beneath him into one great cauldron of churning white water. And Drew Harmon, perhaps, would ride the giant waves that broke a mile from shore along a remote strip of ceremonial land the Indians called Humaliwu, the place of the big water, the place where legends die.

It was a matter of some speculation among the locals. The man had been bitten there in the early spring. It was not clear if he would ride the big water again. Some were afraid that if he did, and did so consistently, others would follow, and the Indians would not only have the fisherman and one another to contend with, they would have the *wagay* in wet suits with jeeps and surfboards as well. But Travis had seen the big water. And he knew something of the land which surrounded it. *Oo-ma-ha,* to any who went there, Drew Harmon and his spooky wife among them, and he comforted himself in the belief that there would not be many takers.

3

The flight Fletcher expected to meet was due in at eight fifty-five. Eight fifty found him still inching along Century Boulevard on the last leg to LAX. It was a particularly ugly morning, vintage L.A., the sky thick with coastal haze and smog, the color of dirty concrete. Fletcher gazed upon it with some mixture of wonder and disgust as a steady stream of jets thundered above him—one of them no doubt bearing his charges from the islands.

The plan was relatively simple. What Heart Attacks required was a strong northern swell, of the variety that had made the North Shore of Oahu famous, and, in fact, they had selected Waimea Bay as one of their indicators. The Bay went off, Heart Attacks should follow, in approximately forty-eight hours. Theoretically, a man could surf the same swell in both locations. Sonny Martin and Robbie Jones would attempt it. It was Fletcher's job to meet their flight and get them to Sweet Home where they would connect with Drew Harmon.

Fletcher still found it hard to believe that Drew Harmon would agree to such company. For that matter, it was hard to believe that Drew Harmon had asked for pictures. The man had, after all, been down that road before and Fletcher would have thought him done with it. When he had voiced this concern to Michael Peters, the man had shrugged it off. "Drew Harmon and Heart Attacks," he'd said. "What was I supposed to do, say no thanks?"

Fletcher supposed this would have to be his position as well. What Harmon wanted with pictures was his business. Fletcher knew quite well what he wanted. A good spread and a good story. And though he had needled Peters over his choice of pros, Robbie Jones was, in fact, a smart move. They were lucky enough to get good surf, having sufficient talent in the water would prove critical to what Fletcher was after. There was little doubt Robbie would be up to it. As for Harmon, no one had seen him surf in more than a decade. He was certainly too old for the slash-and-burn antics of the pro tour. In big waves, however, strength and experience might make up for speed and flexibility. And if both men surfed well, it was like Peters had said—the young charger and the old lion, in mysto California surf. For Fletcher, it was the stuff of new beginnings. With luck, he might even get himself back on a masthead. There would be a monthly retainer. A salary. He had certainly been there before. And he would play it a little smarter this time around. He promised. He made a pact with the concrete-colored sky. He was a grown man and he intended to comport himself as such. And come the winter, he would go to the islands. He would get himself a pair of baggy shorts and a straw hat. He would get one of those big 600s and he would shoot from the beach. And in between sets he would chat with the other photogs lined up on the sand and in the evenings he would play some cards and smoke a little weed and retire early. No more off-beat commentaries on the sport's demise. No more dumb moves. It was so simple, really, a small thing for which to ask.

Once inside the airport, Fletcher parked in one of the outside lots and hurried on foot toward the terminal. Checking the first screen he came to, he found the plane already down and went directly to baggage claim. The first thing he saw upon entering the room were the boards. Two bright blue hard-shelled traveling cases, long enough to suggest guns, stood propped against a concrete pillar not far from the luggage carousel.

He soon picked out his charges as well. They were standing with their backs to him, dressed as if from the islands, in sandals and baggy plaid shorts and sweatshirts much like Fletcher's own. Robbie Jones seemed recently to have shaved his head and the foolish thing, tanned by a tropic sun, shone like an acorn in the muted florescent light. Sonny Martin stood beside him, his shaggy yellow hair gone white at the ends falling to his shoulders.

It was Sonny who saw him first, turning to check Fletcher out with a pair of slightly bloodshot eyes Fletcher found emblematic of an entire generation—cool and dead and knowing, void of compassion; although it occurred to him as he approached the carousel that perhaps he was being too hard on the boy. They would, after all, be spending the next week or two together. Who could say? Perhaps they would even bond in the cold waters of the Pacific.

Sonny offered a limp handshake. Robbie Jones nodded, then turned to pull a brightly colored nylon stuff bag from the carousel.

"Check it out," Sonny said, his hand falling loosely to his side as he nodded in the direction of Robbie Jones. "Dude's had a tough flight, man. Found his ex dancin' at the Staide."

"Give it a rest," Jones told him.

Sonny laughed and shook his head. "Chick was up there big as life, showin' her snatch to some Japanese tourists. Peters kept trying to get her to come down to our end of the bar, but she knew it was us and wouldn't do it. Peters was gonna give her a quarter to pick up with her cunt."

Robbie Jones had managed to shoulder his gear. He moved with the stuff between Fletcher and Martin, addressing himself to Martin. "I said give it a rest." He was the taller of the two surfers. In fact, Fletcher was somewhat surprised by his size. His most vivid recollection of the boy dated to the contest in Huntington Beach, the headbutting incident in the parking lot. The picture etched in Fletcher's mind was that of a skinny white kid with shaved sideburns wobbling around like some Arkansas service boy high on crank, one step removed from mental retardation and born to be bad. The youth now before him had filled out through the shoulders, acquired a suntan and an earring, and would not, Fletcher believed, have passed for one of the few and the proud. His progress, however, did little to invite optimism regarding the week to come. It was, Fletcher feared, going to be a long one, and he hoped that the storm indicators were right on, that they would not get weather with it, that he would be able to get the shot and get out. A kind of nightmare scenario presented itself: the weather no good for shooting, but another swell on the way. Days spent waiting out the rain in some crummy motel while Sonny Martin talked about girls picking up quarters with their cunts. For the present, however, Robbie seemed to have shut Martin up. Fletcher helped them with the gear and they exited the baggage claim area in silence.

"So how were the islands?" Fletcher asked them. They had come to a red light in front of the terminal. Cars crisscrossed before them. Horns blared. The air was heavy with the stench of traffic.

"They were the islands," Robbie said.

Fletcher led them to his van. He put down the board case he was carrying and opened the rear doors.

"Whose ride?" Sonny asked.

Fletcher told them it was his.

"That's too bad," Sonny said. "If we had a rental we coulda rolled it."

"This one looks like it already has been," Robbie said. "A couple of times."

Fletcher just looked at them. "It'll get us there," he said. It was his plan to head up Interstate 5, then cut over to the coast at Redding. He figured they were looking at anywhere from twelve to fourteen hours. He was assuming they would crash with the Harmons. By this time tomorrow morning, he might well be holding a world-class big wave in the viewfinder, looking for his shot. The prospect was enough to generate a few butterflies.

Across the sidewalk from where they stood an airport shuttle bus pulled away from a loading zone, depositing in its wake a pall of churning black smoke that spread quickly to envelope a pair of elderly white women standing at the curb.

Sonny Martin watched as the bus drove away, then turned, fixing his companions with a glazed smile. "Bitches got dusted," he said. "By exhaust."

"I got shotgun," R.J. told him.

The drive from Los Angeles into California's endless midsection was in fact less painful than Fletcher might have imagined. His companions, spent from a night of cards and strippers and out of blow, went to sleep in a way that reminded Fletcher of the way his daughter had slept on drives with him and his wife. Martin crawled into the back with the board bags and gear and was not heard from for two hundred miles. Robbie Jones put his bare feet on the dashboard, his head against the side window. He drooled and snored but was otherwise silent, leaving Fletcher to contemplate the endless miles of farms and cow pastures and John Deere bailers casting unknown chaff upon the prevailing westerly winds, very much by his lonesome. In fact, there was not a word exchanged between them from Los Angeles almost to Sacramento, where Robbie Jones awoke with a pained look on his tanned face and announced it was time to clean out his dick. Also he had to take a leak.

Fletcher himself was hungry and made for the first restaurant he saw, an Anderson's split-pea soup joint—a goofy concoction of rock and wood complete with pillars and steeples from which brightly colored flags snapped in a stiff, brassy wind above a parking lot filled with cars, minivans, RVs, and assorted citizens in tractor hats and jeans.

Robbie Jones pulled a backpack out from beneath his feet and began to rummage in it as the van bumped up the drive and rolled into the lot.

"What do you mean wash out your dick?" Fletcher asked. His curiosity had gotten the better of him.

Sonny groaned from among the board bags and camera gear. "Oh, man," he said. "Wait till you see what this dude did to himself."

Fletcher got a look at what Robbie had done to himself in the bathroom of Anderson's, as did any number of horrified citizens. The guy had had his unit pierced. A golden penis stud protruded from the organ, right to left, exiting bloody holes on either side which oozed with some unholy combination of water, blood, and pus.

Robbie took his act to a sink where he proceeded to clean himself with some sort of antiseptic wash. A pair of teenage kids stopped to gawk at it until a paunchy-looking guy in aviator shades and a tractor hat said, "Jesus Christ," and ushered them out.

Fletcher himself viewed the operation with a kind of horrified fascination.

"Fool had to sign a waiver when he had it done," Martin told him. "The thing never works again, he can't sue."

"When does he get to find out?" Fletcher asked.

"Check this," Martin said. "The fucker can't have sexual intercourse for nine months." The kid laughed and shook his head, as if the idea were unimaginable. Fletcher feigned incredulity as well, but, in fact, the idea was not unimaginable at all. He had about a six-month run of celibacy going himself, though it was not something he would have ever admitted to the likes of Sonny Martin.

"Women weaken legs," Robbie Jones said. He stuffed the bloody organ into his pants, and swaggered out of the bathroom in search of food.

Half an hour later saw Martin and Jones well into a serious soup-eating contest. They had discovered "The Traveler's Special"—burgers and all the split-pea soup one could guzzle. They were currently on bowl number seven, with no end in sight and the waitress getting nastier by the bowl.

The waitress was a plump blonde with glasses and the kind of beehive hairdo Fletcher had not seen in his end of the state in fifteen years. At bowl number eight, she ventured to tell Robbie Jones that he reminded her of Beltar, the cone-headed alien from the *Saturday Night Live* television show.

"She means the one into mass consumption," Martin said. He turned his bloodshot eyes on the waitress, wiped a trail of split-pea soup from his chin, and grinned.

The waitress placed a hand on her ample hip. "That's the one," she said.

"Hey, baby," Robbie Jones said. He said it without looking up, still focused on the bowl of soup before him. "I did it for your precious love."

The waitress grimaced and started away.

"Oh, hey." It was Sonny Martin who called to her. "Miss. You want to bring us some more of those crackers? These are all gone." He held up a small wicker basket from which a few crumbs tumbled to the tabletop.

The waitress kept walking, her nylons rubbing together with an audible swishing noise which brought a smile to the face of Sonny Martin.

Fletcher addressed his food.

"So, Doctor," Sonny said. "Did Harmon really throw some bouncer out of the Biltmore in Waikiki?"

It was the first any of them had spoken directly of either Drew Harmon or the wave they intended to ride. Fletcher looked at the youth seated opposite him in the green Naugahyde booth. "He did," Fletcher said.

Sonny looked at him with some wonder. "That fucker's what, twelve, fifteen stories . . ."

"Actually, he didn't throw the guy off the top."

"I thought it was the observation lounge."

"They called it that. It was really just this patio area off to one side."

Sonny looked disappointed.

"The thing was still a couple of stories up there," Fletcher pointed out. "There was a pool below it and Harmon managed to hit the thing with him."

But the light had gone out of Sonny's eyes and he'd gone back to his soup. Fletcher supposed that anything short of twelve stories would simply not suffice. The kid had seen too many movies. He had become a sophisticate.

"I saw that guy in the water once," Robbie said. "It was about my first trip to the islands. He was still there. It was the year he rode Himalayas for the first time. He was paddling in from some place. I don't even know where. The Bay was happening and he had been out someplace else and he was paddling back in. He went for this wave and some guy snaked him. Didn't know who it was, I guess."

"Wha'd he do?" Sonny asked.

"He waited for the guy to paddle back out, knocked the fucker off his board, and broke off all the guy's fins with the heel of his hand."

Sonny Martin laughed. "All-right!" he said.

Robbie Jones chewed thoughtfully on the last of his burger, then addressed himself to Fletcher. "How you gonna shoot this place?" he asked.

"Harmon told Peters there would be a boat."

"What kind of boat?" Sonny asked.

"Peters didn't say. He just said there would be a boat."

"Yeah, well, that would be okay with me," Sonny said. He looked at Robbie.

"Be okay with me too. But I'm not so sure you can believe the fucker."

"Why's that?"

" 'Cause Harmon's known as something of a bullshit artist, isn't he?" The boy was looking at Fletcher.

"He's been known to fuck with people now and then. But I would suggest you don't say that to his face."

Robbie sneered at him around a mouthful of food. "There's not a boat, you're in deep shit, aren't you, Doc?"

In truth, that was exactly what he was in, but he was reluctant to discuss it with Robbie Jones. "No boat, I'll have to paddle out and shoot it from a board."

"Tricky," Robbie said. "You gonna double check your film this time?"

"Don't worry," Fletcher told him. "I got you covered." At which point he left them to their gruel and went outside. He made for a phone booth he'd seen in the parking lot.

A stiff wind whipped at his clothing. It came as a welcome relief after the murky restaurant with its stench of recycled air and fried foods. He found the sun already in the western half of the sky, the shadows lengthening upon the asphalt, the cars aglow in reflected light.

He stood in the booth which was open on one side. He stood with the wind in his face and dialed the harbor patrol in Crescent City. The outside buoys, he was told, were showing at seventeen feet with fifteen-second intervals. Small-craft warnings had been posted from the mouth of the sound to Mendocino Point. It was going to be a big one, and it was on the way.

Having little desire to return to the restaurant, Fletcher elected to wait out the soup-eating contest in the van. He swallowed a pill and got out his old road atlas, opening it to a map of Northern California. One could see at once why the place they sought had proven so elusive over the years, for it was situated somewhere at the edge of a large extant of land which swept gracefully into the Pacific. The northern reaches of this expanse were colored in green to indicate national parkland. Much of the coast, beginning in the north at a point called Neah Heads, was colored in pink, as were the banks of the big river which spilled into the sea near the southern end, and these were named as three distinct reservations—the Hupa, the Yurok, and the Tolowan. As for the rest of it, there were simply great expanses of white—public lands, uncut by roads, empty save for the two black dots near the southern end, south of the big river. Of these, one was the state correctional facility at Scorpion Bay, the other, the tiny town of Sweet Home.

The face which this piece of land presented to the sea was craggy and broken. The possibilities for surf were obvious. Most inviting, however, was a long, narrow point ending in something resembling a foot. It was the westernmost tip of the westernmost section of coast the state of California had to offer. A wide, natural bay ran back along the instep of the foot, and one might well imagine a large north swell hitting somewhere along the heel then running down the sole to break upon the bay. Fletcher took this configuration as what his book had called the Devil's Hoof, though on the map it was named as Humaliwu and colored in pink.

The town of Sweet Home maintained its lonely vigil over this land from the edge of a small harbor situated very near the mouth of the Klamath River but some miles south of the long point. All in all, it seemed to Fletcher a wild and lonesome enough place, home no doubt to eccentric pot farmers and Big Foot, the beast. And now home to Drew Harmon as well, if the man was not just fucking with them, if there was really a wave there to interest him. If there was, Fletcher sincerely hoped that he'd found a boat to go with it.

Fletcher had put away the map and was checking his film when Sonny Martin and Robbie Jones exited the restaurant.

"Thirteen bowls," Martin said.

"Two full cartons of soda crackers," Jones added.

"Only one drawback," Fletcher pointed out.

"What's tha...

...will... ...s."

...ked at him.

...bbie Jones said, "is the stuff will make you

...one of his glazed smiles. "No way," he

...already behind the wheel when Sonny

..."Yo, Doctor," Sonny said. "Looks like

...an."

...that he had not heard this correctly. H... ...oked into his side mirror. He could see both of them back there. Robbie had gotten to his knees and Fletcher could see the boy's bald head pointed in his direction like some giant, flesh-colored dildo.

"He's right," Robbie called. "Shit. I knew we shoulda had a rental."

Fletcher got out and looked beneath the old Dodge. What he saw was a huge puddle of water from which a tributary of modest proportions ran a short distance to the right before dribbling into some kind of drain. Had the lot been angled in the opposite direction, Fletcher might have seen the water when he walked out of the restaurant. Not that it would have made much difference. He would have been spared the boy's commentary, was all.

At last, Fletcher straightened and looked around. There was a Union 76 station about a quarter mile away, near the freeway on-ramp. With luck, the van would need nothing more than a hose, the station would have one. He said as much to the boys. Sonny was already in the back, supine on a board bag. Robbie had gotten a wrist rocket from one of his packs and was looking around for something to shoot. "Yeah, right," he said.

Fletcher started toward the station. He went among the more fortunate vehicles of the other patrons, past gleaming Winnebagos and Kings of the Road replete with radar screens and television antennas and lawn chairs and bicycles strapped to their roofs. He passed an outdoor fruit stand where snow birds dressed for golf clamored for fresh strawberries and the scent of newly picked peaches was heavy on the fall air. It was an uphill walk, and he moved as if on a collision course with an enormous sun before whose face a patchwork of vaporous cloud had already begun to spread. The clouds rose from the coastal range that skirted the freeway to the west. They spilled over the crests of the ridges and sank among the canyons and lent blue shadows to the folds of the hills, where Fletcher took them as some advance column of the storm they had come to track.

4

Between her seventh and tenth years, Kendra's father had taken her to seances and there were times when she believed that she had picked up something at one of them. It occurred to her, on the morning in question, that the something was in the room with her. The realization startled her and she woke from an unsound sleep. Upon waking she found it gone. There was only a troubling shadow across one part of the room that she did not care to look at, and not till the shadow had dissipated entirely, she knew from experience, would she feel it safe to get out of bed.

She was still waiting it out when the telephone began to ring. She rose with some trepidation. The shadow retreated before her, gathered itself into a small dark place at that point where the walls and floor all joined, and remained there, a stain upon the morning. Kendra lifted the receiver and placed it to her ear.

"Jesus H. Christ, don't tell me, you're sleeping days again."

Kendra recognized the voice as that of Pam, the cook from Cassady's. Pam was one of the few people with whom Kendra had become friendly since moving to Sweet Home. Pam was a part-time cook, a part-time bluegrass musician, a dart enthusiast, and a New Age witch.

Kendra looked at her clock. To her dismay she found that it was two o'clock in the afternoon. "Apparently," she said. In fact, she had spent the night with Travis's books, with sorcerers and shamans, and retired with the dawn. She could hear the other woman laughing. Kendra stared from the small window above the sink in her kitchen. Beyond it lay the fog, making even the potted plants on the deck difficult to see. Beyond the deck were the trees. But she could not really see the trees. Just a dark place in the fog. The sight of the afternoon displeased her and she looked away.

"Well," Pam said, "I guess maybe I don't blame you. I lived in the death coach, I would probably stay up all night and sleep all day too."

"You've already got the stay-up-all-night part down."

Pam whinnied, then coughed loudly into the phone. "You got that right," she said.

Kendra said nothing. She looked once more into the fog. Upon reflection, she supposed Pam was calling to tell her about her gig at Bodine's.

"So," Pam said. "You going to be at Bodine's tomorrow? Or are you going to sit up all night and pitch the cork for the cat?"

Kendra tried for a moment to think of something clever to say, but nothing came to mind. In the end she simply said she would be there. "Be there or be square," Pam told her.

When Kendra had replaced the phone she went rather unsteadily to the sink. Drawing water for tea, she saw the note Drew had left for her the day before, reminding her to get butane for the trailer. They were already on the last tank and the little red flag at the top indicating the tank was nearly empty had begun to show two days ago. The note was damp and stained and stuck to the drain board, almost lost amid the clutter of soiled dishes.

Above the sink, she saw that Drew had taped one of his weather charts to a cabinet door. She found the charts unreadable, a grid of swirling lines and tiny numbers. Drew cut them from the paper. He often photocopied them and made marks on them. The one before her had a series of small red lines drawn across the humps of several isobars. At least she thought they were isobars. One could never be sure. She could, however, interpret the red marks. The marks meant Drew had found something to interest him. They meant he was tracking a storm. It might mean that they would have company as well, for she knew that Drew had been talking to some people from a magazine. There were going to be visitors, a photographer, professional surfers. Kendra found the whole thing vaguely distasteful.

When she had finished with the tea, she pulled a leather jacket over the clothes she had slept in and went outside to see about the tanks. There were two of them. They were short and fat and had been painted to look like giant ladybugs. It was the work of the trailer's former tenant, the one murdered by Marvus Dove. The two had apparently quarreled behind a bar. Marvus was believed to have followed her home, cut her throat ear to ear with a rigging knife, and left her to bleed to death on the kitchen floor. Found two days later at Neah Heads with blood on his boots, Marvus had asserted his innocence then hanged himself at his earliest convenience. Amanda's landlord had driven down from Brookings, scoured out the trailer, and put it up for sale. It had been sitting empty for two weeks when Drew bought it and put it on his land.

Kendra took the tank from the front of the trailer and started with it down the long flight of stairs. The fog clung to her face and filled her lungs. Rheumatism and consumption. The Shaker missionaries had found them the principle ailments among the indigenous inhabitants.

The indigenous inhabitants had blamed these ailments upon evil spirits, Skwai-il chief among them. "You must not do wrong," the Tolowans were reputed to have told their children. "Skwai-il will see you, and take you as his dwelling place." She supposed the children had been frightened. She would have been frightened.

It was all in the books Travis had lent her. Skwai-il, Kitdongwes, sorcerers and shamans. As Travis had suggested, the latter were generally women. Spirits would come to them while they were in trances and put a pain into them. In order to heal, however, the pain need be paired with another, and it was this they were to go in search of, alone, to remote and sacred places. Some of these were high in the mountains, some upon dangerous cliffs above the sea, and here they would stay, and dance, awaiting the arrival of the spirit and the second pain. When it came, the intensity was such that the shaman would temporarily lose her senses. She would retire to a sweat lodge where the pains would become a slimy substance that in time might be expelled from her body.

Kendra found herself moved by this image of the woman, dancing alone in some sacred place, awaiting a pain. She went so far as to imagine that this might have something to do with why she walked in the woods, in a dead girl's clothes. The books, of course, had nothing to say about that. They didn't tell her what she wanted to know.

Perhaps, she thought, upon reaching the mud at the foot of the stairs, if she had not miscarried. If Drew had not been bitten. If she had not been left alone for days at a time. She could, in fact, envision another life here—some gleaming, untraveled road. As it was, she found herself thrown back upon unpleasant memories. She felt privy to what the trailer had seen and what the steam cleaning had failed to wash away. She had taken to sluggish days and wakeful nights, to the sound of rain on the tin roof while she pitched the cork for the cat that had been the dead girl's and that had been taught to fetch. And now there were to be visitors. It was an absurd proposition. Drew had promised big waves, a secret spot. If they took the pictures, where was the secret? Unless it was like the Indians had said. They took your picture, you lost your soul. That might be something, the picture the thing itself. Like seeing an aura. They could bring that off, she thought, they might get more than they had bargained for.

By the time she reached Sweet Home, the fog had turned to a light drizzle and she decided that a glass of wine was in order—a little something to ward off the chill as she waited for the gas. She dropped the tank at Mike's Travel Land for filling and proceeded to Bodine's Tavern.

It was three o'clock in the afternoon and there were only four cars in the lot. Kendra parked beside Pam's brown Honda Civic and went inside, out of the rain. She could hear them at the dartboard as she climbed the stairs. An Iris Dement tape played softly in the background—a song about sweet forgiveness. Kendra stopped when she reached the landing. She listened to the sound of a dart striking the board. The sound was followed by a chorus of laughter that momentarily drowned out the music.

From somewhere in the dark interior of the bar came the sound of an ice machine spitting cubes into a tray. The song ended. Pam's voice rose out of the void, some derogatory remark aimed at the weekend's competition. Darts was considered a large time in Sweet Home. Bodine's had a team, as did most of the other bars. There were leagues, tournaments, trophies, good times. Kendra had been invited to try out. She had declined, of course. She was that way. Tournaments would be won and lost. Trophies would change hands. It would all happen without her.

A toilet flushed in one of the johns behind her. A man she did not recognize stepped onto the landing, buttoning his jeans. The man was dressed like a logger, the heavy black pants, plaid shirt, suspenders, caulk boots. The man had unruly blond hair and a beard. He was not unattractive. He stared at Kendra for a moment, looking her over, then smiled. Kendra turned and went into the bar.

She caught Pam in mid-throw, left leg straight, right leg back and bent at the knee and ankle, toes touching the ground. Pam was a big-boned woman, and the pose—Kendra had seen it many times—always struck her as slightly ridiculous.

Kendra waited at one end of the bar, so as not to disturb Pam's concentration. The throw was apparently on the money. Pam was in the act of waving her fist in the air when she caught sight of Kendra in the dim glow of the cigarette machine and stopped short, staring with such intensity Kendra was compelled to look over her shoulder. When she turned back to the room, she found Pam approaching her.

The larger woman took her by the arm and guided her to an empty table with such dispatch she was barely able to nod a greeting to the two men with whom Pam had been playing, although when she did, she had the feeling that they were looking at her in an odd way as well.

"What is this?" Pam asked her. They were seated against the wall, in a black Naugahyde booth. From the street below Kendra was able to make out the sound of traffic, tires on wet asphalt, the distant patter of rain on metal roofs.

"What?" Kendra asked. She was aware of the two men glancing in her direction, then looking away.

"Christ on a bike," Pam said. "Don't you know who you looked like, standing there?"

Kendra said nothing. The woman shook her head.

"You looked like Amanda," she said. "I mean you looked just like her. The clothes were bad enough, you had to go for the haircut too?"

"I guess." Kendra fingered a strand of hair, tucking it behind her ear. Until just yesterday, her hair had been long and black. In Eureka she'd had it cut short and added a reddish tint. There had been a few pictures of Amanda in the trailer, and Kendra had taken one with her to the salon.

"What did Drew say?"

"Nothing. It was just like with the clothes. The tattoo. He doesn't say anything. He just leaves. That's part of it."

Pam looked at her for a moment. "You should get away," she said. "I'm serious. You should get out of Sweet Home, get away from Mr. Macho Man, and get out of that stupid trailer."

"Perhaps," Kendra said. "We could have a little wine."

Pam went to the bar and came back with a bottle and two glasses. "I'm serious," Pam said.

Kendra sipped her wine. She watched as Pam's brother pinned a dart to the board.

"You need a break. Go to Seattle for the winter, or San Francisco. Get a job."

Kendra had had a job once, in Raleigh Hills. She had worked as a receptionist in a dental office. It seemed like another life to her now, and the prospect of doing anything remotely like it again was, at the moment, inconceivable. She placed her purse on the table and took something from inside it, a manilla envelope containing a check for fifty dollars. She pushed the check across the table for Pam to see.

Pam looked at it, raising her eyebrows.

"I sent one of my arrangements to a floral shop in San Francisco. They sent me that. There was a note asking for more."

"No way."

Kendra nodded. For months now, since her miscarriage, she had been collecting things from the woods. Papery hornets' nests, bundles of dried yellow yarrow and dried kelp, driftwood and lichens and dried bear grass, horsetail reeds and river roots. She found that these might be fashioned into arrangements. It was her belief that people might pay her for them. Still, the check had taken her by surprise. She watched now as Pam held it to the light, finally placing it on the table between them.

"I don't know," Pam told her. "I mean, it's cool, but somehow I don't think time alone in the forest is what you need."

Behind them three men had entered the bar. "I shot the son of a bitch right through the spine," one of the men said. He was an older man, with white hair, a red-and-black flannel shirt. "The motherfucker just kept running, up the fucking hill. Just charging." The men bellied up to the bar. Pam went to draw their beers.

When she returned, she took one of Kendra's hands with her own, turning it to look at the month-old tattoo.

"So what's next? The nose ring?"

"Don't laugh," Kendra told her. "I'm considering it."

"Considering it, my ass. I see you with one of those, I'll drag you to the loony bin with it." She let go of Kendra's hand.

Kendra raised her glass—a mock toast. The other woman remained impassive.

"I hope you're not going to tell me you're still looking around for that detective."

Kendra sighed, lowering her glass. "A lost cause," she said. "Anyway, Travis says they wouldn't hire a detective. They would hire a *heedee*."

"A what?"

"A sorcerer. I thought maybe you would know the word."

"Jesus. They should save their money."

"That's what Travis said."

"Travis McCade?"

"I was trying to get him to tell me who it was. I didn't feel that I could ask the Doves. I figured Travis would know. He has that office."

Pam rolled her own cigarettes and she set about rolling one now. "Did you tell him about what you found?" she asked.

"Not yet." Kendra took some more wine. With alcohol, she could always feel it right away, the smallest amount. "He loaned me some books," she said. "I thought, maybe, when I give them back . . ." She allowed her voice to trail away.

What she had found was a little surfboard. She'd found it among Amanda's things, in a small box filled with costume jewelry. It was only a few inches long, made of redwood with a flat deck and a V-bottom, and she knew it to be a model of a particular kind of board once ridden in the Hawaiian Islands. She knew this because it was what Drew did. She had not known him to make miniatures but he did not deny it was something he had done. When she asked him about how it came to be with Amanda's things, he had been less forthcoming. He would only say that it must have gotten put there somehow when they were moving, and she had begun to have a bad feeling about it. She had also, for reasons that were still not altogether clear to her, begun to wear the dead girl's clothes, and Drew had begun to spend a great deal of his time in the shack by the river, with his template drawings and his weather charts and his old wood.

Pam placed her cigarette on the table. "Let me tell you something about Travis McCade. The guy's got two kids by two wives. I've known him since high school. The man thinks with his dick. You start hanging around him, he'll get you into trouble."

"Like I'm not in trouble already," Kendra said. She took a sip of wine, aware of her pulse in her temples.

Pam studied her in the dim light of the bar. "Have you been doing those exercises?" Pam asked. "The ones I showed you."

"You mean the spells?"

"I mean the meditative exercises."

Pam had given her a number of books. *Drawing Down the Moon. The Spiral Dance. Witchcraft, the Sixth Sense.*

"I tried the one with saltwater."

"The saltwater purification ritual. That's good. Water washes. Salt preserves. You should do that on a regular basis. How did it make you feel?"

"Sick. You wind up drinking the water."

Pam rolled her eyes. At the bar the men were calling for another round. On the tape deck Iris Dement had been replaced by Charlie Daniels.

"You don't drink it. You sip it. One sip . . ." Pam rose to serve the men.

In fact, the ritual had not made Kendra sick, because she had not gotten so far as the drinking part. She had, however, filled her ritual chalice with water. With her athame she had added the three mounds of salt and stirred it, counterclockwise, holding the chalice in her lap. She had set about letting her fears, worries, doubts, hatreds, and disappointments surface in her mind—a feat that, in her case, required some commitment of time. She had done her best to see them as a muddy stream flowing from her body as her breath rose and fell, tried to see them dissolved in the ritual chalice—which, in this case, was a mug from the Chart House restaurant in Haleiwa. She had held the cup before her, trying to feel her body drawing power from the earth, letting the power flow into the salt . . . which, according to the book, was to be done until the water began to glow with light. Which was where she got stuck. Her chalice refused to glow and the water was only cloudy like dishwater, and rather than feeling deeply cleansed, she had only felt deeply foolish. She had ended by pouring the water down the sink and drinking one of Drew's beers instead.

"You got to get off this kick," Pam told her. She had returned from the bar. "They found the man with blood on his boots, for Christ's sake . . ."

"And then he hanged himself."

"You think he was innocent, he would hang himself?"

"The guy was no doubt some loser. You're a loser long enough, you start thinking like a loser. He probably figured he was an Indian . . ."

She broke off as Pam was only shaking her head. "Don't give me that," Pam told her.

A moment passed between them. Pam picked up her cigarette. She placed it between her lips and lit it.

"What if he didn't do it?" Kendra said. "The papers said he and Amanda knew each other. So what if he came by afterward? What if he found her, but he was afraid? Because he was an Indian. Because he knew what people would say. What if the guy that did it is still out there . . ."

"What if you're living with him?"

Kendra could feel the baseline of the music in her blood. "Yes," she said. She believed it was the first time she had said it aloud and her inclination was to stop here, to consider what doing so had done.

"Look. If you think that . . . if you think anything like that, then that trailer is the last place you should be." Pam paused for a drink. "Personally, I think Drew is an asshole. I doubt he had anything to do with this girl. Why would he buy the trailer, for Christ's sake?"

"It would be his."

"What?"

"I mean . . . in this weird way . . . it would be his. He would want it." But she was only half thinking about these answers. Her mind was still upon what she had said before. Yes, she had said, yes.

Pam blew smoke through her nostrils. "That's one weird answer," she said. She gave it a moment's thought. "Something is happening here," she announced. "I think you should see Deborah, maybe."

Deborah was a Caucasian woman who lived in town. The women in Pam's circle seemed to believe she was adept at reading auras. Kendra had her doubts. Nor was she altogether certain she wanted someone looking at her aura. She found the prospect faintly distasteful, the kind of thing her father might have indulged in.

"I'm serious, Kendra. There's something here you ought to get to the bottom of. And it doesn't have anything to do with Drew. Or Amanda, or that fucking trailer you spend too much time alone in. It's something with you. Deborah might help. The coven might help. The rituals might help . . ."

"Pam. Please. Give me a break."

"I'm trying to."

"Deborah watches *Melrose Place* on television, for Christ's sake. I've seen her."

"What is it, really?" Pam asked her. "Afraid it won't work, or afraid it will?"

Kendra found herself smiling.

"Now what?"

"I don't know. Nothing."

"Come on. What?"

Kendra drank her wine. "Maybe it isn't all gardens and faery queens," she said. She was set upon by the sudden desire to be gone. She took the check from the table, creased it down the middle, and slipped it into her purse. "He'll never find it here," she said.

"He?"

"The mad professor."

Pam looked confused.

"You know, Felix the Cat. The cartoon."

"I remember the cat. That's about it."

"Well, there was this mad professor. He was always stealing Felix's bag of magic tricks. And then Felix would have to steal it back. And he would fold it into a triangle and stick it into his side. And he would say, 'They'll never find it here.' "

Pam shook her head.

"It was a joke," Kendra told her. "I saw the check, I flashed on the cartoon . . ."

Pam turned to the men at the bar. She looked at Kendra. "Stay here," Pam told her.

Kendra watched as Pam went once more to the cooler, at which point she made her exit. She was really rather reckless about it, no doubt rude as well. She was halfway down the stairs before she realized she had not paid Pam for her share of the wine. But she did not want to go back up and she decided it would have to wait.

She was in the parking lot, getting into her truck, when she saw the logger again. It was the man from the landing. She heard someone call to her and when she turned she saw the man leaning against the side of a truck. She was not sure what the man had said. She saw another man move around from the back of the truck. The rain had picked up. The afternoon was growing dark and there were two men.

Kendra slid quickly behind the wheel, then drove without looking into the path of an oncoming logging truck. She heard the horn at about the same time she saw the immense vehicle bearing down upon her. Her mind seemed to snap a picture of it, something she would carry to look at later—the driver, in some attitude of panic, hunched over the wheel, wrenching it toward the bar, the cut logs swaying as if made of rubber. She believed she shut her eyes, expecting impact. The driver missed her, however, and when she saw him again, he was on the running board of his jackknifed rig, middle finger extended, as the afternoon broke about him into shimmering liquid sheets.

Kendra drove on. She crossed the river and entered the woods and not till she came to the gravel road that would carry her back to her husband's land did she realize she had forgotten the butane tank. Clearly, she would not go back for it. In its absence the death coach would be quite cold. By morning she would be able to see her breath and there would be no hot water for the shower.

She sat for a moment at just this point in the road. To the left the road curved uphill and into the big trees. To the right it fell away, among the spruce and poplar, and even with the windows up and the engine running, she could hear the rain-swollen river sweeping past her, wide and rapacious and unclean.

She turned off the engine that she might be alone with the sound of the water. She sat with her hands atop the wheel, behind windows streaked with rain. Gazing upon the floor of her truck, she saw that her purse had toppled from the seat, that the little wooden board had slid from it and lay now amid the clutter. If only he had not reacted as he had when she confronted him with it, when she had worn Amanda's clothes. If only he had dismissed it and carried on as before. But things were set against them here. She had known it from the start. Their coming had awakened a sickness. And then one night a girl had died. Just somebody. A girl in an alley arguing with a man. She rested her forehead upon the wheel. Perhaps it was her, she thought. Perhaps it was only her mind fucking with her. It wouldn't be the first time. A little electronic stimulation applied to the posterior of the right temporal lobe, you might get voices, music from unseen harps. Stimulate the middle gyrus, you might get Yahweh and burning bushes. A little indigestion, you might get Marley's ghost.

And yet when Pam had asked her, she had said yes, as if his guilt were a thing one could be sure of. And her of all people. She looked once more at the board. The sight made her vaguely nauseous. She opened her door and stepped into the rain. There was a spell in one of the books—it was one of the cleansing spells, a spell for self-acceptance, for the absolution of regret. She tried now to remember how it went. The rain poured down upon her hair, plastering it to her head. She wheeled about in the mud at the edge of the embankment that dropped down toward the water, casting her circle in the air. In the mud she drew a pentagram and stood facing the north, for the north was the most powerful direction, the direction of mystery, of the unseen. She drew a dark stone from the mud and pressed it to her forehead. "I am the mother of all things," she said, which was all she could remember, and at which point it occurred to her that she was drunk on her ass. She pressed the stone to her head a moment longer, hard enough to hurt, then threw it toward the water on its way to the sea.

5

The van needed a water pump. The station was able to replace it
but the surfers lost three hours. By the time they passed the
junction with 580 and the turn to San Francisco, the sky had begun
to color. It was dark when they hit Redding. They stopped here for
food, then picked up the road to the coast. It was a long and winding road, and about an hour and a half into it, Fletcher's van blew a
tire. Unhappily, he was without a spare.

At this point, they were about three miles outside a town called
Dutch Gulch. They walked the three miles only to find the town
closed for the night. They walked the three miles back and slept in
the van. Actually, Fletcher slept in the van. The others slept outside,
beneath a stand of trees some ways off the road. Fletcher woke early
to find Robbie Jones defacing a state mileage sign with his wrist
rocket. It was noon by the time they had dealt with the tire and gotten something to eat.

Fletcher could feel his future unraveling along with his vehicle.

There were directions to Drew Harmon's house, but no phone number. Apparently the man had harbored some objection to giving it out and there was no way to tell him they were running late. He could, however, call Michael Peters. This he did. Peters was still in Hawaii and Fletcher called collect.

"What is it?" Peters asked. "What's wrong?"

"We've been having a little trouble with the van," Fletcher said. He was standing in a cramped booth at the back of a ratty little station, staring into the groves of pine that surrounded the town of Dutch Gulch. The day was cold and gray, and the tops of the trees were lost in cloud.

"Oh, for Christ's sake," Peters said.

There was a kid in bib overalls standing out in back of the station, hitting a rusted piece of farming equipment with a hammer.

"Is it serious?"

"First a water pump. Now a tire. We'll get there."

"What's that?" Peters said.

"What's what?"

"That banging. I can barely hear you."

"It's some kid," Fletcher told him. The kid looked to be about sixteen. He was still hitting the piece of equipment, grinning foolishly at Fletcher.

"Can't you tell him to shut the fuck up?"

"I believe he's retarded," Fletcher said.

Peters fumed for several moments in silence.

"Listen," Fletcher said. "I just wanted to let you know, in case Harmon calls you, wondering where we are. Tell him we'll be there sometime this afternoon." He fairly shouted, to make himself heard above the kid.

"You should be in the fucking water right now, Doc. The damn ocean's on fire. You should see it over here."

"If he calls," Fletcher said, "just tell him."

Peters started to say something else but Fletcher hung up. It was the first thing he had done that day which pleased him. He went past the kid with the hammer and around to the front of the station, where they were prepared to hit the road once more.

"Wha'd he say?" Sonny asked.

"He says it's going off like crazy over there."

"Shit, man," Robbie said. "This sucks."

The sky darkened as they approached the coast. They drove among magnificent scenery punctuated by sorry little towns hunkering among the trees as if they were no more than the detritus of some grander and larger thing which had passed unseen in the night. They took turns at the wheel and finally it was Robbie who did most of the driving, because, he said, just sitting there made him bored. Fletcher, on the other hand, discovered that he was quite content among the bags and board cases. The beer and muscle relaxants helped. In fact, he was sleeping soundly when, late on the second day of their trip, they rolled into the tiny town of Sweet Home.

He woke to the steady drumming of rain on the metal roof of the van. He was quite alone. When he crawled to the passenger side window and looked outside, he found himself parked before a two-story building sporting a large wooden sign which named it as Bodine's Tavern.

Half a dozen men stood beneath an overhang which ran the length of the bar. The lot before them was streaked with puddles in which a gray sky found reflection. The men were of a kind. They wore plaid shirts, heavy dark jeans, and dark suspenders. Most were bearded. None were what you could call small. They seemed to regard the van with some curiosity.

Fletcher was slightly disoriented. He could not immediately say how long he had slept. He was about to get out to look for his charges when he saw them exit a door and pass among the men.

The boys had a six-pack apiece and Fletcher watched as they came down the steps and splashed through the puddles toward the van. He saw the men watching them as well, all six of them, lined up as if they were no more than mock Paul Bunyans cut from wood and cleverly painted.

"We're here," Sonny said.

The two surfers entered the van with great fanfare, shaking rain from their clothes, reeking of beer and tobacco.

"Not quite," Fletcher told them. For he was awake now and he could see that the road had led them inland. It remained to find the coast and Drew Harmon's house.

Peters had provided a map. Fletcher took it from one of his packs and unfolded it in the back of the van. The map indicated a bridge on the outskirts of town and just past it, a narrow road leading to the coast.

They found the bridge, crossing it slowly as the rain-swollen river thundered beneath them. Fletcher squatted between the two front seats. The map suggested the road to the coast was very near the bridge, and, in fact, such a road soon presented itself—a narrow strip of asphalt that ran off among the trees, then forked in two directions almost at once.

They sat at this intersection, peering into the thickening gloom while the rain hammered the van and Fletcher fumbled with his map. Predictably, the thing said nothing about choices. In one direction, the road was hard-packed white rock and appeared to curve back toward the river which lay now to the south. The other road turned north, was straighter and still of asphalt. It seemed the obvious path and they took it.

Fletcher had to tell Robbie twice to slow it down. Martin grinned and hung on. The rain came hard, then backed off quite suddenly as the road corkscrewed toward a flat place where a number of wrecked cars sat in a field of grass and a dirt road ran up toward a trailer with a ramshackle room-addition dangling from one side above a muddy sinkhole. The addition appeared as a mutilated appendage someone had mistakenly thought to save rather than amputate.

Robbie stopped the van. In the road before them, a pair of stricken-looking ducks waddled out of the bush in the company of two equally sorry-looking chickens and made for the opposite shoulder. Martin suggested to Jones that he see how many of the fowl he could run over. Before R.J. could act on this suggestion, however, a young girl came from somewhere out of the grass in pursuit of the birds. She wore a flowered dress, which was wet, and high-topped white workout shoes. Her black hair was wet as well and hung in shining strands around her face, and Fletcher was given to understand that she was an Indian, that, in fact, they had driven onto the reservation and would not find Drew Harmon's place on this road.

He said as much to R.J., but it was the last light of the day and there was a break in the rain. They could see an end to the trees as well, and a kind of light in the sky that spoke of the ocean, and both Robbie and Martin wanted a look. The fact of the matter was, Fletcher wanted a look too, and when the girl and the birds had pushed off into the bush, they continued along the road.

They passed more trailers like the one the girl belonged to, together with a variety of modular and self-made shacks of all shapes and sizes yet all in the relatively same sorry state of disrepair, and, given the rain and the mud and the dripping trees, all looking very much alike—gray and drab, with the hulks of cars and small fishing boats and various appliances rusting or rotting around them in concentric circles until each had become a small junkyard unto itself and above whose patched and sagging roofs, the occasional trail of gray smoke could be seen spiraling into a gray sky before gray woods, so that the entire scene appeared as a badly done water-color in which the various pigmentations had been lost to too wet a surface. With the disappearance of the girl, however, the men seemed to have been left quite alone, and they drove the rest of the way to the sea and the light, unchallenged. The road bent upward, ending in a muddy turnout where they parked and went on foot to the cliff's edge, for their first look at that part of the coast they had come to explore.

The mouth of the river lay beneath them. It was wide and mud-died with crescents of rocky beach on either side bending back toward impossible shorelines which, in many places, were strewn with mighty logs heaped one upon the other like broken telephone poles. Most of the logs lay parallel with the coastline, though here and there others pointed toward the sea, which at this precise moment was of a uniform gray color, though the sky above it was filled with a pale golden mist out of which a declining sun appeared opposite the three surfers, showing itself for a brief interval in that space between the water and the clouds like some tarnished medallion but losing shape even as they watched it, as if the sea itself bore some responsibility for its dismemberment.

At the edges of the beaches, there were thin fingers of wet sand made purple in the fading light and above the sand and rocks and scattered logs, forest-clad bluffs crumbled into the sea, their broken parts forming any number of small jagged islands dark with living greenery, and from which individual trees could in places be seen jutting upward, or outward, at angles which suggested the skeletal remains of sailing ships broken upon the shore.

As for the break itself, the swell lines were windblown and confused, crisscrossing at treacherous angles around the muddy mouth of the river where patterns of white water gone to the color of old brass in the failing light gave evidence of strong currents.

Fletcher could see Robbie Jones roll his shoulders beneath his nylon parka. Beads of water rolled from his tanned head and disappeared beneath his collar. "Gnarly," he said.

"So where's the spot?" Sonny asked. "Can we see it from here?"

"Beats me," Robbie said. "What about it, Doc?"

Fletcher was uncertain. His book had talked about the long walk in, but he assumed that the authors had gone in from the public lands to the north, avoiding the reservations. "That's why we need Harmon," he told them.

"Supposed to be by the river," Sonny said.

"You bothered to look at a map yet?" R.J. asked him. "There's about six rivers empty'n out all over the place up here."

The three men continued to study the sea beneath them.

"Well, I don't see shit out there," Sonny said.

"You ain't seen shit because you cain't see shit," a voice told them. The voice was distinctly male. The words, cast in exaggerated hillbilly twang, seemed to issue from somewhere to their left and slightly below them.

"An' you cain't see shit if you don't know shit. An' you don't know shit."

The three men turned in the direction of the voice.

"What the fuck?" Sonny said.

A shaggy apparition had appeared at the cliff's edge, moving to meet them out of the gloom, although nearly inseparable from it as it was draped head to toe in military green canvas. They watched as this phantom scrabbled along a steep and narrow trail leading up from the river.

In time the man reached the bluff upon which they stood, swinging a shadowy, bearded face in their direction. "Reminds me of Saint Philip and the eunuch," the man said, dropping the hick accent, shaking rainwater from a huge poncho. "And the eunuch saieth unto Philip, 'How can I understand without someone to guide me?' "

The man studied them for a moment as if in expectation of some answer. When none was forthcoming he came toward them once more and there was, Fletcher thought, something about the way he moved. He moved slowly and with some stiffness. He moved in the manner Fletcher had seen certain professional athletes move when their playing days were done, as a man sharing an acquaintance with pain, and when he had gotten close enough, Fletcher saw that it was Drew Harmon.

"So I'm sittin' on my dock all nice and dry and I see these three eunuchs standin' in the rain tryin' to read the water, and this little voice says, look here, hoss, this must be these same three assholes you've been expecting. Gotten themselves lost, of course. Missed the morning glass. Now you better get your ass up there and tell 'em what they're looking at and what to do and where to stand before they fall off the fucking cliff and squirrel the whole deal." He paused for a moment, resting his hands on his hips.

"So I guess I'm supposed to ask, what you eunuchs are looking for out there, anything in particular?"

Jones and Martin exchanged looks. Fletcher made eye contact with Drew and offered a hand. "Been a while," he said. In fact, he was still trying to reach some accommodation with himself with respect to the man planted before him, for he would not have picked him out of a crowd. He was still big, of course, tall and broad-shouldered, but what Fletcher remembered was a man possessed of movie-star good looks, tall and lithe. He could still picture him blasting down the Kam Highway on a BSA Lightning Rocket, the wind in his hair.

Drew Harmon squinted down on him from beneath the brim of some kind of outrageous rubber seaman's cap. The object was the same military green as the poncho. It sported earflaps and a chin strip that Harmon had knotted in a bow and over which his shaggy beard extended in a dripping point. The man looked like a cross between some West Virginia hillman and something from a children's illustrated *Captain's Courageous*. The eyes that studied Fletcher were small and bright, and, it occurred to Fletcher, as the man's hand enveloped his own, slightly deranged. He saw as well that the man did not recognize him.

"Jack Fletcher," Fletcher said.

"I knew that," Harmon said, although his expression did not change. "Dr. Fun. And you've got company."

Fletcher nodded at the men standing slightly behind him. "Robbie Jones, Sonny Martin."

Sonny Martin shook hands with Drew Harmon. Robbie just nodded, his hands thrust deep into the pockets of his parka.

"So," Harmon asked. "You eunuchs looking for anything in particular, or are you just enjoying the weather?"

"Take a guess," Robbie said.

Harmon just looked at him. The look was not particularly friendly. Two alpha males in the same crew, Fletcher thought. Always bad news.

"Just wondered what we could see from up here," Fletcher said. "We knew we must've taken the wrong turn back there when we found ourselves on the reservation, but we wanted a look at the coast before the sun went down."

"Can you see it from here or not?" Sonny asked.

"See what?"

"Shit," Robbie Jones said.

"What? Shit? You want to know if you can see shit from here? You're standin' in shit, chrome dome."

Robbie Jones looked at his feet.

"Heart Attacks," Sonny Martin said.

"Ah, Heart Attacks. That place." Drew Harmon laughed out loud. "You mean to tell me you believe everything you read in those stupid magazines?"

Sonny Martin looked at Robbie Jones. Jones was staring at Harmon, his hands still pushed into the parka. Harmon looked at him. "What about you, Mr. Jones? You looking for Heart Attacks too, gonna snag yourself a big one, maybe?"

"Depends on whether you're gonna show us where it is or stand around and bullshit all day."

Harmon tried to look chastened. The light in his eyes prevented it. "Oh hey, I forgot. This is serious shit. I mean we got photogs. We got pros. For Christ's sake, man . . . I mean, Jesus, we don't get this kind of treatment up here. I musta forgot my manners." At which point and without further conversation, Harmon pushed past them toward a stand of trees at the north end of the turnout.

The three surfers exchanged looks. They watched as Drew Harmon disappeared among the trees without looking back. Sonny looked at Robbie and shrugged. "May as well," he said.

Robbie Jones spit into mud and said, "Fuck." At which point the two headed for the trees, hurrying to catch up. Fletcher followed.

The trees were tall and thin with pale bark and dripping limbs and once beneath their cover, Fletcher found that the ground began to turn upward once more. Drew Harmon picked his way among the trees, leading them quickly along a twisting path that ended abruptly at a narrow ravine creasing an otherwise impenetrable wall of earth and stone.

The ravine was shallow and muddy, laced with the gnarled roots of trees and chunks of rocks. A miniature river trickled in a series of tiny switchbacks along its bottom. Their guide did not hesitate but started immediately up the ravine, using the rocks and roots for hand- and footholds as if they had been placed there for that purpose alone.

Fletcher kept up the chase, though he found the ravine tough going. He wore an old pair of running shoes whose tread had long ago worn smooth. He slipped numerous times on the slick roots and muddied rocks and was thankful that there was no one behind him to witness this spectacle or to hear the sound of his breathing, which had become quite labored. In fact, there was a point in his ascent at which Fletcher fell so far behind, the others were lost to sight and he was left quite alone in the darkening ravine, alone with the dripping trees, the thunder of distant surf, the sound of blood in his ears. There was even a moment in which he imagined that he might, in this fashion, lose his way and in consequence was seized by a momentary panic he took as quite absurd but was seized by it nonetheless.

He pushed on, of course, eventually emerging from the ravine to find himself on a grassy bluff overlooking the sea. It was here he found the others, waist deep in a thicket of manzanita, intent upon the ocean below. It was an odd little tableau. The two younger surfers were looking toward the water. Drew was looking too, but with his arm pointing in the direction of the sea. Fletcher could hear the big man talking as he approached.

"Sets've been comin' in maybe twenty minutes apart. Intervals should decrease by morning. Should clean up too," Drew said. "We're getting the rain off this little pissant low coming up out of the south. The swell's out of a monster system to the north. Isobars packed just right." The man's face broke in a ragged grin. "Prettiest thing I've seen all season."

Fletcher made a place for himself in the manzanita. It was indeed a fresh vantage point, and from it he was able to see a large crescent-shaped beach dipping inland just north of the river, forming there a kind of bay which had till now been hidden by the shoulder of land they had just climbed. He saw as well what held the attention of the men around him, for the swell lines were clearly delineated, moving as Drew had predicted, out of the north, approaching the bay in such a way as to eventually wrap around its northernmost end then sweep across it toward the headlands at the mouth of the river. He saw too a series of large, jagged rocks rising from the water maybe half a mile from land, in the northern quarter of the bay, and even as he saw the rocks he heard Drew Harmon say, "Okay," and he knew it was the rocks to which the man had been pointing at all along, for he could see quite clearly that something had begun there. He could make it out, even from this distance, in the failing light. The water had begun to boil at the base of the rocks, drawn seaward by some great force. And he saw that a wave of considerable size had begun to build at the mouth of the bay, another quarter mile beyond the rocks, yet drawing deeply enough off the bottom to so alter their appearance.

The peak of the wave was enormous, its pocket perhaps fifty yards across, its crest a boil of whitecaps whipped by the wind—a tremendous amount of water rolling toward the coast. The question was, would it break? For it had a lumbering, sluggish way about it, as if it might roll toward the coast indefinitely, alternately building and flattening, finally dumping its load in some useless shore break of wasted power. Quite suddenly, however, even as he and his companions looked and wondered, they saw it find the reef, and they saw it jack.

Someone sucked in their breath. Fletcher believed it was Martin. Drew Harmon laughed. The wave went top to bottom with what had to be a thirty-foot face. It was hard to judge with nothing out there to give it scale. The wave continued to suck out around the peak even as they watched it—huge and hollow as the shoulders suddenly began to line up, feathering north and south but with the ride clearly a right-hander, peeling away from the rocks toward the mouth of the river, and when the first of the lip came crashing down to meet the turbulent Pacific, Fletcher could feel it in his feet, moving up into his bones from the ground beneath him. He was aware of Drew Harmon at his side, checking his watch. He would, Fletcher knew, be watching for intervals.

There were three waves in the set, with twenty-second intervals between the waves. No one spoke. They watched as the last wave thundered toward the rocks, at which point Fletcher was aware of Drew Harmon chuckling once more. "Welcome to the North Country, boys. Hope you brought the Rhino Chasers."

"That's it?" Sonny asked. "That's Heart Attacks?"

"You get caught inside, you'll call it Heart Attacks," Drew told him.

"That beach," Fletcher said, pointing toward the bay. "That's what they call Big Sandy?"

"It's big and it's sandy," Drew said.

"I thought there was some big boulder field you had to cross to get there."

"Who told you that?"

"I read it in a book."

Drew just looked at him. "Which book was that?"

Fletcher was a bit reluctant to name the book. He was aware of Jones and Martin looking at him. "*A Wave Hunter's Guide to the Golden State,*" he said.

Drew was grinning at him. He grinned at Martin and Jones as well. A moment passed. No one spoke.

"How do you get out?" Sonny Martin wanted to know, and Fletcher guessed that Heart Attacks it would be, boulder field or no, and was a little embarrassed that he had thought to question it. He was, after all, in the presence of the book himself, the man who had ridden them all.

Drew Harmon now pointed back toward the mouth of the river. "It's hard to see in this light, with this wind chop," he said, "but there's really a pretty good rip running out of the river. You just ride it out. You got to snake around some on the inside bars, but you got some current pushing you. Once you're past the inside stuff, the current bends south. You paddle out of it, then angle back across the bay and start looking for your lineups. I use the big rock and a point north you can't see from here. It's really not that hard getting out. Holding position is something else. You don't want to take off behind the peak."

"No shit," Sonny said. "Peters said something about a boat."

"A boat?" Harmon acted genuinely surprised. When he saw the expression on Sonny's face, he laughed out loud. "What, you afraid of a little paddling?"

"No, it was just that Peters said you said there would be a boat. I was just wondering . . ."

Harmon silenced him with a wave of the hand. "Don't get your balls in an uproar," he said. "I got the whole thing covered. Boat was here waiting for you this morning."

"How does the boat get out?" R.J. asked him.

"Right out the river mouth," Harmon said. He made a gesture with his hand, cutting the damp air.

"Must be some boat."

Drew rolled his shoulders and rubbed his hands as if taken by a sudden chill. "Swell's building. I've seen fifty-foot faces out there."

As Drew spoke, the last of the sun slipped into the sea, and with its passing, the wind kicked up fresh and cold and the rain with it, hitting them full in the face.

"You eunuchs can hang around if you want to," Harmon told them. "But I wouldn't recommend it. Locals can get downright nasty. Firewater, you know." The man rubbed his hands together, chortling to himself. "Might get yourselves scalped." At which point he exited the manzanita as might a bear moving through the wood and started back down the ravine.

Fletcher and the two surfers followed. When they reached the turnout, they found Harmon already starting down the trail from which he had appeared. He spoke to them as he went, not bothering to turn around to see if they were there or close enough to hear.

"Go back to the other road," he called. "Follow it to the river." He said something else but the wind took it.

Fletcher and the others were left in the mud, in the gathering darkness.

Martin said, "What?" He was looking at Fletcher when he said it, as if Fletcher was supposed to know.

"He said follow the road to the river."

"Yeah. What did he say after that?"

"Hell if I know."

"Christ."

Robbie Jones spit into the mud. When he spoke, it was to the river. "This is the guy's supposed to show us the ropes?"

"Man's some host," Sonny said. "Really knows how to make you feel at home."

"Fuck him. I say we go into town and find something to eat."

Fletcher shook his head and started toward the van. "We'd better do what he says, we're gonna find his place before it gets any darker."

Robbie Jones stopped, touching Fletcher on the arm. "Whoa," he said. "Is that oil under your van?"

Fletcher felt a sinking sensation in his stomach. He walked quickly to the van, then knelt to look beneath it. He saw nothing but rainwater. When he looked up, Robbie and Sonny were laughing at him.

"Had you going," Robbie said.

Fletcher brushed the mud from his knees and got behind the wheel. "Ha, ha," he said.

Sonny and Robbie climbed in after him.

"This Harmon dude is something else," Sonny said. "Makes you wonder why he bothered to invite us in the first place."

"He doesn't give a shit about us. He invited the doc, here. He wants the pictures. Peters was the one invited us. That right, Doc?"

Fletcher started the van. "I suppose so," he said.

"So tell us, Doc." It was Sonny who asked. "What does a guy like that want with pictures?"

Fletcher was a moment in replying. He stared into the darkness now covering the reservation but out of which a few faint lights had begun to flicker. "That's what no one knows," Fletcher said.

6

They drove back the way they had come, finding the fork and the gravel road. It was a washboard road filled with ruts and potholes. It took them to the river and led them along its bank. In time, they came to a wooden landing and this was where the road ended.

Fletcher was not sure exactly what he had expected to find here. You had Drew Harmon. You had the Great Northwest. The man had taken a bride. A rich girl. It had been so postulated and agreed upon before the trip was even begun. At the very least, Fletcher had expected a house. Possibly the work of Drew's own hand. He would learn that Drew had felled the trees himself and milled the lumber. The house would be placed upon a hillside with a view to the sea.

What lay before him in the gathering darkness was so far removed from such fantasies, Fletcher's first impulse was to believe he and his companions had gotten themselves lost again. Had it not been for the rusted-out van bearing a pair of surfboards lashed to the roof, he would have looked for a place to turn around without bothering to stop. The van and the surfboards, however, suggested that he had come to the right place. Still, he sat for a moment behind the wheel, surveying the scene before him.

"This is it?" Sonny Martin asked.

"Looks like."

"Any of these Indians surf?"

"Look at the boards," Fletcher said.

One could see enough, even in the poor light, the length and thickness, the line of the rail. The place, on the other hand, looked like what they had seen on the reservation. The old van sat before a wooden landing that extended into the river. The landing fronted a clapboard shack whose windows had been broken and patched with scrap lumber and whose sagging shingled roof had been mended in tin. From the front of the shack a pathway led to trees and a steep hillside where stairs might be seen climbing toward a rickety deck set before an ancient house trailer. At length, Fletcher killed his engine and got out of the van. Robbie and Sonny got out with him.

"Shit," Robbie said. "I thought this guy was supposed to be somebody."

"Look at it this way," Fletcher told him. He felt compelled to defend the man, though, in fact, he supposed his disappointment even keener than that of his companions. "It hadn't of been for guys like him, guys like you wouldn't be making squat."

Robbie Jones said nothing.

Fletcher continued to look at the trailer. Clearly there would be nothing here to place alongside Michael Peter's Biarritz tale. No fur coats and no Mercedes.

"So what now?" Sonny asked.

The shack showed no signs of occupancy. Above the trees an outdoor light burned at the door of the old trailer.

"I guess we try that," Fletcher said. He nodded toward the light.

"Jesus."

They had stumbled along the darkened path and come to the base of the stairs when Drew Harmon called to them. Fletcher could not say where he had come from. When he looked, the man had simply appeared on the trail behind them. He held a flashlight in one hand and a grocery bag in the other.

"That ain't the way," Drew told them. "It's down here."

He turned and started back down the path from which they had come.

Fletcher, who had been in the lead, was now in the rear. He looked once more toward the flight of stairs. It was longer and steeper than he would have imagined. He was about to follow the others when it suddenly occurred to him there was someone standing on the deck.

He saw that it was a woman, or so it appeared in the gloom. She was near the door. He believed her arms were folded about her chest. She seemed to be looking toward the river. He was still staring when a voice came to him from among the trees.

"I said, that ain't the way," the voice said.

Fletcher turned. Drew Harmon was standing on the path with his flashlight and bag. Martin and Jones were somewhere behind him in the shadows.

"That your place?" Fletcher gestured toward the stairs with his head.

"That's my place," Drew said. "But we're staying down here." He waited until Fletcher showed signs of following him before turning to the path once more.

Fletcher stole a final look at the trailer. His angle had changed and he saw the woman was still there. He could see the yellow light upon her hair. But he did not look for long, as Drew Harmon was waiting, and soon she was lost among the trees.

The shack was one room, maybe twenty feet square. There was a wood-burning stove against one wall, an ancient circular thing made of cast iron with ornate iron doors. It rested, in violation of all building codes Fletcher was familiar with, on a rough wooden floor. The room was lit by a single bulb attached to a cord wrapped about a rafter.

"You want to piss," Drew told them, "do it in the river. You want to do anything else there's an outhouse in the trees. You can use one of these to find your way." He pointed to a pair of flashlights by the door.

"That's cool," Sonny said, to no one in particular.

In the center of the room was a surf board Fletcher had not seen the likes of in many a year, or perhaps not at all, for the materials were of another era, redwood and balsa, yet the lines were those of a modern gun. It rested on a pair of sawhorses, sleek and shining in the light of the naked bulb.

There were other boards in various stages of development propped against walls or placed standing, tail down, in racks which had been made of two-by-fours nailed hastily together. Other racks held planks of wood. Balsa. Redwood. Other woods Fletcher could not name.

"This was my grandmother's place," Drew said. "Built in 1894. I been using it to shape in. Someday I'm gonna build my own place up there above where the trailer is. I got the site all picked out. You can see the river mouth from there. Right now we're living in the trailer."

Fletcher nodded. They had grouped around the board on the sawhorses. Sonny Martin ran a finger along the rail.

"Where'd you get this?" Martin asked. "A museum?"

Drew Harmon just laughed. "Not hardly. Had to go all the way to Ecuador to get that balsa. You can't get the shit in big enough sticks in the States. Took me another eight months to get the stuff up here. The redwood is strictly from old growth timber."

He stepped to one of the racks and pulled out a plank. The piece was solid redwood, ten feet long. Fletcher reckoned it must have weighed at least two hundred pounds. Harmon handled it as if it weighed no more than a third of that. He spun it on one end and propped it against the others, still racked. "Check this," he told them. "It will blow your mind." He ran his hand along several scars laid crosswise to the grain. "You know what those are?"

When no one answered, he smiled. "That's the scars from a springboard," he said. "That's where some old logger drove his springboard into the trunk. There was still ten feet of the tree left in the ground. Wasteful as hell. I know a guy with a salvage license. We go into the woods looking for stumps. We find one, he slices me a piece off the top. Thing was three hundred pounds of solid wood when I started on it. But I wanted to save those scars. I get done, they're gonna be right there in the board, under the glass job."

He stood back, holding the board at arm's length, admiring the old wood that was indeed quite impressive.

"That's where the magic comes from," he told them. "It's in the wood." He gestured toward the board on the sawhorses. "You paddle out on that . . . the spirits will smile on you."

He slid the plank back into the rack and went to his workbench where he set about removing what he had brought in the bag—two cans of tamales, two cans of chili, two six-packs of beer, and some hot dog buns.

"We'll crash here," Drew told them. "We'll hit it early. First light."

"May as well break out the shit," Robbie said. The two surfers went outside where it had begun to rain once more.

Drew Harmon watched them go. He was at the workbench, opening cans. His parka was pulled back now. His hair was wet and he had twisted it into a ponytail that rested on his broad back.

Fletcher remained by the board. He looked around the shack. There was a hot plate on the workbench. A chaise lounge pad had been laid upon the floor with a sleeping bag on top of it.

Drew nodded toward the departed surfers, his back still to Fletcher. "That kid R.J. He the kid won the Masters this year?"

"Two years in a row."

"What's the payoff on that little item now?"

"I'm not sure. I think he made thirty, forty grand."

"Shit." Drew Harmon dumped the tamales in with the chili and placed the mess over his hot plate in a battered aluminum pan. "You know what I got the year I won that thing?"

"A trophy."

"A fish dinner at Ahi's."

Fletcher listened to the rain on the tin roof. There was a stack of old surfing magazines on the floor by the sleeping bag together with a bottle of drinking water.

"We get some waves, I'd like to get pictures of all three of us riding my boards. What do you think?"

Fletcher looked at Drew. The man had his back to him.

"Fine by me."

"I think there could be a market. This is the new frontier up here. You know that, don't you? Undiscovered country. You need the right equipment to go after it on."

Fletcher considered the board on the sawhorses. It was a ten-foot gun of serious proportions. The number of people requiring one like it would be minimal. He kept the observation to himself. He watched as Drew Harmon stirred his tamales and chili. "You know I got an expense account for this trip. There's someplace in town you and your wife would like to eat. . ."

"I don't go into town," Drew told him. He turned to look at Fletcher. His hair was pulled back flat against his skull, streaked with gray about the temples, and Fletcher could see the crow's feet webbing the skin around the big man's eyes, much, he imagined, as it webbed the skin around his own. Too many years of sunlight on the water, too many hours spent searching for those outside sets on seas made molten before harsh and declining suns.

"Nothing there but a bunch of redneck bars," Harmon continued. "Kind of places I can't go."

When not booming at someone, or clowning with his exaggerated hick accent, Harmon's voice was, in fact, quite soft and well modulated, belying somehow the power of its owner. It was in this soft voice that Harmon now spoke, enumerating in all seriousness a considerable list of things he could not do. He didn't go out at night. He didn't drive much. He did not seek out the company of others. Surfing, of course, provided the exception to these rules. One might drive in pursuit of waves. One might go out at night, if only to arrive at a given spot in time for the dawn patrol. The rest of it was bullshit.

Fletcher's first impulse was to think of the woman he had seen at the top of the stairs. He had taken her for Drew Harmon's wife and he wondered what she thought of these rules, for it seemed to him as if they did not allow for much of a social life. "Why not?" he asked.

Drew Harmon looked directly at him. "Can't," he said. "There's people out there . . ." He looked toward the door where, at just this moment, Sonny Martin had appeared. The boy held a duffle bag in each hand. At his back, the sheets of rain, illuminated by a light above the door, shown about the outline of his shaggy head as might some dime-store halo.

"There's people I can't be around," Drew continued. "People that will get me into trouble."

"Jesus Christ," Sonny said. "It ever quit raining around here?"

"Move the fuck out of the way," Robbie called out from behind him. "You're lettin' it all in."

The boys came on, dragging gear, the door slamming behind them.

"He's just pissed," Sonny Martin said. "Found his ex dancin' at the Staide. Picking up quarters for Jap tourists with her cunt."

Robbie Jones set his bags down, spun around with a lightning-fast wheel kick, and planted his heel in Sonny Martin's solar plexus. The stricken youth made a great show of staggering about the room as if looking for someplace to toss his cookies.

Drew Harmon was still at his stove, a pot in one hand, a spoon in the other. He turned to Sonny Martin and Robbie Jones, as if seeing them for the first time. "Jesus," he said. "This is what they got out there now?" He seemed genuinely surprised.

"It's what the boss sent," Fletcher told him.

Robbie Jones ignored them. On the wall opposite the workbench and hot plate were shelves filled with books and videocassettes. A small television set mounted by a VCR was perched there as well, among a clutter of books and magazines. Robbie read a couple of the titles out loud.

"*The Art of Wave Riding. Hawaiian Surfboards.*"

"Just about everything ever written on the subject," Harmon told them. "That's the goal, get it all. You look, you'll even see Lord's study on hydrohulls for the U.S. Navy."

Robbie Jones just looked at him.

"That's the book Simmons got his hands on back in '46. What made the modern board possible, you think?"

Harmon winked at Fletcher, for it was clear Robbie Jones had no idea who he was talking about. Robbie Jones returned to the case. "You got videos too," he said.

"Them's that's worthy."

Robbie pulled one from the shelf. He passed it to Sonny Martin. "Check this," he said. "He's got the Doc's movie."

"Let's watch it," Sonny said.

"Fuck it," Drew Harmon told him. "Let's eat."

When they had polished off the tamales and chili and eaten the buns and drank the beers, they turned in early so as to be ready for what the morning might bring. They crashed in sleeping bags on the floor of the shack. Fletcher drifted easily into a drug-induced sleep but woke sometime before dawn.

He awoke soaked in sweat to a moment of pain and confusion. Eventually his surroundings became clear to him and he was aware of the rush of the river beyond the clapboard walls, the far-off moan of what he took to be a foghorn sounding in the night. The next thing which became clear to him was that he had lost the feeling in his right hand. As he worked it open and closed little flashes of pain moved up his arm and into his neck. He sat up slowly on the thin mat, squeezing his right hand with his left. What was called for, he decided, were pills. He had placed his backpack and water next to him for just such an occasion, but as he began to dig through the pack it occurred to him that he had left the drugs in the van with his film. Cursing softly, he pushed the sleeping bag from his legs and got to his feet. He pulled on jeans and shoes, took one of the flashlights Drew had left by the door, and went outside.

The night was cold and damp, filled with the scent of pine and the sweet rot of the forest. He crossed the landing and went down into the mud. The river thundered at his side. He used the flashlight to show him his footing, but, in fact, he could have managed quite well without it. The rain was gone and the moon had come to ride squarely above the river, bathing the night in a silvery light.

He stood for a moment at the back of the van, drinking in the sight. The moon was nearly full and the river wound toward it as if it were a thing one might walk on and the moon itself a place that might be so reached. He opened the door of the van by rote, his mind still on the river, and was halfway in when someone groaned at him.

Fletcher was taken completely by surprise. He jumped backwards, banging his head on the roof of the van.

He heard someone say "Shit," and when he looked once more into the van he was greeted by the sight of Robbie Jones. The boy was quite alone in the darkness, seated on an overturned plastic bucket, his male member cradled in a white handtowel stained with blood.

"Shit," Robbie said again. He was hunched forward, one hand raised to ward off the light.

"Jesus," Fletcher said. For, in fact, the whole thing made for a rather disturbing spectacle. "Are you all-right?"

"Thing hurts like a motherfucker," Robbie told him. "I think there might be something wrong with it." He lifted an edge of the towel to reveal his organ, which did in fact appear in worse shape than the last time Fletcher had seen it.

"Is there anything I can get for you?" Fletcher asked.

Robbie Jones just looked at him. "Yeah. You can get me a new dick."

"You want some of that stuff they gave you, that solution?"

"That's what started the fucker bleeding, when I washed it out."

Fletcher stood at the door, in his T-shirt and jeans, in the damp night air.

"I'll be all-right," Robbie said. "Just leave me alone for a while. It sort of hurts when I talk."

Fletcher nodded. He grabbed the bag with the pills in it then looked once more at Robbie Jones. "You want the light?" he asked.

Robbie just shook his head. He appeared to be undergoing some kind of spasm.

Fletcher swung the light toward the trees. "They said it could do this," Robbie told him.

Fletcher was nearly back to the landing when he saw the girl. She would have been easy to miss, a dark place in the night. He saw her at the edge of the path he had earlier followed himself, the one leading toward the stairs and the trailer. She had been watching him. He was quite certain of it, and when she saw that she had been found out she started into the trees. Fletcher prevented it. He took her for the woman he had seen on the landing and he meant to have a look. "Hello," he said.

The woman stopped. Fletcher had turned off his flashlight but the moon was on her face so that even in the darkness he could see that she was quite striking in appearance. She was wrapped in a dark coat that fell to her ankles. Her hair was black and cropped short.

"You must be Drew's wife. I'm Jack Fletcher."

"The photographer."

"How did you guess?"

He saw the woman shrug. It was hard to know her age in the darkness. She was young, he thought. Not yet thirty.

"You're a friend of Drew's. The others would be too young."

"Not a friend, exactly. We knew each other in the islands."

"The glory days."

"I guess," he said to her. "They have become so."

"So that's what this is? You get to go back?"

"Go back?"

"Relive your youth."

Her tone seemed vaguely disapproving.

"Drew wanted pictures. We came."

"So you did."

"You always up at this time of night?" It had occurred to him that she was alone in the forest at an unlikely hour.

She looked at the river. "Pretty much."

"A creature of the night."

She looked at him a long moment then. The river roared at his back. He saw bats cross the face of the moon, tree to tree. They might have been drawn there as in some animated feature. When he looked again, she had given him her profile.

"Well," she told him. "It's late. Or is it early?"

"I don't know," Fletcher said. "I've lost track."

It appeared to him that she smiled a little when he said that.

"Maybe it's those pills."

"Vitamins," Fletcher said.

"The shadow knows," she told him.

Fletcher laughed. "I'm supposed to take your picture," he told her. The idea had just occurred to him.

She stopped once more and looked at him. "Who said that?"

"The editor. At the magazine. He's a friend of Drew's too. I think he would like a picture for the article."

"That's idiotic."

"I think it's a good idea. I think we should do it."

"You can't."

"Really?"

"It's a ploy," she said. "You let somebody take your picture, they wind up with your bag of tricks."

Fletcher watched as she disappeared beneath the trees. He remained there for some time. She was certainly not what he had expected. Not a party girl from the islands and he found himself wondering at just where Drew Harmon could possibly have found her, and why.

Eventually he went back to the shed and took his place on the floor. The pills dulled the pain but sleep eluded him. Robbie Jones returned. Fletcher listened as he climbed into his bag. In a short while the young man was snoring softly. Time passed. Perhaps an hour. Fletcher was still awake when Drew Harmon rose from his mat and went out into what was left of the night. Fletcher did not see him return. He remained sleepless, on his back in the sawdust of the shed, awaiting the dawn, thinking of the girl he had seen by the river, thinking of Drew Harmon climbing the long flight of steps to the trailer, perched there among the trees, at the edge of the town they called Sweet Home—though it seemed to him as if Drew Harmon had not found it so, for he was struck by the feeling that something had gone awry in the land of the tall pine. He lay with his thoughts as the fog horn tolled the hour, its mournful call a reminder of what the morning would bring. For they had come to a place without palms or a tropic light. In their stead, Fletcher imagined once more the rocky coastline he had glimpsed from the high trail near the river mouth. He imagined a ghostly cloud break a mile from shore where they would await the dogs of winter, and which beasts, unlike the ones in Fletcher's movie, would be the real thing.

7

Drew came to the trailer before dawn. Kendra was still awake. She had finished with Travis's books and had taken up *The Origin of Consciousness* in the *Breakdown of the Bicameral Mind* by Julian Janes. That and pitching the cork for the cat. She was seated on the floor, a nearly empty wine bottle on one side, an empty glass on the other.

She heard Drew on the stairs. She could tell it was him. He limped a bit after the shark. She watched as he used his key to come in. He started when he saw her.

"Jesus, Kendra. You still up?"

"No," she said. "I'm asleep."

He reached down to touch the book she was holding, tilting it back with one finger that he might read the title.

"This the guy who thinks everyone was schizophrenic?"

"Once."

"He say anything about those of us still are?"

Kendra gave him a thin smile. "He says something like twenty percent of the population will at one time or another experience some kind of auditory hallucination."

Drew nodded. "Great. I guess I still got a few things to look forward to." He went past her and into the kitchen where he began washing his hands in the sink.

Kendra remained on the floor, seated on her cushion. At Drew's arrival, the cat had withdrawn. It was very skittish. Kendra could only imagine what the animal had seen. It seemed to be more afraid of men than of women. It seemed particularly frightened of her husband.

She watched him. His hair was loose and fell about his face. A golden mane in the artificial light. She was reminded of the way he had looked at Hatteras, showing up on his Harley to rent a boat from her stepfather. In a T-shirt and denim, blond hair flying in the wind. Arms cut with muscle. He was exactly the kind of man her stepfather was always warning her about, so that when he offered her a ride she had taken him up on it at once.

He had come to surf in a contest at Cape Hatteras, in waves driven by a distant storm and she had sat in the sand and watched him, as if the mystery of the sea were a thing he had mastered. And on that day, he had surfed better than anyone on the beach, young or old, because the waves had been big and powerful and that was his stock-in-trade and watching, she had sensed that he might touch something in her that had not been touched before. And so he had.

She watched as he bent to wash his face, drawing his hands back through his hair, plastering it against his skull. His face took on the aspect of a bird of prey in the false light.

"I'm gonna take these guys from the magazine out today," he told her. "We should be gone all day." He turned to look at her. "It's a good swell," he said. "The swell of a lifetime."

Kendra only nodded. She had seen the swell of a lifetime many times, in Hawaii, in Bali, in Costa Rica. More often than not it was the swell of a lifetime when it was on the way. Afterward, it was only good. Tomorrow, it would be better. But tomorrow brought wind. An unfavorable tide.

"I met one of them," she said.

"Which one was that?"

"Jack Fletcher."

Drew nodded. "That figures." He smiled. It was not a particularly pleasant smile. She had seen it more often of late. "If there was a woman around, Jack Fletcher would find her." He looked away. "We were always a little alike in that way. What were you doing to meet him?"

"I was walking."

"You were walking by the river?"

Kendra nodded.

"You keep doing that, you're going to meet worse than Jack Fletcher."

"So I've heard."

"You should listen."

"He's the photographer? The one you knew in the islands?"

Drew watched the light breaking above the river. "Yes," he said.

"I thought pictures were bullshit."

"Depends on what you want them for."

"What do you want them for?"

He did not answer directly. He seemed to be waiting on the dawn. "How would you like to get out of here?" he asked suddenly.

When she did not immediately respond he turned to look at her. There was something in his face then, a thing she could not recall having seen before. It took her some moments to put a name to it. When she did, she saw that he was afraid.

"I've been thinking about Chile," he said. "Fourteen thousand miles of coast down there. You can go from the tropics to the South Pole. Talk about last frontiers."

"I thought this was the last frontier."

He snorted. "For California," he said. "This is it. Of course it won't be for long. Not when these guys get done with it," he nodded toward the river. She assumed he was referring to the photographer, Jack Fletcher, and the pros who had come with him.

"Then why invite them?"

"I'm serious," he said. "Chile. What do you think?"

She hardly knew what to say. "That would take money," she said.

"I can get the money, I have a way."

"How?"

"Leave that to me," he said.

"Why? Why now?" she asked him.

He took a step toward her. She thought he might even come close enough to hold her. She could not imagine what that would be like. It had been a good place to be once, a shelter from the storm. But they had not slept together in months, not since the day he'd come home and found her wearing Amanda's things.

"It's all gone wrong here," he said. "Christ, can't you see that? You never sleep anymore. You're out at all hours walking in the woods."

"There are times," she told, "when I feel like I can see what the trailer saw. It comes in flashes of light."

He looked at her for a long time. "You keep this up, we'll be doing Tamarindo again," he said finally. "Is that what you want? You want to wind up in the hospital?"

Just before moving to California, they had attended a legends event in Tamarindo, in Costa Rica. She'd had a kind of episode there. The kind of thing she had suffered on several occasions as a child. There had been flashes of light, unwelcome voices. She'd wound up drugged on Thorazine in a little hospital in San José. Drew had dropped out of the event and broken her out. Doing so had cost him his last sponsor, in part because he would not provide them with the cause. When they'd asked him why, he'd only told them to fuck off. As if on cue, his mother had died and left them the land. It was mortgaged to the hilt. There was no money in it, but it was a place to go.

She told him that she did not want to do Tamarindo again.

This seemed to satisfy him in some way and he put out a hand as if to touch her face. As he did, she drew back. The movement was involuntary and abrupt. She hit the wine bottle with an elbow and tipped it over.

There was not much left in the bottle. What there was spilled in a small trickle as the bottle rolled across a matted shag carpet. For some reason she could not quite bring herself to pick it up. She had wrapped herself in her own arms. She could feel her fingernails digging into the flesh covering her triceps.

Drew's face hardened once more. He bent to pick up the bottle, then stood, holding it between two fingers. "You know, you should really watch it with this shit."

"Why?"

He held the bottle to the light. "Jesus Christ," he said. "This isn't even grape juice, for Christ's sake. It's for wino Indians and coons. You're sitting there telling me about little flashes of light. You keep drinking this, you'll wind up in front of Marvin's Foodmart drooling on yourself."

He set the bottle down on the countertop with enough force to cause a dirty plate to slide into the sink. The plate broke upon impact. She heard the tinkling shards as whispered voices.

"You know it's colder than a motherfucker in here," he told her. "When are you going to get those damn tanks filled?"

"Actually, one is filled. It's just not here."

"That's a good one," Drew said. "I feel warmer already."

She watched as he took a pair of water bottles from beneath the sink and went outside. He did not say good-bye and neither did she.

When he was gone, she rose and went to the window. She could see him at the landing, at the side of his rusted-out old van. He was so small there, she thought, so solitary, with his worn-out gear and his wooden boards. She felt herself stirred by a sudden pity, a desire to go to him. He was not an evil man. He was in need of grace, was all, an angel of light. What he had was her.

She thought once more about Tamarindo. He had been her knight there. But in costing him his last sponsor, she had cost him the islands. Not that it was anything she could help. It was an episode was all. She had thought herself done with them. It was what they had told her mother when she was young. They had hung a name on it she did not care to remember. It could manifest itself as a single episode, they had said, a response to stress. The episode in question had followed the death of her father. But then, of course, there could be recurrences. These might be florid or mild. There was always the chance they could become chronic. They shouldn't have said those things in front of a child, she thought. Christ. You spend your life waiting.

She put her elbows on the drain board and rested her face in her palms. He had tried just now to talk to her, to build a bridge, and she had sent him away, as if his guilt were a thing she could be sure of. And yet how could she be, sure it was him and not her, sure of what was inside her head and what was out? She had been through a stressful period here. How was one to know this was not some recurrence? "In mild cases," she had read somewhere. "The voices maybe under the control of conscious attention, as are thoughts." She made her hands into fists and banged them upon her temples, as if to drive the thoughts away.

She went reeling through the trailer to the small bedroom and lay there on her back, bathed in sweat. "I hear them if I attend to them," she said. And again. "I hear them if I attend to them," as a kind of mantra, in accompaniment to her breathing exercises, as the moisture which dripped almost continually from the trees pinged against the metal roof of the trailer—an incessant rustle of whispering voices.

8

In Drew Harmon's shaping shack, a pale light drifted among the racked planks of exotic woods. An electric motor whirred. Fletcher stirred, blinking into the odd light with some surprise. He had not expected to sleep and when he looked to see if the others were sleeping as well, he discovered that not only had he dozed, but that the others had risen without him, that he was alone on the floor. He rolled to one side, seeking the source of the mechanical whine.

What he found was Robbie Jones. The young man seemed to have achieved a complete recovery in the wake of his episode in the van. He was moving about before Drew Harmon's work bench, dressed in oversized sweatpants and a Local Motion T-shirt. The bench itself was a litter of broken eggshells and empty banana peels, together with various bottled and canned supplements. As Fletcher watched, Robbie turned off the blender and set about pouring a string of brownish liquid the consistency of spent tobacco juice into a large plastic cup.

"Jesus," Fletcher said. "You brought all this stuff with you?"

Robbie nodded.

"Didn't know you were into health foods."

"Body's a temple of the Lord, bro."

Fletcher rose painfully from his bag. He was hoping Drew had made coffee, but if he had Fletcher couldn't find it. He set about dressing in the cold light. "Wonder what the Lord's take on penis studs might be?" he asked.

"What I do," Robbie told him, "I do to His glory."

At which point, Sonny Martin stumbled through the front door. His face was red, his eyes bloodshot, but he was smiling. "I heard that," he said. He had a Twinkie in one hand, another in his mouth, and when he spoke, it was around the Twinkie, a blob of which bobbed on the tip of his chin like some cancerous growth. "They told the fucker," he said. He was pointing at Robbie Jones with the Twinkie. "Man wasn't supposed to beat off for six months. Dude just wouldn't listen."

"Fuck you," Robbie said.

Sonny Martin favored Fletcher with one of his glazed smiles. "Oh yeah," he said, as if he had only now remembered why he had come. "Drew says to tell you, the boat is here."

Drew Harmon was standing on the landing, the river at his back. He was bare-chested, dressed as if in defiance of the chill morning air in only sweatpants and sandals, and Fletcher saw the scars for the first time.

He did not believe he had ever seen any so large. It was, he thought, as if the man had been sewn up with yarn. The marks issued from beneath the waistband of his sweats, crossing his abdominals then wrapping around his side, following in general the outline of the hip. The flesh along these tracks was raised and mottled—a deep purple in the gray light, and for a moment the sight was enough to distract Fletcher from why he had come. In time, however, he saw the boy and remembered all too well.

For Standing at Drew's side and slightly behind him was a thin, dark-haired boy. The boy rose only to Drew's chest. He was dressed in tennis shoes and jeans. He wore a red-and-black flannel shirt and a red ball-cap with a black marlin stitched above the bill. The boy was looking up the muddy bank toward the trees, holding to a length of rope running to an eyehook at his feet, at the end of which an inflatable Zodiac bobbed in the muddy water. At the sight of the boy and the boat, Fletcher's heart sank.

"Beginning to wonder if you were going to make it," Harmon said. He was sporting a cheek full of tobacco and seemed in high spirits.

Fletcher would have liked at this point to ask about the boat, but Harmon had caught sight of Robbie and Martin at the back of the van and stalked off to see what they were riding.

Fletcher followed. In part, because he was curious. In part, because he wanted to distance himself from the boy and the Zodiac, as if by doing so he might alter what had already transpired.

Both of the boys were on Brewers. They were beautiful boards. Martin's was clear. Robbie's was clear with yellow rails. Both were bisected by spruce stringers an inch wide. They bore the Brewer logo—a flower—and beneath it the signature of Dick Brewer.

Harmon deposited a line of tobacco juice into the mud and inquired after the boards' length.

"Nine six," Robbie told him.

"You bring anything longer?"

"They told me the pocket's a lot like Waimea. Nine six is what I ride there."

"You might want something a little longer here. Check this."

He led them to the side of the shack where a pair of guns stood upright, propped against the wall. One was the board they had seen in the shop. The other was very much like it. Balsa and redwood, and featuring a particularly intricate and beautiful design—half a dozen narrow redwood stringers joined at the tail block, fanning out toward the nose in an elongated sunburst.

"You're really going to ride those things out there?" Sonny Martin asked.

"Why not?" Harmon said. He said it in such a way that Martin was momentarily at a loss, as if he had concluded that saying the wrong thing at this point might, in fact, prove detrimental to one's health.

Kem Nunn

"Well, I mean . . . Jesus, man . . . What if you snap a leash? What if you put it on the rocks?"

"I don't wear a leash," Drew told him. "Ever."

There followed a moment of silence. Fletcher almost smiled. The sight of the boy and the Zodiac were the only things that prevented it.

"Let me tell you something," Drew said. "Last thing you want out there is a light board. This ain't da tropics, brah. Water's heavier, denser. Harder to push through, harder to bury a rail. I made these boards to ride this break with. You get out there. You'll see."

There was a moment in which the only sound was that of the river. "I'll stick with the Brewers," Robbie said, and so saying turned and walked back to the van.

Sonny watched him go. He looked at the boards. He looked at Drew Harmon. At last he shrugged. "Me too," he said. He turned and followed Robbie Jones.

Drew Harmon watched them. "You do that," he said.

With Jones and Martin gone, Fletcher returned with Drew to the landing. He could feel the surge of the river here, feel it in the vibrations of the old wood beneath his feet. Drew looked at the van.

"Dickweeds. They'll come around. Wait and see."

"So, Drew," Fletcher heard himself saying. He was looking at the Zodiac. "Is this the boat?"

Harmon stared a moment longer in the direction of the van. At length, he turned to the Zodiac and then to Fletcher. He nodded his head yes and said, "No, that's not a boat."

Fletcher hesitated, not quite sure what to make of this response. Perhaps he had been misunderstood. But the man began nodding again before he could speak and said the same thing. "That's not a boat," he said. At which point it became clear to Fletcher that the guy was simply fucking with him.

"I was hoping," Fletcher said, "for more of a boat."

Harmon nodded. "I know just what you mean," he said. "I guess we're all hopin' for a little more of something." He bent to a canvas bag on the landing and tugged at its zipper. A wet suit and neo-

102

prene booties spilled onto the deck. Harmon nodded toward the suit. "You got one of these, you might want to put it on."

There seemed little point in discussing it further. Fletcher looked at the boy one more time. He was standing as before, holding to the line, his eye on the trees. After that, he went up the bank and around to the back of the van. His hands felt stiff and cold in the damp air, and it occurred to him that he was scared.

He found Sonny Martin already dressed in the latest of cold-water fashion, a red-and-black O'Neil Heat Seeker complete with booties and gloves and a black neoprene cap with a red stripe down the center which he held in one hand. The stuff appeared supple and warm and Fletcher found himself lamenting once more the loss of his hood. He'd pulled one of his stuff bags to the edge of the van and set about undressing, when he noticed Robbie Jones several yards away, his wet suit covering his legs but turned down at the waist to reveal his back, which was long and narrow but corded with muscle and decorated with an elaborate tattoo. A crucified Jesus hung from his thoracic spine to his lumbar, the Christ's bleeding palms extending as far as his shoulder blades, and beneath the Christ's hands were letters, blocked out in a style Fletcher associated with the Chicano gangs of East L.A. The letters sat one above the other, stacked along both sides of the boy's rib cage. It took Fletcher a moment to make out what the letters spelled. Eventually he saw there were two words—TRUE LOVE.

Mr. Jones was, at this particular moment, down on both knees at the edge of the forest, his shaved head bowed. Fletcher's first thought was that the guy was sick, and he looked around to find Sonny Martin pulling on his cap. "He all-right?" Fletcher asked.

Sonny glanced over his shoulder. "He's cool. He's sayin' his prayers."

"Nice tattoo," Fletcher said.

"Yeah. First he just had the Jesus on there, then he got those words. He told his girlfriend it was for her."

"The one now dancing at the Staide?"

Sonny Martin smiled. "The one picking up quarters for Jap tourists with her cunt. What a bitch."

Sonny jerked his chin strap tight then stopped and looked

toward the landing. "How about those scars?" he asked. "Fucker was damn near bit in half." He paused, observing the river where it ran to the sea. "Right out there, I'll bet ya."

"Maybe we all ought to say some prayers," Fletcher said.

Sonny Martin just looked at him. "Fuck that," he said. He made a slight adjustment to his cap, then sauntered off in the direction of the dock.

Fletcher was some time at the van, assembling his equipment, and when he came with it down the muddy bank he found the others already in the boat. The Indian boy was in the middle of the stern end, seated before the engine. The others had positioned themselves at the boat's three corners with the fourth open for Fletcher.

He came aboard with his gear dangling from both shoulders. He felt at once the cold water rippling beneath him. He felt the boat shift with his weight. There was an awkward moment as he fought to remain upright with the weight of his gear pulling him in one direction while the boat moved in the other. He might have gone down, but Drew put out an arm and Fletcher used it to steady himself.

Harmon laughed as Fletcher regained his balance, then took his seat. "I remember that," he said. He was nodding toward Fletcher's orange housing. "I remember that housing from the islands." He turned to Martin and Jones seated in the stern on either side of the boy. "He lost that thing once," Harmon told them, "on the reef at the Pipe."

"We've heard the story," Robbie said, and from there they traveled in silence along the river for perhaps a mile before coming within sight of its mouth.

Here the boy made for a narrow strip of exposed shoreline on the northern bank. The water grew slower as they approached, due in part to an arm of rock which extended some yards into the river to form there a kind of miniature breakwater. The bottom appeared shallow and sandy, and the boy was able to bring the Zodiac to within a few feet of the beach, at which point Drew Harmon clambered over the side. He called for Jones and Martin to follow, and Fletcher was given to understand that it would be him and the boy from here on out.

"We'll never get this thing over the bars with all of us in it," Drew said. He was looking at Fletcher when he spoke. "We'll hike to that point on the north side of the bay. It's the shortest way out. We'll have the current with us from there. The way I figure it, you two can set up on the south side of the peak." Harmon smiled. "You should be staring right into the pocket. But watch the lines. The peaks can shift. You don't want to get caught inside."

The Zodiac bobbed and heaved as Jones and Martin followed Harmon into the water and soon all three men were wading toward the shore, the big boards beneath their arms.

Fletcher had only nodded when Drew spoke and he watched now as the three surfers moved away. He couldn't help noticing that neither of his two traveling companions had complained about getting out of the Zodiac, nor had either of them spoken to him or looked in his direction before going over the side. He watched as they splashed through the shallows and disappeared quickly among the trees, quite content, no doubt, to take their chances paddling rather than risk the river mouth in such a craft and when they were gone, it was just Fletcher and the boy, alone on the river in the rubber boat.

The boat was bisected by a pair of braces to be used as seats. The boy was already in the center of the one in the stern. With his companions gone, Fletcher now moved to the middle of the one in the bow. He was aware of the boy watching him with a steady liquid stare, and it occurred to him for the first time that Drew Harmon had not introduced them. When he had situated himself and found the boy still staring at him, it occurred to him as well that the boy was waiting for some command, that, in fact, he was in charge. He found the revelation dispiriting.

Fletcher could not quite bring himself to speak. He nodded to see what that would do, then took some comfort in the smoothness with which the boy swung them around, pointing once more toward the mouth of the river. He could not, however, take much comfort in what he saw there.

The tide was down and the bars appeared quite shallow. In fact, from his position at the bow of the little boat, he could see nothing but row upon row of white water, and beyond that row upon row of waves that seemed to line up quickly out of nowhere. The waves turned slick, muddy faces toward a rising sun, then sucked out to pound the bars with the sharp cracking of light artillery. The sound could be heard as something quite distinct from the rush of the river or the distant thunder of the big outside sets which, from their current vantage point, could not even be seen but only imagined.

Farther up river, Fletcher had noted one or two canoes, manned by fishermen, drifting in the early light. This far down, however, he and the boy were quite alone. Overhead, the sky was beginning to blue, but at the river's edge patches of fog still clung to the banks, and as they approached the mouth, a fine, steady mist thrown off by the sea settled to cake the eyelashes and lips, but in spite of which Fletcher found his own mouth quite dry, with his tongue thick and swollen against it.

The boy, as it turned out, was quite good with the Zodiac. He kept them in constant motion, turning first to the left, then to the right, snaking his way through the conflicting waves, making always for the shoulders, gunning up the faces of at least two inside grinders Fletcher guessed to be well overhead and which, if timed incorrectly, would certainly have dumped them on the bars, making for a cold and tricky swim.

In spite of the boy's skill, however, Fletcher was also aware of the rather sickening way the inflatable boat had of bending back upon itself as the boy pushed it up the face and of the way it bent back the other way as it bridged the peak and of the ripples of cold water which he could feel even through the neoprene booties, and he was quite certain that Drew had been right. The small craft would not have born the weight of four men and a boy through the white water, but would have foundered on the bars.

Once outside the boy swung the boat north, taking them past the headland Fletcher had climbed the day before, allowing a first look at the bay and the distant point. The sea was deeper here and the Zodiac rode easily on the ground swell, smooth green water rushing beneath the bow as overhead the sky continued to clear with the sunlight pooling upon the water.

Chunks of driftwood bobbed in the light, together with beds of kelp, some bearing various crustaceans—bright spots of pink or orange which had been loosed from their moorings by the power of the swell, and on at least two occasions, sea lions raised sleek dark heads to look at them as they passed, and Fletcher was reminded of what he had seen on the landing—the scars wrapping Harmon's body like the seams of a baseball. He had not heard about the man being bitten, but clearly this is what had occurred. And this was as good a place as any—the very heart of what surfers called the Red Triangle. The fish came to the mouths of the rivers to spawn. The sea lions came to eat the fish. The great white came to eat the sea lions, and being of poor sight, were wont to get the occasional surfer as well, though generally these were spit back out when the mistake had been so noted and thereby leaving some, like Drew Harmon, to tell the tale.

Such lines of thought were, of course, counter-productive, and Fletcher set about preparing his equipment the better to drive them from his mind. He fooled with his light meter and gauged the angle of the sun. There were bumps on the horizon but as yet no sets. He heard the boy say something behind him and turned to see that he was pointing toward the shore. Fletcher followed the boy's finger with his eye. What he saw were three dark figures on boards angling toward them from the point, and as he followed their line of attack, he saw the first set beginning to build on the reef.

He had no doubt he and the boy were still well off the shoulder, but there was no way he was going to quell the beating of his heart as the set began to build, no way to escape that adrenaline rush you got from seeing a truly big wave from ground zero. It never looked quite real to him. And his first reaction was always the same and had been for twenty years; he could never quite believe he was putting himself in its way.

Fletcher had been around long enough to know the drill. The surfers would hang back a little on the inside, wait out the set, then sprint for the outside. Once outside, the trick was in knowing where to wait. The advantage enjoyed on this particular morning by Jones and Martin was that they were surfing with someone who had already charted the break and could show them their line-ups. It would be up to Fletcher and the boy to find their own.

It was to this end that Fletcher now set himself, and he watched as the first wave of the set passed over the reef and began to break. At close quarters, it was an unnerving spectacle, and yet a thing to behold, full of terror and fluid beauty. The amount of water involved was such that it was like watching a piece of the earth become liquid, as if in some cataclysm, or at the hour of creation. The wave rose first with great mass, like a hill, but this hill was made of liquid, in constant flux, and even as you watched it, it would change its form, turning itself to a long dark wall as the face went vertical and then beyond vertical as the crest began to feather and finally to pitch forward, to strike the water far out in front of the face—thus creating the vaunted green room of surfing myth—the place to be if you were to be there at all, on a board, at the eye storm, encompassed by the sound and the fury, bone dry in a place no one had ever been, or would be again, because when the wave was gone the place was gone too and would exist only in memory, or perhaps, if the right person was there, in the right place, with the right equipment, it would exist on film—a little piece of eternity to hang on the wall.

There were five waves in the set. Fletcher reckoned their size at twenty-five feet. A pair broke perfectly and could have been ridden. Three others broke in sections that were too long to make—sections of two, maybe three hundred yards—and when a section like that would go off, Fletcher was aware of the little beads of water that had gathered along the sides of the Zodiac jumping with the impact—suggesting no doubt some principal of physics he had, in his present position, no desire to contemplate at length.

When the set had passed, he and the boy looked at each other. For a moment, Fletcher felt at a loss, as if in need of a translator, at which point, it occurred to him that this, of course, was ridiculous.

"We're going to have to get closer," Fletcher said. He made an effort to sound casual about it, as if this was business as usual.

The boy nodded. He turned in a more northerly direction, running almost parallel to the coast. He did not, however, give the boat much throttle, suggesting, Fletcher decided, that he understood what was needed but was in no great hurry to get there. In fact, Fletcher might have said the same for himself and he made no move to speed things up. But he had seen his shot and it had given him something with which to cut his fear. The hunt had begun. It was something he had not experienced in a long time and it was good, he thought, to have it back. It was good to be here.

The sea was smooth in the wake of the set, and Fletcher was aware of the three surfers angling toward the line up from the north even as he and the boy angled in from the south. He watched as the three men stroked to some invisible point of Drew's choosing then stopped and swung themselves up to straddle their boards. He held up a hand for the boy to cut back on his throttle and the boy did so. He and the boy were now even with the surfers, separated from them by a hundred yards of ocean.

It was his general plan to keep them in his sights, to hold south and west, then move in with the next set. He would set up on the south side of the peak, fifty yards from the impact zone. He would shoot with the sun at his back, lighting the wave at its highest and most dramatic point, then ride up and over a still unbroken shoulder as the wave passed by. The boy would have to gun it to get them over the shoulder, but it was nothing he had not already done on the bars and Fletcher did not anticipate a problem. Afterward it would only remain to negotiate the mouth of the river at the session's end.

"This is good," Fletcher told the boy. He lowered his hand. "We'll wait right here."

The boy nodded, cut back on his throttle and raised the engine, allowing them to drift. Fletcher could find no suitable line up to the north, but to the south, there was a large island at the mouth of the river, and it seemed to him that if they held to its westernmost tip, they would be about right.

Turning toward the bay, he found them at the south end of a long strip of sand, and he picked that point where the sand ended in rock as his second line-up. He said as much to the boy. "Here and here," he said, and he showed the boy the tip of the island and the end of the sand. "We stay between these two points. Next set, we'll move in a little closer. You just head right toward them." He waved at the surfers. "I'll be taking the pictures." He held up the camera for the boy to see, as if this would make him understand. "But as soon as I say go, you give it the gas, turn us out to sea, and get us over the shoulder." He paused a moment. "Just like you did on the inside. That was good, how you got us over those bars."

The boy smiled at him when he said that and Fletcher thought maybe this would work after all. The boy remained silent and Fletcher went back to fiddling with his stuff. He worked now with the lens, sighting through it, adjusting his focus. Through the lens, he could see the surfers very clearly, seated on their boards, a few yards apart. He could see Robbie Jones and Sonny Martin talking to one another. He could see Drew Harmon slightly apart, arms folded on his chest, eyes on the horizon.

He checked his watch and his line-ups. They had moved too far north along the sand and he said as much to the boy. The boy tilted his engine so that it was back in the water and made a little circle, bringing them back on line. Fletcher nodded. He looked at his watch once more, checked his light meter, and sighted through his lens.

It was always odd, he thought, these little moments of calm on a big day. He felt the sun warming the shoulders of his wet suit. He put down the camera and reached over the side of the boat. He splashed his face and hands, allowing the water to roll down his back, as he had begun to sweat in the thick suit. He looked at the boy. The boy was checking the line-ups, holding to them. He gets it, Fletcher thought. He's going to do all-right. At which point, Fletcher saw him look out to sea, and he saw his expression change.

Fletcher followed the boy's gaze. He was just in time to see Drew Harmon flatten himself on the deck of his board and begin to windmill toward the horizon. Jones and Martin followed suit and Fletcher felt his heart jump. It did not seem to him that they should have to paddle with such intent less they had been too far inside, and he looked toward the horizon himself and saw that, in fact, things had taken a turn.

A wave had begun to build and its peak had indeed shifted and it was further outside than he had anticipated. He looked at the boy, telling him to go, but the boy had tilted the engine out of the water and was now having difficulty in getting it back in. Fletcher moved to the stern to see if he could help and when the boy looked at him, he could see that the boy was scared.

The engine was hung up on something and when they got it into the water, it stalled. Fletcher watched as the boy tugged at the starter line. It was a short line and a one-man job and it was the boy's engine. Fletcher sat back on the rubber seat, striving to master his fear. They were still, he reasoned, far enough south to be well off the peak. Even with a stalled engine, they might ride out a wave or two. Surely it would start in the end. It was the thought with which he sought to console himself as the first gust of an offshore wind kicked down upon them from the mouth of the river.

Fletcher looked at the boy tugging furiously on the line. The wind was cold and dry, laced with the scent of pine. It suggested high pressure and clear skies. It was all he could have asked for. It was also pushing the rubber boat in a northerly direction and he knew that if this continued, if they did not get under power soon, they would be in deep shit, the blessing become the malediction. He looked toward the beach, as if he might have some say in the matter, and it was while he was looking that he heard someone yell. It was a kind of war whoop echoing across the water. Fletcher knew it to be the voice of one of the surfers, and he knew only too well what it meant and he turned to the sea. What he saw there was a wave as large as any he had yet been forced to deal with in thirty years on the water.

The thing seemed to stretch from beyond the point to the mouth of the river—one endless dark wall which, when it hit the reef, would no doubt blot out the sky. Already it was beginning to draw from the depths, adding exponentially to itself even as Fletcher watched it, and it was here that he heard the second war whoop and that he saw the surfers. There were two of them and he believed it to be Jones and Harmon.

Harmon was scratching for the lip, trying to make it over the top. Robbie Jones was behind him, but even as Fletcher watched, he saw the kid swing the board around and begin to stroke toward the river mouth, paddling for all he was worth in an effort to overcome the water flowing back up the face to meet him. To Fletcher's astonishment, the kid was going for it. He was trying to catch the wave.

It was an impossible moment. Fletcher had no doubt the kid was undergunned, that he was already too late into the wave. There was a good ten feet of water above his head, another twenty below him, with the wave just about to jack as he got to his feet. Instinctively, Fletcher went for his camera.

The wave face was dark with the amount of water it contained but with the sunlight splitting the last thin bands of cloud, lighting up the yellow rails of the Brewer gun and the red stripes of the wet suit in such a way that, as Fletcher brought the scene into focus, he could actually see the colors reflected on the face of the wave, and suddenly he was drawing a bead on Robbie Jones. Even as the boy jerked on the starter line. Even as the wave bore down upon them, because in some dark corner of his head, Fletcher knew very clearly what he was looking at. The only shot ever taken from the water at Heart Attacks. In epic conditions. A rider up. The thing he had come for. He saw his shot and he pulled the trigger.

It was really quite perfectly done. Robbie Jones was on his feet, crouched slightly with the board bucking beneath him but driving cleanly down the face of the wave. Fletcher held him in frame, leading him slightly, firing away, aware now too of yet one more sound—something apart from the thunder of the wave, the clicking of the camera. He was aware of the absurd sputtering of the Zodiac's outboard as it kicked to life and yet even as he put out his hand in anticipation of its acceleration, the foolish thing leaped beneath him.

Fletcher's hand, extended backwards, caught at the craft's rail. The rail in question, however, was wide and fat, made of synthetic rubber, slick with spray, and it afforded no purchase. Nor was there time for a second grab. Just like that and Fletcher was going over, still clutching the old orange housing he'd once risked his life to save, ass first into the icy Pacific.

9

Fletcher's first impulse, upon sinking beneath the surface, was to believe this was not happening. He had been thirty years a waterman. Only a kook of the first order would get caught looking, would fall out of the boat half a mile from shore, his camera still in his hands. The thought, however comforting, was a fleeting one and quickly erased by the sub-fifty-degree water which filled his head and he knew that he had indeed taken the fall, that he'd done it in the path of one of the biggest waves he had ever had to deal with, in shark-infested waters, hundreds of yards from a beach upon which no palms swayed in tropic light.

The second thought that came to him was that he would survive. He was no stranger to the open ocean. He had rolled waves for thirty years and he would roll this one. At which point, he rose to the surface and looked once more into the teeth of the dark monster already beginning to feather before a luminous sky and he was not so sure. The urge to panic rose in his chest. He felt it as a physical presence, a dull pain which sapped the strength from his arms. Still, he knew what to do, and he knew that knowing it was the key. Or rather, he wanted to believe that knowing it would prove the key. While one voice outlined a course of action, another cursed him for his ineptitude, calling loudly for panic and surrender, as if, by drowning, he could simply call the whole thing off. Fletcher gathered himself before the approaching wall of water. He took two or three deep breaths, held the last one, bent himself in the middle and kicked out with his legs, swimming for the bottom.

He held the old orange housing before him, kicking hard, hoping to get deep enough so that the wave would not suck him back to the surface. The water grew colder with each kick, and darker. He could see no more than a few inches in front of his face when he felt it come. It came first as a movement in the ocean around him. And then the explosion, prenaturally low. A thing felt more than heard. A function of blood. A promise of what was to come. And yet when the turbulence hit, it did so out of all proportion even to what he had expected. The camera was jerked from his grasp. His wet suit filled as the frigid water flushed down his back. His first thought was that the damn thing had burst a seam, that it would carry him down, as surely as if he had been encased in concrete.

There was no swimming against it now. The shock waves buffeted him as though he were some badly outclassed fighter pinned to the ropes, his sense of direction lost to the sea. Again, he sought to cling to a single thought, that it was a question of time—twenty seconds, max, and that though these twenty seconds might seem an eternity, he had been here before. This too would pass. At which point he began to flail, clutching at handfuls of water, clawing in what he could only hope was the proper direction, forgetting everything save the desire to breath.

And in time it came. The release. The blackness gone to gray, the sudden explosion of sunlight and sound as his head broke through the layers of foamy water, ringing as if from a blow. His first thought, however, was for the next wave, and instinctively he turned toward the reef where indeed the second wave of the set had already begun to build and he saw the boy for the last time.

The Zodiac had managed somehow to ride over the top of the

first wave, for Fletcher saw it quite clearly, not fifty yards ahead of him. He could see the boy sitting in what appeared to be some attitude of calm at the stern of his craft in his blue pants and red flannel shirt, his red ball-cap. The Zodiac, however, showed no indication of having regained power. It was simply sitting on the face of the wave, about midway up, with the crest already beginning to feather above it.

One could see what was to come. The thing was inevitable and Fletcher turned from it. Once again he dove. And once again he felt it come, the distant thunder, the pressure in the ears. This time, however, he got under it. Maybe it was the thrashing he had taken on the first wave, making for an inspired effort. Maybe the second wave was simply smaller. He allowed himself a momentary respite and for a moment he simply drifted, allowing his air to take him up. But he was deep and once more the need for oxygen pushed him, kicking and clawing for the surface, dreading what he would find there, for he did not believe he could roll a third wave. Nor did he know if the turbulence was pushing him toward the shore or only holding him in place. When he surfaced, however, the sea was awash once more in light, and there was nothing on it save the movement of the swell itself, which might be seen as an undulation of the horizon, as if some procession of unnamed beasts roamed there, skulking in the blue light.

He felt the cold now, as he had not felt it before. It was a gnawing thing. It worked upon the bone. He fought once more the almost overwhelming urge to panic, to simply thrash wildly, but set out instead with a measured stroke, offering himself instructions on hand position and follow-through, keeping his head down, breathing, at least for the present, on every other stroke, in some attempt to escape the impact zone before the next set could find him there. He had gone some distance when he became aware of a voice booming at him from across the water. What he saw was Drew Harmon. The man was stroking toward him on the deck of his big wooden board, a bright blue O'Neil hot lid in place over his outsized head, his nose and beard dripping water, his eyes full of demented light.

The man stroked up to him, pulled himself up to straddle the board, reached around behind his back, and, like the magician in a magic show, produced a single Churchill swim fin which he proceeded to pass to Fletcher. Fletcher received it with fingers from which any feeling had long ago departed.

"Swim for the point on the north side of the river mouth," Harmon shouted at him. He waved at some rocks Fletcher was able to see only when the ground swell had raised him to sufficient height.

"Don't let yourself get pulled past those rocks," Drew said. "You get caught in the rips at the mouth, you're going back out to sea."

And so saying, the man was gone. He flattened back out on his board and paddled off toward a distant line-up. Fletcher, for his part, had not said a word. The thought occurred to him that he was perhaps, at this particular point, incapable of it. Eventually he tried. He managed a kind of grotesque call. He found his voice was hoarse with the cold and weak, and he did not believe that the man had heard him and did not himself have any clear idea of what he was trying to say. Perhaps he was trying to tell him to look for the boy. Perhaps it was for himself that he called. But the man was gone, and Fletcher was alone once more with his blue hands and his ice-cream headache and his Churchill swim fin, which, eventually, he managed to work on over his bootie and with it in place he began to swim. He swam for the rocks and the beach he could not exactly see.

Fletcher made shore some fifteen feet from the rocks that marked the mouth of the river. Whether he would have made shore at all without the fin was a matter of some debate. In all probability, the current would have carried him past the rocks and into the rip which, in turn, would have carried him back to sea. And that, he was quite certain, would have been the end of him. He did not doubt that the fin had saved his life.

His legs, it seemed, had checked out already, for when he tried to stand they went out from under him at once. He went to all fours on a steep section of beach where rags of foam lay glistening like snow drifts in the sun, and the icy water, reluctant to let go such a tasty morsel, tugged at his arms and legs, threatening to pull him back once more. At last, however, the water withdrew, sweeping back down the steep bank of sand, raking at the myriad of tiny shards so that they rattled one against the other as might the instruments of some mariachi band sent in mockery of his arrival.

Fletcher made for higher ground on all fours, his camera gone, the Churchill fallen from his foot, his nose dripping water. He made some progress but eventually was caught from behind by yet one more onslaught of white water and foam. For though the swells on the outside reefs came in sets separated by lulls, the wave action on the inside bars was incessant and Fletcher was knocked flat, then dragged on his stomach back into the trough from which he had come, then pitched forward once more and rolled for several seconds up and down this treacherous incline like a piece of driftwood before regaining his position on hands and knees. He crawled more wildly this time, without regard for the spectacle he would no doubt have presented, had there been any to witness it.

He crawled among splintered timbers and piles of kelp from which clouds of black flies rose at his approach. Soon there was dry sand clinging to his wet suit. Yet even here he continued to crawl, not trusting himself to stand or to look back from where he had come, and in fact might have crawled for some distance had not the unlikely sound of an engine brought him to a halt. He looked back along the beach toward the northern end of the bay and saw there an aging primer gray pickup bouncing across the rocks and saw at the same time two dark figures running before it.

In a moment, he was able to make out the colors of their wet suits and saw that it was Sonny Martin and Robbie Jones. They were without boards, pumping with their arms to aid them though the sand, or using them for balance among the rocks so that one might, from a distance, have taken then for some outlandish form of seabird seeking flight with black, featherless wings.

Fletcher rose unsteadily to his feet. He could see the truck more clearly now, could see there were people in the bed, could see their flannel shirts, their dark, flowing hair. As he watched, one of the figures leaned suddenly from the bed and threw something. Fletcher could not say what it was but he saw Sonny Martin stumble and go down.

Robbie Jones came on, offering a single piece of advice as he passed. "Run," he said. And Fletcher did.

They splashed into a shallow channel of fast-moving water at the mouth of the river where Fletcher went into a hole and did something to his ankle. He stumbled and began to swim. Fortunately, it was not necessary to swim far, as the water, though not deep, was cold and fast-moving. Soon, however, he had come to the pile of rock he had earlier that day named as an island and used as one of his line-ups.

Robbie reached the summit before him. Fletcher could see him as he began to climb, scrounging amid the sea grass and razor-sharp crustaceans for handholds among the rocks. He saw that Robbie had managed to salvage a day pack and, from that, his wrist rocket, that even now he was in the act of launching stones in the direction of the beach. In time, Fletcher joined him. They had come to a level place among the stand of trees which capped the island.

"What the hell is this?" Fletcher asked. "What's going on down there?"

"Fuck you," Robbie said. He was a moment in looking for more rocks with which to arm himself. "I shouldn't have even told you to run, man. I should've let them have you."

Fletcher just stared at him. He could see that the boy's face was scraped on one side and that his eyes were gone quite mad.

"You lost the fucking kid," Robbie said. "You get out there with that fucking kid and you can't keep him out of the impact zone. I thought you knew your shit, man. This kid's gone, dude. And these fuckers think it's our fault." He fired off another rock in the direction of the truck. "They got Martin," he said.

Fletcher was momentarily awash in a dawning comprehension, of what had transpired, of how his part in it would be perceived. "What do you mean, they got him?" he asked.

"I mean some fucker cold-cocked him with a piece of wood."

Fletcher nodded, for he had seen as much but worried that Robbie was referring to some new atrocity just witnessed.

"He's still down there," Robbie said.

Fletcher looked toward the beach. He found it blurred by sea spray and refracted light.

"The kid lost his engine," Fletcher heard himself say. "He lost power."

"Bullshit, man. I saw you fall out of the fucking boat."

Fletcher stood in his wet rubber suit, on his bad ankle. He would not, he decided, be required to defend himself before the likes of Robbie Jones.

"You weren't there," Fletcher said. "I was."

"No shit."

At that moment, a volley of what could only be gunshots rang out from the beach. Robbie and Fletcher dove for cover behind the rocks as a number of bullets slammed into the trees high above their heads. They watched as a huge owl broke from its perch and flew screaming into the sun.

"Jesus Christ," Fletcher said.

"Cop to it," Robbie told him. They were seated now on the stiff winter grass which grew among the rocks, their backs to the stone. "The kid's gone. You blew it. And we're fucked."

1 0

Travis was up with the dawn. The council of tribes was scheduled to meet that night and he had intended to tidy up his notes from the last meeting, as he had offered to act as unofficial secretary. But he was finding it difficult to concentrate. In fact, his mind kept slipping back to his meeting with Kendra Harmon. This annoyed him. Surely there were more productive things to concentrate upon. The problem, he concluded, was that his life had become one of routine. The women he saw from time to time tended now to be of a type, middle-aged divorcées, perverse mirror images of himself, with children and mortgage payments and health complaints. Everyone drank. And though the girls still got prettier at closing time, he had learned through experience it was best to be alone in the first light.

At length he stood up, for he had been seated at the kitchen table, and went to the old stove that had belonged to his grandmother and was equipped with a narrow compartment in which one might keep a small wood fire burning. He added a few sticks of kindling then went to the sink to draw water for coffee. The seas were high again today. He could hear the thunder of the waves from his kitchen.

He leaned back against the counter, surveying the cluttered room. It was not much different, he decided, from many of the reservation houses. Artifacts, which had once been his grandmother's, competed for space with the trash of the present. A television capped by a battered set of rabbit-ear antennas occupied one corner. Various magazines and newspapers lay strewn about the floor and furniture, which tended to be of the thrift-store variety. On one wall, there were a pair of old hand-carved pipes and a photograph of his grandmother in a plain cotton dress, wearing the beads he'd been asked to bring to the Jump Dance. On an opposing wall he'd hung a painting of an Indian maiden. She had been painted on black velvet, framed in gold, and Travis had picked her out at a Hupa crafts fair, the proceeds from which had gone to build a gymnasium for the Hupa school. All of which served in some way to elevate her, at least in Travis's mind, from the trashy to the sublime. She was seated on a rock, her buckskin skirt parted to reveal a great expanse of shapely thigh. Her profile was to the viewer, her head tilted slightly upward, her sleek black hair thrown back. Her eyes were fixed upon some high and distant place. She was barefoot, a rawhide band around one ankle, suggesting captivity narratives and maidens in distress. As he looked at the painting now, he found that she reminded him of Kendra Harmon. Something was amiss down there on the river, and, at some point during the night, he'd decided that he should do something about it. She had, after all, come to his door, a bird with a broken wing. In fact, he had thought of little else during the past forty-eight hours, so that when his phone began to ring just now, his first impulse was to believe Kendra Harmon was calling for him.

At such an hour, this was highly unlikely, and yet he managed to hold the possibility in his mind as one might hold the flame of a candle, cupped in the palm of one's hand to shelter it from the wind. The gesture gave him reason for hope. He found in it some small victory of the heart over the forces of entropy and quiet desperation.

Unhappily, it was not Kendra Harmon on the phone. It was Denice, the girl he had hired for the office. She was calling from the reservation and the moment he heard her voice, he knew that something was wrong. There was trouble on the river, she told him. David Little from Johnstons had been seen there in a rubber boat with Drew Harmon and several white men. A number of Yuroks had gone to investigate, her brother among them. Denice had seen them driving away in Bean Dip's white Toyota, and she had seen that they were armed.

Travis left quickly. It was the kind of thing which might well come to nothing. Drew Harmon was not a fisherman. David Little, however, was Hupa, and Travis could not imagine why he would be with Drew Harmon on the river at dawn. Harmon sometimes surfed near there, at a big break north of the mouth, but he had not been known to require the aid of Indians or rubber boats. And then there was the specter presented by Bean Dip and whatever crew he was carting around in his truck. Travis knew most of them, by sight if not by name, the ones who'd dropped out early to take up careers as petty thieves and small-time drug dealers. He knew Bean Dip by name because he was one of the few Travis had been able to catch in the act of vandalizing his office. The boy was no more than sixteen years old and the thought of him at first light in the throws of some speed-induced dementia and packing a piece was not reassuring. It was Travis's hope that by putting himself on the scene he might stop something before it started, and it was only when he had come within sight of the river and heard the sound of guns that he understood he had been too late.

He parked in a muddy turnout that marked the end of the lower road. He jumped from his truck and began to run. He ran toward the coast, his boots tearing holes in the loose soil. The trail ran downhill, through coffeeberry and poison oak. It passed among a stand of coastal alder still holding to the last of their leaves and came finally to an immense pile of logs it was necessary to traverse before reaching the beach but from whose summit the beach was plainly visible. And it was here, atop this stack of seaworn timber, that he was afforded his first glimpse of what the morning had wrought.

A number of Indians were grouped around a Chevrolet pickup Travis recognized as belonging to Goffer Mayhew, a local Yurok empowered by the BIA to enforce the fishing boundaries. A vehicle could indeed be gotten to the beach via a fire road some miles to the north, but the beach was tricky business and Travis could see that Goffer had managed to run himself aground on an outcropping of stone where the truck now sat with one rear tire spinning slowly in midair. There were other Indians on the beach as well, but these were strung out along the sand where it fell away in a long shallow decline and hence more difficult to see clearly. Most appeared grouped around a dark shape that hunkered in the mist at the water's edge, and though he could not see this shape well enough to name it, he could see enough to know that he did not like the looks of it. It looked like death, he thought, even before he had given it a name or seen the figure on the rocks.

It was an Indian from the truck who drew his attention to the man on the rocks. A boy in khakis and a flannel shirt came suddenly from behind the old Chevy, darted across a rocky stretch of sand, and kicked at a prostrate figure—a blond-haired man in a gaily colored wet suit. Travis saw the body jerk with the kick, then fold in upon itself.

The boy delivered a second kick, then ran toward the truck in a crouched position as if he too were afraid of something. Travis was trying to guess what the something might be when one of the truck's headlights suddenly disappeared in what, for Travis, was a soundless explosion of glass. This, in turn, was followed by the hollow crack of a rifle, and he saw that the truck's owner, Goffer Mayhew, had himself climbed into the bed where he now stood sporting a red bandanna and sighting over the cab with a Winchester 30/30. He appeared, Travis thought, to be aiming toward a stand of trees on a small island situated at the mouth of the river not a hundred yards from where the Indians had gathered on its northern shore. On a minus tide, the island might be walked to. At the moment, it was separated from the mainland by a fifty-yard trough of fast-moving water.

Travis left his spot on the woodpile and went once more into the brush, following now the path of a small stream which ran to the beach, arriving finally at that place where there was nothing more to separate him from the morning's devastation.

The Indians, as Travis had noted, held the beach. An enemy he had yet to see had taken the island where, by some means, a wrist rocket perhaps, they were able to launch stones with sufficient speed and accuracy to provide cover for the prostrate figure now occupying that no-man's land between the truck and the island. Further to the west, where the beach angled down toward the sea, the dark shape Travis had glimpsed from the timbers still hunkered in the mist, and he saw it now for what it was—the tattered remains of David Little's Zodiac.

The craft, or what was left of it, sat where it had no doubt been planted by a powerful shorebreak, impaled upon a jagged outcropping of stone though the lacy fringes of spent waves still reached out to brush it, beckoning it back to a more watery grave.

The Indians had collected about these two objects, the truck and the Zodiac, thereby dividing themselves into halves. Of the group which had gathered around the Zodiac, most were women. Some wept openly. Others held to the hands of small children, blank-faced before a rising sun. There were several older children there as well, who had come on their own, unattended, or who had broken from their parents and scampered about the beach as if at play, for unlike the men at the truck, these were well beyond the range of the rocks. A pair of rust-colored mongrels ran alternately among the children and the adults, pausing now and then to sniff at the remains of the inflatable boat. The coats of the dogs were wet and had begun to give off steam with the coming of the sun.

Travis's trail had brought him to the beach very near the truck, and when Goffer's rifle fired again, Travis could see the weapon's recoil. He could hear the men shouting, calling out conflicting coordinates in frustrated attempts to direct fire, as Goffer was operating with the sun in his face rather than behind him and who, in any event, was not known as a marksman, or even a passable dart player.

Travis looked once more at the figure in the sand. The man was clearly alive but also clearly injured, perhaps seriously. He would have to be gotten to soon. Though how this might be accomplished in the face of the flying rocks was not immediately apparent. On the other hand, Travis did not imagine the man's cover could last for long, at which time it would be the men at the truck who would have to be reckoned with, for clearly some great wrong had been done here and they meant to have recompense.

It was a tricky situation and Travis was some time behind the last of the brush. He was thinking about his next move and how best to play it in light of these difficulties when he caught sight of Drew Harmon.

The man was running up the beach from the sea. He was coming fast, with long, powerful strides and before Travis had done little more than register his arrival, he was already past the Zodiac and among the men. Travis felt himself freeze, as if in expectation of some further calamity. What he saw, however, were men parting to make way for this *wagay* in their midst. Upon closer inspection, he supposed that he could not blame them, for the man came on with great authority and in general, it was as it had always been among his people. They knew true craziness when they saw it and were apt to respect it, or at least to give it clearance.

He supposed the man had taken them by surprise as well, for Harmon had fallen upon their flank and leapt at once into the bed of the truck so as to be beyond their reach, though unless they had been able to act as one, Travis thought it unlikely any could have successfully opposed him on their own, or even in concert with another.

Goffer turned when the truck heaved beneath him but he was way too slow. Drew Harmon had the rifle. He pulled it toward him and then back in a rapid motion. Travis saw the stock hit Goffer in the face. The Indian would have done well to let go. He hung on, however, and when Harmon pulled again, in a kind of twisting motion, the Indian was flung completely out of the truck and planted face first in the sand. Harmon was left in the bed, the rifle in his hands, swinging it in a wide arc as the men around him dove for cover.

Travis moved quickly then, out onto the sand, waving his arms. He saw the rifle swing toward him but he remained upright, his arms in the air. The men made way for him. He heard someone call his name, but he ignored them. Goffer Mayhew was pulling himself out of the sand. The rifle had broken his nose and split his mouth. Goffer was trying to put the nose back together with a thumb and forefinger, spitting blood and teeth into the beach.

"Goddamn little pissant in those trees," Drew said. "We don't get that fucker out of here, someone is going to get killed."

"Someone already has," one of the men said.

"It wasn't them that did it," Drew said. "Let 'em take their guy and go."

Travis was somewhat amazed at Drew Harmon's demeanor. He'd pulled his hood away from his head. There was a dark light in his eyes, with the veins and muscles standing out on his neck where it strained at the collar of his wet suit, but the man's voice was calm and he was talking about pissants in the trees as if he and Travis had come to the beach to do no more than cast their bait into the surf.

"Who is it?" Travis asked.

Harmon ignored the question. A rock creased the roof of the cab. Drew ducked and cursed and shouted toward the island, though it seemed to Travis that his words must have been taken on the wind, which, like the sun, was in favor of the shooter in the trees. He was answered by a second rock.

Drew turned, squatting on his haunches, the cab at his back, the rifle across his knees. "Kid must be blind as well as stupid," he said.

"Good aim for a blind man," Travis offered.

Drew just looked at him. "I tried to get to them on the board," he said. "Currents pulled me way the hell over to the other side of the river. I had to paddle all the way back around the bay to get in here."

Travis looked toward the sea, lost for a moment in simple astonishment at this feat, though Drew himself had spoken of it as if he had done no more than dog paddle around some placid lake. It was the Indians who answered Travis's question, crowding about him, speaking all at once. The *wagays,* it seems, had come to surf. David Little had been paid to take them out. They wanted photographs. It had gone badly. The boat was lost. David could not be found. While Drew stayed out to continue the search, three of the surfers had come to the beach. There had been an argument, a fight. At least two of the invaders had fled to higher ground. The standoff had begun.

"We've got to get them off the land," Drew said.

Travis nodded. The present situation was barely under control, and he suspected there were already other men going for guns. If someone was shot here, federal agents would come. People would be fucked with. And that was never good.

"Tide's still high," Drew said. "If you were to get your ass out there in a boat you might get 'em off the rock before it turns."

The plan was not without merit. Travis knew these people. They would not leave the beach. It was their beach. He looked over the men grouped around him. They were not bad people, he thought, a few fishermen, a few loafers and drinkers, a few delinquents. He saw them in the misty light of the beach, in their jeans and khakis and flannel shirts worn too big and untucked over T-shirts. He saw the knit caps, worn at the eyebrows as if they had made a quick inspection of the outside world and chosen as their models the very ones most likely to ensure their own demise.

"How bad is he?" Travis asked. He was looking now at the young man who had fallen.

"Don't know," Drew said. "I'll look. But he ought to see a doctor. I can tell you that right now."

Travis was thinking this over when he caught sight of Bean Dip, together with Denice's brother among the men. To his great horror, he saw that Bean Dip was indeed armed. The butt end of a small caliber revolver could be seen sticking out of the waistband of his jeans, and even as Travis watched, he saw Bean Dip pull the gun. His first thought was that Bean Dip would drawn down on Drew Harmon. Bullets would fly. Any number of people would be killed. Instead, however, Bean Dip stepped out onto the sand and began firing rounds at the island.

Travis got to him quickly, seizing him by the wrist. The youth's arm felt no bigger around than a yardstick in his hand and when he twisted it, Bean Dip let go the gun.

"Are you crazy?" Travis asked him.

Bean Dip responded by trying to kick him in the balls. Travis gave him the heel of his hand up alongside his temple and set him down in the sand. He felt a rock pass his ear. Close. He could hear it sing. He reached down and grabbed the kid, dragged him to his feet and stepped back, getting both of them behind the truck. Bean Dip shook loose, spitting and cursing, demanding his piece.

Travis flipped open the chamber and dumped the remaining shells on the sand. He stuffed the empty gun into the waistband of his own trousers and looked at the men grouped around him. "Okay," he said. He tried to make himself heard, and he saw that most of them were looking at him. "We don't want the feds out here. I'm gonna try and get those guys off the reservation. You see me out there, you back off."

The faces which stared back at him were, for the most part, impassive. Still, he thought, they would do it, could the *wagays* be removed. He looked once more at Drew Harmon.

The man was still hunkered down in the bed of the truck, his hair in wet tendrils draped over his shoulders, an odd half smile playing about his face as if this last little scene with Bean Dip was something acted out for his entertainment.

"You got about two hours before the tide turns," Drew told him.

Travis just looked at him. He wondered if the idea that any of this was his fault had ever entered the man's head, but he did not suppose so. Guilt was for lesser men. A sign of weakness.

"I'll tell you what," Travis said. "I'll make it just as fast as I can."

Drew Harmon grinned at him. "You do that," he said.

Travis stared at the grinning face, taken with a moment of profound contempt, for the man's arrogance, for the ignorance which accompanied it. Had Mr. Harmon taken the time to learn a little more about the people he had come to live among he would not have hired a Hupa to bring a boat through Yurok waters, and at least some of the morning's troubles would have been averted. Nor, Travis believed, would he have been so complacent just now, for in truth there was a good deal more to be worried about than the turning of the tide.

The men on the beach were Yurok. David Little had been Hupa. His people came from a particularly bad place deep in the interior of the reservation. In time, the word of this thing would spread. It would reach even into those places without phones or electricity where a certain breed of men with guns and idle hands might leave untended their meth labs and fields of contraband long enough to come downriver, drawn by the promise of sport and a taste for mindless violence. Travis knew these men, as much, that is, as one could, for they were of a different sort from these on the beach and could not truly be known by anyone of this world, for theirs was the vestige of some other, and all he could say of them with certainty was that they would not be so easily reasoned with, or held at bay, even by the likes of Drew Harmon. There was, of course, little point in going into any of this with the surfer. One might as well tell it to the wind. And so it was that having said his good-byes to the men, Travis turned and made his way back through the manzanita with the beach grown silent behind him, save for the sound of the waves which continued to rage and moan as if they had not yet heaped sufficient calamity upon the land.

Travis kept a boat on the river, an aluminum-hulled skiff with a Johnson outboard. The boat was stored on the dock of an old friend, a Yurok barber by the name of Carl Sugarfoot. The dock was about a mile and a half north of the mouth. Travis reached it quickly in his truck and soon he was on the water, motoring toward the sea.

The island upon which the surfers had stranded themselves was known locally as the Witch's Rock. Travis had visited it many times. He'd camped and picnicked there with each of his wives. As he approached it now, upon sun-spangled water, it was impossible not to think of those times, or to see it as a perfect day for such an outing—a thing to be undertaken with a bottle of wine, in the company of a young lady. Kendra Harmon came to mind. He was imagining what that might be like as the island drew near. He put in at a tiny cove on the southern side, then tied his boat off to a tree that jutted from the rocks at an angle perpendicular to the water below. It was an easy climb from this point, and soon he was looking down on the grassy bowl at the center of the little island which was shaped something like a squat volcano.

The surfers were just about where he had expected to find them but he was some time in watching, wary of getting nailed with a rock. Given the number he'd seen pelting the beach, he had supposed both men were in some way armed. He saw now this was not the case.

One of the men seemed to have injured himself. He was stretched out on his back in the grass, his hands laced behind his head, but he'd pulled off one of his booties, as if to examine his foot. The other man, however, was getting off enough shots for any two men. He was a lanky, well-muscled youth with a shaved head and a huge tattoo which covered most of his back. Travis was afforded a look at the tattoo, as the man had peeled his wet suit down around his waist. He saw too that he had been right about the wrist rocket. The kid would scrabble about on the rocks like a spider on speed, collecting ammunition, then rise to fire, occasionally getting off some kind of hoarse scream as well, though between the roar of the surf and the rush of wind, his words were, for the most part, incomprehensible.

Travis waited until the surfer was looking for rocks to make his entrance into the grassy bowl. He did so with his hands raised, palms out, in what he assumed to be some universal gesture of peace and goodwill.

The man on the ground saw him at once. Travis saw him sit up, then call something to the kid with the wrist rocket. The man on the ground was probably close to Travis's age. He looked to be fairly tall himself, a bit lanky, like the kid, but a good deal softer around the edges. His hair was straight and brown and fell to the collar of his wet suit.

"I'm here to help," Travis said.

"Help what?" the kid asked him.

Travis was a moment in staring at this bald-headed *wagay*. He could see where the boy might be a problem.

"Name's Travis McCade. I work for the local Indian council. I've come to get you and your friend here off the reservation."

"Those fuckers packed my bro, man."

Travis watched as the kid bent quickly to collect a rock.

"You have to understand that this is their land," Travis told him.

He was doing his best to remain calm. He was aware of the man on the ground watching him. "All they want right now is for you to leave. They wanted to hurt your friend, they could've shot him by now."

This seemed to give the boy pause. Travis turned to the other man. "Are you all-right?" he asked.

"Twisted my ankle. It's not that bad. Just how do you propose to get us out of here?"

"I have a boat," Travis told him.

"What about the guy on the beach?" the man asked.

"Drew is down there now. I give him the signal, they will let him get your buddy into town."

"How do we know this isn't some trick?" the bald surfer said.

"If it was a trick, I'd be packing and you'd be dead," Travis told him. Having said this, he crossed the bowl and went up into the rocks from which the kid had shelled the beach. He could see the truck and the men below. He waved his arms and shouted. In time he saw Drew Harmon stand up in the bed of the truck, the rifle held aloft in one hand.

"That Harmon?"

Travis turned to find that the kid had followed him into the rocks, that he was squinting toward the beach.

"Yes it is. You'd been payin' attention to what you were shooting at, you might've seen him sooner."

"Yea, an' get myself shot," the kid said.

Travis left his perch and went to look at the other man's foot. The guy was already pulling on a bootie, but Travis could see the ankle was swollen and starting to bruise. He supposed the man was right, that it was no more than a sprain. Still, he thought, it might be necessary to give him a lift to the boat. He said as much to the kid.

When he got no answer, he turned to find the boy struggling back into his wet suit, still on the rocks. He had put the wrist rocket on the ground, but now, with the wet suit zipped, he picked it up once more. When he saw Travis looking at him, he said, "What?"

"Your friend," Travis told him. "We may need to give him a lift."

The kid laughed. "You can lift him," he said. "He's no friend of mine."

Travis performed a slow double take. He looked once at the man on the ground, as if some confirmation of these words were needed, then back at the kid. He was in time to see the boy's hands at work with the wrist rocket. He could guess what was coming. He was just too slow to do much about it. The rock itself was invisible. It came as a flash of light, a settling into shadow, as the stiff winter grass rushed to meet him.

11

Fletcher witnessed the stoning of the Indian with no small amount of horror. He saw the man bring a hand to his head and he saw his knees buckle. The man wobbled and went down. He dropped to one knee before rolling onto his side and then his back.

Fletcher turned to Robbie Jones.

The youth was standing with the wrist rocket dangling from one hand. "Wasted that fucker," he said.

Fletcher was silent with disbelief.

"I'm outta here," Robbie told him. At which point he sprinted across the grass and disappeared among the trees.

Fletcher watched him go. It occurred to him that perhaps he'd best go as well. If anyone else were to come upon this little scene, they might well assume Fletcher had felled the man himself. Things might go badly for him. But there did not seem to be anyone else around, and Fletcher could see that the man was already attempting to right himself. Fletcher finished with his bootie and got to his feet.

The man who had identified himself as Travis McCade was a thickset man with black hair starting to gray at the temples. As Fletcher reached him, the man had managed to bring himself to a three-point stance. He was supporting his head with one hand, the elbow braced upon his knee.

Fletcher asked if he was all-right. When there was no response, he moved closer. He reached to touch the man's shoulder. When he did this, the man shouted. He brought the hand that had been on the ground up in a kind of backhanded swing. The blow grazed Fletcher's cheekbone. Fletcher leaped backward, tripped over a rock, and landed on his ass. The man, pulled off balance by the force of his swing, made a kind of pirouette on one knee and landed on his ass as well. There followed a moment in which the two men, so seated, regarded one another across the grass.

"You've got to believe me," Jack Fletcher said. "I had no idea he was going to do that." He could see the other man trying to clear his head, blinking and grimacing. He saw as well the man was possessed of a silver front tooth, which flashed now and then in the sunlight.

"I'm tryin' to save your ass," Travis said at length.

"I can see that," Fletcher told him.

"Christ." The man got slowly to his feet. "Where is he?" he asked.

Fletcher nodded toward the trees.

Travis looked in that direction, cursing beneath his breath, then setting off at a slow jog.

Fletcher followed, limping along as best he could.

It did not take long to reach the edge of the island and soon the two men were looking down on the aluminum skiff.

Travis appeared greatly relieved to see it. "I was afraid the fucker had stolen my boat," he said. He turned to the currents of fast-moving water which swept past on either side of them. "Where do you think he went?"

"Swam for it, I imagine."

"In that?"

Fletcher nodded.

"Christ. He's drowned, most likely."

Fletcher disabused him of the idea. It was his opinion that any number of things might one day claim the miserable little fuck. It was just that the sea was not among them.

Travis worked his way down to the skiff. "Come on," he said. "You get in, I'll cast us off."

Fletcher remained where he was. When Travis had gotten the line out of the tree, he stopped and looked back at Fletcher. "You coming?" he asked.

"I need to know something," Fletcher said.

The man just looked at him.

"That kid that took me out . . . Do you know . . ." He stopped as Travis looked away, then cleared his throat and went on, seeking to master his voice as he did so. "I just thought . . . As long as Drew was still out there . . . that he might still find him."

"He's gone," Travis said. "Your friend found nothing."

Fletcher looked to the trees on the north bank where earlier that morning he and the boy had dropped the surfers. It might, he thought, have been in some other lifetime, so long ago did it seem just now, and he looked upon the darkening trees, their limbs set like those of supplicants before the sun, and he listened to the sound of the big waves detonating on the outside reef. Huge Heart Attacks in epic conditions. The thing he had come for. The thing that was to have put it all right.

"Come on," the man told him. "You want out of here, let's do it now."

They went in silence for some time after that, Travis reading the river, guiding them smoothly before the current. It should have been him, Fletcher thought, watching the man before him. It should have been him, in this boat. He would have gotten the pictures. The boy would still be alive. "That boy," Fletcher said at length. "Did you know him?"

The man was silent, watching the water, as if the question was an unwelcome distraction. "David," he said finally. "David Little."

"I'm sorry," Fletcher said. "I'm sorry about what happened." He was thinking of what Robbie Jones had said to him, that he had lost the boy, and he was wondering if he had. "The magazine said there would be someone here with a boat. I didn't know it would be a kid. I didn't know the boat would be a Zodiac."

"The magazine?"

"*Victory at Sea.* It's a surfing magazine. They hired me to come up here, shoot the place. They said Drew could get us in."

Travis studied the river in the autumnal light. "Yeah. Well, I would say, he got you in."

"The boy . . . David . . . He lived on the reservation?"

"David was Hupa. His people are further up the river. He could have gotten himself shot just being down here."

"How's that?"

"Fishing rights. Yuroks have the mouth. Hupas have what's up there." He gestured with his chin toward that place where the river faded among the shadows. "Someone could have thought he was fishing."

"Why would he risk it?" Fletcher asked. "Why would he try taking that thing out in that surf?"

Travis shook his head, as if he thought this a stupid question. He rubbed his thumb against the insides of his fingers in a gesture which suggested money. "Why do you think?" he asked.

"The magazine wasn't paying him. I suppose Drew could have offered him something."

"It wouldn't take much."

"His folks are poor?"

"Take a look around you, man."

They were come now out of the shadow and into the sun that lit the eastern bank. Drew Harmon's landing loomed before them, its deck low enough to be washed by the small whitecaps driven before the wind.

As they drew near, Travis reached out with one hand to pull them even with the dock. The aluminum hull, still carried upon the river's current, rubbed against the old wood. Fletcher was aware of the other man looking toward the trees, toward that place where the roof of the Harmon's trailer might be seen as a piece of reflected light.

"If you see Mrs. Harmon, tell her to stay in tonight. Tell her to stay off the river."

Fletcher nodded. "You think there will be more trouble?"

"I would say you could go to the bank with that."

The boat continued to bob on the spangled water. Travis put a finger to his head. He was sporting a nasty-looking welt above one eye where the rock had creased him. An inch to the left and the thing might well have fractured his skull. Fletcher watched as he scooped water from the river and splashed his face with it. When he had done that, he looked over the shack at the landing, the empty stairs leading into the light.

"You don't suppose that shithead who nailed me could've made it back here yet, do you?"

"I don't see how."

Travis let his breath out slowly. "I must be getting old," he said. "You see the fucker, tell him to stay clear of the reservation."

"I will," Fletcher said.

"I should say the same to you. I sincerely hope this is it. No more pictures."

"It's not likely," Fletcher said. He put a hand upon the wooden dock. "I want you to know I feel real bad about what happened out there today."

Travis only nodded.

"I realize there's nothing I can say. Still, I keep thinking . . . wondering, I guess . . . if I should say something to the boy's family."

"What?"

"There must be some tradition here," he said at length. "Some way the tribes had of dealing with accidental deaths."

"The guilty party would present himself to the family of the one who had been killed. The family might do one of two things. They might kill this person. Or they might work out some method of making recompense. The guilty person might work for them as a servant for some period of time. He might give them something . . ."

Travis broke off. In fact, he was not quite sure why he was saying any of this. What was the point? "Look," he said. "I know you feel bad. But believe me, there is nothing you can do here except cause more trouble. The boy's family is from up the river. It's another world up there. You would not be understood. You'd be lucky if you got back in one piece."

"No recompense?" Fletcher asked.

"Chances are, you'd never get the chance to find out."

Fletcher suspected what the man said was true. What did he know of these people, or they of him? "It's a tough one to walk away from," he said.

Travis looked toward the river, in the direction of the sea. "Just tell the girl," he said. "Tell her to stay in tonight."

Fletcher said that he would. He could see the man was anxious to be gone. And why wouldn't he be? Bad karma, after all, was not something people generally rushed to embrace.

1 2

Travis watched the photographer limping across the wooden deck as he drifted once more upon the current. He sincerely hoped the man could be counted upon, that he would find Kendra Harmon and deliver the warning. He hoped as well that he had discouraged him from going off in search of David Little's family. It was an absurd notion, and he could not imagine what the man could possibly hope to gain by it.

The image reminded him of Kendra Harmon inquiring after the *hee-dee,* and it seemed to him for a moment that white people were forever requiring things of Indians. First, their homes and lands. And now their benediction. It was vision quests and absolution they wanted now, as if come to some bankrupt place of their own making, it was time to turn to the gates of the city, to the desolate reaches beyond, time to seek their enlightenment among the lepers. Travis wished them luck.

As he moved back down the river Travis thought of a story Frank had picked up from an old medicine man on the lower Elwa. The medicine man had worked out a scam for the *wagays* who came to him in pursuit of their vision quests. He made blood runners out of them. He told them they had to take off their clothes and run naked through the woods. The funny part was, they did it. Through nettles and poison oak, over sticks and stones, ran themselves bloody then went round quite pleased with themselves while the natives laughed behind their backs. Eventually some idiot ran into a ravine and killed himself. The old man gave up his racket. Said he hadn't realized how insane the *wagay* really were. "Crazy sons of bitches," he told Frank. "Gives you to understand how they came to fuck everything up in the first place."

Travis hoped that his blood runners would show more sense. But already the day had been a close call. Had the *wagays* not made it to the island . . . Had Drew not been able to protect their friend . . . Had Travis himself not been there to fetch them . . . An abyss yawned before him. And this was only the beginning. He was certain of that. It was why he had not taken the time to tie off the boat and look for Kendra Harmon himself. Because time was set against him now. There was a storm brewing, and if one could not exactly control it, one might at least track its progress. One might take precautions.

It was to this end that, when Travis had finished with the boat and loaded his truck, he did not go home as he would have liked, for he was tired and his head hurt. He drove instead to the Golden Ox, the establishment being a bar on the outskirts of town frequented by Indians. For if he was to monitor the situation he needed to know the talk on the river, and the Golden Ox was as good a place as any to start.

The Golden Ox was a single-story structure set well off the road among a stand of redwood. The bar's owner was an old Indian logger named Bone. Bone lived in a small trailer in back of his bar, and on this particular afternoon was himself his only customer, a situation Travis was inclined to read as a bad sign, as it was quitting time, and though not many of Bone's regulars had jobs to quit, Travis would have expected a few more in attendance.

Bone was seated on a stool as if awaiting service when Travis came into the room, which was low and dark and usually smoky as well, but which this afternoon was only poorly lit and smelled of beer, spilled and gone sour.

The old man regarded him as might an aging parrot, his head tilted to one side, his face shaped around a certain brand of laughter Travis found peculiar to many of the older Indians along the river, as if they were privy to some joke of which you happened to be the butt. The thing to do, he had learned, was to laugh along with them. Sometimes the laughter was silent. Sometimes, particularly in public, and particularly if there were strangers present, the laughter was loud and rude and accompanied by a good deal of pointing and name-calling, as if indeed each of you were the butt of some joke and each knew it, and knew what it meant, and knew as well there was little one could do but laugh, as if this were the last act of courage to which one had been reduced, though whether Travis was alone in this assessment or had company he could not say, because it was not something one talked about but only something one did, and so it was that he went about aping as best he could the old man's grin and seated himself next to him and requested a beer.

Bone slapped the bar with the flat of his hand and limped off to fish in his cooler for a bottle of Budweiser, which he opened and placed before Travis.

Travis nodded. Bone got a beer of his own and sat down next to him. The men drank their beers in silence and Bone got up and got them two more and they drank those. It was not, Travis knew, Bone's way to come immediately to any point. Nor would he do so himself.

"Frank was in here this morning," Bone said at length. "Wants me to come upriver for the dance."

"You going?"

"Shit. Nothing up there but bugs and poison oak. He says you're going, though. Says you're going to bring your grandmother's beads. Says you're going to dance."

Travis drank his beer.

Bone laughed at him. "You got to lay off that shit, you're going to dance."

"If I'm going to dance."

"Frank says you are."

"There are some things Frank don't know."

"He knows," Bone said. The men sat for some time in the silent bar, working on their beers.

"So where is everybody?" Travis asked.

"Big do up at the Moke's."

Travis nodded. He could not say that he was pleased with this news. Nor could he say that he was surprised by it. The people of the reservations were splintered into many factions. On one very basic level, however, there were two. There were those willing to work for change within the system. And there were those who would take things as they were, who would collect their food stamps and tend their weed and wait on the apocalypse. The evening in question would find one of these groups at the gathering of the tribal council where the matter of the new constitution was up for debate. The others would party at the Moke's. And then there were the ones like old Bone, who Travis knew would attend neither, but would pass the dark hours alone, retiring only when the alcohol had done its work. For they considered the one gathering a waste of time and the second, evil.

For Travis, the course seemed clear enough. In thinking about it, he supposed the Golden Ox would have been too easy. Still, he was in no immediate hurry to be gone. The long drive upriver in the dead of night was not something he looked forward to. As a consequence, he sat with Bone and watched in silence as the old man shuffled around the bar for more beer, which Travis received in silence and drank in silence, watching as the last of the light drained from the narrow slice of sky made visible through the front door set ajar before it, until finally, it was the old man himself who spoke, saying no doubt what had been on his mind since Travis had sat down beside him.

"I hear you was out there today," Bone said.

Travis nodded. "I was with one of them just now," he said.

"Which one was that?"

Travis sighed. "The one that lost the boy," he said.

An hour later found Travis deep within the Hupa reservation. The forest rose on either side of him, climbing toward the crests of distant ridges, hiding the moon, casting the narrow road which skirted the river in abject darkness. As a consequence, he drove slowly, with time to think. He thought about his conversation with Kendra Harmon on the day she'd come to ask about Marvus Dove. He had tried to frighten her with bits and pieces of the old stories. He had given her the books, saying that what he knew was so contained. But in this he had lied. The stories were not just in books. They were in the blood, and blood was deep here, old and swift like the river itself, so that driving its bank, he heard once more the voices of his people. The voices did not come to him in his office, in the light of day. Or if they did, they came only as memory, faded by time. It was different here, by this river, beneath these trees, in this darkness. The voices were rude and strong once more.

The Hupa had once been known as the Romans of the Pacific Northwest. The Yurok, the Tolowa, the Tataten had all paid tribute to the Hupa, and the cold-blooded nature of the raids in which they had swept down the river to carry away captives had long been a great source of terror to the other tribes. Among themselves, however, direct confrontation with an enemy was often avoided. They preferred the black magic, the invisible arrow, the incantatory chant. Some preferred them still. It was yet one more source of division among his people.

The drowning of the boy would prove no exception. At the council meeting, there would be talk of litigation and high-priced attorneys. On this night, however, that was not the talk which interested Travis. Though he had not said as much to the photographer, he knew something of the boy's family. They came from a remote part of the reservation where the black magic still flourished, where the dried salmon hung in the smokehouses, where the graffitied rocks read "Hupa Stoners" and "Fuck the Police." And while the talk of litigation would no doubt come to naught, the bad talk might well bear bad fruit. It was talk of a lost past, an apocalyptic future painted bright on crank and Budweiser, and harm was what came of it.

Eventually, a handful of lights appeared among the trees. Travis turned onto a narrow gravel road at the end of which he came upon the ruins of what someone had once intended as a fishing resort but which had been taken by sloth and the river, so that all that remained now was a bare concrete slab and a brick wall across which someone had spray-painted the words "Hupa Stoners."

Travis parked in front of the bricks and got out of his truck. As he did so, the darkness closed in around him. It was a cloying thing, filled with dampness and the sounds of the river. There was a stand of trees some fifty yards from the spray-painted ruins. The river curved there and the trees touched its bank. A faint light issued from their midst, and Travis knew them to mark the home of an old Hupa known as the Moke.

The Moke was a clan leader of some repute, noted principally for two things: his smoked salmon and his righteous weed. He was pushing seventy, still fit and trim though how exactly this could be after all his years of bending the elbow and chasing skirt Travis could not quite understand. All he was certain of was that the old man would outlast him. He had been seventy years on the river and he knew its ways better than most. There were some who said he was a *hee-dee*. A rumor which, in the light of day, at the edge of the strip mall which housed Travis's office, might elicit a smile. In the darkness of the forest, at the side of the Moke's river, such a smile would be hard to come by.

As Travis started toward the light, he heard music. It was the music of the tribe, of the drum and bow. He passed between two junked cars, a rusted Trans Am and a Plymouth Duster whose colors had long ago worn down to the metal, and which, by the light of the moon, appeared identical in color and had been so for just about as long as Travis could remember.

In time he was greeted, first by a pair of dogs and then by a young woman he knew to live with the Moke. The woman's name was Delores and she was college-educated and not unattractive, though alcohol had begun to make her fat. He spoke to her and she to him. They were standing now beneath the mountain alder that ran to the house, and he could see that between the house and the shed used for smoking fish, someone had strung up a big Roosevelt elk that had been skinned. There was a fire near the animal, and he could see what looked to be several painted figures dancing about the flames. It was a primitive little scene. An apparition from the past, conjured out of ectoplasm on the breath of the river.

Travis stood with the young woman in the shadows.

"That's some Roosevelt," Travis said.

Delores took a cigarette from the pocket of her T-shirt and put it to her mouth. As she lit it, she cupped her hands about the match, briefly illuminating her face from the underside, allowing Travis to see there a wry smile and hard lines he had not noticed when he had seen her last. He watched her nod as the light went out, blowing smoke toward the sky.

"Who got it?"

"Jimmie and Deke."

"How far did they have to go?"

Delores took another drag on her cigarette. "About as far as Ted's Bucket of Suds." She gave him the wry smile and he saw that she had broken a tooth. Not long for the Moke, he imagined, and he supposed that she knew it too. "They were on a beer run. Elk was nosing around a Dumpster in back of Ted's. Jimmie jumped out and shot him."

Travis looked toward the firelight, the dancing shadows. As he did, he noticed for the first time a vehicle parked on the far side of the flames. It sat beneath the trees not far from the smokehouse, and he saw that it was some variety of homemade house car. He took it for the remains of an old American-made station wagon someone had thought to convert to a truck by cutting away much of the rear end. In the resulting bed, they had erected a kind of cabin, complete with a steeply pitched roof along whose spine one might discern the edges of wooden shingles, like the dark teeth of a saw before the moon. In another time or place, Travis might have found the sight a comic one—an Okie shack put to wheels. On the evening in question, the car's effect was quite the opposite and he viewed its black and crooked silhouette with some degree of dread, for it struck him as just the kind of thing one might well expect from upriver. When he turned to ask Delores about it, he found that she had already moved off, that she was scolding a half-naked child, holding to the child's arm with one hand while balancing the beer can and cigarette in the other. Travis found the pose a prophetic one and when he had seen there would be no further conversation between them, he left her and went closer to the fire.

That he was able to move freely among these people was one of the few things he had accomplished here. He had managed a reputation. He had found many of these men work, though few had kept it. Still they knew him to be fair-minded and they knew that he was not afraid of a fight. An ex-con by the name of Davies had shown up at the office early on. The man had ostensibly come looking for work, but he'd come drunk and rude as well and Travis had gone after him, right over the top of his desk, and driven him off with his fists. Of course that had been nine years ago, and Travis had been more enthusiastic and wilder then himself, in love with a Hupa woman and inclined to party—all traits which had made him welcome or at least tolerated in most corners of the reservation. He had taken some pride in this. He had thought it an auspicious beginning. But it was nine years and two wives from where he stood just now, and much to his remorse, the old fire had dwindled considerably. The job was a job, and he had not gone over his desk for anyone in some time.

Thinking these things, he nodded to a number of men as he moved among them. It was well, he thought, that they had not been there today, on the island, to see him beaned by some bald-headed *wagay* with a slingshot. He was working his way around the perimeter of the fire for a better look at the car when a hand took him by the wrist.

"Got us an elk," someone said.

Travis reached down to shake the man's hand. He had gotten close enough to the car to see the plates were so old they were black with yellow letters.

"Got us a big elk," the man repeated.

The men around him nodded. There were four of them seated on a log. They were dressed in workboots, khakis, and flannel. The man who had spoken was named James. He was seated next to a man named Bob and another man called Mousey, who had done time at the correctional institute at Scorpion Bay. Travis looked at the fourth man as well but the man was not known to him.

"James," Travis said. He let go of the man's hand. "You still working at the yard?"

James laughed. "I flunked my test," he said.

By this, Travis assumed he had failed a drug test. The other men laughed.

"Elk's got a lot of fat on him," Bob said. "Gettin' himself ready for winter."

Travis looked once more at the skinned animal. He saw indeed that its body was heavy with fat, white and waxy by the light of the fire, and it was then that he spotted the Moke.

The old man was among the dancers. As Travis watched, the Moke came swooping toward him, his arms spread as if in flight. A carved eel hook swung from one hand trailing a feather, describing an elongated figure-eight upon the cool night air, and he saw the paint on the old man's face and his white hair which he wore long and braided, and his dark eyes, and he saw the old man was laughing at him.

Beyond the dance sight, a door stood open at the side of the house and Travis could see there were people inside. The blue light of a television flickered among the shadows. Snatches of organ music drifted across the sagging steps to inhabit what spaces there were between the sawing of the bow and the beating of the drum. Travis watched as a number of men exited the door and passed among the shadows on their way to the smokehouse. He studied their movements, trying to decide if there were any he knew, but the Moke had finished his dance and come to stand beside him, clapping him on the arm by way of a greeting.

"Travis McCade," the old Indian said. "What brings you to the river in the middle of the night?"

Travis turned to the man before him. "Bone told me there was a party. I came to see why I wasn't invited."

The old man laughed at him. He waved at someone beyond the ring of firelight, calling loudly for beer and fish. In a moment a young girl appeared. Travis was offered a can of Budweiser and a stick of smoked salmon, which he accepted, then followed the Moke toward the steps and the door through which the men had just exited, as the old man was suddenly eager that he see the Polaroids they had taken of the elk before they had skinned it, so that he might appreciate the magnificence of the beast which had been unfortunate enough to wander onto the parking lot of Ted's Bucket of Suds and get himself shot by three men on a beer run, allowing them to skin him and dance over him, to imagine for a night, at least, that the old ways still lingered along the banks of the big river.

The house was dark except for the light of the television and smelled of tobacco and pot and beer and salmon. Moke went to a lamp near the big propane heater and soon a dim light fell upon the shadows. He passed a stack of photographs to Travis.

Travis thumbed through them, admiring the size of the elk. At his back, the television continued to blare, a game show in which the contestants tried to win money by answering questions.

There were a pair of high school–aged girls in the kitchen and a young boy Travis recognized as one of the Moke's nephews. Moving a bit to his right, he saw Bean Dip there as well. The boy was sporting a bruised cheek and talking to a pair of men Travis did not know.

The men leaned against a yellow, smoke-stained wall. Travis made one for a Tolowan. He was of medium height, thin and wiry with the narrow pointed features Travis associated with that race. They were a coastal people from north of the Yuroks. This man had a particularly unwholesome appearance. His hair was long and straight and hung about the sides of his thin face as might the locks of some witch in a child's fairy tale. The man's hair was almost completely gray, though Travis guessed the man was not much older than himself.

Travis looked for a moment at the Tolowan, but it was the second man who interested him. For this man was clearly Hupa, and Travis guessed he was from upriver. He had that look about him, thick, powerfully built. A capable man. His black hair was pulled back into a long ponytail. He had a somewhat wispy mustache and another patch of hair beneath his lower lip. His eyes were sullen, dark and quick, and when he saw Travis checking him out, he straightened and turned so that just his shoulder was still touching the wall. Travis finished with the pictures and handed them to the Moke.

"He's a good elk," the old man told him.

Travis nodded. When he looked back into the kitchen, he was in time to see Bean Dip nod in his direction. He saw the thin man smile. The Tolowan was missing his two front teeth. In their absence, the man's smile became quite demented. The Hupa was only staring, his eyes showing nothing at all, save a smoldering insolence.

When Bean Dip saw that Travis was looking at them, he favored him with an insolent smile of his own.

"*Wagay*'s in deep shit," Bean Dip said. He said it loudly enough that his voice might carry above the music and the television. "Elk's a sign, man. We gonna take back what's ours. Make it plain to the people."

Bean Dip was slurring his words, swaying slightly in the light of the kitchen, as from the television in the living room there came a wild burst of applause together with organ music. An excited white woman jumped up and down on the screen as several Indians watched impassively from the Moke's couch.

"Bean Dip's got a troublin' mind," Moke said.

"We don't need more trouble." Travis said. He said it loudly enough to be heard by everyone in the room, but he was staring at the Hupa. The man held his gaze, a slight smirk playing around the corners of his mouth.

Travis was aware of someone talking but he did not bother to look. He was suddenly light-headed with hatred, with the possibility of physical violence.

The intensity with which this feeling took him was, in fact, quite surprising, no doubt dangerous as well. Slapping down a pup like Bean Dip, as he had done on the beach, was one thing. The Hupa in the kitchen was something else, and probably more than Travis was up for. Still, he could feel the sweat breaking about his temples and he was aware of a new silence, as if others were just now becoming aware of this exchange of vibes, and watching to see what would come of it. What Travis knew was that it had slipped beyond his control. His physical condition not withstanding, he would go with this man if that was what it came to, as if, in fighting him, he might assault that which was most pernicious among his people.

It was only Bean Dip who seemed to miss what was happening. He took the bait as if this were only a thing between himself and Travis.

"We didn't bring trouble," Bean Dip said. "They did." He waved at the darkness beyond the walls.

"Same as it ever was," intoned the Moke, as if this were the final word. And just that quickly the moment had passed. People turned away, resumed conversations. There would be no fight between Travis and the Hupa, not just now.

"Take a beer," Moke said, passing him another. "Party with us."

Travis took the beer. "You know they're meeting tonight," he said. There was no challenge in this, only a certain weariness, and yet he felt compelled to say it, addressing himself to the Moke.

The Moke only smiled at him. "What they need me for," he asked, lapsing into a kind of false Indian speak, giving Travis to understand his arguments would get him nowhere, for, in fact, they had been down this road many times and always to the same end.

"You could be of help," Travis said. It was pointless, of course, but he would play it out. He would have his empty gesture. "You could lead. You're a man of influence."

Moke continued to smile, as if this were some merry surprise. "Me?" he asked.

Travis smiled back at him. There was little else one could do. "You," he said.

"No way, I'm too dumb."

Several people laughed.

Moke saw that he had his audience. "That's what they tell me. They tell me I'm a dumb motherfucker. Dumb Indian, they say."

"Who says?"

"Everybody says. But now we have this elk."

The old man put a hand on Travis's arm, ending the debate.

Travis allowed himself to be turned from the kitchen. As he did so, he heard a screen door slam. He looked back into the yellow light but Bean Dip and the strangers were gone. In another moment, there was the sound of an engine starting on the yard. When Travis moved to look, however, the old man prevented it, his hand tightening upon Travis's arm with a grip that belied his age.

"Bean Dip's been upriver," the old man whispered, as if this were a thing meant for Travis's ears alone, though, in fact, Travis suspected everyone on the premises knew as much and had since that afternoon.

"He's come back with some bad men."

From beyond the door, Travis could hear the sound of tires in the mud, and he knew that should he look now, the house car would no doubt be gone. The old man had slowed him just enough, as if its departure was something Travis was not meant to see. One might, of course, ask the Moke about it. But then one might ask the river as well.

"There's bad people upriver," the Moke continued. "I don't like them. You know that. You know what they do up there. I've told them I don't want any of that here."

"Who's in the house car?" Travis asked.

Moke shrugged. "Still, they come here. What can I do?"

Travis looked at the old man. There was a light in the old man's face, the silent laughter.

"If those men were some kin to David Little, would you tell me?"

"How would I know?"

"Don't give me that. I'm serious about this. You know what trouble will mean."

The Moke smiled at him. "You worry too much," he said.

"So who was in the house car?"

"Ask them yourself. They'll be back. Just another beer run. Maybe they'll get themselves another elk, huh?"

Travis looked into the blackness beyond the door.

"Come on," the old man said. "We have an elk. Dance for him. This is where those assholes at the council ought to be. They ought to be dancing."

They went outside by the fire. Travis saw that the house car was indeed gone. He found Mousey seated on the log where he had first seen him. He nodded after the departed car. "Where'd they go?" he asked.

Mousey looked at the Moke then at Travis. "Beer run," Mousey said. "They'll be back."

"Go down to the smokehouse," Moke said. "Bring me my pipe."

Mousey went off among the shadows. In a few moments, Travis saw him coming back with the Moke's bowl. The old man lit up, drew deeply, and offered it to Travis. The sweet scent of dope rose on the damp night air.

Travis looked at the offered pipe.

"Come on, Cousin." Moke said. "We have an elk. Party with us."

Travis sighed. He took the pipe, drawing as deeply as the old man before him. The men would be back, he told himself. They had an elk to party over. And who could say, but that this might not be just the ticket, open the old inner eye, as it were. It had been a long day and the thought of Drew Harmon and the sorry photographer and the geek who had hit him made him suddenly more tired than he could say, so that partying with his mother's people was perhaps the thing after all, and before long he imagined he would even dance. It would not be anything like the Jump Dance to which his true cousin had invited him. It would, in fact, be its opposite number, performed without sense or meaning, an ode to nothing. Under the circumstances, however, Travis deemed it appropriate to the day's events and in fact he found the Moke's weed much to his liking, and in time he drank more beer and ate more salmon and stripped off his shirt and danced half-naked around the fire with the night air and the dampness of the river cool upon his sweating flesh, and at some point, just before the sky had begun to pale above the trees and the moon lay half-devoured upon the broken spine of the Moke's smokehouse where the salmon hung in coral-colored-strips like so many icicles the color of human flesh, it occurred to him that the house car bearing the bad men from upriver had not returned, and that it was against his better judgment he had gotten stoned and danced like a fool around the Moke's dead Roosevelt elk that had itself been fool enough to get itself shot in the parking lot of Ted's Bucket of Suds.

1 3

As was her custom, Kendra slept past noon. She woke to light streaming through one of the trailer's narrow, rectangular windows. The room's other window remained covered with a thick shade. She lay for a moment on her back. She was trying to decide if she was alone. It was a dangerous little game. In time, however, she concluded that she was indeed alone. It likes the fog, she thought. It's stronger in the dark. At which point, it occurred to her that she had no clear idea of what she meant by "It."

She propped herself on one elbow and peered from the window. The sun had come to rest upon the crest of the ridge opposite her own. As a consequence, the river had been turned to gold flecked with shadow.

She rested in this position, struck by the impossible nature of what lay before her. For it was a thing not always apparent. Hidden in fog, cloaked in precipitation. And then there were those moments when the shroud parted and the landscape lay naked to the eye, and there was nowhere, she thought, where the collision of land and sea appeared more recent or had given birth to a more violent beauty.

In time she got out of bed. She had slept fully clothed and added only a silk bomber jacket with a dragon on the back that Drew had bought for her in Bali, and that she had found to be a good weight for hiking. She used this to cover the black silk blouse and black pantaloons with the red stitching that had been the property of Amanda Jaffey.

Pulling on the jacket, she caught sight of her reflection in the mirror hung upon the closet door. When the girl in Eureka had done her hair she had finished with a comb and gel, telling Kendra that, really, she had such good bones, she could get away with anything. She supposed that with the comb and styling gel she had looked rather trendy, but she had not bothered with them since and had no desire to do so now. She would go about ragged and unkempt and if there were good bones there, they were lost to her. She thought of that photographer from the magazine, Jack Fletcher, the one who had wanted to take her picture. She wondered what he would want if he could see her by the light of day. Would he see good bones? Or would he see what she did? Still, she thought, the look suited her and when she had collected her gear— her lantern, her knife and gunnysack and water—she went with them into the golden light.

She was halfway down the stairs when she caught sight of the man at the dock. In time, she saw that it was the photographer, Jack Fletcher. He was quite alone, seated with his face to the sun, his legs in the water.

It did not immediately strike her as odd that the photographer was alone. She assumed the others would be somewhere nearby, coming in, perhaps, by another route, as everything would be done according to some plan of Drew's, and she had seen a long time ago that his were worked out in accordance with thoughts all his own to which none were privy, save perhaps the elements of wind and tide with which his life was bound.

She put her things into her truck which was parked near the foot of the stairs and went to the dock. It was not her way to be friendly with strangers, but she was curious about these pictures and what it was Drew wanted with them.

"Hello," she said.

The man turned slightly but did not get up or look her in the eye.

"It went well?" she asked.

He looked toward the water, giving her to understand that things had not gone well at all.

"We lost the boy," he said.

She was aware of a coiling in her belly, of a shadow placed above the water.

"What boy?" she asked.

He stood then, and turned to face her. It looked to her as if he had been crying, for his eyes appeared puffy, ringed with red, though she supposed the wind and sun and salt might account for these things as well.

"The Indian boy. The one Drew hired to take me out." His voice broke and she decided she had been right, that he had been crying.

"That's terrible," she said. "It's awful. Do you know his name?"

"David Little."

She knew the name. He was from upriver. He couldn't have been more than fifteen or sixteen.

"That was the boat?" she said. "The boat Drew got to take you out?"

Fletcher nodded.

Kendra felt sick. "It's not even a boat," she said. "It's one of those rubber things. Drew used it once to float some lumber down the river. David helped him."

Fletcher said nothing. The wind chop lapped against the wood.

"How did it happen?" she asked.

"We got out okay, but the kid lost power. There was some sort of problem with the engine. We got caught inside on a big set . . ." His voice trailed away.

"And you're okay."

The man just shook his head. "I had a wet suit," he told her. "I knew what to do." He looked at her with his red-rimmed eyes. "I was with him," he said. "In the boat."

She saw then that he believed it was his fault. Kendra knew better. The truth fell upon her as might a blow. "And Drew?"

"I don't know. I mean, he's okay. I just don't know where he is right now. I assume he's getting help for Sonny."

"Sonny?"

"One of the pros. Some of the Indians saw what happened. There was a fight on the beach."

Kendra found herself pacing the weathered landing. She looked toward that place where the darkening river disappeared among the folds of the hills, winding its way inward, toward the heart of the reservation, the home of David Little. She was aware of the photographer watching her, and she stopped to look at him.

"I just keep thinking there is something I ought to do," he said. "I mean, I was the last person to see the boy alive. It seems to me I should go to his family, that I should tell them . . ."

"What?"

He shook his head. "I don't know."

Kendra looked on him with some pity. Though it struck her that there was something of the fool about him as well, with his rubber suit and his red-rimmed eyes. She'd seen that he was favoring a leg when he'd gotten to his feet. Probably he had been hurt in some way. Well, she thought, he'd come on a fool's errand and he'd been found out. There was blood on his hands now and he would have to live with it. Her pity derived from the perception that he would not do so without remorse.

Drew, on the other hand, would already be planning his next session. She thought briefly of asking the photographer if he'd gotten his pictures, and if he had, did he think them worth the price. But there seemed little point in chastising him further. Drew was the one she should ask, and yet even as she imagined this exchange she could feel some resolve hardening within her. For she had put such questions to Drew before and could by now guess the answers before the asking.

She moved quickly then, across the mud and into her truck. When she had closed the door, she saw that the photographer was walking toward her. She could see him in the rearview mirror, his hand raised as if to beckon her back, but she saw no need for further talk. She started the truck and drove away, gravel pinging in her wheelwells, her windshield covered by the mists which rose from the river, and it seemed to her as if something was in the air. Energy flowing downhill. She saw it in the flight of a deer. An owl before dark. "*No bueno,*" she said. And again, "*No bueno,*" as the river rushed to the sea.

She went along a winding dirt road, deep into the reservation. An orange light churned among the trees, dusting the rusted cars, the gutted appliances, the moldering house trailers. In time, she lost the sound of the river. She came around a curve where the road she was on intersected with another.

The junction was marked by a weedy lot and a rambling wooden structure, a company store. There was a sign above the roof: "Ted's Bucket of Suds." There was a pair of well-used pickups parked in front. Kendra pulled in beside the other trucks and parked.

She had never been in this store, and, in fact, she had been warned away from such places. They were not, she had been told, frequented by whites, nor were whites welcome here. Still, she was feeling reckless. It was the death of the boy. She felt unclean, compelled to place herself in harm's way.

As she got out of the Toyota, she could see there was something dead in the bed of one of the trucks—a dog, or perhaps a coyote, its fur burned away to reveal bone, a death's mask of interlocking fangs. Her passing raised a cloud of flies, some of which seemed to come right for her, circling her head, trapping themselves in her hair. As a consequence, she fairly stumbled up the sagging steps, swatting at the air as the flimsy wooden door banged shut behind her.

With the closing of the door, she found herself confronting a handful of Indians. The men were standing along a counter behind which another Indian operated a cash register. They were all looking at her as if she were an object of great curiosity, and, in fact, she supposed her entrance had gotten her off to a poor start. A dingbat from the woods.

She made an effort to compose herself, to go about her business. At which point it occurred to her that she had no clear idea of what her business was. She had come in because she had supposed she shouldn't. There was really no more to it than that.

She felt them watching as she started through the store. She seemed to be headed toward the cooler. The floor fell away beneath her feet at a ridiculous angle. Fluorescent lights flickered and buzzed above her head. There were no windows in the room, though beyond the screened door, she was aware of the late light in the dusty lot. She felt the men watching as she passed among the shelves, which were made of rough pine slats, sparsely stocked with a variety of canned and paper goods.

By contrast, she found the cooler filled to overflowing. A cornucopia of alcoholic delights. She selected a bottle of white port wine. It was a an idiotic purchase. She believed she'd heard Drew joke about drunken Indians, white port and lemon juice, and, in fact, she got some of that as well. She found some in a plastic yellow lemon not far from the wine. She took these things to the counter. There was sweat in the palms of her hands as she fumbled with her wallet. The men watched. No one spoke.

She was not thanked for her purchase and she did not thank anyone in return. The things she bought were not bagged. She collected them in the crook of an arm and went with them into the light. The blood burned in her face. The truck's door swung shut behind her with a hollow pop. A child's toy. She lurched from the rutted lot, grinding gears, the bottle of white port rolling across the seat to bump against her thigh.

She worked that evening along the shoulders of an old logging road, moving in series of elongated curves that took her some ways into the forest, then back to the road, so that it was the road which guided her. It was a steady uphill climb.

The first time she had worked this location, she had gone only about a quarter of the way to the ridgeline before turning back, exhausted. Tonight, she would not stop until she had reached the top. There was a grove of redwood there, the arrow-straight trunks made unearthly in the moonlight, and a high meadow from which she would be afforded a view of the river.

She took pleasure in these things, in her knowledge of the landscape, in her ability to make the long climb. They were small victo-
ries, yet hard won. And now there was even a check, a sign that she
might make a go of things here after all. The thought came to her
as she cut the stalks of several reeds, taking them with a sharp knife
close to the ground, then adding them to her bag. She thought as
well of how these things so gathered might change with the season
and of how a circle of events might be so cast and of how one might
place one's self within this circle. Then she thought of Drew, and
his wanting to go to Chile.

The notion was suddenly as transparent as a child's story. But
then these were her finest moments. Maybe it was nothing more
than the endorphins, but she was granted a certain lucidity here.
The voices were down there. Chile, for Christ's sake. There was no
way she was buying that last-frontier routine. She knew what he
wanted. He wanted a home and a family, on his mother's land. A
house made of redwood with a view to the sea. What he wanted was
here. He had said so too many times. And even though she had
miscarried, the doctors had told them there was no reason they
could not try again, no reason they could not succeed. And there
was no reason for Drew to suddenly bail and run to Chile. No reason she could think of, except one, and there was nothing pretty
about it.

She had come now to the redwoods. She rested her back against
a trunk and drank some of her water. She had told him Chile would
take money and he had said he could raise it. There was no money
in the property they owned. Selling it would only pay off the credi-
tors. It had something to do with the pictures. She was sure of it.
Why else would he have invited these people? Why else would he
have risked the boy's life in the open ocean? And what if he managed it? she thought suddenly. What if there was money? She saw
him in a doorway, flushed with light, a pair of tickets in his hand.
And what if she said no? The idea struck her as a bolt from the blue.
She righted herself and hiked the rest of the way to the meadow
with its view of the river—a fixed ribbon of light among the trees, as
breathtaking as she had imagined it. The sight consoled her. Why, if
she were to work through the fall, she might be ready by Christmas.

At which point, it occurred to her that she'd best stop and think these things through. "Ready for what?" she asked.

The answer presented itself as an auditory hallucination. The voice was located somewhere above her right temple, but she knew better than to look. "Time for you to leave," the voice said. The voice was vaguely familiar and she decided it was the shaulin priest from the beginning of the *Kung Fu* television show. She made this connection with some disappointment. Moses had Yahweh and burning bushes. She would have to make do with television.

She was back at the truck before she thought to question this occurrence. The voices weren't supposed to be up here with her. Theirs was the world below. It was the deal they had struck. She found the bottle of wine she had purchased at the reservation store on the seat where she had left it. She broke the seal and took a drink. It was ghastly stuff. One could see at once how it might rot the brain. Still, she thought, a celebration was called for, in spite of what she had heard, and she thought once more of the plan which had come to her on the ridge—that by Christmas she could have plenty of arrangements. It was true, she thought. It was a thing that could be done. If Drew went to Chile, he would go alone.

It was hard to imagine it beyond that. She had, after all, never really been on her own before. It was hard to image how Drew would react. She drank and drove, scarcely aware of what she was about, flushed with an excitement she found difficult to trust. She seemed to recall reading somewhere that one in her condition might experience the onset of an episode as euphoria. But then, as near as she could remember, no two doctors had ever been willing to agree on exactly what her condition was. One had prescribed tranquilizers, another, intermuscular shots of vitamin B_{12}. Her father had favored seances and exorcism. But once he had made them swords out of wooden toilet plungers and they had hacked at tree limbs and called them orcs and celebrated a great victory. She supposed he was not all bad. In a fortnight, he had killed himself in a barn.

Eventually Kendra came within sight of the river once more. In fact she came upon it quite suddenly, as the logging road she had been following ended abruptly after a steep descent among manzanita upon a two-lane strip of asphalt. Once arrived at this intersection, she was some time in placing herself, for she found that she had exited the woods at a point much further east and north than she had anticipated. But then the logging roads were like that, one never did quite know where one was. It made for a good number of surprises. The trick, she had learned early, was to make sure one entered their red-dirt labyrinth with a full tank of gas.

Still, she was quite taken aback to find just how far inland she had come. Nor could she recall at just what point she had erred, or at what nameless intersection she had borne right instead of left. Perhaps the wine had something to do with it. Perhaps it was the ruminations, or the rush of excitement which had accompanied her newfound resolve.

At any rate, she was here now and the course, at least, was clear. She put the river on her left and pointed toward the coast. She had no sooner completed this maneuver, however, when she saw that she was not alone on the road. Almost at once, a pair of headlights filled her rearview mirror. The lights startled her for one did not expect company at this hour and her first thought was to distance herself from them.

For the moment, however, she held speed, examining the lights, first in the rearview mirror and then in the side mirror, as it seemed to her there was something peculiar about them. Upon further examination, she saw that it was not the lights themselves, but rather the thing they were attached to that was peculiar.

She could not, even with the help of the moonlight, say exactly what it was that trailed her along the river. Her first impulse was to believe it was a car being followed by a house. She supposed it was something someone had made at home. One saw such outlandish vehicles now and again around the reservations—school buses converted to house cars, worn-out Cadillacs pressed into service as pickup trucks. Whatever was following her seemed particularly absurd, a tall peaked roof wobbling along before the starry sky as the headlights followed her own through the curves above the water.

Clearly her truck was the more nimble of the two vehicles. She might have pulled away quite easily, and yet she lingered, watching the house chase the car through one more curve. It was, she concluded, a bit like watching the dish running away with the spoon. T'was the wine, again, she thought. Already it had done her wrong once tonight. She helped herself to one more tiny sip.

"Now go," she said. The woods, after all, were no place for games. Suppose she had a flat? The thought was marginally sobering and she rolled down her window, ushering in the cold night air, then reaching out with one hand, and turning it, that she might wave with her fingers. "'Bye, you all," she said. And she pushed in the clutch and shifted to fourth, leaving the headlights behind.

14

Drew Harmon had installed an outdoor shower on his dock. There was nothing fancy about it, no shower head, just an open pipe. Cold water only. When the girl had left him, Fletcher used it to wash away the salt. That he had been unable to issue Travis's warning seemed only one more feature of a day gone obscenely awry. He peeled off the wet suit and stood naked in the freezing stream, remaining there for some time, as if to spite himself, or as if the water might somehow wash away the sight of the boy in the boat, alone on the face of the wave. When that didn't work, he threw on his sweats, got into his medicine bag and washed down a sampling of what he found there with a pair of Drew Harmon's beers.

He was sleeping unsoundly in the back of the old Dodge when he heard them come. He heard an engine, the slamming of doors. A light swept the windows. He thought suddenly of what Travis had told him, that there would be trouble. Voices issued from the forest.

He fumbled in the darkness for something that might serve as a weapon. He was crouched there with a tire iron, bathed in sweat, when the back door swung open and the light rushed in.

"Look here," a voice said. "The Doc's finally cracked."

The voice belonged to Drew Harmon. Fletcher put down his tire iron and crawled outside. There was a vehicle of some sort on the road. Fletcher believed it to be a truck, but all he really saw were the taillights vanishing among the trees. He was still trying to shake the adrenaline pump to which he had wakened, standing barefoot in the muddy lot. "Where did you come from?" he asked.

Harmon nodded toward the road. "Town. We had to hitch a ride back."

Drew Harmon was dressed as he had been that morning, in the parka and shorts. The hiking boots had been replaced by sandals.

"Glad to see you made it," Drew told him. "The kid here seemed to think you might've drowned trying to get off that rock."

"I had help," Fletcher said.

"Told you." Drew was looking over his shoulder at Robbie Jones. The kid walked past them and took something from the van.

"How did I know?" Robbie asked. "The motherfucker looked like an Indian to me."

"He told you what he was there for," Fletcher said.

"Yeah, well, the motherfuckers packed my bro, dude. I saw it."

Fletcher shook his head. "You could've killed him," he said.

Robbie shrugged.

"He's right," Drew told him. "The one guy tryin' to help us and you hit him with a rock. From now on, you watch it with that kind of shit."

"Or what?" Robbie asked him.

"If you'd pulled that shit in front of me, I would've torn your fucking head off. That's what, chrome dome. We understand each other?"

"You can try," Robbie said. "Anytime."

Drew Harmon watched him for a moment, then turned to Fletcher and laughed out loud. "Pity the fool," he said.

Robbie Jones strode off in the direction of the landing, where he squatted in the glow of an outdoor light affixed to the side of

Drew's shack. He set about eating a power bar, his eyes fixed on the river.

"He's really something," Harmon said. It was hard to tell if he was amused or pissed off.

Fletcher looked around. "Where's Sonny?" he asked.

"He's okay. Head took a couple of stitches. He wanted to go home so we took him to the bus station."

"Why the bus station? We got a van right here."

"That wasn't it," Robbie Jones said. He was passing them once more, headed for the van and another power bar.

Fletcher watched him, aware of a spasm somewhere back of his breastbone. "What does he mean?" he asked.

Drew Harmon smiled at him in the moonlight. "He means you still got some pictures to take."

The surfers took council in Drew Harmon's shaping shack. Propane lanterns burned among the stacks of old wood. A map of the California coast lay spread upon the floor, anchored at the corners by cans of beer sweating in the muted light of the lanterns that had been set to low. The sound of the river raged beyond the clapboard walls and boarded windows.

Drew Harmon had shed the parka. He was bare-chested, seated in his baggy shorts on the floor, his legs tucked beneath him. He stabbed at the map with a thick finger, speaking enthusiastically of buoy readings and swell direction. Fletcher studied him with some wonderment. Looped on pain pills and beer, bone weary, he was as yet unable to reconcile this scarred and leering figure before him with the drowned boy. Surely, he thought, these images could not partake of the same reality.

"We're in the window," Drew was saying. "There's no question about it. Look at this." He placed a ruler upon the map, angling it in opposition to the coast. "Buoys are already starting to show. Weather report says winds in excess of a hundred and thirty miles an hour. You know what that means."

Fletcher found that the big man was looking at him. "Category five . . ." he began.

"What it means," Harmon said, cutting him off, "is that ye'd better have some big balls on ye." He bent once more to the map. "This is coming our way," he said. "And there's not a motherfucking thing in front of it."

Fletcher followed the line with his eye. He could see where Harmon had marked the mouth of the river, and he could see that the point at which the ruler intersected with the coast was some ways north. What, in fact, Drew Harmon was really pointing at was that finger of land Jack Fletcher had studied in his van, the westernmost point on the westernmost piece of real estate the state of California had to offer.

"What you're trying to tell me," Fletcher said, at length, "is that what we saw today . . . that wasn't Heart Attacks. Heart Attacks is . . ." He waved at the map. "Up here someplace."

Harmon just laughed at him. "What do you think?" he asked. "You think you can drive up some country road, walk up a path and find Heart Attacks?" He laughed once more. "People have been looking for this place for years. Christ. You were the one telling me about the rock field . . . The Devil's Hoof . . . Shit, man, I've seen that book. And yeah, those two assholes came close. They'd had a swell to show them they might've even found it. Open your eyes, brah. Look around and smell the roses."

Fletcher could not quite bring himself to speak. The man was right, of course. He had been a fool. He had, after all, said it himself. "He likes to fuck with people a little," he had said. What he could not know was whether the man was fucking with him before or fucking with him now. The blue eyes gave away nothing.

"Listen, man," Harmon told him, "the river mouth gets good. It gets big too . . . in case you hadn't noticed."

Fletcher heard Robbie Jones laugh. The youth had been quiet till now, wrapped in sweats, knees drawn up, eyes intent upon the map. The trouble, Fletcher saw, was Robbie'd had his taste. Fletcher had seen it, seen him bucking down that face, and he saw as well that Peters had called it . . . "The real thing," Peters had said. Like the Drew Harmon of old, and here was Fletcher caught between them, a pair of junkies on a drug run. Once he might have been right there with them, ready for anything. At the moment, he felt little more than tired, alone somehow with the death of the boy.

"You'd gotten here when you were supposed to, we would've been there, man. Way it was . . . I got a look at how the river mouth was handling the swell. It was perfect. Plus, the weather was working out. We had a shot at clear skies, morning glass . . . Why not go for it? I figured it would be a good test run. How did I know . . ."

"Mr. Pill Head was going to fall out of the boat and lose the fucking kid," Robbie said. He looked at Harmon. "That what you were going to say?"

Fletcher picked up the first thing he found. It was a bar of wax, and threw it at Robbie Jones. The article bounced off the kid's bald head and skidded across the room.

Robbie Jones lunged for him across the map. The only thing that prevented him from getting there was Drew Harmon, who seemed to catch him in mid-flight with one arm and set him back down. "Whoa," he said. "Save it, both of you. You want to fight when we're done, be my guest. Right now, I need you healthy. You came for Heart Attacks and I can get you there. I can guarantee we're gonna get it big. We may even get it clean."

As he was saying these things, he pulled another piece of paper from the hip pocket of his shorts. Robbie and Fletcher continued to glare at each other. Fletcher supposed he should have been happy that Drew was there to stop the thing. Clearly, he was in no condition to be fighting. Still, visions of choking the life from Robbie Jones's simpering face remained to tempt him.

"Look at this," Drew told them. He had spread what appeared to be a weather map cut from the newspaper across the larger map of California. Fletcher was still staring at Robbie Jones. He could see that a red welt had risen on the kid's head where the bar of wax had struck him.

"I said look at this," Harmon said. "Check the fucking isobars. And now check this." He moved his hand in a circular motion some ways inland. "They're calling for more high pressure, just like we had today. You can see it setting up." He slapped the map with the palm of his hand. "All just for you, Doc. This doesn't give you a hard-on, go kill yourself."

Fletcher looked at the map. He looked at Drew Harmon. "You should've told us," he said. "You should've laid this out before."

"Why?"

Fletcher went looking for an answer. None presented itself.

"I liked that kid," Harmon said at length. "It's too bad he fucked up. So boo-hoo, fuck you. Now what I need to know is if you're gonna go home with your tail between your legs, or if you're gonna get your butt out at Heart Attacks and take some pictures?"

Fletcher was aware of Robbie Jones snorting derisively in the background. "What with?" Fletcher asked. "I lost the only rig I had."

"I got a camera."

"What? A Brownie?"

"A Minolta."

"What kind of lens?"

"It's not one of those big motherfuckers, if that's what you mean, but I got a housing."

"What you're telling me is that I'm gonna have to shoot from the water."

Drew Harmon sighed. "What I'm telling you is this. When the shit hits the fan, a man need make accommodation. Way it was supposed to work was, we were going to strap that Zodiac to the van. We were gonna drive up here." He poked at the map. "We were going to hike in from Neah Heads. It ain't going to work that way now. We're going to avoid Neah Heads like the plague. We're going to hike up the coast. It will take longer, but we can get there. You're gonna pack an extra board. You can paddle out and shoot from that if you've got the balls for it. If not, you can shoot from the rocks. Least you'll get something. You don't have the balls for that, then say so now. We'll drop your ass off at the local bus depot and you can sit there with Sonny Martin and feel sorry for yourself. We'll take the fucking pictures ourselves."

"Is this still Indian land?" Fletcher asked.

"Tolowans."

"You think that's smart? These people are pretty pissed off."

"Shit. These people are always pissed off. It's a full-time job."

"This guy from the Indian Development Center seems to think this is something special."

Harmon dismissed the idea with a wave of the hand. "Shit, man. You been listenin' to me or not? We're in the window, bro." He pointed once more at his homemade map. "You got a swell. You got Heart Attacks, and you got talent in the water. You want to lose your shit to a few drunken Indians and go home empty-handed, be my guest. But I'll tell you this, you may as well get happy with the weddings, 'cause that's all you're gonna get."

Fletcher sat before Drew Harmon's map, in the muted light. He stared into the darkness beyond the door.

"What about your wife?" he asked.

"What?" The man seemed genuinely surprised.

"It's gonna be safe here, for her?"

The man just looked at him. "They don't come around here," he said. "They tried. I slapped a couple of 'em silly and now they stay away, but as far as that goes, I can leave her a note. She can stay with friends in town. That make you happy?"

Fletcher shrugged. "Who told you about the weddings?" he asked.

Drew Harmon was a moment in responding. He was busy folding his map. "Word gets around," he said.

Fletcher nodded. The man was right, of course. Word did. He thought of the long drive home. He pictured himself in the alley in back of his apartment, bone-tired and empty-handed. He tried to imagine what would be next. The truly frightening part was that he could imagine it all too clearly.

"When do we go?" he asked.

"Ten minutes do you?"

Fletcher felt slightly ill. He had been counting at least on a night's sleep.

"It'll take me that long to get my gear and leave a note. We'll camp on the beach and start in the morning. We're gonna have to make tracks to do this right." The man looked at him. "I hope you're up for it." Fletcher expected some crack from Robbie Jones, but the boy's eyes were focused on some middle distance known only to himself.

Fletcher rose and went outside. He went for some way along the riverbank. It was the direction taken by Kendra Harmon, and he saw that her little truck had not come home. He was left with the feeling that the girl had run away from him.

In time, he turned from the road and looked to the river, to the blackness of its northern bank, trying to imagine what lay beyond. For it seemed to him that he had glimpsed it, that first afternoon, in the gloom and drizzle. A gray and rocky wasteland, run to some last place of land's eventual ending, and it occurred to him that, for the first time in his forty-four years, he had come to know regret.

TWO

THE
CAPTIVE'S
TALE

15

By midnight, one could no longer see the stars from the landing that marked Drew Harmon's property. A heavy fog had rolled in off the ocean. It seemed to pour from the mouth of the river as if the river itself were some herald of bad tidings. "You live and die by the weather up here," Drew was fond of saying. By which he meant the surf conditions were fickle, dependent upon many variables. And though Kendra could still not read his weather maps with their meticulous notations, she had, over the course of time, mastered some of the basics. She knew, for instance, that on the night in question, the fog was all wrong. It told her the ridge of high pressure her husband had been predicting had, in fact, broken down.

Not that such setbacks ever really deterred him. And as she drove across the muddy lot which bordered the landing, she could see that such was the case now. A boy was dead, another injured. The clear skies were gone. But the old van was gone as well and Drew with it, and she did not doubt that he had gone surfing.

The photographer's van was where she had last seen it earlier that afternoon, suggesting that when all was said and done, he had gone too. That would make three of them out there, she thought, hunting their wave in the fog. She supposed that Drew had taken them up by the Hoof, to a big place he had found there. It would take them at least three days to get in and out, longer, she supposed, if they found what they were after. She would be alone. The thought even occurred to her that she might be gone when Drew came back, but then remembered that her leaving would require money. Christmas, she thought, feeling once more the complex surge of emotion which now accompanied the word.

She parked in the mud, then walked through the fog to the landing, that she might stand at the water's edge, breathing in such scent of the sea as was borne upon the river. The big horns that marked the harbor entrance had commenced to moan. The dirge they toiled seemed omnipresent in the fog. She thought once more of euphoria as the precursor to despair, wondering at why this should be so, and if it necessarily was.

She still held her keys in her hand. There was one on the ring which fit the door of the shaping shack and she used it now, turning away from the river and going inside. She was not sure why. She carried the sack with her clippings over one shoulder. A few embers still glowed in the wood stove and a dim red light spread about the room. She stoked the embers with an iron poker, then threw in a few sticks of kindling. They caught at once, suggesting the men had not been gone for very long. The light of her small fire was yellow and uncertain and set the shadows to dancing. She saw Drew's mattress on the floor, his water bottle, his magazines. She moved among the stacks of old wood and came to stand in front of the rolltop desk that had once belonged to Drew's grandmother and had come with her by way of the Horn, landing at Sweet Home when there was yet no harbor there to speak of and so was borne, like the old lady herself, upon strong arms and shoulders over the very waves her grandson would one day come to ride.

She was looking rather absently over the books and magazines, the charts and papers and videocassettes all neatly arranged in their wooden shelves when one in particular caught her eye. It was entitled *The Dogs of Winter*, and it bore the name of the photographer, Jack Fletcher. She pulled it from among the others and slipped it into the VCR perched atop the small television, which was itself perched atop the desk.

She started as the room filled with light—the small screen exploding with color. She had been expecting waves. What she got were Day-Glo alligators scattered like so many fallen logs, red tongues lolling beneath black plastic eyes. And these she found surrounded by yellow submarines and giant toadstools like something from beyond the looking glass, a hallucinogenic forest of pinks and yellows and greens, from the midst of which a huge sheet of water began to spew from four metal sluice gates.

She watched, a hand to her mouth as this impromptu river shot down a blue concrete runway to collide with a curved concrete wall. She watched as the water rolled up the face of this wall, arcing to form a long, perfectly shaped wave of chlorinated turquoise water, a wave big enough to stand in, she thought, and then noticed that someone had. There was a person in the water, surfing atop a kind of foam man. It was a thick-chested white kid, a kid so white as to suggest that much of his life had been spent beneath a rock, or perhaps here, in the shelter of this mechanical blue barrel. At that point she heard a voice she now recognized as Jack Fletcher's.

"Duane Cravens, New Braunfels, Texas," Jack Fletcher said. The camera pulled back to reveal a suntanned and smiling Jack Fletcher. He wore a blue ball-cap with the words "Dr. Fun" stitched above the brim.

The doctor was positioned upon a metal catwalk, talking to the kid, Duane Cravens, now standing just below him, waist-deep in the brilliant turquoise water.

"So, Duane," Jack asked. "You ever surf in the ocean?"

The boy managed a sly smile. "Neow way," Duane said, his accent a muted Texas twang. "Fish piss in the ocean."

"Not to mention sharks."

"Damn straight," Duane said. "This friend of mine went up to Northern California. He saw this guy get bitten. Fucker bit the guy right in half then started spitting things out."

"Jesus."

"No shit."

"You happen to know if the guy lived?"

Duane was a moment in thought, as if this answer required some consideration. "He lived," Duane said at length. "But the guy was totally hassled."

Dr. Fun appeared perplexed. "Hassled?" he asked. "By whom?"

Duane looked a little perplexed himself. "Oh, man," he said finally, shaking his head at the doctor's having missed the obvious. "By the shark."

Kendra was on her way out of the shack when she heard the sound of something approaching the landing. It came by way of the road leading down from the bridge and the highway. Instinctively she drew back, holding the door open a crack, so that it was by this aperture that she saw it come. And it was, she saw, the thing which had trailed her along the river. There was no mistaking it. She saw it now for what it was—an old station wagon with the rear cut away, allowing for a small house to be built where the back seat and trunk had been.

The object came rolling down from among the trees, its engine popping and hissing, springs creaking. It might, she thought, have been the runaway calliope of a traveling roadside attraction, and she watched with some combination of fear and amazement as it rolled to a stop a short way from the landing. She watched as two doors swung open, as three men stepped out into the mud. For a moment, they stood there, looking about, as if to take some stock of their surroundings.

Briefly, she entertained the notion that they were simply lost, that not finding what they had come for, they would climb back into the thing which had brought them and go away. But her heart told her no. And though she could not see them clearly in the darkness, her instinct was that they were from upriver, that they had come about the boy. One wore a pointed hat, and beneath it, shoulder-length hair. Another was a big man. He wore a kind of poncho and there was something strapped to his leg, for she saw him bend to adjust it in some way. A third man said something to the others, and she saw him wave toward the river.

It seemed to her, at this point, that there were two things she might do. She might stay in the shack, hoping somehow to hide there, or she might make a run for it. There was a deer trail just west of the stairs that led to the trailer. The men would no doubt see her. But the angle was in her favor. She would have a good head-start. If she could beat them to the trailer, she would have access to a phone. There was a weapon there too, an old shotgun that had belonged to Drew's grandmother and which Drew had once shown her how to use.

There was not much time to decide. The men had begun to move. She took a breath, shoved open the door, and ran. She heard one of the men shout but she believed she had caught them flat-footed. She paused beneath the cover of the trees, for an instant, long enough to hear the sound of pursuit—though still some ways down. She had her lead. She turned and went on, pushing through the blackberry and stinging nettles which pulled at her clothes and lashed at her skin. She felt the bag containing her clippings fall from her shoulder. She stumbled among the gnarled roots and patches of dew-wet grass, coming in time to the rickety wooden landing built to front the old house trailer where it hunkered among the tall trees, only to find there that she had been outfoxed after all.

It was the Hupa who met her. He had guessed her destination, and while his companions chased her along the path, he had come by way of the stairs to the landing at the trailer's door, so that when she stumbled from the woods, he was there to meet her, though it may have been that she surprised him almost as much as he surprised her. For though it cannot be said what he expected to find, it can only be stated that the moon had, at just that moment, begun to show through the fog, and it was by this light that he saw her—all black and white, with lines of blood drawn across her skin where the nettles had scratched her, with her chest heaving and eyes wide and spiderwebs alight with dew in her hair, so that even a man like him, who had long ago abandoned belief in anything more mysterious than blood, was, upon first sight, at such an hour, in such a place, willing to take her as a visitation.

There was only one seat in Drew's van, and that was an old lawn chair he had placed behind the steering wheel. He had neglected, however, to bolt the chair down. In consequence, the invention made for highly unstable seating, and every time he went around a corner—which he was wont to do in excess of posted speeds—the chair would tilt up on one or two legs, swinging this way and that, with Drew hanging on to the wheel, turning the old van, and balancing himself at the same time, and in so doing, making a circus act out of every bend in the road, while at the same time, using his free hand to punctuate whatever discourse he was at that moment in the middle of. For the fact of the matter was that Mr. Harmon had, in his advancing years, become something of a professor.

It was a new wrinkle in the man's act, but Fletcher could see how it had happened. He could imagine the solitary hours of hiking and surfing, of felling trees and shaping boards, the hours spent seated in cold deep water, holding to all but nonexistent line-ups through shifting fogs and raging offshore winds. He could imagine him out there by his lonesome, plotting storms by campfires, rising in the still dark of a new day to drive yet more hours in his rusted, heaterless van, its walls covered with weather charts and infrared satellite photographs of the coasts of California and Oregon, and other photographs of perfect empty waves—not a surfer among them—arriving finally at some remote outcropping of stone to be marked and charted until he had marked and charted every reef and point, every cove and cloud break, had studied how each broke on differing swells, at differing tides, watching from unhikable cliffs, squinting toward some always distant horizon, and all the time with only himself for company.

What the man had hatched out of all this solitude was a kind of crazy quilt of a world view, stitched together from disparate parts. Nor was he inclined to show much sympathy for listeners. His thoughts were not arranged or edited along any discernable line but spewed forth in an intense but haphazard fashion, with much of his terminology left undefined. Ideas sprang from any number of arcane sources. He had, for instance, managed a kind of union between Terrance MacKenna's notion of history's fractal mountain and that of Miklos Dora—a.k.a. Da Cat, the king of Malibu's rogue wave. It being Professor Harmon's contention that, in fact, the Rogue Wave was the transcendental object at the end of history, that wave height, water density, speed, and intervals existed in a kind of Pythagorean flux, creating as it were a surfer's cabal, the mysteries of what might only be plumbed with strict attention to a kind of cultus involving the grains of ancient woods and their arrangement along the lines of the ancient boards unearthed from the Hawaiian caves and charged with the magic of the Hawaiian kings.

The man could go on about these ideas at great length, and no doubt had. Typically, Fletcher suspected, with only the metal walls of the old van with their weather charts and satellite photos and empty waves for company. On the evening in question, however, these self-same walls were providing him with a captive audience in the form of Jack Fletcher and Robbie Jones.

Fletcher's principal line of defense was silence. Which was all-right with Drew, as the man was not much of a listener. It was the tortured landscape of his own mind that he was most interested in transversing. Others were invited to follow, as best they could.

Robbie Jones, on the other hand, was a restless listener in his own right, with his own poorly formed ideas on a wide variety of subjects. Nor was he a man to hide his great light beneath a bushel. As a result, the two men butted heads often. The subject of board design was a particularly sensitive issue. "But I've been there, dick-weed," Drew Harmon would say. "Been where?" would come the nasal response, and Harmon would dictate once more the details of his last visit to the basement of the Bishop Museum on the island of Oahu, of how he had gone equipped with white cotton gloves, of how he had been allowed to prowl among the stacks.

"It was all there, man. Alias, Olos, Hot Curls, Balsas. I felt like Howard Carter when he opened up Tut's Tomb. You know what the bastard said when they asked him what he saw?"

Drew paused, waiting for a response that did not come. For his part, Fletcher had no idea what the bastard had said. Harmon smiled. "He said, 'I see wonderful things.' "

Drew laughed.

"I been to the Bishop Museum," Robbie Jones said. "That's one big whale they've got there."

Drew craned his neck, staring into the back of the van. "Whale? You hear me talking about a whale? I'm not talking about a god-damn whale. I'm talking about surfboards." He shook his head and looked back into the night.

"There I am, man, right in the middle of all this . . ." He pawed at the night with one of his big weatherbeaten hands. "This, stuff. And one of the coolest things there is this 1930s redwood. I mean, this one really breathed."

As Harmon talked, he described the various design features not only in words but with his hands as well, chopping and slicing the air, at times letting go of the wheel altogether, bringing the old van back on line only when two wheels were already off the road, but doing so with a certain effortlessness, one which bespoke a set of reflexes Fletcher imagined had served him well through some thirty-odd years of riding the world's biggest waves, and which, in the end, put Fletcher's mind to rest. The man would not drive off the road and kill them in some ditch. Such was not his fate.

"The bottom design was really very similar to today's boards," Harmon said. "Complex as shit, considering it was shaped with an ax. It started me thinking. This board was carved from a tree. It was alive once. You could see it in the grain of the wood." Harmon paused. "And when I picked it up, something happened. That's all I can say. There was like this sound coming up through the timber. I swear it sang to me."

"Wha'd it sing?" Robbie Jones wanted to know.

Drew Harmon shook his head. "Jesus. I don't know, man. Pure energy."

"Sounds to me like you were on something, dude. Why don't you pull over, I gotta flash."

Harmon looked unhappily toward the road. "Shit. Flash out the window, Junior. We got a storm to catch."

Robbie Jones just stared at him. "You're shitting me."

"I'm not shitting you. You gotta piss, do it out the window. What do you think? You think I'm your momma drivin' you to the beach? You think there's anybody out there to see you?"

Robbie Jones cursed and got to his feet as best he could in the confines of the van and pushed open one of the rear windows, where, after more fumbling, he managed to get his dick out of his pants and into the night so that, in time, Fletcher was treated to the sound of Robbie Jones's urine pinging against the side of the van. At which point, Drew made a hard right and Robbie Jones toppled away from the window, landing first on his ass and then his back, urine spraying in all directions as Drew hooted and rolled down his window to usher out the stench, and Robbie rolled and swore and clutched at himself, having apparently hooked his penis stud on something as he fell, jerking the mutilated appendage hard enough to draw blood.

Drew looked over at the kid rolling around on his floor, noticing the blood and the penis stud for the first time. "What kind of faggoty bullshit do you call that?" he asked.

But Robbie Jones was too busy pissing and moaning to answer. Fletcher looked away. He clung to the stack of wet suits he was using as a seat and banged the back of his head on the metal wall of the van as Drew rounded one more curve, as what the next few days had to promise presented themselves to him in all of their terrible glory.

Drew Harmon drove on, for a time, down roads that still had names to them but coming finally to roads no one had thought over long enough to name. Roads torn violently from hillsides and ridges, the earth taken right down to the bone so that the rusted-out old van rattled and shimmied, following its own corkscrewing headlights into places where only people long dead and loggers had gone before.

It was a patchwork landscape they passed through here, a motley collection of clear cuts and burns, of recent Forestry Service plantings wherein spindly young trees of remarkably uniform dimensions were laid out in neat, Christmas tree–farm rows, their fuzzy limbs laced with dew. Here and there, they would see some older stand of timber rising up black before the black night, and to which Drew was inclined to point, calling out the trees by name. Douglas Fir. Cedar. The ubiquitous hemlock. And all the while negotiating intersections known only to himself, driving them deeper into the heart of the wilderness.

By the time Harmon at last parked in a rutted turnout on the side of a logging road, they had been gone from the river for close to two hours. Fletcher climbed stiff-legged from the back of the reeking van. On one side of the road was a great clear cut, the timber having been harvested for as far as the eye could see, nor had anything yet been planted in its place, and the moon rolled high and white above a black and barren landscape punctuated only by intermittent mounds of dirt and ash and blackened tree stumps left moldering like the tombstones of some ancient and forgotten race. In stark contrast to this bleak scene, and yet separated from it by not more than eight feet of rocky ground, there rose up, on the opposite side of the road, a wall of virgin forest, a tiered web of foliage impregnable to light, as well as to men, and along whose uppermost edge even the stars surrendered their light.

"Enough to make you believe in Bigfoot, the beast, ain't it?" Drew Harmon asked.

He was watching Fletcher watch the dark woods. Robbie Jones stood a few feet away, still cursing beneath his breath, apparently tending his unit.

"We walk from here," Drew said.

"Walk where?" Robbie Jones asked him.

Drew pointed toward the wall of blackness. "There," he said. And he went to the back of the van and opened the doors and began to remove their gear. Fletcher went with him.

Each man carried a pack with food and water, together with a sleeping bag, a wet suit, and a board. Fletcher carried a camera as well and Drew asked how his ankle was, for he had gotten a look at it before leaving and had wrapped it in an Ace bandage.

Fletcher said it felt okay, and, in fact, it did feel better than he would have imagined. How it would hold up was another matter, but he guessed he would find out soon enough.

"It ain't that bad," Drew told him, shouldering a pack. "Just keep it moving."

Robbie, having finished with his business, stood looking at the boards shimmering in the moonlight. They were Drew's boards now. Robbie's had been lost to the locals, and if he wanted to ride Heart Attacks, he was going to have to do it on one of Drew's big guns. He bent to pick up a board, testing it for weight. "I owe you one," he said.

"Oh, hey, don't mention it, brah. They put your picture in the magazine, you tell them how good the board worked."

"I'm not talkin' about boards."

Drew ignored him. He was turned now toward the moonlight and Fletcher got a good look at his face for the first time since climbing into the van, and it seemed to him as if the man had aged considerably during the course of the drive. There was a weariness about him Fletcher had not seen in the shaping room by the river, and as he stared toward the moonlit clear cuts, his face appeared lined and drawn. At last, however, he turned toward the dark stands of timber and when his voice came to them, there was an edge to it, that of a weary parent scolding a slow-moving child.

"Come on," he told him. "I want to hit the beach early enough to get some rest. We got some miles to cover in the morning, we're gonna make Big Sandy by tomorrow night." And so saying, he snatched up a lantern from the back of the van and started with it into the trees.

What followed was, for Fletcher, a kind of hallucinogenic experience, lit by the strobe of Drew Harmon's lantern, complete with dripping sword ferns, and mushrooms the size of serving platters, and moss-covered cedar which, in places, showed trunk diameters of more than twenty feet. There was little time to admire these wonders, however, as Drew set the pace, driving them through the woods in one long, forced march. It was all Fletcher could do to keep up. His ankle was soon throbbing away and he slipped often, as the ground was cast in darkness and veined with tree roots made slick as icicles by the incessant drip of the forest. There was of course no question of stopping. He slogged on, without complaint, a steady downhill trek, following at times the beds of tiny gullies where his feet splashed in running water, trying always to keep up, to follow the dancing light, lest the darkness swallow him whole and one nightmare take the place of another.

And so the time wore on, and the night with it. Nor was there any movement of moon or stars to mark its passing, as all that was hidden from them here. By that canopy of living growth which concealed the sky. And concealed as well the pale red glow which, at this very moment, had they been perched atop some clear-cut ridge rather than sunk in the heart of the wood, they might have observed staining the sky above the old trailer that had belonged to the murdered girl, then purchased at a reduced price and moved to the banks of the Klamath.

17

Travis awoke stiff and hungover, having slept on a couch on the back porch of the Moke's. He woke to gray skies and the sound of the river. He shed the dirty wool blanket with which he had covered himself and walked to the front of the property where he saw at once that the house car had not returned.

He cursed his lassitude in the cold gray light and picked his way among the empty beer cans and the bones of animals to where his own truck sat parked near the oxidized Duster. Looking back toward Moke's he could see a thin line of smoke just beginning to curl from a rusted vent, but the house itself, like the morning, was silent and gray and showed no obvious sign of life. He saw that several Indians had spent the night near the blackened remains of the fire but had yet to regain consciousness. He saw too the remains of the skinned Roosevelt elk already drawing flies where it hung beneath the cedar at the entrance to the smokehouse, and he thought that if they were smart, they would put it in with the salmon, but then being smart was not their way. Although he guessed they had been smart enough to fool him, and when he had seen enough he got into his truck and drove away.

He drove back along the road which skirted the river. The water looked high and cold, the waves formed by its speed bearing silver crowns in the early light. He saw a pair of men in fishing vests floating on the water in an aluminum drift boat, though aside from their vests, they showed nothing else in the way of gear, nor did they row, but were content to drift with the current, and might, for all the life they showed, have been no more than chunks of wood carved into the shapes of men. As Travis went on, however, he was aware of their heads turning together to mark his passing, though no hand was raised in greeting, neither his nor theirs.

When he reached the interstate and the bridge which spanned the river, he was set upon by a not-unexpected sense of dread, for what he saw there was a small caravan exiting the gravel road that skirted the lower Klamath. Out in front, there was a car belonging to the Sweet Home Police Department. Behind that there came a flatbed tow truck bearing a bronze Dodge van Travis believed he had seen before, parked at Drew's landing, and even at the distance from which he first saw the cars, he could see the van had been gutted, windows broken, tires slashed. It hunkered atop the flatbed as might the husk of some gigantic and ruined insect. Behind the truck came the entire tribal police department of the lower Klamath—Jerry Blacklage and his deputy, Jim Lemon. The Indians rode in Blacklage's green-and-white Bronco with a gold sheriff's star on the door.

Travis pulled to the shoulder of the road, watching as the little procession climbed up from the river and turned toward town. When they had passed, he fell in behind, flashing his headlights. When the police chief saw him, he pulled over, allowing the caravan to proceed without him, disappearing finally into the fog that had thinned but not yet burned from above the town.

Blacklage was a tall, fleshy Indian from Portland. He wore his summer tans and aviator shades in spite of the fog. He had been trying to work his way south for the past decade and still applied for postings on the reservations around San Diego, but the jobs in that part of the state were hard to come by, and Sweet Home was as far south as he had managed to get. His principal accomplishment to date was the posting of a thirty-five-mile zone on a short strip of interstate where it crossed the reservation. It was where he spent most of his time, sipping Diet Cokes, dreaming of sunlit beaches, and handing out traffic citations to unobservant citizens. He had been known to absent himself in times of trouble.

His deputy, Officer Lemon, was an enthusiastic young Hupa recently graduated from the state university in Humboldt County. He had been less than six months on the force, and, for the most part, Blacklage kept him chained to a desk at the tribal center, plowing through the backlog of paperwork which had been collecting since the chief's arrival from Portland. Travis suspected that if there was anyone pulling for Blacklage's transfer any harder than Blacklage himself, it was Jim Lemon. The three men met between their respective trucks.

"What?" Travis asked.

Blacklage removed his aviator shades. He looked, Travis thought, even more unhappy than usual. "Vandals," Blacklage said.

"The Harmons?"

Blacklage nodded.

"Anyone hurt?"

"Don't know. Doesn't look like it. There's no one there."

"Kendra's not there?"

Blacklage shook his head.

"Know anything about who did it?"

Blacklage nodded in the direction of the departed caravan. "The cheese dicks think it was kids. The Posse maybe. Maybe the Stoners. Harmon's had trouble with them before."

"Burned one of his storage sheds."

"Yeah, well, this time they got the whole place."

Travis stared at him.

"You want a look, come with me." He put his shades back on. "I wouldn't mind a walk-through without those guys looking over my shoulder." He nodded once more in the direction of the town, then seemed to remember something and turned to his deputy. The young man had been standing to one side, listening intently to the talk.

"Why don't you take the Bronco and follow Charlie in," he said. "I want to make sure they put that van where we can keep an eye on it. Travis here can bring me back."

"Right," Lemon said. He snatched the keys from Blacklage's hand and walked quickly toward the Bronco.

Travis watched him go. "You ought to let that kid do something once in a while," Travis said.

"That's what I'm afraid of," Blacklage told him. "I'm afraid he will do something. Makes me nervous every time I let him out of the office. He has ideas."

"He's young," Travis said.

"That's my point. I'd like to see him get old."

Travis and Blacklage rode together in Travis's truck back down the gravel road. They parked at the landing. The shed was partially burned. Higher up, however, Travis could see that the trailer had been burned out completely, the trees around it scorched.

The chief pointed at the blackened remains. "Butane tanks hadn't been empty, the fucker would probably have blown."

"That could have been one hell of a fire."

"Could have been anyway, somebody hadn't of seen it, we'd had wind instead of fog."

"Christ. Who would do such a thing?"

Blacklage shook his head.

"You find any graffiti?"

Blacklage shook his head once more. "I found this," he said. He went into his shack. When he came back, Travis saw that he was holding something in his hand. His first impulse was to believe it was a severed finger. Upon closer inspection, he saw that it was a piece of dried salmon.

"You don't get stuff like this in the stores," Blacklage said.

"No, you don't."

Travis looked at the dried fish. It came, he was quite sure, from upriver. Perhaps from the Moke's smokehouse.

"Where'd you find it?"

Blacklage nodded at the shack. "Was in a beer can I found sitting there."

The two men walked to the shaping room together. The wreckage was quite complete. Shredded books and tapes littered the floor, some of it burned, some of it turned to confetti by the water that had put out the flames. The sight made Travis slightly nauscous. He went to a fallen television set and VCR. He saw there was still a cassette in the box. He reached to pull it out, but found it jammed, perhaps fused by the heat. Looking at the back, he saw Jack Fletcher's name on the spine. He stood and went outside.

"I don't think this was the Posse or the Stoners," Travis said. He told Blacklage about being upriver. He told him about the men he had seen at the Moke's.

"Crankster gangsters."

Travis shrugged. "Up there, who knows. I would say they were some kin to David Little."

"You ask the Moke?"

"Sure."

Blacklage heaved a sigh. "Yeah, well, there's no sign anybody was hurt here. I would say Drew must be out on one of his trips."

"What about his wife?"

"She ever go with him?"

"She has."

"There you go."

Travis said nothing.

"Looks to me like we're just going to have to wait for them to come back. We'll find out if they know anything then."

Travis had no immediate response. He was bone tired, and he could not really say what he thought ought to be done. There was no way of knowing where Drew had gone or when he would be back, or if his wife was indeed with him. There was no point in asking the Moke, and certainly no point in saying anything to the officers from Sweet Home. The reservation was not their jurisdiction. If there looked to be trouble Jerry Blacklage could not handle, they would call in the feds. Travis had seen the feds. They would come with guns and dogs. Before they were finished looking for whatever it was they had been called in to look for, they would find half a dozen excuses to send half a dozen more Indians off to places like Scorpion Bay, and the black stake of recrimination and reprisal would be driven ever deeper in the heart of the very thing Travis would have hoped to heal. And so it was that he stood in the misty light, looking up the hill at the charred remains of the old trailer while Blacklage mumbled something about getting into town to do something about the van, for it had been towed out upon his order.

Travis just looked at him a moment, uncomprehending in his weariness. "Why'd you do that?" he asked at length.

" 'Cause there was still stuff on it," Blacklage told him.

"What kind of stuff?"

"Everything, pretty much. Engine. Parts . . ."

"You mean it was vandalized but not stripped?"

Blacklage nodded. "I figured I'd get it out of here before it was."

"That doesn't strike you as odd?"

"What, that it wasn't stripped?"

"Been kids, they would've taken everything. You know that."

Blacklage shrugged. "If there was time, if something hadn't scared them off. Like I said, I don't see as how there's much we can do but wait. Harmons'll be back."

"You hope they'll be back."

Jerry Blacklage just looked at him. "They'll be back," he said.

The men got into Travis's truck.

"You say anything to the cops from Sweet Home?" Travis asked. "About the salmon, or the van not being stripped?"

The police chief smiled. "You shittin' me?" he asked. Travis nodded. He started the truck and drove away.

Travis went twice that day to the trailer by the river. The first time with the chief of police, the second time by himself. It was after he had gone home and showered and tried to sleep. But the sleep would not come, and something had begun to eat at him. He had the feeling that they had missed something. He could not have told you what. A detail. A sign to be read.

He drove back along the rutted dirt road, coming within sight of the landing and Kendra Harmon's truck. It was difficult for him to imagine that she had gone with the surfers, though she had accompanied Drew at times past, for she had told him so, told him of Drew's interest in remote spots with difficult access, and yet the sight of that little truck appeared to him as some omen of evil luck.

He parked near it and got out. He found the doors unlocked. There was a bottle on the seat. White port. Half full. Surely this was not how she steeled herself for those moonlit hikes in the forest. And yet why would someone else have put it there, not yet empty? He began to move around the truck, circling it in ever-widening loops until, at length, he had come to the deer path and found there an unusual number of tracks. Someone had been up this trail quite recently, he thought, for the tracks were fresh and deep, suggesting, he concluded, that someone had come this way in a hurry. Moving on, he found further signs of some hasty ascent, broken stems, crushed leaves. In one place, he came upon a piece of a black, silky fabric impaled upon a thorny branch. He took it between a thumb and forefinger, moving the fabric beneath his skin. It was hers, he thought. How could it be otherwise? He went on once more, halfway to the trailer, where, as the last piece of some demented puzzle, he came upon the things she had collected, the horsetail and mushrooms. The yellow yarrow. He found them dropped and spilled from their bag as if they were nothing less than the brightly colored entrails of some small thing taken in the night.

1 8

With the coming of the morning, Kendra saw the men clearly for the first time. There were three of them and she saw that they were Indians. One was no older than a boy, dressed like a cholo. She believed she had seen him before, in town, or around the reservation. The others were strange to her. One was skinny with a narrow, pointed face and long white hair. The other was big. Not tall, but thick-chested and thick in the arms and thighs and neck. His hair was long and braided. He wore a long drooping mustache and a patch of hair beneath his chin, and she knew he was the one who had surprised her at the trailer.

When she had seen him on the landing, she had run. She had not gotten far. She had been taken quickly and with great force. The other way she was taken did not happen then and there, but later, on a filthy mattress in the back of the homegrown camper. Which was where she was just now, the vantage point from which she viewed the men.

They were hunkered about a small fire from which gray smoke spooled away into a wet gray morning. There was coffee that they laced with alcohol, and someone had apparently made a run into town because there were Egg McMuffins and Tater Tots and biscuits and sausages that she could smell wafting through the cracks in the bare plywood walls and through the sliding glass windows which had been left open to the chill morning air. She could smell the trees on the air as well as the food, and this came as a kind of perverse reminder that indeed another world continued to exist beyond these warped and splintered walls, thought it seemed to her now, in light of what had transpired, that her entrance to that world must surely have been revoked and would remain so from here on out.

No one thought to offer her any food, although she did not believe she could have eaten anyway, as her mouth was still sour with rancid jissim and her throat sore and her body bruised and bleeding. Eventually she was given to understand that what they were talking about was her. They were trying to decide what to do with her, now that they had her.

The boy apparently favored pushing her off a cliff.

"Everybody knows she walks in the woods at night."

"You pumped enough paste into her. They'll see what happened before she got pushed."

"You pumped some into her yourself."

The skinny one favored taking her deeper into the woods where no one would find her.

"That's deep."

"Deep like I was up her ass with it."

"Yeah, all three inches."

At length, however, the big man, who till now had been squatting on his haunches and poking at the fire with a stick, said what he wanted and she saw right away that that was how it would be.

"We take her," he said.

The skinny one seemed to like the idea. She was watching them from the mattress that covered the floor of the plywood room and that, in fact, was its only article of furnishing. She saw the man take hold of his crotch, moving himself about in an obscene fashion.

"What then?"

The big man looked up, annoyed. "What do you think, what then? We fuck her in front of her old man. After that, we have some fun."

The boy chewed on a doughnut. The skinny man looked toward the car and caught her looking. He favored her with a toothless and demented smile. He grabbed his crotch once more, this time pointing to it for her benefit with the thumb of his free hand.

"Humaliwu," the man said. "The place where legends die." The name seemed to amuse him but Kendra recoiled when she heard it, for she knew now that she had been right in her assessment of Drew's plans. Most likely, he had left one of his notes for her, taped to the trailer door. The Hupa had found it. It was how they knew, and she could see now that these men meant to go there as well. And, as if in some perverse counterpoint to this revelation, she saw for the first time that the men were armed.

They had moved around some and she could see rifles propped against a fallen log not far from their fire. One of the guns was exposed to the air, the other was encased in a soiled buckskin sheath with fringe on it as if it were a relic of some Wild West show.

She supposed this should not come as any big surprise to her. Still the sight of the weapons sickened her in a way the mere knowledge of their existence might not have. For in seeing the guns, she could see as well where this would lead. She could see its end in its beginning.

"So what about her?" the boy asked.

Kendra drew back into the interior of her box. She pushed at the rear door with her foot but found it locked. Outside the men continued to talk. In time she heard them coming to the car. She thought that maybe they would come for her but they didn't. She lay on her back on the soiled mattress as the car started and drove away.

It was a rough ride, leading her to assume they were holding to the logging roads and as the light drained from the windows she concluded that they had come within the shadows of tall trees. She did not raise herself to look. She had no desire to call attention to herself, for she felt that she was being watched, that something was on her, the darkness, perhaps. The thing she had seen moving in the trailer, collecting and dispersing, laying in wait for her across the years. It had all come down at last. She would be undone here. She and Drew and the surfers with them.

19

Fletcher woke to the sound of Drew Harmon's voice. He woke to utter blackness and was some time in placing himself. Had not some hand been there, in the dark, to shake him awake, he might well have thought he had never slept at all, for he had continued to hike even in his dreams, slipping and sliding, through the surreal dark and drip of the forest, following a distant, dancing light, and come finally to a beach so shrouded in fog that even Drew Harmon's lantern had shown them little of it but where they had heard the crashing of unseen waves and tasted the sea and gone about making a shelter of sorts among the driftwood to shield themselves from the night.

Upon reflection, he supposed that this was where he was just now. He was no longer scouring the beach like some blind worm. He was on his back, in the thing they had made. Having settled this for himself he closed his eyes and rolled onto his shoulder.

"For Christ's sake, Doc. You dead, or what?"

Fletcher looked into the blackness. He watched as a piece of the roof was lifted and tossed away, revealing a pre-dawn sky across which some tepid gray light had begun to bleed. A dark shape hovered above him. He set up slowly, the sleeping bag falling from his shoulders. A Pop-Tart was thrust into his hand.

"Eat this," a voice told him.

Fletcher decided that he was not altogether well. With the Pop-Tart in one hand he crawled out onto the wet sand, finally settling upon a wet rock while Drew Harmon rolled his bag for him and assembled his pack. Fletcher could see him there, a dim shape in the fog.

"I ain't gonna do this for you every fucking morning," Drew told him. "Tide's coming up fast. We need to get around a point up yonder before it peaks. We've got a minus seven at three this afternoon. I'm hoping to hit the rock field by two. We can do that, we can make Big Sandy by the end of the day."

Fletcher took a bite of the tart. He was attempting to process this information. At length he began to fumble in the pocket of his parka for a pill. The articles could be heard rattling in their plastic container.

"What the fuck's that?" Harmon asked him. He had finished with the packing and was standing in front of Fletcher, holding his gear.

"Vitamins," Fletcher told him.

"Take 'em later."

"These are the kind you gotta take right now," Fletcher said. He managed to free one from the bottle and swallow it with a mouthful of cherry-flavored pastry.

"You haven't gotten old on me, have you, Doc?"

"It seems to me a man should try everything at least once," Fletcher told him. He slid off his rock as Drew stepped around behind him, helping to get the pack onto his back. "If only," Fletcher continued, "to get a complete picture of the resources of the planet." He was suddenly feeling a bit giddy with false bravado, inclined to quotations.

Harmon tugged at the straps of his pack, then hung a board bag over his shoulder. Fletcher put a hand upon the rock to steady himself against the weight. The prospect of dragging this shit for an entire day, over miles of beach, was suddenly unimaginable. A wave of panic swept over him, erasing the bravado of only moments before. "Looks like we lost that high-pressure system," he said. He felt it necessary to say something, if only to break the feeling which gripped him. Perhaps the big man would agree. They would call the whole thing off. It was only sensible.

He was aware of Harmon looking him over, then turning to stare off into the gloom. The man had wrapped his head in a large bandanna and might, Fletcher thought, have passed for a figure of another time, the ghost of Blue Beard perhaps, come back to scour the beaches for something he had lost.

"It's mother nature fucking with you," Drew told him. He gave one of Fletcher's straps a final pull, then turned his attention to Robbie Jones. The boy had hoisted his own gear and was now standing some way off, a shadow in the fog, eager to be off. "Okay," Drew told them. "Let's do it." It was how they began.

The beach they were on ended after a short walk and they began to climb. For Fletcher it was a hellish ordeal. He was always in the rear. Climbing with the pack would have been bad enough. The board bag rendered it close to impossible. On several occasions he banged the thing into the rocks, or hooked it in such a way as to be thrown off balance. At such times he would lose his footing, jamming his shoe into a crevice, or immersing it in a swirling pool of frigid water. Had there been some ledge from which to topple, he would no doubt have fallen to his death. As it was, the way was never very ledgy, but seemed to proceed along corridors cut from stone. At times these corridors would lead them up and over things, and at other times they appeared to be right at sea level, splashing over rocks made slick with sea grass and sharp with crustaceans, and sometimes even through vast tide pools with bottoms of sand though the sea itself seemed always to be some distance away, for rarely could Fletcher sense its surge or feel the spray of breaking waves. Though with such limited visibility, there was really no way to make much sense of anything. There was no end in sight, nor, for that matter, was there a beginning or a middle. There was only the going on, the next place to put a foot, the next crevice set among walls of stone.

The thing that was most certain was that without Drew Harmon to lead them, they would have been unable to proceed at all. That the man had come this way often enough to negotiate such paths in such conditions was a kind of tribute to something. Though whether these skills spoke of dedication or insanity, Fletcher would, at that moment, have been hard-pressed to say. It was all he could do to hold up the rear and he was aware that often, upon rounding some corner, he would find the others, awaiting his arrival. There were other times when he would meet Drew Harmon coming back to find him, lest he wander off down some wrong turn and the sea take him, and at such times he knew that he was slowing them down, though no word was spoken of it, neither by Drew Harmon, nor by himself. There would just be this dark shape looming up among the dark rocks, in the dark light, beckoning him on, and Fletcher would hoist his gear and shuffle ahead and the journey would continue. And in time, he even managed an image with which to sustain himself. It was the image of the boy in the Zodiac. For in the aftermath of what had befallen him at the river mouth, Fletcher could find no suitable place in which to position himself, neither here, nor in the days to come. As a consequence of this dilemma, there arrived a point in which this painful groping among the shadows came to seem quite right and proper. He took it for an act of penance, the first, no doubt, of many.

By midday they had climbed over more rocky points and traversed more coves than Fletcher cared to think about, but the pills had done their work and he had shaken off the cold. The sun had burned a hole in the sky and the wind had been kind to them. Still, he was aware that he was slowing them down. The beaches were often pitched at steep angles that he found hard on both his back and his ankle. At first, Drew had tried to hurry them along. In time, however, he seemed to resign himself to Fletcher's pace, though ofttimes Fletcher would see him looking at his watch, and then toward the sea, as if studying the progress of the tide or the capricious antics of the fog which, though it had burned from the immediate coast, could still be seen laying in a thick bank not more than half a mile off shore and from which point it would roll toward them now and again before thinning and retreating, as if to mimic the motion of the sea which heaved beneath it.

At times, they hugged the beach. At other times, they went higher and deeper into the woods where they would pick up some piece of trail which, in the end, would generally lead them back down to yet one more cove bordered by more outcroppings of rock.

Now that they could be seen, many of these coves were quite beautiful, with white, unmarked sand, and where the water was shallow, it went often to the color of some fine gem, and starfish could be seen clinging to the rocks like lilies in the field. It was finally to one such cove that Drew brought them and announced it as their next camp.

"It's still early," Robbie Jones said.

Harmon just shook his head. "We were too slow," he told them. "We get around this next point and we're into the rock field."

"What's that?"

"It's where you don't want to get stuck on a rising tide."

"It's where those guys in the book got stuck," Fletcher said.

"They almost got stuck there," Harmon corrected him. "They got lucky is what they got. They got a flat ocean. They'd had a swell, they would've done two things. They probably would've seen Heart Attacks. And they would've drowned."

Fletcher dumped his backpack and board bag and seated himself on a rock, wiping the sweat from his face. He looked around at the little cove. They had first seen it some ways back, from the edge of a cliff. In time, they had made a steep and treacherous descent, following the path of a small waterfall as it tumbled a hundred feet to a narrow creek that opened into a sandy beach. At one end of this beach, there was a huge rock from whose center the elements had cut a twisting arch and toward which Drew now pointed.

"We'll do better on the other side," he told them.

Fletcher shouldered his gear one more time. "What about those trails?" he asked. "The ones those guys in the book used? We couldn't camp there?" He supposed he was hoping to make some show of having gotten with the program. Though in point of fact, he was spent, and the words had a hollow ring, even as he spoke them.

Drew Harmon just looked at him. He was still wearing the bandanna and beneath it his face was reddened and streaked with sweat. The blue eyes, however, still burned with their savage light, and for a moment Fletcher thought the big man might call his bluff, or reprimand him in some way for their failure to cover the ground he had intended. In the end, he simply shrugged and looked at the water. "We could," he said. "Trouble is, we wouldn't gain that much. We'd still have to wait out the tide and it's a crappy place to camp. Much nicer here. Besides that, there's surf."

The argument so settled, Fletcher followed his two companions toward the portal cut from stone and through which an expanse of pure white sand shimmered in the light.

"Beach is deeper here," Drew called as he led them into the rock. "We'll stay drier."

Fletcher followed. He passed through the wind-sculpted stone and into the light, where he saw at once that they had indeed come to a fine stretch of beach, deep and wide, remarkable for its lack of driftwood or dying kelp, although beds of the stuff could be seen glistening in the sunlight a scant fifty yards from the shore. When he looked back in the direction from which they had come, he could see Harmon had been right, that to go further would be risky, that indeed the tide had already begun to turn. For he saw the first lacy fingers of white water as they reached out to touch the wind-sculpted rocks, and he could see that in another hour or two, the sea would indeed seal the portal behind them.

When he turned back to the beach, he found Drew Harmon watching him. The man was standing some ways up the sand, the board bag and backpack still dangling from his shoulders. He waited as Fletcher slogged on up into the dry sand, then nodded toward the rising tide. He looked at Fletcher and he smiled. "No one gets out of here alive," he said.

2 0

By three o'clock of the day on which he had gone with Jerry Blacklage to the trailer, Travis was on his way to see the chief of police once more. He had not yet reached a conclusion about what ought to be done but he was beginning to have some ideas. He carried with him a partial map he had fished from the floor of Drew Harmon's shaping shack, and he figured it was time to talk. He would liked to have talked to someone other than Jerry Blacklage. Under the circumstances, however, Chief Blacklage was all he had, and he would have to do.

Travis drove off the highway and down among the trailers and modular homes of the Lower Elwa, all hunkered amid their piles of cast-off debris, their rusted refrigerators and cars sunk to the axles in mud and weed, and came finally to the big steel-roofed building of the tribal center.

It was going on Halloween, and as Travis got out of his truck, he found himself walking in the midst of costumed children, of midget

Wolfmans and Barney Rubbles and Casper the Ghosts. They scampered about his legs in cheesy store-bought costumes, depicting the full range of Saturday-morning television heroes. He nearly tripped over a three-foot Incredible Hulk in an effort to gain the stairs through the press of the children, and he found in the sight of them cause for a profound depression. "G.I. Joe will see you dead," he told them, but they were making noise, and, in the end, he supposed, it was for himself that he spoke.

He crossed the main floor of the tribal center and proceeded down a narrow carpeted hallway where he came to the door marked Tribal Police. There was a paper pumpkin covering the window and, beneath that, a small skeleton dangled against the door. Travis opened it and went inside.

Jerry Blacklage was alone in the office, seated behind his desk. He was downing a pair of Eskimo Pies and a can of diet cola when Travis came in. He tossed the Eskimo Pie wrappers into the trash can, patted his paunch, and shrugged. At which point he held up the can of diet soda.

"Only two calories per can," he said.

Travis seated himself opposite the chief. He looked around the room.

"Lemon out on point?"

"I got him on the highway. Least that's where he's supposed to be."

By this, Travis assumed, the boy was watching the speed trap.

"You know, for someone who grew up around here, you'd think that kid would show a little more savvy. I mean, there's some things you fix and some best left alone."

Travis nodded. "Yeah, well, I hate to say it, but I think we've got one on our hands that's going to need fixing."

A shadow crossed the chief's face, but he listened as Travis told him of what he had seen. He told him about the trip back to the trailer, about the tracks, and about the clippings from the forest he'd found scattered across the deer trail.

Blacklage shifted his weight but made no move to speak.

"I didn't go back out to Moke's," Travis said. "I didn't want to take the time. But I'll tell you this. I will lay you odds it was those guys in the house car from upriver who trashed the Harmon place."

Jerry Blacklage pursed his lips and looked at the ceiling. "What you're trying to tell me," Blacklage said, "is that you think these crankster gangsters from upriver took the girl."

It was the first time Travis had heard it said out loud, and he found that he didn't like it much. But it was what he thought. He took the map from his pocket and spread it across Blacklage's desk. The map was stained and torn but it was readable. Travis pointed to a boot of land sticking into the Pacific. The spot had been marked and there were notations in red ink written upon the ocean.

"I think Drew's gone up here," Travis said. "I think he's taken those surfers from the magazine and they've gone to the Devil's Hoof."

"That's reservation land all the way. You think he'd try that, after what happened?"

"I think he wouldn't give a shit about anything except the waves."

Blacklage looked at the map and shook his head. "That's a long way from nowhere." He drummed the desktop with his fingertips. "Damn. You know it's not a hell of a lot to go on. I take that story to the Bureau, you know what's going to happen."

Travis knew. Bad Indians from up the river. A kidnapping. Enough to bring out the guns and the dogs.

"It would be bad if we called them and you were wrong," Blacklage said. "If the girl was with the surfers."

This was true. Travis stood and went to the wall at the side of Jerry's desk. There was a map of the reservation there. It was a good deal more readable than what he had taken from Harmon's floor and showed clearly the land extending into the Pacific, the great bay which lay to the south.

"There might be a way of finding out," Travis said.

"What? If you're right about the girl?"

"I could find out if she was with the surfers or not." The idea was taking shape even as he spoke.

"How's that?"

"Go out and look."

"Shit. You couldn't leave now. It's too late. You leave tomorrow, you'll spend the whole day just getting there."

"Not with a boat. You can motor up there from the harbor in a couple of hours. I was thinking, I might prevail upon the old man to run me up there first thing tomorrow. He could drop me off in the bay. I could kayak to the beach."

Blacklage was up now too, looking at the map with Travis.

"You ever kayak out there?"

"No."

The two men were a moment in studying the map.

"I don't know," Blacklage said. "I wouldn't want to try it."

Travis listened with growing impatience, with Blacklage, with himself. It seemed to him that he'd mishandled just about everything so far, and he shook his head. "We need to find out," he said. "Those guys shouldn't be out there anyway, not after what happened. And if Kendra isn't with them, then fuck it. Bring on the feds. The sooner the better. Meantime, it wouldn't hurt to start looking for that house car."

Blacklage snorted at him. "Needle in a haystack," he said.

This was true. There was a network among the reservations, a brotherhood of miscreants. Men such as these might move like ghosts among the old logging roads and backwoods camps. The fact that the car had not been licensed in more than a decade spoke of the paths taken by its owners. Still, it was something to do. He said as much to Blacklage.

The man had gone to a little refrigerator he kept at the side of the desk, removing from it a fresh diet cola. He opened the can with a loud pop. "Damn," Blacklage said. "Of all the people that photographer had to drown."

21

The men had still not offered Kendra food. She had been in the wooden box since the advent of her capture. Hours now. She could not say how many. Nor had the men offered her any opportunity to relieve herself. Apparently they did not think of her in those terms.

They continued along the rough roads, though at one point the ride had gotten smooth and the tires had begun to hum. She had raised herself a bit then, to look from a window. There was little to see save trees. She judged they were headed north, although this was only to be expected if what they said was true, that they were taking her to the Devil's Hoof. It was a poisonous thought. In time, however, even that pain seemed to recede before the need to empty her bladder, and she began to cast about beneath the wooden shell for something she might use to this end.

She undertook this investigation surreptitiously, as she had no desire to draw the attention of the men who sat only a few feet away, all three riding in the front seat and separated from her by means of a plastic shower curtain which had been shortened and hung upon a rod and which, at this moment, was only half covering the rectangular window that had been cut between the camper and the car.

She managed her search from the fetal position, from beneath the coarse blanket, at intervals snaking out a hand or foot to lift some piece of canvas or push at a box. For though the mattress upon which she lay took up most of the camper's floor space, there was a fair amount of junk piled around it.

Eventually, she came upon an old five-gallon can that she thought might work. It smelled of chemical residue but it was empty and the top had been cut away. It was only when she had rolled the thing toward her, and squatted above it, hunkered as tightly into one corner as she could get, the old blanket still covering her shoulders, that she discovered the top had been removed with tin snips, leaving behind a number of jagged edges, and it was on one of these that she cut her thigh, allowing her blood to run into the can along with her urine, which burned badly enough to suggest an infection.

The smell was bad too and soon filled the interior of the plywood box and the men caught her at it. She saw a hand on the shower curtain, and she heard one of them say something. The others laughed. She tried to move, then lost her balance, for the logging roads were rough, filled with ruts and curves, and when she fell, she cut her leg once more and the can rolled away from her, dumping her urine across the already soiled mattress upon which she had been plundered.

When next she looked toward the front seat, she found the skinny Indian watching her. The man was peering at her from between the shower curtains, his toothless grin framed by yellow daisies and guernsey cows, as if she were the object in some carnival peep show in which the usual roles had been reversed and it was the citizenry placed in dioramas arranged for their various humiliations, with the freaks come to gawk in demented wonder.

They came late that afternoon to the Tolowan reservation at Neah Heads. She knew the place, for she had visited it with Drew.

The tribe ran a campground there. It was located in the coastal range and looked out over the beaches which lay north of the long point. From the camp, it was a day's hike back to the Hoof's south-facing slopes where a series of trails led down to the beach the surfers called Big Sandy.

There were clapboard cabins here that the Tolowans rented in the summer, to tourists and hikers and even a few surfers come to explore the rocks and beaches to the south. In summer it could be a busy place. She and Drew had come for the last time on the Fourth of July when the Tolowans were selling firecrackers as well as their beaches. It was the occasion on which her hike up the little river valley had been cut short by the pit bulls she'd told Travis about. Still, around the camp, the air had been scented with gun powder and a festive mood had prevailed. She and Drew had watched sunsets and fireworks from a high place above their cabin, at rest in the grass, a bottle of wine between them. But the summer was past now and the cabins sat empty in the wind above a distant, steel gray sea. It appeared, however, that at least one of the men was known here by someone, as they were given one of the more remote cabins for the night. It was a flimsy clapboard affair, damp and uninsulated.

Kendra watched as the men built a fire. It was a poor excuse for heat. The cabin remained cold and unless you were sitting on top of it, the stove was little match for the north wind whistling through the cracks in the rough, slatted walls. She hated it that they had come here, to a place she'd shared with Drew. Must you take every memory? she asked of no one. Will nothing remain unspoiled? There was no response to these questions, hallucinatory or other-wise. The men, in fact, had very little to say to her. Much of their time was spent oiling and cleaning the two rifles she had seen that morning. One belonged to the big man, the other to the boy. The big man's looked the more efficient of the two, with a long barrel and a big telescopic scope mounted above the stock. The boy's seemed small by comparison but each took great care in the main-tenance of his piece, and, in time, the talk turned to shooting and how upon arrival at the cliffs they would be looking down on the beaches and the men below.

They talked of strategy as well, and she was given to understand it was their intention to kill anyone they could but Drew outright, and she saw that it was their intention to save him for last that they might make sport with his wife before he died.

In Neah Heads she was given something to eat for the first time, cold jerky, canned beans, and beer, which was what they ate themselves and she tried but was unable to keep it down.

"Bitch is worse than a dog," the big man said.

When they had stopped laughing at her, they stuck her back in the plywood box while they finished with their food and their guns in the meager heat provided by the stove, and she was left to the cold and the coming dark, alone with the certain knowledge they would come for her again when they were ready.

She wrapped herself once more in the old blanket for she had begun to shake uncontrollably. She sat with her back to the wall, pressing herself against it, trying to force her mind to do something. It had never been a very dependable organ, even under the best of circumstances. She thought, at the very least, it could oblige her by providing some abyss into which she might fall. But there was nothing and she remained where she was, aware of each torment. She drew up her knees. She placed her forearms across them and pressed her brow to the backs of her hands. She closed her eyes. The wind was in the trees. Something thumped against the truck. She thought at first it was them, but when she looked, there were only the shadows deepening beneath the trees, an advancing darkness before which she was quite powerless. She could not hide in drink or reach for a light. She felt the panic as heat and constriction. She closed her eyes once more, then opened them quickly, for it seemed to her as if she had glimpsed something after all—a shape in the darkness, a thing she had never seen before, yet surely, she thought, he had been there all along. Maybe she had never looked. Maybe it was the fever. But she saw him now, with a sudden clarity, as if he were the supplicant, she the hieratic witness to his entreaties. It was so simple, really. One need only embrace him to make it so.

• • •

In time they came. It was the skinny man with white hair, the Tolowan with the toothless grin, that she saw first. For being the most eager, he had gotten there ahead of the others and jerked open the door and that was how she saw him—framed as a scarecrow in the last purple light. She watched as he sought her out, then saw him stop short, stammering to himself as the others joined him, so that in a moment all three of them were there, gaping, in various stages of drunkenness and undress, in the weird half light which was neither day nor night, for she had put a little something over on them and what they saw was not exactly what they had come for, or had expected to find.

She was quite naked and bruised, with blood still on her thighs from the things they had done, but she was seated on the horsehair blanket with her head bowed and when she turned toward them, they saw that she had drawn on her forehead a pentagram with her own blood. Her arms she held crossed in the attitude of skull and crossbones, and her eyes were fixed on some place they could not see.

"What the fuck . . ." the skinny man said.

"I have eaten from the drum," she told them. "I have drunk from the holy basket. I have passed within the bridal chamber. You come in, you can meet my friend."

2 2

The surfers lolled about their little beach for the rest of the afternoon. They ate dried fruit and soybeans. The surf, Drew predicted, would come with the rising tide. Upon arrival, he had indicated rocks at the north end of the cove, proclaiming that by late afternoon, they would be under water, and that, in their place, a clean right-hander would begin to rifle off the point.

Fletcher had little interest in such things. He had come for Heart Attacks, and finding it was all that mattered. For the moment he was content to break out the soma and Percodan.

Harmon saw him with the pills and wondered what they were. Fletcher told him.

"Stuff will make you old before your time."

"Already happened."

"You ain't givin' up, are you, Doc?"

"I was givin' up, I wouldn't be here."

"You think you shoot Heart Attacks, they're gonna let you back in?"

"Let me put it this way," Fletcher said. "I got a kid, an ex-wife, and a whole shitload of bills."

Drew Harmon nodded. He studied the ocean before them, the play of light upon the waves. "Let that be a lesson to you," he said.

When Harmon had left him, he lay on his back. The sand was warm here. The drug put him in a dreamy state. He began to study, from this position, the unnatural collision of earth and sky. For the cliffs were set here upon an incline, pitching forward above the sand, cutting patterns from the sky and so appearing, in that angle from which Fletcher viewed them, as the edges of continents, replete with inlets and peninsulas and jagged bays. The sky became the sea, upon whose surface thin rages of cloud swirled as might distant storms, allowing Fletcher to find in all of this an inverted reality. A fun-house mirror upon whose surface the land bowed and the sea undulated, but from which he and his companions, being of little consequence, had been omitted altogether.

The view interested him, and, in time, he decided to shoot it. He did so lying on his back, framing what he found to be the most interesting angles. Drew Harmon came over to watch. He had a large black bound notebook with him and Fletcher could hear him as he shot, the scratching of pen upon paper. Neither man spoke and for some time, each went about his own business.

Eventually, the sun came to the edge of the rock and burned the color from the sky. Fletcher stopped shooting.

"You find something to interest you?" Harmon asked him.

"It's the angle of these cliffs," Fletcher said. "The rocks against the sky."

"Think they'll put it in the magazine?"

"Who gives a shit?" Fletcher said.

Drew Harmon nodded. "It will be so noted," he said, and Fletcher could hear him once more, scratching in his book.

In time, what Drew had predicted came to pass, and with the rising of the tide, a clean right-hander did indeed materialize where the surfer had said it would, and with the sky just beginning to color in the West, Drew and Robbie broke out their gear and stood naked on the beach, pulling on wet suits.

This done, Robbie Jones prayed while Drew stretched. Eventually, the big man stopped long enough to look at Fletcher. "Grab a stick, man. Get yourself a few waves."

Robbie Jones was done praying. He looked at Fletcher and laughed. "Guy's a pillhead, dude. What if he drowns?"

Drew just looked at him. "This ain't a contest, ass munch. It ain't a photo shoot, either. This here's a little go out among friends."

"I didn't know he surfed," Robbie Jones said.

"There's a whole shitload of stuff you don't know," Drew told him. At which point, Robbie Jones got mad and went into the water by himself.

Drew looked down on Fletcher once more. "What about it, Doc? You gonna get wet or you gonna stay on the beach and pop pills?"

"The pills sound good," Fletcher told him.

"Screw it," Harmon said. "Get a stick, man. Get wet. It's good for the head."

So saying, Drew jogged off toward the water's edge and Fletcher was left alone on the beach. He watched as the two men paddled off toward the point. The sight pained him, for it was approaching what had always been one of his favorite hours of play—that hour in which the sun was low in the sky, so that in paddling out, one was apt to lose it now and again behind the lines of approaching swells, only to find its light burning through the lip of a translucent face, an hour when the winds might be seen as blowing sparks from the tops of the waves.

As a consequence of Drew's words, of the time of day, of some instinct latent within him, Fletcher began to study the break before him with some degree of seriousness.

The right-hander Drew intended to ride appeared as a sly little fucker, with boils still showing on the faces where the waves passed above the rocks. But right out in front, a mushier little wave had begun to develop, peaky enough to allow one to go right or left, mushy enough to promise a forgiving take-off, yet sectioning into a shorebreak just fast enough to be fun, maybe, for an aging hipster with a bum ankle and a bad back. So that in time, without ever having anticipated that he would, Fletcher too was naked on the beach, struggling into a wet suit as the wind washed his chest and shoulders, and where, after performing a few quick stretches, he picked up one of Drew Harmon's big guns with which he might have ridden waves in excess of thirty feet, and marched off with it toward the four-foot slop now shimmering before him in the cool fall light.

As anticipated, the take-off was forgiving, which was a good thing because Fletcher felt himself rising in sections, unbelievably slow, but once on his feet, it was all there—the board planing across the face of the wave, collecting speed as the face steepened, and suddenly he was into a little crouch, pushing the board through the fastest part of the wave like a bird in flight, without a sound, save for what the lip made striking the water behind him.

Fletcher continued to work his wave. The rides multiplied. He grew accustomed to the way the big board planed the surface of the water. He found that with its weight, the line of its rail, he could get in early, then hold a high fast line.

The cold was punishing at first but in time a kind of clarity set in. He saw with a fresh eye the lines of the cliff, the sharp angle of the rocks, the last light finding reflection upon a purple bank of sand. But it was more than seeing these things, it was a joining and therein lay the rush. It failed to matter that he was middle-aged and out of shape, practicing little more than the fundamentals on an undistinguished wave. He had come to a place of great beauty but it had taken the waves and the act of riding them to grant him communion. It was a simple truth and it was ever so and he had been too long without it.

Eventually, he lost his take-off spot to the tide. But by now, his confidence was up and he paddled out to the north end of the cove, in front of the rocks, though the boils had by now disappeared from the faces of the waves.

"Dr. Fun," Drew Harmon said, as Fletcher pulled himself up to straddle his board. "Where you been hidin' out?"

They surfed for perhaps another hour. They did so mostly in silence, trading waves as the sun passed from behind a thick band of cloud to sit opposite them on a far horizon, a great orange buddha losing his shit to the sea. Afterward, they built a fire on the beach and stood around it with their wet suits peeled to their waists, warming their hands and chests, then turning to warm their backs before peeling off the cold, wet rubber and pulling on clothes in a hurry, as the wind had grown stiff and cold.

It was while they were yet dressing that Drew called their attention to a sudden boiling and splashing off the point not far from where they had surfed, and it seemed to them that at least one dark shape broke the surface, although with the wind chop and declining sun, it was, from their angle of observation, not totally clear what had transpired.

"Shark taking a seal," Drew said. He was squinting in his customary fashion toward the darkening sea.

"No way," Robbie Jones said.

"What do you think it was?" Harmon asked him.

Robbie Jones looked at the spot. "You really think so? That's right where we were sitting, dude."

"No shit."

They looked toward the water once more.

"That's right about where the reef would be. That's their way, you know. Fuckers love ledges and shelves and reefs, deep water close to shallow, gives 'em something to hide in. Never know the son of a bitch is there till he bumps you, or bites you, whichever comes first."

Drew seemed to find in this some cause for amusement and stood chuckling to himself as the flames of their fire scattered sparks to the wind.

"Mother nature for you," Drew said. "Bitch is just full of surprises."

Fletcher pulled a parka on over his sweatshirt. Robbie Jones was still looking at the water. Drew, still bare-chested so they could see the scars, squatted before the fire, stoking it with a stick.

"Japs caught themselves a pregnant female," Drew told them. "Three, four years ago. First one, ever. Seventeen-footer. They cut the bitch open and guess what they find? Ten full-term, four-foot long embryos. And guess what else they find? In the babies' stomachs? Teeth. The babies' stomachs were full of these tiny teeth."

Drew looked at them and smiled. "Little fuckers are swimming around in the womb, eating each other. Eventually only a handful of the strongest survive. The thing is a predator before it's even born."

Drew poked at his fire a last time and looked at Robbie Jones. "What does that say about the old peaceable kingdom?" he asked.

When Robbie didn't say anything right away, Drew laughed one more time. "I saw somebody had done a parody of that painting," he said.

"Which painting is that?" Robbie asked him.

Harmon shook his head. "The peaceable kingdom. You know, all about how the lamb will lie down with the lion and the child will play upon the hole of the asp. That's the painting. What I'm talking about is a print. A parody of the painting. All the animals in it were eating each other. Kind of how it is, don't you think? You or them. And only the strongest survive."

"Hey, man. What you see around you isn't God's plan. Man fucked up, the whole deal went wrong."

"What? You're telling me animals didn't eat each other, fish didn't eat each other, bugs didn't eat each other till man fucked up?"

Robbie Jones shrugged. "What I know is this, dude. The world is in the power of the wicked one. That's why it's stored up for destruction."

"The fire next time."

"Damn straight."

Drew smiled. "So tell me this, hot shot. The Man burns the place down, what are you gonna do for waves?"

Robbie Jones just looked at him. "Well, shit, man. I guess I'll just have to play me a tune upon the hole of an ass."

"That's asp, dickweed."

"Same difference," Robbie Jones said.

Drew Harmon looked at Fletcher. "How do you talk to a man like that?" he asked.

"I don't," Fletcher told him, and he walked off a little from the others and stood watching the dark ocean, stained with blood, and his thoughts returned to the boy in the red-flannel shirt, even as the moon began to strike the water with a silver light. When he turned to see it, however, thinking that, in fact, it might be quite full, he found he could not, that given his position on the beach, at the foot of the cliffs, the moon itself was hidden from him and he was left to imagine it, moving like a thing of prey among the gibbet shapes of trees which marked the ledge high above them and which, together with the sea and rocks, made their prison complete.

23

Things went badly for her that night in Neah Heads, almost as badly as they had gone the night before, with the exception that one abstained, and of the two who did not, she was able to note a change in their demeanor. They were less raucous though more inclined to violence as if now there had been an upping of the stakes, an engagement of wills. It was a frail thing, this barometric change she claimed as victory. She supposed it had been purchased at some cost she could not yet name but she would think about that later, and when they had left her for their fire and drink, she turned her attention to her surroundings with a sense of purpose she had not known before.

There was no way out of the box. She had grown used to that idea. For though it was a ridiculous thing to behold, it had been built by someone who knew how. The narrow sliding-glass windows might have been broken but they were too small to crawl through. The rear door was solid as a piece of oak, leading her to wonder if she was the first to be held prisoner in this place, and if she was not, what had become of the others.

The hole which had been cut between the driver's compartment and the camper was even smaller than the side windows. One might, however, get an arm through, and this is what she did. She had the idea that she was after something and she would know it when she found it. By getting her shoulder into the small opening she was able to paw about over much of the front seat.

Save for the tears in the vinyl upholstery, there was little to feel. In time, however, she came upon what felt to be a paper bag. She could just touch it, with the tip of her little finger. She twisted and stretched, pushing the plywood edges of the hole into her armpit and neck. For a moment or two, she worried that she might get herself stuck and be found out, though she supposed there was not much more they could do to her. In the end, she managed an edge of the bag between the tips of two fingers. It was enough to drag it closer, and finally to pull it through the narrow opening.

It was quite dark in the box now. When she had spilled the contents of the bag across the mattress, she set about examining each object, guessing at its nature as might a blind person. Among these things was a book of matches and when she found this she sat with it in her hand for some time. After some consideration, she drew the curtains. She put the articles back into the bag and placed the bag in a corner until she had managed to get enough of the mattress off the floor to cover the window which faced the shack. This done, she struck a match that she might see more clearly what she had found.

What she had, aside from the matches, were these: a bag of peanuts, a pack of cigarettes, a set of Desert Storm flash cards, a plastic harmonica, and a man's wallet. She put her back to the mattress, struck another match, and examined the contents of the wallet. She found that it contained forty-two dollars, a Band-Aid, and a driver's license.

It was the license of the skinny Indian. Surprisingly enough, he wore false teeth in the picture and looked slightly less deranged. She saw that his name was William Longtree. He was five feet, ten inches tall and weighed 150 pounds. He was thirty-five years old. She found this difficult to believe. She would have guessed he was fifty, at least. And yet, upon reflection, it seemed odder still that he should have any age at all, that someone had once thought to give him a name, that indeed he was some mother's son, or that he had ever been anything other than the mutant shape she had observed in the night. The observation caused in her a momentary pang of sorrow, though she could not immediately say what this sorrow was connected to, or from what well it had sprung, for in her eyes he had ceased to be a man. And yet even so, she thought, he was not so very much older than she. And thirty-five was young to die.

It was of course, a rash plan, but she was past caring about any of that. She had come to a place beyond the reach of reason. Her deal had been cut and it was with the darkness. She might have burned down the camper and herself with it, if only to cheat the men from their sport, but that would still leave the men on the beach with no one to warn or protect them, and whatever Drew might be, or what he might have done, he had taken her once from a bad place, only to be repaid with her silences, her spasms and hallucinations. And so it was that she tore a piece of cloth from the blanket. In this she wrapped the matches and the driver's license and tucked them into the waistband of her pants. The rest of the things she put back in the paper bag and returned it to the front seat of the truck, and after she had done that, she took the mattress away from the window and lay in the dark. "Rebellion is as the sin of witchcraft," someone said. But she answered, "I am a secret agent of the moon. *Spirita sancta.* Holy, Holy, Holy."

24

The surfers rose in darkness, as they had on the previous day. Once again, Drew was pushing them. The first low tide came early and it was his intention to be across the rock field by midday.

They passed almost without seeing, and certainly without being seen. They went among stone corridors and fishers slick with lichen. They went among rocks sculpted into every conceivable shape and form. Some were as sharp and pointed and perfectly round as if they had been fashioned for the railway spikes of a world much larger than the one into which they had so fallen. Others were huge and round and smooth as marbles, while still others had been broken into shapes too fantastic for the naming, and they passed among these as if they were portals or doorways to other times and other places, though always on the other side, the scene was the same as that which they had left behind.

By mid-morning the fog had thinned somewhat and they came to a long, narrow stretch of beach at the foot of tall cliffs and found here a strange sight, for there were perhaps a dozen deer in this place that seemed to have fallen from the cliff and now lay dead on the sand. They looked to have been that way even on a higher tide for several of the deer had seaweed draped over them, but there were no other marks on them and they lay in various attitudes of repose with their eyes unseeing and open to a distant sun.

They went by the deer without speaking, as if in the sight of these dead animals some portent was contained which none cared to name. Even Drew had nothing to say, though Fletcher did see him stop long enough to make a note in his black book, and after that they went on.

In another cove where the sand was steep and black and flecked with shards of shell and rock made golden in the sun, they came upon the body of a small whale that had been attacked and killed by sharks. Huge bites had been taken from the whale's body, and these were now black with congealed blood and covered in flies, and the stench was terrible so that they went quickly and in silence once more. Nor did Drew stop to write anything in his book. Though later, when they had stopped for something to eat and were seated on a series of rocks that ran for some ways into the ocean, the older surfer took out the book once more and commenced to write.

Fletcher asked him if he was making a note about the whale, and Drew said that he was.

"What else is in there?" Fletcher asked.

Drew flipped back a page and read from his book. "November the fifteenth, 1995. Pelicans. It was surfed on a plus-five-foot tide, on a northwest swell. The waves were a consistent six feet with an occasional eight-foot set. I had two companions with me, Robbie Jones and Jack Fletcher." He looked up from the book. "You'd have to cross-reference this entry with one of my earlier logs in order to get more information on Pelicans. But everything's been laid out. I've drawn maps, noted trails . . ."

"Shit," Robbie said. "You could blow this part of the coast wide open, you let those get out."

Drew Harmon looked at Fletcher. "Smart boy," he said.

"What did you say there about the whale?"

"Just that it was taken by a shark. I make notes of any shark activity I find."

"You find much?"

Drew laughed. "They don't call it the red triangle for nothing. You paddle out up here, you're part of the food chain." He paused, looking back in the direction from which they had come. "Those deer were something else. I've never seen anything like that."

"You put that in the book too?" Robbie asked him.

Drew just looked at him. "You know your Bible?" he asked.

"I know it, some."

"So what did it make you think of, all those dead animals at the foot of the cliffs?"

Robbie was sitting some ways off, wrapped in a plaid sweatshirt with a gray hood covering his shaved head. Fletcher watched as the gray hood bobbed in the gray light. "Jesus putting the demons into the swine," Robbie said at length.

"Exactly so," Harmon said. "The mad man among the tombs. That's what I put in the book. The Gospel of Mark, chapter five." At which point the big man looked out to sea, and when he spoke again it was to quote scripture and this is what he said: "Ofttimes he had been bound with fetters and chains, but the chains were snapped apart and the fetters were smashed and nobody had the strength to subdue him, and continually, night and day, he was crying out in the tombs and in the mountains and slashing himself with stones."

Robbie Jones had half turned on the rock to regard the older surfer. His shaved skull sticking part way out of the hood was awash in light, and he did not, Fletcher thought, appear altogether sane himself.

"The grace of God is available to everyone," Robbie told him.

"You don't believe in unforgivable sin?"

"Apostasy."

"Nothing else?"

"Murders, adulterers, thieves, liars. This is what some of you were. You have been washed clean in the blood of the lamb. Everything," Robbie Jones said, "can be forgiven, if one seeks forgiveness. Except for the sin of apostasy, for speaking against the blood of the Christ."

Drew Harmon was some time perched upon his stone. He had

closed his book once more. "What does the law say?" he asked. "The law says, spill no blood."

"What's that?" Robbie Jones asked him.

"Bela Lugosi. *Island of Lost Souls.*"

"Shit, man. I'm talkin' to you about the Bible. You're tellin' me about some movie."

"Maybe that's all it is, eh, bro? It's all a movie. A seduction of light."

Robbie Jones shook his head in disgust. Drew Harmon turned to Fletcher and winked. He had a Pop-Tart in one hand and there were crumbs on his beard. It seemed as if he was about to say something else when suddenly he held up a hand and told them to listen. What they heard was a deep, distant boom echoing across the water, and Drew Harmon did not have to tell them what it was.

"Is that it?" Robbie Jones asked.

"Is that what?"

"Heart Attacks."

Drew Harmon shrugged. "You think this place is easy to find?" he asked.

"I just asked if that was it."

"Yeah, well, lots of people been askin' that one for a long time. This it? This it?"

Unhappy with finding himself mimicked, Robbie Jones moved away to sit by himself at the edge of a tide pool.

Drew Harmon took no notice but continued to talk. "It's sacred land there," he said. "The Indians knew it. Like the Hawaiians knew it about Waimea. The wave's as big as Waimea, but longer, deeper, way more sections. You can ride this wave for half a mile. More, maybe."

Fletcher looked at Robbie Jones hunkered there in the cold light, a lone buzzard dressed in plaid, perched upon a barren rock before a barren sea. If he was following what Drew said, it didn't show. If Drew cared, that didn't show either. He appeared to be talking as much to himself as to either of his companions.

"You've never seen a wave like this," Drew told himself. "Like J-Bay, only the size of Waimea." He took a large bite from a Pop-Tart, gazing thoughtfully upon a milk white horizon. "Why you need the longer board, the extra weight, carry you through those sections."

As Drew talked, Fletcher sought to hold once more, in his mind's eye, the maps he had studied in the course of the trip. What he remembered were colors, the green of national park and the pink of Indian land running in a patchwork quilt over a field of white, running north from Sweet Home and encountering no other road or town but running right on across the border—a fifty-mile stretch into the state of Oregon. Drew had called it a day hike, but already they had hiked for the better part of two, and as Fletcher sat listening to the big man talk, he was struck by the uncomfortable feeling that what the man was describing was something he had hoped to find, rather than something he had found. This thought was followed in quick succession by another—the absence of photographic evidence, the insistence on the part of some who had been here that Heart Attacks was no more than a rumor—like the photograph of the rogue wave Miklos Dora was said to carry in his wallet. He had till now taken Drew for, if nothing else, a knowledgeable guide. Still, his newfound paranoia would not leave as bidden, and he looked once more at the big man at his side, hoping perhaps for some assurance. What he saw was a kind of gargoyle shrouded in fog, his great shoulders hunched, his eyes narrowed, his red beak of a nose pointing toward a lost horizon, his hair combed back wet above a high and bony brow.

It was not, Fletcher decided, a pretty sight, and he turned from it. Still, he thought, his fears were absurd. Surely the man would not have dragged a photographer and two pros this far north, made promises he would be unable to keep, risked having himself portrayed as a fool, without having seen this place somewhere outside his own head. At which point, Fletcher was made aware of a sound and thought at first it some product of the sea, so high and keening and random did it seem to him, and he looked about for its source, only to discover that it came from Drew Harmon himself, that the man, lost in thought, oblivious to those around him, his eye on the reckless sea, had, in fact, begun to make a kind of humming sound, a song to himself.

2 5

The men came to her with the dawn. The fog and drizzle came with them but she concluded she had been right about the change in their mood. They appeared more solemn in this light, and more haggard, as if this were an ordeal they not only had inflicted but had come to share in as well, though none would ever say it in just that way. It was possible, of course, that she misread them. They were a day's hike from their kill and maybe it was this that made them different. Blood, after all, being the star around which their world had been made to move. But she did not believe it.

There were no attempts to make sport with her or even to look her in the eye, save for the big man, the one who had abstained, and his eyes were as dark and dead as some creature of the sea from whose sight the light has been forever hidden. She was given beef jerky and water and told to get it down and keep it there because there was a long way to walk, and this she did.

They drove just a short ways after that, to the far end of the reservation and the trails leading south. They parked in a turnout before a trail head. The morning was still gray and cold, and theirs was the only car.

The trail head was marked by a pair of signs. One read: "Caution. Unmaintained Trails. Hazardous Cliffs." The second was quite large. It contained the line drawing of a shark and read: "Use Caution. Dangerous Beaches. Strong Undertow. Rip Tides. Sleeper Waves." As if this were not enough to discourage the average bather, the sign contained as well the listing of at least half a dozen shark attacks dating back to 1975.

Kendra studied the signs, recalling the first time she had seen them, here with Drew, and how she had found in them cause for concern. But Drew had only laughed them off, telling her it was his kind of place. And so it had proved to be. She remembered her sense of awe at the conditions he would paddle into, of how he would be lost to her for hours at a time. In the beginning, there had been no exploring for her. She had stuck it out right there on the beach, straining for the occasional image of her husband, gliding down the face of some huge wave far from shore, as if by so doing, she could insure his safe return. With the passage of time, however, she grew to accept his prowess with the waves, his return as a given. It was then that she would set off on adventures of her own, returning to the beach at some agreed-upon hour, sure to find him there as well, jogging along the sand to meet her, chilled to the bone, eyes flushed with a wild light she had taken as evidence of that secret thing he took congress with in a world she could only dimly imagine. And perhaps this was so, though she was inclined here and now, on the morning in question, to believe that what she had glimpsed there was more than the thrill of the hunt. It was darker than that, she thought. It was the image of the other she had seen, burning through—the light, perhaps, to which Amanda Jaffey had been treated in her final moments. It was an aspect, she concluded, of the fate to which she had been consigned, that she should see it so.

When the Hupa and his two companions had selected what gear they meant to take they started out. In time they arrived at the grassy bluffs which ran finally to the cliffs of the Devil's Hoof. The trails turned here, veering now toward the beaches of Big Sandy, following the outline of the hoof. It was a barren, windy place. And though they were still too far away to see it, they could hear the sound of the waves upon the rocks and smell the salt in the misty air.

They came several times upon the bones of animals, entire skeletons, some still showing patches of fur, others bleached white or decomposing in the sea air. Kendra went in the clothes she had been taken in, the blouse and pantaloons that had belonged to a dead girl before her. She still had her hiking boots but the jacket she had worn into the woods seemed to have been appropriated and she had not seen it since. For a time she was bothered by the cold. She was bothered too by the nettles which grew here, woven among the stands of grass, for the pantaloons were thin and had been badly torn in a number of places. The nettles, she discovered, had the effect of making her legs itch and then go numb, but eventually, fatigue brought her to a place where the walking was as sleep-walking. Twice she fell and received for her troubles a kick to her side or hip. Both times, William Longtree helped her to her feet. At length, she began to talk. She would say anything that came into her head. She told them of the evil principle. He was called the king of darkness, she said, and he dwelt in the land of darkness surrounded by his five eons, the eons of smoke, fire, wind, water, and darkness . . .

Her captors would only shake their heads at this talk and make lame jokes but were, she believed, troubled by her as well, and so she walked and spoke her gibberish, this when she spoke at all, although the gibberish seemed to play in her head constantly, in rhythm to how she walked, along a gradually descending trail, through the long stretches of grass and wind and the bones of animals. And all through this long hike, the big man went always in front, his rifle unsheathed now, its large scope mounted, and from time to time during the day he would stop and sight through the scope, occasionally leading some seabird as if he meant to bring it down. At such times, the other men would stop and watch, but the big man never fired the gun. He would sight for a moment, as if satisfying himself about something, then sling it over his shoulder once more and go on, and the others would follow and Kendra would go on as well, with her numb legs, and with her gibberish, which in time did not seem like gibberish at all but the truth as she knew it.

26

Travis had spent the better part of the night packing. At one point, he had paused long enough to call each of his ex-wives, telling them that the children should be kept away from the river just now, nor should any outings be planned that would take any of them very far into the woods. When they had assured him that his wishes would be honored, he'd returned to his packing, where, after some consideration, he'd added a .45 automatic and a pair of clips. The stuff would supply unwelcome weight but he did not doubt that the men from upriver would come armed, and including the gun had seemed a good idea to him at the time.

Standing now at the side of his pickup, beneath a morning sky the color of a dead television screen, he considered the decision once again. It was a question of weight. The kayak was, after all, a recent acquisition, his experience in it thus far limited to a few local coves in small surf. On the morning in question, he would already be carrying more weight than ever before, and he considered yet again the particular configuration of land and sea he would this day hope to traverse.

He'd always felt that the Devil's Hoof was shaped more like a boot than a hoof, the toe of which extended into a great natural bay. It was Travis's intention to have his father take him as far as the bay. For as long as they kept with the lee of the Hoof, he reasoned the old man would be able to put him out and come about with minimum exposure to the big swell pushing down from the north. Travis would then kayak to the beaches, upon which he fully expected to find Drew Harmon and the others.

The plan had more or less made sense to him upon conception. Now, standing in the dark and cold, adding the weight of the gun to the gear already lashed to the deck above the small storage compartment, he was less certain. It all seemed a little crazier by the cold light of day, the simple truth of the thing more apparent—that without the involvement of Kendra Harmon, he would no doubt be willing to follow the sheriff's lead, to curse the surfers for their persistence and wait on their return. It was the girl who had him up at dawn. If she was in danger, he wanted to know it. If she was with the surfers on the beaches, there was the prospect of a day in her company, on the trails leading back to the Heads. And so he put the gun into a Gore-Tex stuff bag and set about tying it to the deck of his craft, which was itself tied to the bed of his truck, and, all the while, in some interior chamber, grinning at himself like some jackass at the window, content in the secret pleasure that he was not like his wives, grown plump and complacent in their ordered lives. In the end, he was still a gambler, a believer in mad romance.

He found his father seated on a stool at the Marlin, a coffee shop favored by local fishermen. It was a place in which they might pass the time with one another for company, waiting out storms and fog banks and red tides. The room was all fishnets and turquoise Naugahyde, with large picture windows fronting the harbor which, on the morning in question, lay unseen beyond the greasy plate-glass and smoky air.

"I don't know," his father said. He blew on his coffee as Travis seated himself at his side. "Fog's a bastard and there's a storm coming. Outside buoys are showing at twenty feet."

Travis looked at his reflection in the plate glass. He ordered a cup of coffee.

"Think maybe you'd better shit-can it for the day," his father told him.

"Bay's generally pretty sheltered. Fog might even be better there."

His old man looked at him over his cup.

"Damn. You must want out there pretty bad."

Travis shrugged.

"How you gonna get back?"

"Walk."

"To town?"

"Campground at the Heads. I know a few people there. I'll bum a ride."

His father nodded. "Let's watch the fog," he said. "I expect it will lift."

By noon, the fog had burned off in the direction of town but still lay heavy on a rolling ocean. Travis felt called upon to point out that the old man knew the waters, that he was equipped with instruments and not likely to lose his way between the harbor and the bay.

The old man looked at the harbor.

"We wait too long, we may get a storm."

At last, the old man sighed. He put out the last of his cigarette and led Travis down to the docks, where his trawler rocked in the gentle swell of the harbor. They carried the kayak between them. The old man had said nothing but had watched Travis unleash it from his truck with a dubious eye. A large gray-and-white gull studied them from atop a concrete piling. The bird gave them twenty feet of dock before departing at their approach.

Travis's father went on board and started checking over instruments and firing up his engine while Travis pulled in the buoys and coiled the deck lines—chores learned as a boy, when his father still entertained notions of his son following in his footsteps, this when a man might still make a good living from the sea. But that time was gone and both men knew it, so that it was just as well Travis had grown tired of the stink of fish and gone off to school instead and come home to counsel desultory Indians because there were still those in abundance, with grievances aplenty, some of which were aimed at men like Travis's father and some of which were not unlike those harbored by the old man himself. And both men knew this too, in a way that made talk of it superfluous.

They had little company as they made for the channel. A few fisherman waved to them from the docks. An old man who lived on a tugboat he'd turned into a kind of houseboat and had since Travis was a boy, stood out on his deck with his old black dog and shouted at them and wanted to know what McCade thought he was going to catch in a storm and laughed at them.

Travis's father waved back, and Travis looked at the old man and his old dog on their old green boat that had been the same color since he was a boy and, in fact, did not look as if it had seen a new coat of paint since he was a boy, and he said as much to his father.

"Isn't that old man ever going to die?" he asked.

His father studied the channel, squinting now and then toward the swell lines running like hills across the horizon.

"He'll die," his father said. "It's just that he'll come to both our funerals first."

Travis nodded, wondering if this would prove the case.

They had by now reached the harbor entrance where the great buoys, covered in rust and the droppings of gulls, lurched about like drunken Salvation Army supplicants ringing their bells, beckoning them entrance to some refuge of the deranged.

The seas were indeed high, and even without rounding the point at Devil's Hoof, the old trawler took on a corkscrewing motion as it plunged steadily north, climbing the faces of the ground swells, then sliding down their back sides to meet the hump that followed and which, at times, was apt to bury the bowsprit altogether, washing the decks with water, eliciting a hoot from the old man. Travis found in these things an unexpected exhilaration as well, for it had been some time since he had been on the open sea, and for a while his spirits ran high, the trepidation he had felt in his driveway all but gone.

They ran with the fog bank well off the starboard bow, with the coast visible to port. Coming within sight of the big bay, however, they cursed, and Travis felt his high spirits wilt upon the vine for they saw that, in fact, the bay was filled with cloud. It rolled before them in great billowing sheets, as if this were the place from which the entire bank had sprung and they had come to some chimney stack leading back down to the molten core of the planet.

Travis watched his father shake his head, consulting instruments as they plunged into the fog. He set the running lights and a small foghorn to signal any other boats of his presence, though it seemed highly doubtful there would be any to hear. He cut back on his engines as the water smoothed beneath them, giving evidence that they had indeed entered the bay.

"No way," his father said at last. "You can't go off into that."

"Maybe we could circle in and out a couple of times. Maybe we'll get a break."

His old man shook his head. "Got your mind made up, don't you?"

Travis stared into the fog. He felt a sudden gust of wind upon his cheek. He turned to the old man.

"We'll make one circle."

In perhaps twenty minutes, at a more westerly point than Travis would've picked, they came to a hole in the fog. A yellow-faced sun burned through the mists, striking the ocean and one narrow band of coast where a pair of sandy coves presented themselves among the rocks, and Travis elected to go.

"I guess you're old enough to call your own shots," the old man observed, though it was clear he didn't like the looks of things.

"I guess so," Travis told him, and set about pulling on his wet suit and strapping his gear into his kayak, then hitching himself to it by way of a cord and Velcro ankle strap and attaching the paddles to his wrist in the same fashion, so as not to be separated from either in case of a spill, because one was no good without the other.

He shoved the plastic boat over the side and went in after it, hitting the cold water on the rise of a swell alongside his craft, then pulling himself quickly on board. The kayak was the kind you straddled rather that sat down in, and with one final look at his old man he began to paddle hard for the coast, lest the fog rush in and swallow what he aimed at.

For his part, Travis's father was not long in watching his son. There was a storm coming and he was eager to be gone, and so the two men moved off in opposite directions with no more than a look, though each carried with him the image of the other. What Travis saw was an old man, a solitary figure on the deck of a working man's boat, and he thought of the years his father had spent in just that fashion, alone upon the sea with a wife and daughter buried and a desultory half-breed for a son. As for the old man, he went with the image of his only son, headed toward some distant cove, dwarfed by an immense groundswell, yet pulling with a skilled and powerful stroke—a feat, he supposed, in which a father might take some pride—and he wondered what it was his son thought so important that he was willing to risk himself in such seas but had long ago given up asking such questions, as he had yet to have one answered.

And so it was that if one were to view this entire section of coastline from the air, from Scorpion Bay at the south to Neah Heads at the north, one would see a huge chunk of ground some fifty miles in length bulging into the Pacific, punctuated at its center by that arm of land known as the Devil's Hoof.

The land that formed this western outpost was a barren, windswept thing. The trees would not have it. There was only grass and rock and a little coastal scrub ending in harsh cliffs that tumbled toward rocky beaches—a rookery for migratory birds made white by their droppings, home to sea lions and seals, a breeding ground for the great white sharks which, on a clear day, might be seen circling from the rocks high above the sea. The Indians had called it Humaliwu, and they had buried their dead above its grassy plains. The whites had called it the Devil's Hoof. They'd left it to the Indians and built their town on the little harbor to the south.

And if, on the morning in question, one were to have viewed this stretch of coastline from the air, or with the eye of a god, one might have seen three separate groups of pilgrims, two by land, one by sea, traversing slowly this dented landscape, following their varied paths, yet meant, one would see, to converge, as if in dance. Though what pattern these steps might weave, or to what end the dance might come, it would not be so easy to say, lest one be some Demiurge as well, and thus able to order these patterns as might the caller in a barn dance, and so dictate both set and step in accordance with the intentions of the Darkness.

27

By midday, the surfers had at last traversed the long field of rock and come finally to a great stretch of flat sandy beach. To the north, a point of land might be seen as a vague outline in the fog. The land appeared to stretch for some distance into the ocean, forming, as it went, the northern end of a great natural bay.

Fletcher was relatively certain that they had arrived at the place, though it was hard to see much in the fog. Nor had the great booming sounds they had heard earlier come to them again, neither on the hike across the last of the rock field or here now, on this stretch of sand. Still, if the arm of land they could see reaching westward was not the Devil's Hoof, it was hard to imagine what else it might be. The elements were accounted for, and Fletcher called these things to Drew's attention.

The big man only nodded. "We'll get waves off that point," he said. "Probably what we heard earlier. The place is fickle as hell. I'll tell you this, you wouldn't want to try and paddle out there just now.

There's a rip runs out of this bay on an outgoing tide you wouldn't believe. I've never been able to figure it out. There's that estuary we crossed back there, but it's not that deep. I mean, you get caught in this mother you'll think you're at the mouth of San Francisco Bay or some damn place. But then this whole area is a little weird."

"What do you mean, weird?" Robbie asked him.

"Got a charge on it," Drew said. "You spend enough time out here, you'll feel it. I mean, look at the place. No one's ever used it for anything. Not even the Indians."

The three surfers stood for some time in silence, surveying the desolate landscape into which they had come. When Fletcher had seen enough he dumped his gear on the sand and lay down. His back was killing him and he wanted to stretch it out. He began by pulling one knee to his chest and then the other.

"What's with the Doc?" Robbie Jones asked.

Drew Harmon squinted down on him. "Back," he said. "What's with yours, Doc?"

"They don't know," Fletcher said.

Drew Harmon nodded. "Sounds about right. But that don't keep 'em from askin' for their money, does it?"

"Bill's always right on time. It's like death and taxes."

"Where'd you hurt it?"

"Mexico."

Drew nodded. "Fractured three vertebrae in the islands a few years back. Some fucker's board came over the falls on me."

"I hoped you kicked his ass," Robbie Jones said.

"Actually, I wasn't in condition to kick his ass at the time. Ain't seen him since."

"Shit. Some fucker does that to me, he'd better fucking kill me. He doesn't, he's dead meat."

Drew Harmon lifted his shirt to reveal the patterns of stitch marks running around his side and back. "This guy fucked me up even better. I didn't kill him either."

Robbie Jones observed the scars standing out like train tracks in the desert. "That's another story," he said.

Drew Harmon looked down at Fletcher. " 'Another story,' he says. You know what they called the 1916 Harley-Davidson? The silent gray fellow." Harmon nodded toward the sea. "That's what I call these bastards. The silent gray fellows. You see one, you kick his ass for me." He was looking at Robbie Jones.

Robbie Jones looked at the ocean. "So. This it?"

"Is this what?"

"Don't give me that shit."

Harmon rested his hands on his hips. "We'll see," he said.

Robbie Jones was somewhat incredulous. "We'll see," he repeated. "We've been hiking for two days."

"What? You got some place to be?"

It occurred to Fletcher that Robbie Jones looked just a little bit worried for the first time.

Drew turned to Fletcher once more. "He doesn't know what I'm talkin' about, does he?"

"What's that supposed to mean?" Robbie asked.

"Means you're too young. You still think you're gonna live forever. Ask the Doc. He knows. Those silent gray fellows. They're out there. Lying in wait. Under reefs. Hidden in shadow. In the end, they get you. Don't they, Doc?"

Fletcher looked up at the two men standing above him, one hawk-faced and reddened, a viking too long among the waves, the other tanned and shaved bald beneath a gray hood, a tiny golden cross dangling from one ear as if he were the acolyte of some apocryphal order.

"They do indeed," Fletcher said.

When Fletcher had gotten off his back, he found that Drew Harmon had wandered down toward the wet sand where he had embarked on an elaborate series of stretching exercises of his own. Robbie Jones had climbed atop some rocks, the better to observe the break. Fletcher could see his parka and sweats, blue against the gray stone, as if a painter had touched the morning with his brush, then gone away grieving. In time, Fletcher joined him.

Robbie Jones noted his approach but said nothing. Fletcher squatted beside him and looked toward the sea. The fog was still quite heavy, and the waves appeared as gray humps moving against a gray sky, a species of sea life no one had heretofore thought to name. As the tide had begun to rise once more, the waves did not break upon the reef but rolled silently through the fog, only to lose themselves in the deep still waters of the bay.

On the beach below, Drew Harmon could be observed in the performance of a peculiar kind of side stretch. He stood with one hand arced above his head, the other braced upon his hip. As they watched, he moved slowly from side to side, appearing as might some mutant crane about to take flight.

"Guy's nuts. You know that, don't you?"

It was the first time Robbie Jones had spoken directly to Fletcher in some time. Fletcher continued to watch the man below, leaning this way and that, balanced upon one leg.

"For Christ's sake," Robbie Jones said. He was looking at Drew. "This is about the most fucked-up trip I've ever been on. Except for maybe that time we went looking for this island off Mexico. We found a guy with a sea plane said he could get us there. He takes us out and drops us off. He's supposed to pick us up in two days and there's not a wave in sight, just rocks and about a million seagulls all the time shitting on everything. We spent two days holding our boards over our heads to keep the shit off. Son of a bitch never did come back. We finally wound up hitching a ride with some fisherman. That was pretty fucked-up too."

"I can see where it would be," Fletcher told him.

"What does this guy mean, 'we'll see'? Does he know where this place is or doesn't he?"

Fletcher shook his head. "I don't know," he said. "Could be he's still looking for it."

Robbie Jones appeared to give this some thought. "We're a long fucking way from nowhere, you've noticed that?"

"I have."

"There could be half a dozen Heart Attacks out here."

"Or none at all."

"So what's his trip? Why are we even here?"

"Drew Harmon and Heart Attacks. What was Peters gonna do, say no thanks?"

"Yea, but if this jerk-off doesn't know where the place is . . ."

"He seems to know where everything else is."

"Well . . ." Robbie started to say something else but the words appeared to fail him.

Fletcher just shook his head. "He's up to something," he said. "It has to do with these wooden boards, the logs he's kept. You didn't know the guy in the old days. I did. He was always a scam artist, and this is beginning to smell like a scam to me. But I can't figure the angle. I mean, it might have something to do with selling these wooden guns."

"Shit, man. How many people do you think are going to want one of those?"

"About six."

"I'll tell you what I think. I think the guy's lost it. Maybe it was the fucking shark or something. I mean, we got those waves at the river mouth, I thought maybe we were really onto something, but this . . ." He waved toward the colorless beaches where Drew Harmon continued to stretch.

"Well, according to the book, this has got to be the Devil's Hoof. We don't get something wrapping around that point out there, I don't see any reason to go on."

"What if he doesn't see it that way?"

Fletcher gave this some thought. It spoke directly to his own paranoia. "Maybe we go home without him," he said.

"You're shittin' me. You think you could get back out the way we came? That guy knows every trail. Every tide."

"There might be another way. If this is where I think it is."

Robbie Jones just laughed at him. "Dream on dude. You think you can find some trail 'cause you read about it in that stupid book?"

"They got the boulder field right. Harmon himself admitted there were trails."

"The trouble with the trails is, you got to find them."

"Harmon said it was about halfway."

Robbie Jones spit over the edge of the rock he was perched on. "Yea, well, I just hiked it, and I didn't see shit."

"It was foggy and we weren't looking."

Robbie Jones shook his head. "You want to bail on your own, be my guest. You ask me, you'll find those trails same way you got that kid out of the Zodiac."

Fletcher got to his feet. "Have it your way," he said. He started back down the trail that led to the beach. He could hear Robbie Jones say something behind him but the boy's words were lost on the wind.

By late that afternoon, the tide had turned and the waves had begun to break in the bay. As there was no shore break here, no inside bars as there had been at the mouth of the river, there was only the sound of big waves breaking upon deep water and Fletcher and Robbie had soon dubbed the place "Thunder Bay" in honor of this sound, though Drew scoffed at the name and led them in a long paddle across the icy water.

Fletcher brought up the rear, his camera beneath his chin, resting upon the deck of the wooden gun which planed easily across the water, slicing through the small surface chop as if it were the bow of some sleek craft, which in fact it was.

He set up south of the peak as he had done in the Zodiac with the boy. This time, however, he was in calmer waters, still within the lee of this great arm of land which itself provided him with the only line-up he truly required, and soon he was running through film, shooting without difficulty as the surfers began to catch the waves.

The set waves here were big. Fletcher reckoned it at double overhead, but nothing like what he had seen at the mouth of the great river. Though maybe, as the tide fell, the wave would jack more handily across the reef. Or maybe, the swell generated by the storm was not as great as Drew had predicted. Or was not striking at the anticipated angle.

Nor were conditions optimal for shooting, as all was still cast in a murky gray light, but Fletcher was determined to get what he could and so continued to fire away, his fingers blue from paddling, but finding his shots and thinking none were yet equal to what he had seen at the mouth of the river.

He was resting for a moment, as there were no riders up, looking back in the direction of the beach, when something on the cliff ledge caught his eye. First a shard of reflected light. And then a small, bent figure moving among the coastal scrub. He lifted the camera and pointed it toward the cliff. What he saw there was a man with a gun. The man was dressed in denim and plaid, waist deep in a thicket of grass and scrub. He was sighting through what appeared to be a scope of some power and he appeared focused on the sea below, leading something with his rifle.

Instinctively Fletcher snapped the picture, then looked back into the line-up in an effort to see what the man was pointing at. He was in time to see Robbie Jones drop cleanly down the face of a polished gray wall. He watched as the wave steepened and began to pitch. He saw Robbie pull up into a barrel, then watched as the wave collapsed on him. When he looked back at the cliff, he found the man had turned. The gun was still raised, but now pointed directly at Fletcher.

Fletcher could feel a sudden rush of blood, a quickening of the heart. He supposed the thing to do was to dive, get under the board. Inexplicably he remained upright, his eye to the camera, so that for a moment the two men simply watched each other through the two lenses. At which point, the man on the cliff lowered the rifle and disappeared into the brush. He did this quickly, in one fluid motion, so that one second he was there and the next he was gone and Fletcher was very much alone, rocking gently upon a frigid ground swell, his eye glued to an empty cliff in the gray light.

He continued to sit there. He found Drew Harmon on a wave and took another series of shots in the shitty light. Robbie rode another wave as well. Between waves, Fletcher scanned the cliffs. The man did not return. As soon as he was able to catch Harmon looking in his direction, however, he waved his arm, then pointed to the beach, a signal he was ready to go in.

Harmon raised his own hands, palms up, as if to ask why. Fletcher began to paddle. He assumed the others would follow. He started with a measured stroke, but once under way, a kind of delayed panic set in and he pulled as hard as he was able for the distant line of beach, certain now that he was about to be shot. He still could not understand the way he had sat there on his board, staring into the barrel of a gun. One could not call it bravery. It was more a paralysis born of surprise, he supposed, for it occurred to him, scratching for the shoreline, that no one had ever pointed a gun at him before. Nor, he decided, was it an experience he cared to repeat.

Once on the beach, he collected their gear, then dragged it closer to the foot of the cliffs, so as to be hidden from the view of anyone skirting the ledges. When he had done that, he pulled on his sweats and set about gathering wood. He had a small fire started by the time he saw the others walking along the beach from the north.

Drew began talking as soon as Fletcher was within earshot, shouting to him across the beach. "What's the story, Doc? You get bumped out there, or what?"

Fletcher waited until the surfers had gotten closer, for he had no desire to shout. When they had reached the fire, he told them about what he had seen on the cliff.

Robbie Jones looked there now, as if he fully expected to see something. "You're telling me this fucker was leading me with a gun?"

"That's what I'm telling you."

Drew Harmon put his board on the sand and shook his head in disgust. "Some asshole from the Heads. Probably hunting birds."

"The guy was an Indian."

"So he was an Indian asshole hunting birds."

"How about an Indian from upriver? Some kin to the boy who drowned?"

"How would they know where to look?"

"You left your wife there. She knew, I take it."

"I sent her into town."

"I don't know," Robbie said. "I don't much like the idea of some jerk-off pointing a gun at me. I don't care what the motherfucker is hunting."

"There's worse things in the water. Christ, I thought that was what the Doc here was pissing himself over. Turns out it was a drunken red man with a bird gun."

"This wasn't a bird gun," Fletcher told him.

"You know anything about guns?"

"No. But this thing had a big scope on it, I know that much, and I know the guy was pointing it at us."

"So why didn't he shoot?"

"I don't know."

Harmon laughed at him. He had peeled his wet suit down around his waist. Now he picked up a few sticks of firewood and tossed them into the flames, then held his hands out to warm them. Robbie Jones picked up a few sticks as well. The fire grew.

"Forget it," Drew told them. "It's nothing. Anyway, I'd say we're hitting it just about right. Wait till you see what's waiting around the point."

Fletcher was a moment in assimilating this information. He looked at Robbie Jones. The young man was staring at Harmon in a way that was not altogether friendly.

"Really," Fletcher said finally. "Around the point. I thought you said, we got to the sand at the end of the rock field, we were there."

"Shit," Drew said. "Any asshole can hike down from the Heads and this is where they're going to wind up."

Fletcher looked at the empty beaches, the steep cliffs. It was difficult to imagine a crowd.

"This is the obvious spot," Harmon went on. "But you've got to get around the point. There's really a series of reefs up here. This is the first reef, where we were today. There are two others, spaced out to the north. Heart Attacks is the last reef."

"How far?" Robbie asked him.

"Well, shit," Harmon told him. "You can be in Oregon from here in a day. How's that for a joke? California's big mysto spot. Only it's not in California. It's in Oregon."

"Is that what you're telling us now, it's in Oregon?"

"I'm telling you there are three reefs. Heart Attacks is the last one. We get one more minus tide in the morning, we can start out. It's a bitch getting there. It's not that far, but it's a bitch. There's no beach to speak of. You have to go in off the rocks."

Fletcher looked toward the great arm of the Devil's Hoof. At its westernmost tip, where the rocks met the sea, the sky had already begun to darken. In his mind's eye he held once more the map of the coast, the long unbroken run toward the Oregon border which lay to the north, the direction Drew intended to take. He could not believe there was anything there. The configuration of land spoke against it. "Maybe it's time we went back," he said. "Maybe what's around the bend is for another trip."

"What are you trying to tell me, Doc?"

"I'm trying to tell you I didn't come up here to get shot. Travis said there was going to be trouble. I would say that guy on the cliff was trouble, and I would say it's time we got off their land."

"I'll tell you what you came up here to get," Harmon told him. "You came up here to get pictures."

"These pictures must mean a lot to you," Fletcher said. "You're willing to risk getting everyone shot to get them." He might have mentioned his willingness to risk the life of a boy in a Zodiac in huge surf as well, but he didn't. The light in the big man's eyes dissuaded him.

"What I want with pictures is my business," Harmon told him. "Peters told me he had a whole shit load of guys could do the job. I asked for you. We're in the window, man. You know how long we could wait for that again?"

Fletcher was saved from further conversation by Robbie Jones. "You said you could get us there," Robbie said. "As far as I'm concerned, you've been jackin' us off since we got here. How do we know we get around that point, there's not gonna be another point, and then another? I'll tell you something else. I'm gettin' a little sick of Pop-Tarts and soybeans. And I'm getting a little sick of your bullshit too."

Drew Harmon shifted his attention to Robbie Jones. He picked up one more chunk of driftwood. He stood for a moment, as if he might do something with it other than commend it to the flames. In the end, this is just what he did, but he had gotten Robbie Jones's attention. "Let me ask you something, dickhead," Harmon said. "Where were you when I was paddlin' out at Himalayas? 'Cause I sure as fuck didn't see your scrawny ass out there."

Robbie looked into the fire.

"How about Avalanche?" Harmon asked. "What's that, man? I can't hear you. Log Cabins, maybe?"

For a moment the two men just stared at one another. "You got two choices," Harmon told him. "You can stand up and be counted, or you can fade into the crowd. Like your buddy, Sonny what's his name, 'cause I already forgot and so will everyone else. As for you, Doc," Harmon turned his gaze on Fletcher once more, "you got no choices. I brought you up here to take pictures, and you're sure as fuck going to take them. And I don't mean this penny-ante shit you took out there today. You ain't leavin' until you've gotten us, on these boards, in waves that are going to blow some minds. You had a shot at the river mouth and you fucked it up. Now I'm gonna get you into some more, and you're gonna get it done. You understand what I'm telling you?"

Fletcher glanced at Robbie Jones. The boy continued to stare at Drew Harmon. The trouble now was that a challenge had been issued, and R.J. was not one to back down from a challenge. Harmon had the kid's number and Fletcher supposed that in the end, the two would chase each other round the next point and keep right on going. You followed the whole thing long enough, one might even get northern lights. Certainly one would have cold and deprivation. If Fletcher was right about the man on the cliff, one might well expect payback and early death as part of the bargain, though it was not his intention to continue this insanity long enough to find out, and he looked at Drew Harmon, for the man was still waiting on an answer. "I understand perfectly," Fletcher said.

"That's good," Harmon told him. "I'd hate to see our friendship come to a bad end."

They argued one more time that night, over the placement of their camp. Drew wanted to move it out, away from the cliffs that he said were dangerous. Fletcher did not want to camp in so exposed an area. In the end they compromised, moving north, then building their fire among a clump of large rocks that Fletcher felt might minimize their exposure.

When they had finished with what passed for dinner, Drew took up his log book and pen. Fletcher watched from the sleeping bag he'd placed in the slight overhang of one of the rocks. The big man was still bare-chested, sweating before the fire in spite of the cold, his hair spread in a great blond mane upon his shoulders, his expression impassive. He worked this way for some time and the camp was silent, save for the scratching of Drew's pen and the crackling of the flames, together with the incessant excretions of the sea.

In time, however, Drew put down his book. He looked first at Robbie Jones, then at Fletcher. "There was a tribe of Indians lived out here once," he told them. "Where we are, right now. I can't tell you their name, nor can anyone else, as it was a name known only to themselves. At one time, the tribe was quite large. They made their living off the Smith River just north of here. But as the tribes around them caved into the white men, these Indians continued to fight until there were only five of them left. Two men, two women, and a child. This much is known, for one of the women was captured by a group of hunters. The hunters attempted to barter for her release but were themselves killed, with the exception of one man. This was the story he told, that there were five and no more. For he had seen them come down on the camp, one woman with a papoose and two men, all with their skin blackened and their hair singed down to the scalp."

Drew stared into the fire as he spoke. "They lived here, on these beaches," he said. "They walked from stone to stone so as not to leave footprints that might be followed. They left nothing behind them, no fire rings, not a broken twig or a charred bone. Can you imagine that?" He looked up then, as if in expectation of some answer. Receiving none, he went on. "They lived among the rocks for twenty years, and they were never caught, and they never surrendered, and they were never found."

"What happened to them then?" Robbie wanted to know.

Drew sighed. "That should be obvious," he said. "When they'd had enough, they died. But since they were never found, they must have done it themselves. I think one must have disposed of the others, cremated them perhaps, as that was the custom, then took the ashes and swam out. The sea took him and he was the last of his race. Sometimes I think maybe that's what's wrong with this place. It was them. They put something on it."

Drew poked at the fire with a stick.

The others watched him in silence for some time.

"They should've all done that," Robbie said, as if he had been giving the matter some thought.

"Done what?" Drew asked him.

"Fought to the last man, the last woman, the last child."

"That's what you would have done."

"No quarter. No mercy."

"No man can say what he would do in those circumstances," Drew said. "Who can say what the world would even look like to such people?"

He raised his eyes to look at them, for till now he had been staring into the flames. They found his face lit from the underside, hollowed out by shadow, as if what they saw there was not flesh and bone but that which lay beneath flesh and bone, and it occurred to Fletcher that he knew this man for the first time. He's like me, Fletcher thought, a middle-aged man, afraid of what was to come. And yet, even as he thought this, he was aware of a chill running along his spine, for there was another thing there as well, a coiled thing that brooded, barely contained, a thing of which to be afraid.

When no one had proposed an answer to his question, Drew Harmon took up his book and began to write in it once more. Robbie Jones withdrew into his sleeping bag, where he lay with his back to the fire. Fletcher remained where he was, in the shadow of the black rock already dripping in the fog that had rolled in to blanket the night. He thought of the boulder field which lay behind them and the dreary northern reaches which lay ahead. He thought of this place now in light of Drew's story. One could almost see them there, he thought, that party of five, hovering and crouching in their nearly disembodied life among this wasteland of wind and stone. What ghosts must have stalked them. What memories. Twenty years and not a footprint in the sand and nothing to mark their passing, save a story told by the likes of Drew Harmon, who, like all men, could only tell stories that, in truth, were about themselves. This was a story about the man Fletcher had glimpsed above the fire, and of the coiled thing poised to strike. It told, he concluded, of how the one would destroy the other, and if he had any brains left he would take steps to avoid being its witness, for it was also his belief that when the time came, bystanders would prove expendable. As a consequence, he chose to abstain from his pills. On this night, pain would be his ally. When the others slept, he would make his move. What happened after that was anybody's guess.

2 8

Travis McCade was afforded his first glimpse of an attainable landfall along that ragged collection of rock and beach that formed what he liked to think of as the sole of the great boot, well north of the point, miles from the sandy beaches upon which he had expected to find the surfers.

Things had gone badly from the start. His craft, laboring beneath its absurd load, had behaved more sluggishly than he had anticipated. Groundswells pushing at him from behind were apt to wash over the rear deck, at times sinking it altogether. For a while, he'd managed to compensate for this inconvenience through a careful regulation of his stroke, one which allowed him to actually ride each swell for a short distance before it passed him by.

No sooner had he arrived at this strategy, however, than a second, even more serious obstacle had presented itself. The cliffs, he discovered, were not getting any closer. Rather, they were sliding to his right. In fact, he was caught upon some great movement in the water around him. Had he been at the river's mouth, he would have taken it for an outgoing tide. In the bay, in the lee of the hoof, answers had failed him, and there was nothing for it but to stroke and curse, as the mysterious current pulled him from his path of sunlight and into the fog.

By this point, he had been able to hear the sound of breaking waves, leading him to the conclusion that should he continue as he was, he would most likely be sucked directly into the impact zone of the huge waves wrapping around the point. With this in mind, he'd been forced to give up the beaches of Big Sandy altogether, to dump the gear he'd lashed to the deck, and to paddle for the open ocean in the hopes that he might get around the rocky toe of the boot, then make land somewhere along the heel.

It was the plan that had gotten him here, stroking now for all he was worth toward some minuscule, rockbound cove, a mere sliver of sand before whose shimmering surface the fog passed in tattered translucent rages, carried upon a cold north wind as might the vestments of some holy gown torn violently asunder.

He paddled on, his kayak pushed hard against a sudden outcropping of stone, and then another, but him keeping his seat, feeling a wave beneath him and renewing his efforts, in hopes of catching it, which, in fact, proved to be his final act in this theater of ignominy. For the wave was steeper and more hollow than he had imagined, and once in its grip, he found himself unable to hold any kind of line. He dug hard with the end of one paddle, but to no avail. The rear of the kayak swung around toward the beach leaving him sideways, to be sucked up the face then pitched from his boat, dumped hard on a rocky patch of wet sand. The kayak landed on top of him.

For a moment, he was completely stunned and could do nothing more than push away his craft, then lay gasping for air as the white water swirled around him. It was only when he tried to stand, however, that the enormity of this calamity was revealed.

The pain hit him like a brick. He could not say where it had been hiding till now. His knees buckled. The wet sand rushed to meet him once more. This time he stayed put, racked by nausea, unable to say at once exactly where it hurt, for the pain seemed to issue from all quarters with dazzling intensity. In time, however, he looked to his leg.

What he saw there was enough to bring back the sickness—a bulge the size of a baseball straining the black skin of his wet suit, just above his right ankle. The sight panicked him. Surely, he thought, he would die here, and for some time he lay as he had fallen, on the rocky beach, like a thing already dead. With additional time, however, he began trying to think it through, to fight through the pain, to take some stock of his situation.

The kayak was at his side, still attached to his leg by way of his leash, and he was able to take inventory of the things he had saved. Stuffed into the small storage compartment was a day pack containing his parka, his running shoes and sweats, a folding knife, and one small bottle of water. He took some consolation in these things. The dry clothes would serve him now, better than any gun, better even than food. If he could get himself dry and off the beach, perhaps, he thought someone would come, perhaps he would live after all.

An hour later and Travis had gotten himself among the rocks just above the cove. He had managed, with the aid of his knife, to get out of the wet suit and into his sweats, and it seemed to him now there were two things he might do. He could stay where he was, or he could try for the bluffs. In either case, his only real hope was that someone would come looking—when his father had been back long enough, when Travis had failed to show.

In the end, he decided on the bluffs. He had come some distance already and if he could make it to the top, he would certainly be easier to find. Also, it was a thing to do, for he had concluded that labor might serve to take his mind from the pain, as if in pitting himself against the rocks, it was the pain itself against which he fought.

He paused before starting out, thinking once more about why he had come, about his desire to find the girl. He thought too, of the figure he had hoped to cut—the errant protector borne upon the sea. There was, of course, little he could do about any of this just now, save stare into the splintered cliffs before him, lost for some time in simple wonder at how easily a man might die in pursuit of such folly.

The tide rose quickly with the darkening of the day. And though he had managed to get into his dry clothes, Travis soon found he was getting wet again. He had picked a shelf of rock not more than twenty feet above the beach as his first goal, but the going was tougher than he had imagined, moving like a crab across the rocks, dragging his broken leg behind him. It was discouraging work as well, for he saw that there was no way he would ever reach the bluffs. His condition was deteriorating. The shelf seemed to recede even as he reached for it, and he was seized once more by the belief that he would never see the morning, that this is where it would end, in this rookery for birds, lost on a fool's errand. It was with this in mind that he at last gained the shelf and came upon the body.

It took some moments for him to recognize it as such. At first glance, in the failing light, one might have taken the thing for a bundle of rags. Unhappily, the more one looked, the more one saw, and as Travis moved across the rocks, the thing lay revealed to him for what it was. The head was split and rested at an impossible angle to the neck, balanced upon the very edge of the stone shelf. One eye had been sprung from its socket to lay upon a sagging cheek, for there were no bones left to support it. The head's contents had been spilled upon the stone. A gaudy, obscene paint, dark and shining in the half light.

Travis held to the rock, panting for air. The shelf where the body had landed was narrow, barely wide enough to accommodate what had fallen there, though beyond the body it appeared to widen out, ending in a cul de sac of stone. Travis had little choice but to go on. The climb had cost him dearly and there was really no question of inching his way back down. As a consequence, he was a long time at his perch, seeking handholds not fouled with blood, not wanting the dead body to touch his own, and yet finally, in spite of his contortions, pulling himself past it in such a way that his face came within inches of the dead man's, and at just that point, his foot slipped beneath him so that it was the body he grabbed for support.

His hand seized upon a belt, his forearm pushed against broken ribs. An audible groan escaped. The body moved beneath him. The head twisted, the mouth sprung impossibly wide as if in death it might swallow the night. He saw at the same time a shank of white hair which, till this moment, had been pinned somehow beneath the body, saw it unfurl in the gray light, and in that moment knew it to be the Tolowan he had seen as a living man in the Moke's home, at the bank of the river.

He moved quickly after that, pulling himself on his stomach across the shelf that did indeed grow wider before it ended. He moved as far as he could from the desecration he had crawled over until at last he found for himself a fissure of rock and squeezed himself into it, as if he too were something broken, then watched as the night closed in around him.

At some point, out of sheer exhaustion, no doubt, he managed a little sleep. He woke parched and in pain. He saw that the fog had lifted, or that he had crawled beyond it, for the sky was streaked with great billowing clouds. These were shown to him by a secretive, skulking moon that prowled in their midst, and his thoughts turned once more to his bedfellow upon the rock, wondering at how this man had come to be here, and at what this portent might mean.

29

It was late in the day when the Indians reached a spot where it was clear they intended to make camp. The big man went off once more with his rifle, returning to announce that the surfers had made camp on the beach. "Second time today," he said. "'Cept the light was better before."

Earlier that afternoon the big man had left and come back to report seeing the men in the water.

"Could've had 'em right there," he'd said.

"Why didn't you?" the boy had asked him.

"One of them saw me."

"So what?"

"You've no mind for sport, Cousin."

The men repeated a similar argument now. The boy, Bean Dip, was all for going after the men this night. The Hupa favored playing them a little, now that they had them. William Longtree had sided with the boy. "I say take them now," he said.

The Hupa looked at his rifle laid crosswise upon his knees, patting the stock with his hand. "Just remember who's mine," he said.

Kendra thought they would go then, that it had begun. Instead they built a fire and began to drink, and it occurred to her that perhaps this was what came first. In any event, she thought, her time had come. In the morning someone would die, possibly sooner.

Eventually, after some time spent watching them about their fire, and in a voice clearer than any they had yet heard from her, she asked them if she might go some ways off to relieve herself.

"You want to piss, do it right there."

Kendra was silent.

"Maybe she has to take a shit."

"She can take a shit right there too."

The conversation was between the boy and the Tolowan, but at last, the big man, who had been watching, stood up and walked over to where she sat. He shoved her on to her back and when her feet flew up into the air, he caught one of her ankles and pulled off the boot and threw it into the fire. He dropped that foot and picked up the other and did the same with it and when he had finished with the boots, he took a knife from his pocket, opened it with a flick of the wrist and cut her on the heel.

"She won't go far on that," he said. And he let her go.

She limped some ways from the camp, for she had seen a stand of coastal scrub and she passed behind it. One of the men called something after her and the others laughed. She could not make out what was said, but set about right away with what she had intended. For she knew that they would not give her long, and she meant to be found in a certain way.

She cleared a place in the dirt. She drew a circle with a stone, and nine was the number of wheel things she slew in that barren place, and nine was the number of the circle, set with sticks instead of candles because, like the book said, it was the thought that counted and at times one need improvise. She drew pentagrams in the dirt before each stick. She chose a flat rock for a makeshift altar. She tore the pocket from the shirt she wore and bound it around some dried grass and tied it with string as a kind of poppet. She took the driver's license from the waistband of her trousers and tore off the photograph of William Longtree, aged thirty-five, which she smeared with blood in a red pentagram and placed beside the poppet. When these things were done, she removed her clothes and sat naked on the ground, in the skull-and-crossbones position, and she waited for them to come.

Some time went by before she heard their voices and felt the fall of their footsteps. She lit the sticks with the matches she had pirated from the camper. For, as luck would have it, the sun had begun to decline and the moon to rise and already she had seen that it was a waning moon—coming empty of souls after some communion with the sun and best suited for the spell she intended to cast, and she set the poppet on fire, but just apart from the photograph, as she wanted to be sure they found it and when she was done, she commenced to speak. She said whatever came into her head. She spoke in bits and pieces. The pieces were from many places. Some came from Pam's coven where she'd been made witness to aging flower children as they'd tried to erect a cone of power she'd never been able to see as anything more than wishful thinking. Some came from the reading she'd done as her father's pupil, and some from that she'd done on her own. And all the while, as she said these things—for, in fact, one had to say something—other words ran unspoken beneath the cover of her impromptu incantations, a steady unbroken appeal to that thing she had picked up at some long-ago seance. For, if the truth were to be known—and why shouldn't it, here at the end of things—it was what was most real in her life and always had been. There had been no cones of power for her. No blessed enchantments. No ecstasies of the goddess. For her in this life, there were really only two things that ever seemed to count, the dead father and the shadow she had breathed in as a child, and from which, for most of her life, she had recoiled in dread. But now it was the thing to which she appealed, with whatever words she could muster. Beneath this dark moon. And she held the burning poppet to her breast and said, "Blessed be thou creature made by art, by art made, by art changed. Thou art not cloth and grass, but flesh and blood. I name thee William Longtree, and thou art between the worlds, in all worlds so mote it be . . ."

And that was how they found her—naked, before the pentagrams with the burning poppet which had already scorched the skin between her breasts, with her hair all wild and dark and her pale skin streaked with dirt and blood and ash. And they stopped, all three, cold in their tracks, just as she threw the poppet away from her, and one of them swore and stamped on it to put out the fire, and the big man came forward and snatched her by the arm, jerking her to her feet, then finding the blood-smeared photograph and picking that up as well and looking at it.

"Look here, Longtree," the man said. "It's you she cursed."

"Must be that three-inch dick," the boy said.

Kendra looked the big man squarely in the eye. For it seemed to her as if some moment of reckoning had arrived. "It's all of you," she said. "I have cut your lifelines . . ." but was unable to say more because the man slapped her and she went limp in his hand.

It was only for a moment, and then she righted herself with great effort and spoke to him once more. "By air and earth. By water and fire so be you bound as I desire, by three and nine your power I bind . . ."

At which point, the man slapped her once more and dragged her back toward the firelight by one arm, where the man whose image she had smeared with blood was in favor of killing her right then.

The other two laughed at him, but when they brought her near, he backed away, closer to the edge of the cliff, where he began to shout and pace, his thin arms swinging at his sides, his white hair held out before the moon. He went right up to the edge, and she saw him look over it, as if looking for a good place to drop her, and was in just this act when a chunk of ground gave way beneath his feet. He vanished without a sound and the big man let go her arm as if he had been burned.

30

When the Indian dropped her, Kendra ran. She went in the direction of her fire though with no particular sense of purpose. It took the men about two minutes to find her. The boy was all for killing her on the spot and had, in fact, drawn a handgun she had not seen till that moment, when the big man backhanded him. The man had hands like ham butts and the blow broke the boy's nose.

He sat on the dirt, holding his face with his hand. He appeared to be crying. The big man took the gun and stuffed it into his own jeans.

"She's a witch," the boy said. He was still wearing his rifle. It was attached to a strap slung over his chest, and when he hit the ground, she saw the barrel bang him in the back of the head. "She'll kill us all," he said.

The big man kicked him in the chest.

The boy rolled across the ashes of the fire, got to all fours, and, without looking back, staggered off into the night in the general direction of the campground from which they had come, though the place was a day's hike away and the night was young.

The big man watched as the boy disappeared. He looked at Kendra. "Useless little fuck," he said.

Kendra looked up at the man, holding his eye, though he was hard to see in the poor light.

"Is that right?" he asked her. "Are you a witch?"

Kendra did not answer right away. Her head seemed to be throbbing in time to her foot and leg. Thinking was made difficult. Fortunately the man went on without her. "Like to dance in the woods maybe. Eat mushrooms. I bet you got a cat named Morning Glory."

His mode of speech just now surprised her. She had thought him frightened. Maybe she had been wrong. But then he had left her alone on the preceding night, when the others had not.

"We caught some witches out in the woods one night, me and a couple of my cousins. Only these were just a bunch of middle-aged *wagays* running around barefoot. Maybe you'd like to hear what we did with them."

She was trying once more to get her head to work. The only thing that came to mind was what Travis had told her about making them think your magic was stronger than theirs. But it seemed to her as if her magic had just about run its course. At which point, she thought of something else Travis had said. It was a name.

The man had drawn his knife and was standing above her.

She needed the name.

The man touched the blade with his thumb. "You want to hear about the barbeque?" he asked.

"You've got one chance," she told him. "You have one chance to live. You have to leave. Now. You do that, I can take away the curse."

He laughed at her.

"You think it's a joke?" she asked him.

He looked at her for a moment. "I think you've got some guts. I'll give you that. I think you're lucky too."

"What if it's more than that?"

He shrugged. "I guess I'll take my chances. You think I'm really gonna run away like that little shit?" He gestured into the night with a nod of his head.

"You could find out," she said.

He just looked at her now.

"You're Hupa."

"What of it?"

"There's an old woman. A Hupa. Rose Hudson. She lives along a little river. Not far from here."

It seemed to her that his expression changed just a bit at the mention of this name. She was going on intuition now. It was strictly a high-wire act. She had no idea if Ruth Hudson was a Hupa or not, but she seemed to have guessed correctly on that one. If he knew the old woman was dead, she would be finished.

"She can see it," she said. "She can see what I've put on you. She can tell you what it is."

The man looked at her for some time. "I've heard of Rose Hudson . . ."

"Then you know what I'm saying is true."

"I thought she lived in town."

"She lives on the Temple. It's not six miles from here."

The man looked into the night.

She was nearly giddy with pain, with lack of food, with what she was about.

The man squatted suddenly on his haunches, bringing his face close to hers, looking her in the eye. "I don't know the coast," he said. "But I know the valley, further up. I know there's a couple of meth labs up there."

"I've heard that. Rose lives just up from the beach. It's the first house in the valley. Go by yourself, if you want to."

He smiled at her. He was younger than she had thought. She noticed this just now. He was her age. At last, he looked away from her. He hissed then, and shook his head. Finally, he stood once more and walked away. She watched him. She could feel the sweat on the nape of her neck, along her rib cage, in spite of the cold.

When he returned, she saw that he carried the packs from their first camp. He set these by the remains of Kendra's fire from which a few embers still glowed and from which some thin yellow flame would now and then lift itself to lick at the night. The man set about stoking coals, adding wood. In time, a second fire burned above the ashes of the first. Kendra could feel him watching her through the flames. At length, he got up and walked over to where she lay, propped on her elbows. He carried one of the packs. He set it down next to her foot and squatted before her.

She was still quite naked, covered in dust and bruises. For all she knew, she was about to die. It seemed the logical next step. The man reached into the pack and came out with a bottle of water. He took her ankle in his hand and he began to wash the cut. He held the cut open with one hand, pouring water into it from the bottle. He did this for some time. He squeezed it as well, making it bleed. When he had done this for a while, he rested her ankle on his knee and took a lime from the pack. He took a knife from his pocket and he cut the lime in half. He picked up her ankle once more. Again he used his fingers to spread the wound, this time washing it with the juice of the lime.

Kendra made no sound, although her leg jerked as the juice hit the cut. The man's hand was steady as a vice. She watched him as he went about his work. His eyes were as steady as his hand, intent on what he was about.

When he had finished with the lime, he took a small, wrapped object from the pack. He pushed the pack under her leg, using it to hold her heel off the ground. He rose and walked to the fire, picking up a stick as he went, then holding that to the flame until he had ignited one end of it, at which point he came back to where she lay, carrying the burning stick as one might a torch.

He squatted before her as he had done before, and she could see that the object he'd taken from the pack was a bar of wax. He returned her leg to his knee, turning it to an uncomfortable angle.

"Hold it there," he said.

Kendra did as she was told.

He held the wax to the flaming stick. As the wax began to melt, he allowed it to dribble into the cut. It was all she could do to hold the leg in place and yet it seemed to her there was something at stake in being able to do so. When he was finished, she felt herself bathed in sweat and she saw that the wound was sealed in wax.

When the man had finished, he put his things into his pack and returned to the fire where he took something from one of the other packs which had been left there. She saw that it was a blanket. He tossed this to her and she covered herself with it. He watched as she did this, then came and squatted before her once more. He looked at her heel, as if to make sure of his work, and he looked into her face.

"I can't tell," he said, at length. "I can't tell if you're lucky, or if you have put something on me."

Kendra only looked at him.

The man looked away. He looked toward the cliff from which William Longtree had fallen. "We'll go in the morning," he said. "We'll see Rose Hudson. We'll see if you've done what you say. She will know what to do if you have. I will know what to do if you haven't." He stood then, nodding toward the cliff. "There will still be time for them," he said. "They're a long way from home."

When he had said these things he went back to the fire. Kendra watched him. She watched as he took a bottle from his pack and sat with it before the flames. He did not look at her again but she could remember his face. She had studied it closely for the first time as he'd worked on her wound. Though he was a heavily built man, his features were drawn in fine straight lines. He was well-muscled, and the thought occurred to her that, in some other place and time, some other universe, perhaps, she might have found him handsome. Though how this could be, in light of what had transpired, she could not say.

Man looked to the stars, she thought, dreaming of worlds he might one day bridge. And yet each man was a world unto himself, and no two worlds, though bound by different stars, were any more lost, one to the other, than she and this man before her. And there was nothing in heaven or on earth which could alter this, or make it other than what it was.

31

Travis spent the night on the rocks and that was where the surfers found him, wedged into a crevice, his day pack set before him to shield him from the wind. He heard them long before he saw them, and though he could not rightly identify them as the men he'd come to find, he could not imagine who else it would be, in such a place, on such a morning. And so he had gone with his hunch and called out, hoping that it would indeed be the surfers and not the compadres of the man who had fallen.

But they called back to him, and he to them, and in time, he saw them coming, climbing through the fog, small, bent figures moving crab-wise along veins of stone, their surfboards sheathed in nylon bags slung from their shoulders like the shields of some ancient race. He was not sure he could move from his crevice, so long and cold had the night been. He felt locked in place, as if the darkness had turned his bones to stone in its passing.

He watched as Drew Harmon led the way, climbing quickly up

through the rocks. He watched as the man came face-to-face with the body, even more ghastly in the morning light. Or so Travis supposed, for he had yet to look at it closely himself. Drew Harmon scarcely batted an eye. Nor did he contort himself in any fashion so as to get past the obstacle without touching it as Travis had done. Drew simply put out one hand, grabbed the body by the belt which circled its waist and, in one powerful motion, hurled it from the cliff.

Even in his groggy state, Travis found himself shocked by the act, so defiant did it seem. As if the body were no more than a bundle of rags. As if there were no law, neither God's or man's, that would dictate such an item be viewed in some other light, or handled in a different fashion.

The body so disposed of, the big man stood upon the ledge. He removed his pack and board bag, bracing them among the rocks, then walked to where Travis lay. A second surfer followed him.

"Friend of yours?" Drew asked. He nodded toward the fog into which the broken body had fallen, a strange grin on his face.

Travis deemed it the kind of greeting one might expect from Drew Harmon. But he knew that he was the bearer of bad news and thought it best to come directly to the point, and he told them why he had come. He told him about the men from upriver. He told him about the fire, and he told him that he'd hoped to see Kendra with him.

The smile passed from Harmon's face as Travis spoke. When he stopped, the man looked down on him with an expression Travis found impossible to read. "This fire," Drew asked at length. "They burned the shaping room? They burned my wood?"

Travis was a moment in responding, for he had expected the man to ask about his wife. "Most of it," Travis said. "The fire department saved some."

Drew squatted beside him then, his back against the cliff. He looked out upon the fog, in the direction of the sea. The second surfer continued to stand upon the ledge, some ways back. He wore a hooded sweatshirt and Travis could not tell if it was the photographer or the man who had hit him with a rock.

"I was hoping," Travis said once more, "that your wife would be with you." Perhaps, he thought, the man had not heard him. But Drew only looked at him, as if this were a thing he could not quite comprehend.

"What?" he asked.

"Your wife, I thought maybe she had come with you."

"I sent her to town."

Travis told him that her truck was still at the landing. He told him about what he'd found in the woods, the clippings dropped along the deer path. He had the man's attention now and as he said these things, it seemed to him as if something more than the smile drained from the big man's face. What he witnessed there now was the loss of something essential.

"Did you look in town?" Drew asked him. "Did you call Pam?"

"No."

"Then she could be there."

Travis said nothing.

"And you think this was one of them?" Drew asked, "one of these men from upriver?" He got to his feet, nodding at the blood-spattered rocks as if what had been split there was the man himself.

"He was one of them," Travis said.

The muscles tightened along Drew's jaw and he looked toward the upper reaches of the cliff, as if he meant to start climbing at once, leaving everything behind, Travis included. It was then that the other man spoke. He had moved closer and dropped to one knee for a better look at Travis's leg. He'd pushed back his hood, revealing a naked skull, and Travis saw it was indeed the kid who had nearly killed him with a rock.

"You seen this?" the kid asked.

Drew turned from the cliff. He squatted on his haunches, reaching out to touch the leg. He pushed down on the sock, then twisted the foot slightly for a better look.

Travis turned his head to vomit. It was not much more than a thin trail of greenish bile.

Drew Harmon stood up. When he spoke, it was to the other surfer. "Can you get up this cliff with both packs and both board bags?"

The kid just looked at him. "Why?" he asked.

"Because somebody's gonna have to carry him," Drew said.

The kid shook his head, as if the entire proceeding was in some way beneath him, but he set about loading himself down with equipment. He did this perched upon the narrow ledge as if it were nothing more than a sidewalk set above a city street.

"Okay," Drew said. He was looking at Travis now. "We're going piggyback. Least till we get on top. I'm not sure what we'll do with you after that."

"I might be able to walk, you could find me something to use as crutches."

Drew Harmon just laughed at him. "You looked at your leg lately?" he asked.

Travis could not say that he had, nor was he of a mind to just now.

"You're dead weight, all the motherfucking way," Harmon told him. "Only thing that's gonna slow us down is if we run into the assholes burned my place. We find them, I'm gonna stop long enough to rip their lungs out."

It was at about this point, as they were preparing to start out, that Travis noted there were only two surfers here, that clearly no one else was going to emerge from the fog.

When he asked about this, both men turned to look at him.

"He's gone," the kid said at length.

"What do you mean, gone?" Travis asked.

"Bailed," the bald surfer said. Travis saw that he was wearing an earring, a delicate golden cross.

"That what you were doing, trying to find him?"

"Fuck, no," Drew said. "We were trying to make that outside reef break north of the point before the tide came up."

"You have any idea of where he went?" In part, he was curious. In part, he was stalling for time, bracing himself for what was to come.

"I know right where he ran to," Drew Harmon said. But he seemed to take none of the pleasure in this knowledge that Travis would have anticipated. His eyes, in fact, seemed weary beyond measure. "He's gone back to that old logging road runs along the Temple."

"Christ. Why?"

Harmon shook his head, as if the whole thing saddened him in some profound way. " 'Cause he read this book and he thinks it will get him back to the Heads."

"It might have once."

"Uh huh. What the poor dumb shit doesn't know is that the trails from the Heads run out along the Hoof now. The ones he's looking for got washed away in the winter of '83. That old logging road just runs up the Temple River, clear to Oregon, as far as I know."

The bald surfer laughed. "I told him," he said. "That guy's one sorry fuck-up."

"Yeah, well, he didn't used to be."

"He'll get himself killed up there," Travis told them. It was the last he would say for some time. He had begun to shake and he felt himself bathed in a cold sweat.

Drew Harmon studied him for a moment, then shook his head. "He doesn't starve first," he said.

3 2

The Tolowa cabins of Neah Heads were perched on a hillside. The sea one saw from their secondhand, single-paned windows was what lay north of the Devil's Hoof, and there were numerous trails which led down to these northern beaches. If one wanted to visit the Hoof itself, however, there was really only one trail. It was long and winding. It began in the shade of redwoods but came, in time, to the grasslands which capped the Hoof. As the trail neared its end, there were three paths to the beaches below. Two of these led to Big Sandy and were relatively tame descents. The third ended at the cliffs from which the Tolowan had fallen, and if one wanted to get to the rocky coves below, one was faced with an arduous task, for the cliffs were treacherous and steep and had, over the years, claimed the life of more than one unfortunate.

Kendra and her captors had, of course, come to this place. But when the light broke above the mountains, she and the Hupa set off for the first of the spurs, retracing the steps they had taken on the previous day, for Kendra had named this as the quickest path to the beach and therefore the most direct route to the home of Rose Hudson.

As they rose that morning, the sky was clear and struck with color, but below lay a vast fogbank. The thickness of this low-hanging cloudbank was such that it corresponded exactly to the height of the cliffs, thus appearing as a kind of vaporous extension of the land, a great churning plain upon whose aqueous surface the sunrise found reflection. It was, Kendra thought, as if sometime during the night the world had been broken into halves, and she was surprised they had not been awakened by the commotion.

And so it was that as she and the Hupa set off for the first and easiest trail to the beach, they did so without ever knowing that a scant two hundred yards away, beneath the great layer of fog, the men the Hupa had come to kill toiled upon the cliffs. Nor could Drew Harmon know that his wife was within shouting distance of where he labored, for he could see little more than the rocks before him, and even they were blurred by the great white cocoon of emptiness in which he found himself contained.

In time, Kendra and the Hupa made their own descent into the fog. The man had cut a hole in the blanket she'd slept in and given it to her to wear. She wore it like a poncho, a figure from a western movie. He'd made shoes for her as well. At least they worked like shoes, though, in fact, they were no more than bundles of grass bound with strips of cloth, and she could not say what movie these were from, for, until now, she had seen nothing like them.

They ate as they went. Blackberries they had picked near the cabins, and dried sticks of salmon. They came to the beach and followed this to the small estuary where Temple Creek found its way to the sea. They crossed the water on an old log, then picked up the trail that led to the road.

In a short time, they had put the fog behind them once more, and the valley lay naked to their eyes. Though it was the thing which had originally drawn her to it, Kendra found she had forgotten the intimate beauty of the place. Or perhaps she saw it more clearly now. It was a narrow little valley. The foothills which rolled away from it were covered in trees, some still showing leaves of autumnal hue. The banks of the creek were thick with all manner of berry and vine, and these were woven through with poison oak, which, like many of the trees, had begun to color with the season. All in all, she thought, it made for a happy little display. All reds and greens— the stuff of holidays and good cheer.

They passed among groves of Douglas fir, together with a few cedar, their limbs bearded with a gray-green moss. There were other trees too, which Kendra could not name. Many had already lost their leaves and their naked white limbs were forked and woven into the sky as if any movement thereof might wrest their roots from the muddy soil.

The Hupa had hidden the packs in the grass near their camp but he carried the rifle, unsheathed, slung over his shoulder by a black nylon strap. He walked more or less at Kendra's side, but stayed just a step off her pace. She supposed they would have made for an odd sight—the girl dressed in the old blanket, her feet wrapped in rags, her hair short and ragged, the Indian coming just behind, with his erect carriage, his long, braided hair, and his big rifle. He wore hiking boots, jeans, and a plaid flannel shirt, and she wondered what someone would make of them, if there were any there to see it—the risen Magus, perhaps, in the company of the whore of Tyre. But then she supposed it would take a mind like her father's to make that out of it and he was a long time gone.

In time, they came to a small path that did not look like much more than a deer trail, and Kendra made for it.

"This is the place?" she heard the man say. They had not spoken in what seemed like hours. But now she only nodded and pushed ahead. "Rose keeps dogs," she called back to him. "But don't worry. They know me."

It seemed to her as if he made some response to this remark but she did not stop to take note of it. They had come to a small bridge and she could see the trailer. It was all just as she remembered. It rested in a clearing among the trees, its aluminum siding scorched half black, and, as if on cue, she saw the dogs as well, though it seemed to her as if they had added to their number, for now there were three instead of two. The animals came headlong, the day made terrible with their cries. Kendra ran as if to greet them, for it was her intention to play her hand to the very end.

33

Fletcher was betting heavily on the authors of *Surfing the Golden State*. They had described a trail leading down to a boulder field. Fletcher believed he and his companions had traversed such a field. Though it had been too foggy to look closely at the cliffs, he had taken note of their presence, monolithic shapes looming in the half light. The authors had further described the trail as leading overland to the campground Drew had spoken of at Neah Heads. The trail was said to be well-defined but arduous, crossing streams, climbing a mountain. Still, the authors had done it in a day and Fletcher was banking on that, for he had taken little with him. Not that he'd had much choice. Without the opportunity to stock up, he'd come in the clothes he'd slept in, together with a single Pop-Tart and one small bottle of water which he had managed to slip into his sleeping bag before retiring. After that, it was only a question of waiting them out. When he was sure that the others were asleep, he'd made his move.

The fog swallowed him at once. He'd gone along the shoreline, where the water might erase his tracks. He went stone blind, stumbling among slimy beds of kelp, tripping now and again on the odd rock, his feet numb with cold. Still, the plan worked. By daybreak, or what passed for it in this climate, he was seated on a boulder at the beginnings of the rock field.

He had come to the moment of choice. At this point, he could still go back. To go on was to risk everything. The trouble was that to go back meant going on as well. At least in this direction, he was his own boss. Stuffed into his parka was the roll of film he'd shot on Thunder Bay. It was not great stuff, but it would do. There was Drew Harmon and R.J. trading double overhead waves before the steel gray cliffs of the Devil's Hoof. He had left them the camera, just in case they found anything worthy of their efforts. It was Fletcher's belief that what they were most likely to find was more regret.

In fact, the trail was not so elusive as he had imagined. For a time, he had worked his way along the base of the cliffs. This was the hard part, for he was filled with misgivings. His visibility was made poor by the fog. The cliffs seemed unending. His passage was slow and, in time, he was aware of the white water making inroads upon the beach, telling him that the tide had begun to turn. It was his darkest moment. Soon after, however, he came to a place where the cliffs dropped down into long, rounded shoulders and the beach bent inland between them, drawing with it the sea, and so forming a narrow estuary, at the heart of which a good-sized stream ran from among the rocks and brush to join its waters with that of the Pacific.

He was some time in scouting this location, following carefully the path of the water, where, eventually, he came upon a log placed crosswise over the stream. Its purpose seemed unmistakable. Drawing closer, he could see the top worn smooth where boots had passed over it. He went this way himself, climbing into the rocks just south of the log where, in five minutes' time, he came upon a patch of grass cut by hard-packed dirt.

The trail was narrow at first, overgrown in places and yet with each switchback, each gain in elevation, it seemed to grow a little more defined. In time, the fog had begun to burn away as well and he was able to make some sense of his surroundings.

The water he had seen on the beach ran from the bottom of a narrow little valley, a steep V cut between the shoulders of the coastal range. The trail kept within sight of the water, but it seemed to be moving in the right direction. Fletcher felt that he should break into song, so certain was he that he had found the path—a little something from his days at Y camp—a few strains of "When Those Caissons Go Rolling Along," perhaps, for certainly there was no one here to listen, and the sun had broken from the treetops and he was thinking that, by nightfall, he would have found a room somewhere, a hot shower, a phone. He would have begun to put the trip behind him.

By noon, Fletcher's optimism had given way to an exhaustion laced with dread. He was seated once more, this time upon a fallen log. The water was still visible, a silver thread among the autumnal trees, though by now he was some distance above it as his road had begun to climb. It had also, much to his dismay, begun to run in a southerly direction, and he was beginning to have doubts about it taking him to the Heads. He had begun to worry that it was a logging road, and he remembered all too well the labyrinth of such roads Drew had driven on the night they'd hiked to the beach. The sun would set early behind the range to his west and the valley would go cold quickly. He was without provisions or direction. Such were the anxieties which beset him when he heard the sound of gunfire issuing from the valley below. Instinctively, he moved off the log and into the trees.

The shooting went on for some time. There was no mistaking the sound. He believed there were multiple weapons. It was difficult, surrounded by trees and mountains, to pinpoint the direction from which the sounds came, but he believed them to be coming from the west, the direction of the sea. Was it possible, he wondered, that Drew and Robbie had come after him, that they had crossed paths with the man he had seen on the cliff? He did not suppose the man had come alone. There would be others. Scenes of carnage filled his head. His first impulse was to press on, in the hopes of at least outdistancing the shooting. In the end, however, it seemed to him as if some investigation was required.

There were, he decided, two possibilities. Drew and Robbie were in trouble. Or there were hunters about. The latter scenario appealed to him a good deal more than the first. For if the former were true, he doubted there would be much he could do, save witness it. The latter held the possibility of help. He went so far as to imagine himself seated in a pickup truck, a tall cold one in his hand, as the woods receded behind him. A last shot came to him through the trees and he went in pursuit of it.

The going was slow. He was moving downhill now, toward the V of the valley. He followed what he took to be a deer path. The grass was bent beneath his feet and a way had been made among the brush. A narrow, twisting way, and yet a way nonetheless. At times, the tree limbs blocked him and he was forced to go on all fours to stay his course.

Eventually, however, he came within sight of the valley floor. He paused here. A dead silence hung upon the fall air. The trees in the valley showed color and he could make out the silver water of the little stream as it snaked among them. It seemed to him, however, that there was something else there as well, something besides the water that was reflecting the light, and he moved a bit further down the hillside, straining to see through this play of light and shadow. There was a structure of some sort there, he thought, and he went on.

Eventually, he came to a muddy bank made slick with fallen leaves. He was across the river and still some distance away, but he could see now that he was approaching a small settlement. He saw an old house trailer half-blackened as though by fire. He saw a shack in need of paint from whose roof a thin trail of gray smoke wafted into the air.

A short distance downriver from where he stood, he could see that someone had built a narrow, moss-covered bridge it would be necessary to cross to reach the trailer. He approached with caution, mindful that he was alone and unarmed in a neighborhood where trespassers were likely to be shot; wondering, too, if this could have been the scene of all the shooting. In truth, he was hoping that he had been wrong, that the gunplay had come from some other quarter, for he would gladly swap his hunters for the generous, if reclusive, citizen. He was still harboring such fantasies when he reached the bridge and came upon the first of the bodies.

He was treated first to the sound of buzzing flies and then saw the man. He took him at once for the Indian he had seen on the cliff. His hair was long and braided. He was dressed in denim and plaid and a long-barreled rifle with a large scope lay beside him. The man was shot through the chest with what looked to be a large-caliber bullet. His mouth was open and his eyes had rolled back into his head.

The bridge transcribed a little arch as it spanned the creek and appeared to be a work of some craftsmanship. The Indian seemed to have been shot near the apex of this arch, then fallen backward so that he lay now on Fletcher's side of the water.

The sight of the body stopped him cold and he was some time crouched in the mud at the side of the stream. He had the idea that if he moved he was likely to be shot himself, though he could not have said by whom. Nor could he have told you how long he waited.

Nothing happened. There were no further shots and no voices. The day had fallen silent once more, save for the buzzing of the insects and the rush of water across a rocky bed. In time, he rose, his legs stiff from the position he had held. He stepped over the man, moving upward along the bridge that he might at least get a look at the clearing on the far bank. From this elevation, he could see that quite a number of things had been shot. Namely, three dogs, two men, and a chicken. The devastation appeared, at first glance, quite complete. It was only upon further examination that he saw the second chicken and the girl.

The girl was bare-legged, dressed only in a gaily colored blanket. She was seated on the ground, her back to a tree, and she was cradling the chicken in her arms. The bird's head bobbed up and down, and from time to time, the girl would raise her hand to stroke the side of the chicken's neck with the backs of her fingers. The last thing he noticed about her was that she was Kendra Harmon.

THREE

THE
SILENT
GRAY
FELLOW

3 4

Fletcher crossed the bridge and entered the clearing. There was a dead man by the water, a tall, skinny man dressed in red long-johns. The man had a gun belt around his waist and there was a garden hose at his side. The hose was still spouting water. As a result, a tiny, unnamed tributary trickled along the muddy bank to join the stream. Another man clad only in soiled boxer shorts and a bloody T-shirt lay nearby, his face in the dirt, an automatic rifle pinned beneath his belly. The dogs were scattered more or less between the two men.

Fletcher walked among the carnage. He was making for the tree and Kendra Harmon. At his approach, the girl turned to look at him. She stroked the side of the chicken's neck. "I named him Lucky," she said.

"Are you all-right?" Fletcher asked.

"Me and Lucky," the girl said. "We came out okay."

Fletcher stood before her. He looked around. The place was a veritable swamp of bodily fluids. It was quite unlike anything he had seen before. "Christ," he said. He felt a little weak in the knees. "What happened here?"

"I cut their lifelines," Kendra Harmon told him. "What can I tell you?"

Fletcher nodded. It was clear the girl would require attention. It was possible that he would be requiring some himself. At which point, he noticed the buzzards, an entire congregation perched among the trees. They sat with their great black wings held rigidly away from their bodies as if posing for his benefit, bat-winged shadows before a failing sky.

Fletcher supposed he should do something about all of the bodies. Someone, of course, would have to be told. Some appropriate thing would have to be done. And then there was the girl. In fact, she presented a rather alarming spectacle. He could see that some harm had befallen her, but had no clear idea of how to proceed.

He began by offering her a pill. But she would only shake her head, stroking the chicken's neck while looking into the trees. Fletcher took the pill himself. After which, he set about a hurried inspection of the property. Apart from the trailer, there were two structures. A pair of shacks in which he found gardening tools, firewood and burlap bags. An old truck was parked behind one of the shacks. There was a second entrance to the property there as well. A dirt pathway barely wide enough to accommodate the truck could be seen winding off into the shadows in an easterly direction.

The dead men had obviously been living in the trailer, for though the thing had been scorched by fire, the interior was intact. Neither man, however, had been much of a housekeeper. The place was a litter of filth, of paper bags filled to overflowing with discarded tin cans, soiled dishes and half-eaten bowls of dog food.

When he had satisfied himself that there were no phones or much else to interest him, he went back out to the girl. She was still at the tree but the chicken was now walking around in front of her, scratching at the ground. Fletcher knelt at her side. "There's an old truck back there," he said. "You know how to get anywhere from here?"

The girl rested her head against the tree and closed her eyes. "The shamans in these parts were women, and they were meant for receiving pain. When this happened, they would go to a sacred place. They would dance there, until the spirit brought a second pain. For it was only when the two pains had been paired that a healing might be effected."

Fletcher nodded. Obviously, the girl was not thinking clearly. But then she had been through an ordeal, the likes of which he could only imagine.

"I know of such a place," she said. Her face appeared slightly flushed. A light burned in her dark eyes. Fletcher suspected she was with fever. "It's an old Indian cemetery," she continued. "It's on the coast, north of the Heads. I want to go there. I want to dance."

Fletcher gazed into the failing light. The buzzards had grown in number. When new birds arrived, the air was filled with the rustle of their wings. He supposed that, at the very least, the bodies ought to be protected in some way. "Can I ask you something?" he said. He was thinking about the Indian on the bridge. He had begun to for-mulate a theory about what the girl was doing here and he thought it important to find out if he was right or not. "Drew said he sent you into town. How did you wind up here?"

"Some men came to the trailer. I tried to run. They caught me."

"Kin to the boy who drowned?"

"I don't know," she said. "They found Drew's note telling me he'd gone to the Hoof. That's how they knew where to come."

Fletcher looked at the carnage once more. "I saw one of them," he said. "It was that guy back by the bridge. He was on a cliff, point-ing a gun at me."

"I know," she said.

"But how . . ." he began, then stopped as she raised her fingers to his lips. "Don't," she said.

She took her hand away. Her fingers smelled like the woods, and it seemed to him as if they had left a residue he could still taste.

"Okay," he said. "But I think we should get back. The wrong peo-ple show up here, we could be in deep shit."

The girl shrugged. "They've got nothing on me. I cut their lifelines."

Fletcher fingered the vial of pills in the vest pocket of his parka. "Yeah, well, I'm sure they had it coming."

"You're sure I'm full of shit."

"I'm sure you should see a doctor."

She shook her head, then looked away.

"I don't mean a shrink. I mean someone to look you over. You've been through a lot."

"You don't know the half of it," she told him.

They sat for a moment in silence. With the passing of the sunlight, the temperature had begun to drop. The wind smelled of rain. "If we left now," Fletcher said, "we might beat the storm."

"Beat it where?"

"You think you could find your way to town?"

"I told you," she said, "I have no interest in town. I told you where I wanted to go."

It was clear the girl had her mind made up. Short of fighting her, Fletcher was unclear about what to do. "Could we get to this place in the truck?" he asked.

"We?"

"I can't exactly leave you here."

She looked at him for a moment. "There might be a way," she said. "But I don't know how. The only way I know would be by the trails."

Fletcher seated himself on the dirt. He supposed they might weather the night in one of the shacks. The trailer would be warmer, but the thing was too foul for his liking. There was also the prospect of someone else showing up. The thing to do, he decided, was to leave a propane lantern on in the trailer, then he and the girl could hide out in one of the shacks. Perhaps they could sleep in shifts. If anyone showed up, they would see it, they could slip out the back and hide in the woods. Perhaps, he thought, the girl would see things his way in the morning.

"Okay," he told her at length. "We can spend the night here. We'll try to figure something out in the morning."

The girl nodded in the direction of the trailer. "Look't Lucky," she said.

Together they looked toward the water where the man in longjohns lay covered in dirt and blood. The surviving chicken had climbed atop the man's chest. As Fletcher and Kendra watched it, the bird pecked out an eye.

"Dinner time," Kendra told him.

•　•　•

With much effort, Fletcher managed to get two of the bodies into one of the shacks where he covered them with burlap bags. The Indian on the bridge was too big to move very far. In the end, Fletcher rolled him down the bank and buried him in a shallow grave in the soft ground near the water. As for the dogs, he dragged them far enough into the woods where he would not have to witness the feast and left them to the local scavengers.

As he worked, he became increasingly puzzled over what the guy in the long-johns had been doing with a garden hose. The thing had by now run out of water. Following it to its source, Fletcher found a holding tank and a well but nothing else. As near as he could tell, the guy had been doing little more than adding to the stream. But the light was failing him, and, in time, he abandoned this mystery and set about finding them something to eat.

There were a few canned goods left in the trailer—Pork and beans, Vienna sausages and stale soda crackers. Fletcher brought these outside where he and Kendra ate from the cans in the shack they had elected to sleep in. When Kendra had eaten, she went outside and wretched. Fletcher lay on one of the flimsy mattresses he'd dragged from the trailer, waiting for her to come back, wondering at what was to become of them.

In time, a steady rain began. Kendra was still outside. He was about to go looking when he heard her come in. She pulled a mattress as close to one of the walls as she could get it and lay down, her knees drawn up, her face to the tin siding. Fletcher watched her. She had wrapped herself rather ineffectually in one of the sleeping bags he'd found with the mattresses. He waited a moment, then moved to kneel behind her, arranging the bag so that she was completely covered with it. She allowed him to do this, and when he was done and gone back to his own mattress, he heard her thank him.

He had left a lantern burning in the trailer as planned, but it did not, he concluded, make much sense to talk to the girl about sleeping in shifts. He had retrieved the automatic rifle and the .45 from the two men in the clearing—the rifle because it looked to be the most lethal of the weapons, the handgun because it was the only one he was certain he knew how to use without some amount of experimentation. But not once during the night did he bother to look outside.

The cold was murderous—much colder than what he had grown used to on the beaches. Near morning, the girl came to him. "I wonder," she said, "if you could put your hand here." She seemed to be pointing to her stomach. Fletcher opened the bag, allowing her to crawl in with him. It was the first she had spoken since they had eaten and she had gotten sick. He could hardly refuse the request. She placed his hand upon her stomach, but low, below her navel. He could feel something writhing there. A serpent in the garden.

He held her that way for a long while. Anyone would have. They exchanged a few words. She asked him, for the first time, what he was doing here and why he wasn't out taking pictures.

He told her.

"You got scared," she said.

"Yes."

"Of the Indian you'd seen on the cliff."

"That was part of it."

She was quiet for some time. "You were scared of Drew," she said.

He didn't answer right away. He could feel her breathing against his chest. "That was part of it too," he said finally.

He thought maybe she would say more but she didn't. In time, his shoulder began to ache, for the mattresses were pitifully thin and she had brought him to an awkward position. Still, he held her. He would hold her till daylight, he decided, if that was what she wanted, and at some point, he was able to feel the snakes beneath his hand stop their incessant writhing. He knew, however, that she was not asleep.

"Are you okay?" he asked. They had not spoken in quite some time.

"Actually," she said, "I'm not."

35

The surfers made Neah Heads in darkness, in a driving rain. Under optimal conditions, the trip might have taken them six to eight hours. As it was, they did it in closer to twelve, managing the last couple of miles in total darkness, stumbling blindly among the redwoods. For Travis, the hour had little meaning. He had been, at various times throughout the day, dragged, carried, pushed, and pulled. He had ridden on backs and on boards. The time had passed as a kaleidoscope of dreams and half-dreams, punctuated by moments of stark clarity, with pain as his only constant, the star by which to place himself, and it had burned with a brilliance that far outshown that pale and watery impersonator which had raced them across a darkening sky.

The initial climb was the worst, his arms wrapped around Drew Harmon's neck as Drew picked his way among the rocks, climbing toward the bluffs with two hundred pounds of dead weight clinging to his back. The kid followed them. Travis was afforded glimpses of him now and then. With his shaved head and his peaked hood and the huge board bags dangling from his shoulders, he appeared upon the fogbound rocks as might some slightly demented vassal in pursuit of his king. The fact of the matter, however, was that the kid was carrying quite a load, and Travis was well aware that had he been discovered by two any less capable specimens, he would no doubt have been left on the rocks until more help could be found.

Once upon the grassy bluffs, they proceeded in all manner of configurations. At one point, they even tried dragging him in one of the board bags with a wet suit under his tailbone to save it from the rocks. In the end, however, it was Drew who took him once more, draping him over his shoulders in a fireman's carry, then trudging for a mile and a half in the rain and darkness, a steady uphill run among the redwoods to the ramshackle cabins and finally to the tribal center set upon the balding crest of a hill where, by the light of day, it commanded a view of both the redwoods below and the restless sea beyond.

They arrived to find that lines, downed by recent storms, had left the reservation with neither phones nor power. The small building that passed as the tribal center was attended by Art the maintenance man, a burly 250-pounder who, some forty years previously, had gone off to Los Angeles to a brief, undistinguished career as a professional fighter, then come back to the reservation where, for the last thirty years or so, he had worked as a handyman for the campground and tribal center at Neah Heads. It seemed to Travis that someone had once told him Art had fought under the name Art the Red Man Hancock.

On the evening in question, Art the Red Man Hancock had already settled in for the night. He was dressed in his pajamas and romeo slippers. He had a fire going in the big wood-burning stove and a little generator set up to run his television. They were used to power outages in Neah Heads. The Red Man was drinking Old Crow and watching reruns of *The Rockford Files* when the surfers and Travis came banging on his door. When he saw that it was Ruth McCade's boy, he pointed and laughed and ushered them in, where they stood shedding water as if they were themselves storm clouds set upon legs.

Travis attempted some introductions, but Drew brushed them

aside, demanding some link to the outside. The Red Man reiterated that there were no lines.

"You must have some kind of two-way radio up here," Drew told him.

Art said this was not the case.

"Bullshit," Drew said. He pushed past the old man, looking around the room for himself, leaving great puddles of water wherever he went. "You've got something. I know you have."

"What do you think this is?" Art asked him. "A fucking Coast Guard station?"

Drew whirled to face him. "What do you do if you have an emergency? What about that?"

The two men were eye to eye.

"We wait," Art told him. "We're Indians. We're good at it. If you want to wait with us, you can shed those clothes and take a seat. If you don't, then get the fuck out of here, 'cause this is where I live and you're makin' a mess out of it."

Drew left without another word. He shouldered past them and walked back out into the rain. Travis had no idea where he was going, nor was he in a position to ask. He was braced against the door jamb and it was all he could do to keep from falling, but he watched the old Indian. Drew had left the door standing open to the storm, and as Art the Red Man Hancock moved to close it, he stopped for a moment and stood looking into the night with an odd expression on his face, much, Travis imagined, as if he were watching some young *wagay* version of himself striding off to make war with the world.

When Drew showed no signs of rejoining them, Art shut the door and took their clothes and gave them towels and blankets so that they might warm themselves by the fire. He had to help Travis with his clothes and, in so doing, got his first look at Travis's leg.

"This is bad," he said. "Only thing I know to do before morning is to get Becky. She's the nurse from the school. She might have something."

Travis nodded. He watched as the old Indian set about pulling on his jeans and rain gear. After some deliberation with himself, he told Art about the Tolowan he had seen on the rocks.

Art stopped and looked at him. "Long white hair? No front teeth?"

"That's the one."

"That's Whitey Longtree," Art said. "He was up here night before last. Showed up around sundown. Wanted a cabin."

"You see who he was with?"

"No. Shit. This time of year, who cares? I gave him a key to number twenty-five. That's where he wanted. I made a run by there this afternoon. There'd been a fire, but the place was clean. No sign of Whitey. Must of been somebody with him though. I don't think Whitey'd ever clean anything on his own."

"You knew him?"

Art shrugged. "Knew him when he was a kid. He doesn't come around here much anymore. Stays upriver, the way I hear it. When he's not in jail." Art paused to shake his head. "Old Whitey," he said. "Probably been whiffin' fumes. Think there's anything we ought to do?"

"Tell Blacklage, I guess. When we see him."

The Red Man laughed. "Gotta get a traffic ticket to do that. I'll go for the nurse."

Nurse Becky was quite young, or so it seemed to Travis. She had a little black bag with her and walked in shaking rain from her hair like a country doctor called out on a bad night. When she saw Travis's ankle, she made a face which did not make him feel any better, then turned to her bag. "That must hurt like a bastard," she told him.

She shot him full of antibiotics and painkillers. She also bathed and dressed his wound as best she could, though it was beyond her skill to set the leg and she told him so. She told him that, in the morning, he would have to be transported by some means to the medical clinic in Sweet Home.

There was not much to do after that, except wait. The nurse made coffee and Art got back into his pajamas. *The Rockford Files* went off the air and was replaced by *Star Trek*.

"This is a good one," Art said.

"Hey, yeah, no shit," Robbie Jones said. "I remember this one."

"It's the one where they take out Spock's brain," Art said.

"Fuckin' A," Robbie said.

Travis was, by now, prone upon the floor, his leg raised upon a rolled sleeping bag, covered by a blanket. He had another sleeping bag underneath him and a couch pillow for his head. It was how the nurse had fixed him. He was a little ways off from the others, where it was darker, and where Becky thought he might be able to get some sleep.

When she was ready to go home, Becky came over to Travis one more time.

"I hoped you would be asleep," she said.

"I'm close."

"I hope so. You need the rest. It's only a few hours now. We don't have any phone service by morning, we'll have to find somebody here that can drive you. I'm sorry, it's the best we can do."

Travis nodded.

She stood then. She had a big navy blue coat and as she was buttoning it, she looked outside. There was lightning at just that moment and Travis was afforded a look at her face.

"What's with your friend?" she asked.

"Who?"

"Your friend. Out there. The big one."

"You can see him?"

She nodded. "Yeah, I can see him. He's outside."

"What's he doing?"

"Nothing."

"Nothing at all."

She shrugged. "He's squatting down. He's got his arms wrapped around his knees, it looks like, and he's staring toward the ocean. What's his story?"

"I don't know," Travis said. He had turned his head to a different angle and was treated to the unlikely sight of Art the Red Man and Robbie Jones. The two were seated side by side on Art's couch. The kid was wrapped up in one of Art's oversized bathrobes. They had their feet up on Art's table and were eating from boxes of Cracker Jacks, their faces lit by the flickering light of the wood stove, their eyes fixed on the screen above them.

"You think I should try and get him?" the nurse asked.

"I think he'll come in if he wants to," Travis said. His words were punctuated by a rolling clap of thunder.

"You think he'll want to?"

"No," Travis told her. "Probably not. Not tonight."

Fletcher found the girl much restored by morning. It was quite surprising, really. He woke to find her already up, dressed in a flannel shirt and khaki pants several sizes too large. He supposed she had been in the trailer. She'd tied the pants up with a piece of sheet and clad her feet in oversized woolen socks and leather sandals. So dressed, she made for quite a sight—the last of the homeless waifs. She'd picked some berries as well and was quite enthused about the idea of eating them with vanilla ice cream.

She'd also found a hundred dollars cash in an old can, together with a stash of buds. Fletcher was quite happy with the find. It would give him a little something to go with the pills. So armed, they had taken the truck and the chicken, electing to follow the back road away from the clearing. She was still intent on finding the cemetery. The good news was, he had been able to talk her into the truck.

Happily, the truck was an old Dodge Power Wagon. It carried them without complaint through bush and bramble. Branches lashed at the windshield. Mud spattered the hood. At the end of a particularly long and rocky climb, they arrived upon a more reasonable excuse for a road. Fletcher was willing to take it for the fire road he'd hiked on the previous day but at a much higher elevation.

This road led them to the top of a ridgeline from which they were afforded a view of the sea, or at least of the clouds in which that body was so draped. They turned north here and, in another half hour or so of fairly tortuous driving, came to a long, ramshackle building so covered in ivy as to be almost inseparable from the vegetation that surrounded it.

There was a '69 Coupe de Ville sitting out front with its windows missing and great iron-colored rust spots on its hood and trunk. Its tires were missing as well, with the wheels gone to rust and the axles set on blocks. There was, however, a more roadworthy vehicle—a four-wheel-drive Toyota parked to one side of the place and a thin trail of smoke issuing from a stack at the back half of the building, which was arranged, more or less, in the shape of an L. An ancient dog lay near the Toyota, in a puddle of sunlight. At the arrival of the Power Wagon, he raised a graying muzzle and sniffed at the air. The dog was flanked by a pair of chickens scratching at the dirt. "Lucky's cousins," Kendra said.

A sign perched atop the roof gave them to understand they had arrived at the Orleans Grill. Fletcher parked and got out. The place was so covered in ivy, it took them some time to locate the door. The old dog had by now made his way over. Fletcher scratched him behind the ear, and when they found the door and went inside, the dog followed them.

If the outside of the Orleans Grill was unique in appearance, the inside was more so, an eatery and roadside attraction rolled into one. For what they saw upon entering was a long, dimly lit corridor whose walls were punctuated by a series of recklessly constructed dioramas. One featured two female mannequins whose flowered cotton dresses had grown thin as paper with time, and these were bent in attitudes of mute concentration over an ancient Victrola and attended to by a taxidermied two-headed calf whose heads were cocked as if in attention to some master's voice none but themselves could hear. In other booths were other mannequins and taxidermied birds, but most were simply full of junk—mainly consisting of old mining and lumbering tools such as long, two-handled saws with rusted blades and handles rotted with time and bugs.

Fletcher found the place reminded him of the roadside attractions he'd visited in the Mojave Desert as a boy and half expected to find a missing link or alien being but such was not the case. The walls between the dioramas were covered in old sheet music, and at the end of this long hall, one came finally to the Orleans Grill itself—a one-room affair attended to by a fat white woman. A tall, thin male of clearly Native American descent might be seen some ways back, in the murky confines of a windowless kitchen.

The walls of this room were covered with cast-iron skillets upon whose flat, black bottoms the names of various couples had been inscribed in white paint. "Rusty and Sue." "Bill and Bobby." At which point, the fat woman took it upon herself to tell them that they too might purchase a skillet and get their names on it and which skillet, so adorned, would then hang upon these walls for all to see until death might do them part.

"Nice," Fletcher told her, and drifted off once more into the hallway to peer with no small amount of wonder at the dioramas, wondering about how these things had come to be here and what stories they might have to tell, could their poor, dumb mannequin voices be lifted in other than dusty silence, while Kendra Harmon went about her transaction, which included trading Lucky for ice cream and obtaining directions to the old Tolowan cemetery north of the Heads. The fat woman was evidently familiar with the place as Fletcher was able to pick up bits and pieces of the conversation. He could hear the woman talking about road conditions and unmaintained trails, not to mention the uncertainty of the weather, all of which led him to conclude the woman was trying to dissuade Mrs. Harmon, but he'd already tried that one himself and was, by this point, quite confident the girl would get what she came for, which, in the end, is exactly what happened.

The late morning found them outside, seated upon a log placed before the Orleans Grill, and meant, Fletcher supposed, to serve as

Kem Nunn

a kind of curbstone, though he found it hard to believe many tires were stopped by it. On the other hand, there was the testimony of the skillets, so that, for all he knew, they had arrived at some local hot spot and come the weekend, people he could only dimly imagine would show up here to drink and party and pass along the dusty entrance and the attentive mannequins and the dusty two-headed calf which, the fat woman had assured him, was quite real and born to a local farmer and had lived to the size at which he now saw it, as if this was supposed to tell him something about its age—a thing he had scant interest in, for the mere sight of it had been enough to brighten his day.

"So what do you say?" Fletcher asked her. "You think we should get our names on a skillet?"

The girl smiled, eating the ice cream and berries.

Fletcher had rolled a joint and now set about smoking it.

The girl declined his offer to share. Her brain, she said, had never been the most dependable of organs, and she didn't like to fuck with it any more than she had to.

Fletcher nodded. "The course of prudent behavior," he told her. He was suddenly feeling quite content. There was no reason for it. In fact, everything argued against it.

Clouds were passing quickly and in great number overhead, a parade of distended airships set before a blue blaze of sky. Shafts of sunlight fell among the trees. It pooled at their feet and warmed their shoulders, though the wind was from the ocean and spoke of the coming rain the fat woman had predicted.

Fletcher seated himself in the dirt that he might lean back with his elbows upon the log, high on pot and pills, at peace with the world. Kendra stayed where she was. In time, however, she placed the ice cream at her feet and started taking things from her pockets.

"I collected these this morning," she said. "While you were sleeping."

She laid the articles first upon the log. There were flowers she named as yellow yarrow, together with several strands of dried kelp, horsetail reed, and river roots.

As Fletcher watched, Kendra took these in her hands, braiding and wrapping, until she had fashioned a small wreath that one might hold in the palm of one's hand. She gave this to Fletcher. He sat with it in the light, examining the intricate weave of color punctuated by the bright yellow blossoms.

"You need a wire to do it right," she told him. "But that's the idea. The trippy part is, people will pay you money for those and it's all right here, just waiting for someone to pick it up."

Fletcher nodded, examining the small wreath. "It's nice," he said.

"I first thought of that, it seemed like the perfect thing. Drew could make his boards. I could make these. We would live off the forest and the beaches."

"I don't see why not. I don't see why you couldn't."

"You don't?"

"No."

"Because Drew's done something," she told him.

"Done what?"

The girl looked at him for some time. "It's so hard to be sure," she said. "But I am."

Fletcher sat with the small wreath in his hands.

"I think I can see how it happened. It was hard for him here," Kendra said. "The old lady had taken out loans on the property. He wanted so much to make a family, to have a home. I miscarried. He got bitten. There were medical bills on top of the other payments. He'd gone through whatever he'd saved. He was working two jobs. He was scrapping hulls at the harbor during the day. At night, he was driving to Eureka to unload trucks. He wasn't surfing. Eventually he got everything paid off. He had the idea about the old boards. He saved money for the woods. He began to shape. But somewhere something happened between him and this girl. I think it was while he was at his lowest point, working all the jobs. Maybe she made him feel like he used to feel. A distraction. I don't think it was more than that. Maybe she wanted it to go on. Or end. I don't know. She was last seen arguing with a man in an alley behind a bar in Sweet Home. They found her the next day with her throat cut."

Some time passed. Neither spoke.

"I think Drew was that man," Kendra said at length.

Fletcher was not sure what to say.

"You think that's a terrible thing to say, don't you?"

"Only if it isn't true. Did anyone investigate this? Did anyone ever talk to Drew?"

The girl shook her head. "They got someone. Right away. They found this Indian by the name of Marvus Dove in Neah Heads. He had the girl's blood on his boots. When they busted him, he hung himself."

Fletcher looked once more at the small wreath, the weave of color.

"Now you think it's a terrible thing to say." She put her fingers to her temples. "I did. I thought it was a terrible thing to say, to think. The trouble was, I began to see things."

"What kind of things?"

"Little things. I began to see things at night. Like what the walls had seen. Drew bought the trailer she was killed in. It's where we live."

Fletcher had nothing to say about that. It was hard to argue with visions. "Does Drew know," he asked, "how you feel?"

"He knows."

Fletcher sat with this in the tepid light. Clouds shifted above them. The light vanished. He recalled the sight of Drew's shaping shack, the mattress on the floor, amid the sawdust and shavings. He thought of what Drew had told him, that there were places he couldn't go, people he couldn't be around. On the long hike up the coast, he had spoken of unforgivable sin.

"The girl's name was Amanda Jaffey," Kendra said. "She was pretty, part Indian, I think. Kind of a street girl. Except that she had this crappy trailer. When she died, no one came. No one ever took her things. They were still there when Drew bought it. I was looking through them one night and I found this little surfboard carved out of redwood. It was a certain kind, without a fin."

"A hot curl board."

"That's the name."

"It was what the Hawaiians rode, before the Californians showed up with fins."

"I think it was why Drew bought the trailer. He knew about the board. Maybe he knew about other things too. If the trailer was his, no one would ever discover anything else in it."

"Except you."

"Except me."

"Did you ever tell him?"

Kendra nodded.

"And what did he say?"

"Nothing. I wore her clothes and he still didn't say anything. But he began to sleep in the shaping shack by the river. He began to talk about moving to Chile."

Fletcher watched the clouds. When he turned back to the girl, he saw that she was watching him with an intensity he found unsettling. "Why did he call that magazine?" she asked. "He used to say pictures were bullshit."

Fletcher shook his head. "I don't know," he said.

"The morning you left, to go out with the boy, I told him Chile would take money. We're broke, but he said he had it covered. So I wondered about these pictures . . ."

Fletcher shook his head once more. "There's no money in the pictures. I mean, he might have some deal with Peters. But it wouldn't be much. Maybe he thinks he can pick up a sponsor . . ." At which point, he thought of something else and stopped short.

"What?" she asked him.

"The boards," Fletcher said. He rose and walked some way into the dirt road. Christ. The boards of Heart Attacks. He turned to face her. "When did all this happen?" he asked. "When did the girl die?"

"Amanda was killed at the beginning of August."

Fletcher shook his head. "He was going to sell those boards," he said. "The article was just free advertising."

The girl looked puzzled. "But how much could he expect to get for them?"

Fletcher laughed. He couldn't quite help himself. He and Robbie had joked about it, for Christ's sake. But he could see now that they had been wrong. When Robbie had asked him how many people would want one, he was thinking about how many people would buy them to ride. "They're collectibles," he said. It seemed so obvious to him now—the elaborate work with the stringers, the sunbursts and tail blocks. Old Greg Noll Da Cat models were going for ten grand a pop the last he had heard and it was a growing market. So how much for a Drew Harmon signature model, a balsa wood gun with redwood stringers? "He could probably get two to three grand a board," he said. "At least." He was talking almost as much to himself as to the girl. "You invite *Victory at Sea* up for a spread . . . You get the editor to drop a line about how one of the boards might be had . . . That's a hundred thousand free ad bills. And all you need for a quick score is to sell a dozen that are already shaped."

"That's thirty or forty thousand."

"It is, indeed."

"You see," the girl said. She had begun to rock. She had clasped her arms about her shoulders and sat there rocking on the log, the ice cream melting at her feet. "You see."

Fletcher sat down at her side. He found that her rocking disturbed him, and, after some consideration, he circled her with his arm to make her stop.

She leaned into him. Her head came to rest upon his shoulder. He could feel the beating of his own heart, the rush of blood in hidden chambers and he knew that Drew had felt it too, with this girl in his arms. And he could not prevent himself from imagining what must it have been like to lose her. To look in her eyes and see it gone.

"I was going to tell him I wouldn't go," she said. "But then I guess he won't go either, now. Not if he was counting on the pictures."

Fletcher took a roll of film from his pocket and held it out for the girl to see.

"That's him?"

"Drew Harmon and Robbie Jones, on his boards."

"But there's nothing left to sell."

Fletcher craned his neck, the better to see her face. "What do you mean?" he asked.

"I mean the rest of the boards, the wood to make them. Those men who took me—they burned it all down."

"Everything?" Fletcher asked. "Everything that was in that shed?"

"It's gone," she said.

Fletcher looked to the road, to the tall trees, above whose tips the clouds continued to swirl. In fact, the news affected him in a way he would not have imagined, for the first thing which struck him was the enormity of what had been lost—the books, the tapes, the charts, the boards, the wood—a life's storehouse, up in smoke. The second thing which struck him was the image of Drew Harmon. The picture which came most readily to mind was that of the man as he had last seen him, crouched before the flames, with the story of his nameless tribe and of the end they had chosen, and he knew now, with a clarity not afforded him before, that he had been right to leave. Indeed, he had been right to be afraid. "We should go back," he said. "Right now. You should see a doctor." They should probably talk to someone too, he thought, about this thing that had happened, about the dead girl and the little board found among her things. It occurred to him they might start with the man who had rescued him from the island. They could go to Travis, he thought.

He stood, ready to return to the truck, but the girl had him by the wrist. He looked down on her. Her face was turned toward his, the ice cream melting between her feet. "There's a place I have to go first," she said. "I require its blessing."

She was, of course, completely serious.

"I think I require a shower more than a blessing," Fletcher said. "I should think you would want one too."

He was hoping to lighten her mood but she wasn't having any. "No way," she said. "You require this place too. For losing the boy."

He looked down the road. His eyes were clouded with mist. "I should see his family," he said. It was one more reason to go back. "I should tell them . . ." His voice trailed away.

The girl squeezed his wrist. "They will be there," she said.

"They will?"

"Where we're going, are you kidding?"

Fletcher was aware of an unpleasant weight upon his chest. Every rational impulse called for him to go back into the Orleans Grill, to ask for a phone, for more sensible directions. "And after this place," he asked. "After we go there. You'll come back with me then? We'll go back together."

"Of course," she said.

Travis slept fitfully. At length, he opened his eyes to find the floor streaked with sunlight. Turning, he saw, through rippled glass, a blue sky lined with clouds. For a short time, he was alone in the room. Soon, however, Robbie Jones came in, accompanied by Becky the nurse. To Travis's dismay, he learned that Drew Harmon was no longer around, but had gone off with Blacklage's deputy, Jim Lemon.

It seems that Jim had arrived in Neah Heads some time earlier. On his way, he'd stopped at the Orleans Grill, where the owner had told him of an odd occurrence. It seems that around eight or nine that morning, a man and woman fitting the descriptions of Jack Fletcher and Kendra Harmon had shown up there. The woman had wanted to trade a chicken for a quart of vanilla ice cream, then inquired about directions to the old Tolowan cemetery at the north end of Neah Heads. Drew had been insistent that Lemon investigate this further and the two of them had gone off together.

Becky was furious that no one had told the deputy about Travis, but Art had been out and it was not the kind of thing that would have occurred to Robbie Jones, who, in fact, had seen the men go off together. Becky couldn't quite believe it. "You saw them leave?" she said.

Robbie nodded.

"Well, what about him?" she said. She was pointing at Travis. "That deputy should be driving him into Sweet Home, right now."

"They'll be back," Robbie said.

At which point, Becky had thrown up her hands and gone off in search of another driver.

Robbie and Travis were left alone in the center. There was little for Travis to do but wait. And this he did, in the company of Robbie Jones, while the wind railed at the walls of Art the Red Man's living quarters, upon which a badly done portrait of Christ thumped against knotty pine. The picture was hung above the television now showing reruns of *Family Feud*. Alongside the picture there were hung old hand-carved eel hooks and beaded headdresses and old wooden masks, and these shared equal space with photographs of the Neah Heads football team, together with several dusty pedestals upon which small golden men who did not look at all like Native Americans ran above nonexistent gridirons, footballs tucked beneath one arm, the other outstretched to ward off invisible tacklers. The men ran among dust-covered bowls of Halloween candies and two dead rats dressed in hula skirts and mounted upon burls of polished redwood.

As the time wore on, Travis became increasingly worried about Drew Harmon and Jim Lemon. He rested his head on the floor as the game show continued to spill from the television. It was impossible not to hear. White people vied with one another for some kind of ultimate humiliation. "He masturbate with chicken parts," a fat woman said. The audience howled with delight. Her husband looked hurt. "Disgust you to see it," the woman added, playing now to the crowd. The show's host, an edible blonde in a tight skirt, convulsed with laughter, appearing to swallow her tongue. Travis believed himself to be hallucinating. He closed his eyes but he could still see it. The Indian on the rocks. Holes where his brains had been. Behind this abhorrence, an audience of mutants clamored for blood. At which point, he became aware of the face of Robbie Jones peering down on him out of the gloom, capped by its shaved dome upon which the first signs of stubble had begun to appear.

"Hey," Robbie said. "You're the dude I hit, right?"

Travis said that he was. He tried to imagine the particular mind-set which would allow for such a delayed recognition, and found that he could not.

"I'm sorry, man," the kid told him. "I was kind of excited out there. I'd seen 'em pack my bro."

Travis told him to forget it.

"I'm tryin' to do better," Robbie said. "You shoulda seen me before I accepted Jesus as my lord and savior." He offered Travis a hand.

Travis took it. It seemed silly not to. They shook as the wind rattled the walls.

In the end, it was decided that a Tolowan by the name of Balloon Dick Bob would drive Travis to the hospital in his Jeep. The man was a notorious drunk. The road out of the Heads was all but nonexistent, steep and rutted, choked with weeds. A place where drunken Indians killed themselves on a regular basis. Balloon Dick and Art the Red Man carried him outside on a canvas stretcher as the rain began to fall, and he felt the first drops on his face. They struck him as might sparks driven on a wind.

The stretcher wouldn't fit into the ratted-out Jeep, making it necessary for Travis to sit upright in the front seat. Balloon Dick set about tying him in with canvas straps, as the vehicle was short on belts. Art Hancock stood alongside, apparently to make sure things were done correctly.

It had just occurred to Travis that Robbie Jones was missing when he looked up to see the young man running from the hillside behind the tribal center. The Jeep rocked as the young man heaved himself inside. Travis could see just enough through the haze of Nurse Becky's pain pills to notice that the kid was without gear save for one small backpack. "What happened to the rest of your stuff?" Travis asked him.

"It's gone," Robbie said.

"You mean somebody ripped it off?"

"Yeah. Drew Harmon."

Travis twisted in his seat. Pain prevented him from turning as completely as he would have liked.

"You mean he was here, just now?" he asked. He wanted to be sure he had heard correctly, that he was not hallucinating.

"We stashed our stuff in that little storage shed out back." Robbie told him. "I went out there to get it, he was just leaving . . ."

"Now? You talked to him just now?"

"Sort of."

"Well, what did he say? Did they find anybody? Was the deputy with him?"

"I don't know. I didn't ask him any of that shit."

"Did he say anything?"

"Yeah. He said it was coming up, right on time."

Travis was some time in trying to figure out what this meant. Balloon Dick was experiencing difficulty in starting his Jeep. The engine growled but refused to kick over.

"I don't know what he thinks he's gonna get," Robbie said.

"I'm not sure I follow you," Travis said. He was still trying to make sense out of what the kid had told him.

"What's to follow?"

"About what he's going to get."

Robbie Jones just looked at him, clutching at the roll bar above his head as Balloon Dick's Jeep came to life, lurching forward on the rutted road. Travis felt the pain run all the way up into the core of his being and fought back the urge to vomit.

"This wind," Robbie Jones yelled over the engine. "It's gonna be blown to shit. Strictly victory at sea. I could've gone with him, but I thought what the fuck."

Travis saw that he was talking about the surf.

"You mean he was going surfing," Travis asked.

"He had the boards, dude. What can I tell you? The fucker's crazy."

3 8

K endra Harmon had brightened with Fletcher's agreeing to accompany her to the cemetery. But as the day wore on and they approached the location the woman from the Orleans Grill had told them about, she grew silent and pensive once more.

They reached the trail head near midday, beneath a sky gone to the color of pearl, made luminous in two places. Fletcher took one of these for the sun. The other appeared as a kind of reflection he could not recall having seen before. The result of this illusion was such that there was not one sun but a matched pair set upon twin trajectories above a leaden sea. Fletcher called this phenomenon of the two suns to Kendra's attention as they parked among the coastal scrub at the rocky end of the road. The girl stood upon a running board, raised to her full height, as if by so doing, she would be afforded a better view of things.

"It is the job of the sun," the girl told him, "to sort out and refine the light brought to it by the moon. For this is the light made up of the souls of the dead and it has been mixed with darkness."

Fletcher had come round to her side of the truck. She was still on the running board and he was standing next to her, which made them roughly the same height. He was not exactly certain about how to respond and so said nothing.

"What's the matter?" she asked. "Am I scaring you?"

"I think I'm just coming down," he said.

"I think I'm just my father's girl," she told him.

He had no idea what she was talking about. He was looking at the trail before them. It was clearly unmaintained, a steep and rocky descent of indeterminate length, and he was beginning to wonder if either of them were really up for it. He felt compelled to point out that it was not too late to turn back.

"No, you don't," she said.

They went on after that, a long unremitting descent, through coastal scrub and manzanita, the trail nothing but gullies and loose rock that crumbled and slid beneath their feet. It was the false sun they followed here. Fletcher was certain of it and he doubted this sun capable of the kind of separating work the girl had spoken of, for he was only an imposture, a trick done with mirrors. He's like me, Fletcher thought, for it had been his job to separate the light as well, to preserve a little something for eternity, but all he had managed was to drown a boy.

There were times in the course of this hike that Fletcher believed himself to be followed, though by what or by whom he would have been hard pressed to say. The only indication that this was something other than his own paranoia came when once he turned quickly enough to catch sight of a handful of pebbles skittering across rocky soil and which, he was convinced, gave evidence of some unseen figure dogging their tracks. His thoughts went to the Indians who had taken Kendra, for she had spoke of them as men, though in fact he had only seen one at the clearing. When he raised this issue with her, however, she would only dismiss it with a wave of the hand, convinced apparently that she had cut their lifelines as she had said and that having been so crippled they posed no further threat to the living.

The trail went on, through the manzanita and thorns, passing beneath a surprise stand of redwood then coming at last into a stiff, yellowish grass. The grass was ankle high and wind bent, sprinkled with rock and bone and at its western edge one might see mists swirling up out of nothing as if they had come to the very edge of the planet. Though Fletcher supposed it was their destination they had come to, for it was clear they had arrived at land's end and he watched with some satisfaction these mists thrown up by the sea, swirling as they passed, achieving in many cases forms and shapes that only poetry, or perhaps his girl at his side, might have named. But the shapes were transitory and lost to the very winds which had spawned them.

In time they came upon many broken stones set flat against the earth. They saw pieces of old iron fences and mounds of shells bleached white yet polished like mother of pearl and Fletcher was willing to take it for that sacred place the girl had spoken of. He hoped she would find her benediction here but of course he doubted it. As for what the place held for him, he could not imagine it.

39

Travis was occupying a bed in the Sweet Home Emergency Center. He was awaiting transfer to the hospital in Eureka and watching his leg drain by way of a plastic tube run from his foot into a large plastic container marked as hazardous waste when he heard the voice of Jerry Blacklage. Travis was alone in the room and he could hear Jerry in the hall. The chief was inquiring after his health. Travis listened as the nurse spoke in hushed tones about his leg.

There was a compound fracture. An infection. Clearly he would never have made it to Neah Heads had not Drew Harmon been willing and able to carry him. He could not exactly say that he cared for owing his life to a man he did not like. But there it was. Things were as they were. He righted himself somewhat on his pillows as Blacklage walked into the room. The chief was dressed in his summer tans, complete with cap and shades, as if expecting transfer to San Diego at any moment. A man, Travis thought, of infinite hope.

"Hear you got here in Balloon Dick's Jeep," Blacklage said.

Travis allowed that he had.

"Lucky he didn't kill you."

"I got news for you. He damn near did."

Blacklage nodded without smiling. "So, what did you find out?" he asked.

"I found out there's a hell of a current runs from that bay on a minus tide."

"I figured I'd give you another day, then try and get a chopper in here to look for you."

"Another day and I would've been dead."

"So they tell me." Blacklage removed his cap and ran a hand through his hair. "I always thought it was a bad idea." He put his cap back on and looked at Travis. "What's this I hear about Harmon going off with Jim Lemon?"

"Who told you that?"

"I talked to that kid, the bald-headed one."

"Lemon was up at the Orleans Grill this morning. Jenny told him a couple of strange ones had come in, a man and a woman. Sounded like Kendra and that photographer. Drew wanted to go find out."

"I thought the girl was kidnapped by crankster gangsters from upriver."

Travis felt the blood in his face. "I don't know about that," he said. "She had to have gotten out there some way. All I know is, it looks like she's with the photographer now. It looks like they've gone off to that old cemetery north of the Heads."

"Christ. Why would they do that?"

Travis was aware of a sinking sensation in his chest.

Blacklage just looked at him. "What?" he said.

"Wrong answer, Cousin. You were supposed to say you already knew."

"How would I know that?"

"You were supposed to say Lemon had called in."

Blacklage seemed suddenly to get where Travis was going. His face darkened noticeably. "Shit," he said. "I been trying to raise Lemon on the radio all afternoon."

"That's what I was afraid of," Travis said. "That surfer you talked to saw Drew just before we left the Heads. The kid didn't ask him any- thing, naturally, but it sounded like Drew was by himself. And I sure didn't see Lemon anywhere when we were driving out of there."

"Damn," Blacklage said. He walked to the window at the side of Travis's bed. Travis craned his neck to watch. The chief seemed sud- denly quite intent upon the long northern twilight. As Travis watched a coloring sky reflected in the man's shades, he was stricken by the feeling that somehow things were even worse than he had imagined.

In time, Blacklage turned from the window. "Anybody ever tell you about the Doves hiring a private detective to look into the death of that girl?"

It was suddenly quite hot in the small room and Travis was aware of the sweat popping out along his brow, of the bed crawling beneath him. "I heard something," he said at length. "I couldn't believe there was anything to it."

"You remember Jack Lindherst?"

"Racetrack Jack?"

Blacklage stepped away from the window and removed his glasses. "He's been down in San Francisco. Put himself through some kind of detective school."

"Christ. That guy would be lucky to make rent-a-cop. You're not going to tell me that's who the Doves hired."

"Yeah, and I'll tell you something else too. The guy's managed to get the body exhumed. Apparently there was a sister somewhere. She signed some papers."

The two men looked at one another. "They found a couple of things," Blacklage said. "Seems there was some stuff in the girl's hair. Sawdust, to be exact. The deal is, it isn't just any kind of saw- dust. It's balsa and redwood."

"Drew Harmon," Travis said.

"He's the only one I know works with the stuff. It just ain't that common. There was something else too."

He turned from the window to look down on Travis. "Girl was pregnant at the time she was killed."

"They just now found that out?"

"No. The Sweet Home guys saw that when they did the autopsy. It just never got out, was all. Apparently they didn't think it was a big deal. The girl was known to be fast, and they had their man."

"Had themselves a derelict Indian."

"Yep."

"You think they were wrong?"

"I don't know what to think. They exhumed the body just last week. Racetrack's trying to get the case reopened. Apparently this sister he turned up has married into some money. So, who knows." Blacklage spread his hands. "Right now, all the Sweet Home cops want is to talk to Harmon. I mean, as far as they're concerned, it's still Marvus."

"And Lemon knows about all of this."

Blacklage was some time in answering. "Puts a new spin on things, doesn't it?"

Travis turned his face to the ceiling. The chance to clear an Indian, to hang the crime on an unpopular *wagay*. The lure might prove difficult to resist for a zealot like young Lemon. In fact, Travis could envision a particular scenario quite easily. One in which Drew Harmon wanted to head for the cemetery, while Deputy Lemon entertained visions of delivering his man to the cops of Sweet Home. One could envision an unhappy ending as well. He watched Blacklage hovering above him, certain they were partaking of the same paranoia.

"What are you going to do?" Travis asked at length.

Blacklage seated himself in a chair. "I don't know," he said. Travis suspected he'd rather be hanging out on the interstate, nursing his speed trap and dreaming of sunlit beaches. For once, Travis could not say that he blamed him.

"You're going out there, you'd better take someone with you," Travis told him.

"Who'd you have in mind?"

"How about somebody from Sweet Home? They're the one's want to talk to Drew Harmon."

"Shit, I'd rather go to the devil. They'd a done their job in the first place, maybe they wouldn'ta been so quick to hang it on Marvus."

Travis lay on his bed for some time. "Gonna be dark by time you even get out to the trail head, you know that?"

Blacklage nodded. "Yeah, but I can at least look for Lemon's car. I find it and he's not in it, I'm callin' out the feds. Let the fuckers come."

"It's possible Lemon and Harmon went down there together."

Blacklage shook his head. "Lemon would've called in, he was going to be out of touch that long. Something's fucked up."

Travis closed his eyes, listening to the distant, muffled rattle of the forced-air heating system. "There's something else you might want to keep in mind," Travis said. "You remember those Indians I told you about, from upriver? Well, I saw one of them on the rocks above the beach. He was dead. If he and the others were tracking Harmon . . . the other two might still be out there."

Blacklage stood for some time at the foot of Travis's bed. "Well," he said, finally, "I'll tell you what. The only one I'm worried about right now is Lemon. I don't find him, I'm going to the bureau."

"You know what that will mean."

"The hell with 'em," Blacklage said. "The hell with all of them."

When Blacklage was gone, Travis was left alone with his thoughts. He could not believe he had been so out of touch as to have missed hearing about the Doves hiring Racetrack Jack. He had gotten old here, he thought, old and flabby and out of touch. He had thought to stay on top of things and yet he had missed them from the beginning. And now here he was, flat on his back with a tube up his leg, while such furies as he'd hoped to contain were loosed upon the windswept bluffs somewhere north of the Devil's Hoof.

He knew the cemetery they'd all gone off to, if only by dim recollection. The last story he could recall hearing about the place was one involving a family of urban Tolowans who had gone there to scatter the ashes of their grandmother. The grandmother, it seems, had died a very old woman, and she had spent her entire life on the reservation. Her children and grandchildren, who had long ago moved to the city, had nevertheless elected to do what they considered a Native American thing. They'd had the old woman cremated and they meant to scatter her ashes upon the ocean in a sacred place. They had accordingly hiked out past the graveyard to the rocks overlooking the Pacific, but a wave had taken them, the entire family, and none were seen again. Several friends not of the immediate family had accompanied them and had witnessed this occurrence. The surf, they'd said, did not appear to be unusually large that day and the papers had referred to the culprit as a sleeper wave, that is a huge wave which might materialize suddenly out of an otherwise unremarkable sea. Travis knew the cemetery and the cliffs by dim recollection, for it had been years since he had seen it. Still, he knew the rocks in question to be a good thirty feet above the ocean.

He was still thinking about these things when his telephone began to ring. He picked it up. It was his father calling to tell him he was a fool. Travis did not dispute it.

"Guess you ain't gonna be doing much dancing this year after all," the old man told him.

"What?" Travis said. For his mind was still on the cemetery.

"The Jump Dance," his father said. "Looks like Frank was wrong after all."

His father hung up after that. It was a habit he had, of hanging up without saying good-bye. Travis replaced the receiver. In doing so, he was afforded a look at the sky beyond his window. It was quite dark now and he found in it a sudden reminder of his whereabouts on the night before, of his place on Art the Red Man's floor as Nurse Becky peered into the storm, asking if the big man who had brought him would be coming in out of the rain, and Travis had said no, and it occurred to him now, as the first full drops of rain flattened themselves upon the glass, that such indeed was the case. Drew Harmon would not be coming in again. The question, it seemed to Travis, lay only in how many others, bound perhaps by the sheer force of such a man's will, would suffer the storm in his company.

40

The girl danced. Fletcher sat on a rock and watched her. She danced before a gathering of clouds. Twirling this way and that, the khakis and flannel shirt trailing her arms and legs like flags before a tarnished sky. There were moments in which she appeared as quite exotic. A creature from another age. There were times when she appeared as simply deranged. It depended, Fletcher decided, on the light.

Eventually, she elected to stop, but it was too late to go on. Nor did Fletcher have any clear idea what was to come next. There was a kind of shelter built there, a place dug into the ground. A mound of earth had been built up around it. There were some boards on top. Grass grew on the mound. A small, circular opening permitted access.

Kendra said it had been once used as a sweat lodge. There was a circle of rocks inside and the walls, made of cedar and covered with slabs of bark, were blackened with soot.

The afternoon brought rain. Kendra and Fletcher hunkered in the darkness of the earthen room. There was no food and in time he held her as he had before, his hand flat against her stomach. He thought of asking her if the dancing had changed anything, if she had found the blessing she required, but her silence prevented him. She had gotten tired. That was all.

At some point late in the day the rain backed off though the sky remained dark over the ocean. Kendra went once more to the edge of the land where it curled off in a grassy point like a question mark placed above the sea.

Fletcher could see her there, arms outstretched. He saw her spin before the darkening sky. He saw the spray thrown up from the sea below. There were rainbows caught in these plumes of spray and the grass about her feet was green and bathed in the last light where it slipped from among the clouds and fell upon the land.

He was seated on his haunches at the door of the hole and wondering if he ought to go down by the cliff lest the girl stray too close to the edge when he saw the figure moving toward him out of the mist. Again he thought of the men who had stalked them above the cliff and he started. Quickly, however, he saw that this was not the case. For the man had moved closer and he saw that it was Drew Harmon. Fletcher's relief was short lived. Given Kendra's story, one might take the arrival of either as bad news.

One might, of course, doubt her story. Fletcher's inclination was to believe that she had called it. In either case, there was little to do save sit there and he watched as Harmon came on. He looked for Robbie Jones but it appeared as if the big man had come alone. He moved much as Fletcher had seen him on that first day, coming to meet them on the bluffs overlooking the river mouth, with a certain stiffness to his gait, in a dripping parka. He had a pair of board bags slung over one shoulder and a large nylon stuff bag over the other and this was his only gear. When he saw Fletcher hunkered before the sweat lodge he stopped. For a moment the two men simply stared at one another across the wind bent grass. Eventually Harmon altered his course and started up the slope.

"What's the matter," Harmon called. "You get lost?"

The big man was still some yards away. Fletcher did not answer. He got to his feet, then pointed in the direction of the sea.

Harmon hesitated, then turned to look. When he saw what Fletcher was pointing at he dropped his gear and ran. Fletcher watched. He saw Kendra catch sight of her husband. He saw her turn and run back for a ways along the edge of the cliff. He saw Drew follow, then stop, silouetted before the sky. The man seemed to beckon. The woman to hold back. For a time, it seemed to Fletcher that they moved this way, as if in dance.

In the end, Drew caught her up in his arms and carried her as one might a child to where Fletcher waited by the hole. He carried her inside and laid her down. After that he came back to the front of the shelter where Fletcher sat. He opened a board bag, removed one of the long wooden guns and set about filling the bag with handfuls of grass. Fletcher went to help. They worked in silence. When they were done, Drew took the bag inside, presumably for Kendra to lie on.

The brief period of sunlight and rainbows was gone. The darkness had come and, with it, the rain. As Fletcher waited, he noticed the stuff bag Drew had carried still sitting some ways down the slope, and he went to retrieve it. The bag was only partially zipped, and as Fletcher lifted it, he could see there was a gun inside. He believed it to be a .357 Magnum, silver with a black grip. It was sheathed in a black holster attached to a black belt, and the whole rig had a very official look about it. Fletcher was quite sure it was some kind of police issue. He was equally certain that Drew had not carried it on the long hike up the coast. He supposed that some story was contained in the appearance of this object just now, but if this was so, he could not say that he was in any great hurry to hear it. He would wait, he decided, for the light of day, though it occurred to him that if things went badly, he might not hear it at all.

It also occurred to him that he might take the gun for himself, though this might prove a tricky business, as he and Drew were now within sight of one another, the big man having set himself to starting a fire near the mouth of the lodge. Nor could he quite see himself drawing down on Drew Harmon. In the end, Fletcher elected to help with the fire. He placed the bag before the doorway then went about delivering his own sorry offering of damp sticks and driftwood, out of which, through some woodsman's skill Fletcher could do little more than admire, a garden of yellow flame had soon blossomed beneath Harmon's hand to contend with the darkness.

When the fire was lit to his satisfaction, Drew Harmon seized the stuff bag containing the gun and pulled it into the sweat lodge, then retired to the rear. Fletcher remained outside. No one had asked him to. Nor had he been asked to leave. He might have run, hoping to gain the trail head and the battered Dodge. Honor, he believed, dictated some form of vigil, though to what point he maintained it, or to what end it might come, it was not so easy to say. There was the distinct possibility that all three of them would die here. Kendra first, then Fletcher. In the end, he supposed Drew would turn the gun on himself. It was what you heard on the evening news. The way it went.

And so he waited, his parka drawn about him, the rain tattooing his shoulders and skull, though, from time to time, he would turn to the room for a glimpse of some dim movement therein. He could see no more than that, as the lodge was low and long, with much of the rear left in darkness. Nor could he tell with any certainty if two people were moving about back there or only one. The rain and wind were such that any sounds which might have originated in those shadows were lost to him, the movement rendered all the more mysterious in their absence.

He might, he thought, have been swept back in time, made witness to whatever rites this structure had been built to house in the first place, and he would have known no more of those hieratic gestures than he did of these, yet they would have seemed no less mysterious, no less rife with concealed meaning.

In time, however, the movement stopped, and after more time, Drew Harmon came out of the hole and stood before Fletcher, but with his eyes averted, his face to the storm. Fletcher rose himself, for he had been seated before the door.

"She wants something," Drew said.

"What?"

"I don't know," Drew told him. His voice was quite grave. "She wants you."

Fletcher went into the room. It was not high enough to stand in. He went on all fours, crawling to the back. The girl was there, lying on the bag. He had no idea of what to expect. She seemed at rest, though her face was bathed in sweat, and when she opened her eyes to look at him, he saw, even in the shadowy light, that they were ringed with dark circles yet lit with some pale inner fire.

"I think I might try one of those pills now," she said.

Fletcher was not immediately sure about what to say. He supposed he had been expecting something more dramatic. Perhaps he had hoped to be made privy to that which had thus far transpired. But apparently such was not to be.

He fumbled in the pocket of his parka, producing the plastic vial, removing the cap.

Kendra held out a hand. He could feel her fingers brush his wrist. He tapped a pill into her palm.

"Maybe I should have one of each," she said.

Fletcher smiled. Apparently she was more observant than he had imagined.

She had brought herself to one elbow and was watching him.

"I don't know," he said finally. "You think the shamans took pills?"

"I think the shamans were chumps," she told him.

Fletcher gave her the second pill. She washed them down with water they'd purchased at the Orleans Grill, then lay back down and closed her eyes. Fletcher felt that he should say more but he didn't. Nothing suitable would present itself nor would she look at him again, and, in the end, he went back to the door and out into the rain.

Drew Harmon was hunkered there, the water dripping from his T-shirt, for the parka had been cast aside. He held something in his hands, and as Fletcher knelt beside him, he saw that it was an eight-inch diver's knife. First a gun, now the knife, though in fact Fletcher had seen this article before, as Drew had used it from time to time along the beaches to whittle kindling or to scrape something of interest from a stone. He seemed now to be testing the edge with his thumb. "What was all that about?" he asked.

"She wanted a pill."

"You give her one?"

"I gave her two. They should make her sleep."

Drew Harmon looked at him for some time. "She's been through shit," he said.

"Yes, she has."

"That was foolish of me to leave that note. She says she cut their lifelines."

"I wouldn't know about that. The only one I saw was killed in a shoot-out with some other guys up one of the rivers we passed. I had the feeling she had gotten him to walk into something."

"A trap?"

"That's what it looked like. They were all dead when I got there. Everybody but her."

"Must've been that valley, where she got chased by the dogs." He turned to his knife. "That was a hell of a thing to do," he said.

"Yes, it was."

Harmon was silent, examining the knife as if it was an object of great mystery. The image recalled Kendra's story—the local girl found on the floor of her trailer, a death by cutting. Kendra had said she could see how it might have happened, and, in fact, Fletcher could see this too. He had, after all, been in the room that night in Waikiki. He had seen the bouncer thrown from the roof.

The act had always struck him as more careless than malicious—the reckless behavior of a golden child, with the bouncer's water landing just one more indicator of Harmon's luck. But that was all changed now, with the ticket come due up some dark alley in a nothing little town. It would not have surprised Fletcher to learn that the girl had died of a broken neck, of a careless slap thrown too hard, caught at a bad angle, that the cutting had come later—a misguided afterthought in those seconds following the realization that something irrevocable had gone down. And yet even then it must have seemed to Harmon as if his luck would hold. An Indian was busted, then found dead. There must have been a moment in which Drew thought it behind him, an aberration. At which point his wife had found the board and begun to wear the dead girl's clothes and Drew had gone to the well one more time, looking to trade on the past, to sell the boards and disappear into Chile, the myth intact. But now that scheme had failed him as well, leaving Fletcher to wonder at what could possibly come next and to what extent the luck had run out for them all.

"Tell me," Drew said. "You think before you die, there'll be a shining light?"

"I don't know," Fletcher said.

"But you've thought about it?"

"Of late, yes."

Drew laughed at him. "I ever tell you I was born in Sweet Home?"

"No, you didn't."

"Well, I was. My mom got herself knocked up by some logger. When she saw the guy wasn't going to marry her, she headed for L.A. I think she thought she was going to make it in pictures." He laughed at that. "She made it in the bars instead. I never went to school. She didn't give a shit. I drifted down to the South Bay, discovered the ocean. Pretty soon there were people paying me to ride their boards."

"I remember that part," Fletcher said. "The rest is history."

Harmon just looked at him. "Yeah," he said finally. "And now I've come home." At which point, he stood up.

Fletcher rose with him. The moment seemed to demand it. For a moment, Drew looked at him, as if his presence there was suddenly quite unexpected. "Dr. Fun," Drew said. And then he was past. It seemed to Fletcher that the big man brushed his shoulder with his own. Fletcher turned. He saw Drew Harmon duck and go into the sweat lodge once more.

Fletcher felt his knees go suddenly quite weak. He could not say if it was because he had just survived something or if he was about to witness something. Nothing would have surprised him at that moment. There could have been a gunshot, or a scream. He had no idea what he would do in these circumstances. He only knew that he would not be surprised by them. It occurred to him for the second time that night that he might run. He might enter the room himself. He might do any number of things. What he did was stand in the rain, rooted to that soggy soil before the dripping house as surely as if he had been planted there.

Time passed. The fire in the doorway had all but gone out. Fletcher took up a position near the opening. If there were to be sounds of distress, they would not pass unheard upon the wind. But the night was silent save for the patter of the rain, and when, on occasion he would turn to peer into the sweat lodge, there was little to see but shadow.

There was, however, a single exception to this routine, a moment in which, by accident or design, his turning was set in concert with a sudden flaring of the meager fire, its flames fanned perhaps by a gust of wind before settling back into little more than glowing embers. And it was by this light that Fletcher caught sight of an odd tableau, one which seemed, perhaps because of its strangeness, to be conveyed as if by reflection—an image blurred upon an imperfect mirror—for what he saw was Drew Harmon. The man appeared to be on one knee, his head bowed. His back was to the doorway. Kendra was seated almost in front of him. One hand was placed upon the mat they had made for her, as if to steady herself. The other appeared to rest on the back of her husband's head.

Fletcher looked away. The light flickered and went out. It was their moment. Not a thing to be witnessed. And yet, even as he turned from it, it seemed to him as if some accommodation had been reached, though how this could be or at what cost it had been procured he could not guess. He knew only that it spoke to him of blood and recompense. And in thinking these things, alone and in the rain, he found himself quite suddenly thrown back upon his own ties to this unlikely chunk of rock, to a father long since laid to rest, to a distant mother, an ex-wife, a daughter waiting somewhere miles away through the night. And he wondered at what accommodations there might be reached, and for what sins he might yet be called upon to atone. He witnessed a dark-haired boy in red flannel going before the wind, then, drawing the hood of his parka tightly about his head, managed, in that soggy night, to procure for himself a little sleep. He slept as might a soldier in the field, in the face of a storm, at rest before an uncertain morning.

41

The day broke cool and crisp. A light breeze carried the scent of pine, suggesting high pressure inland, an offshore flow. Fletcher felt it upon his cheek. He opened his eyes to a thin band of color spreading above the coastal range to the east.

The sweat lodge was quiet. Turning to look inside, Fletcher found that someone had hung a towel across the opening. At the edges of this article, there was nothing to be seen save blackness. He rose slowly, stiff to the core. Water ran from tiny pools which had collected in the folds of his parka. He was shaking it out when he saw someone walking toward him across the grass. He started, but quickly realized that it was Drew. The man wore a T-shirt, jeans and boots. The clothes were wet and muddied, all of a color in the early light. His long hair was wet and matted, his beard as well. Moving up through the ankle-high grass, he might have passed for something not altogether human. Fletcher watched as the big man moved steadily toward him through the old cemetery.

"Check it out," Drew said, as if he'd fully expected to find Fletcher up and ready for some new adventure. "We got offshores. And guess what else?"

Fletcher felt it then. The waves. Somewhere close they were breaking. One felt their detonations through the ground, as if great pieces of machinery were rumbling across the grassy bluffs. He might have been twelve years old, camping on the beach at Salt Creek. The call was the same. The taste of old metal at the back of one's throat.

Except, of course, that he wasn't twelve, and Salt Creek was a long time gone. He had no idea how long he had slept, or at what point Drew had gone past him to wander the bluffs; probably, he supposed, not much before first light.

"How is she?" Fletcher asked.

Harmon stopped, looking at him as if the question was in some way a surprising one. "She had just woken up when I left," he said, finally. "She was looking around for more of those pills you gave her."

Drew had reached him by now. The two men stood before the lodge as the first rays of sunlight splintered upon the black face of a rocky peak.

"I've just been down to look," Drew said. "Those reefs I told you about, north of the Hoof. You can't quite see the breaks from here but you can see what's out there, corduroy to the horizon." By which he meant swell lines, which, in turn, would mean waves, and, yet, there was, Fletcher thought, an odd note in Drew's voice. It was as if the man were asking, rather than telling, pleading perhaps, that Fletcher share this moment with him, share his enthusiasm for offshore flows and blue corduroy and secret spots, as if, by so doing, the two of them might turn back the hands of time. Just a kid from the South Bay and one from old HB, high on waves, without regrets.

Fletcher was not unmoved. It was simply unclear to him at this point just how much he had to give, and how much was gone forever. "I'd like to see her," he said.

Drew made no answer. He went to the big stuff bag which had been placed outside once more. Fletcher could see there were wet suits inside, and something else as well, the old Minolta in the water housing with which he had shot R.J. and Drew Harmon at the place they had dubbed Thunder Bay. Then he turned and went inside.

Kendra was indeed awake. She had laced her fingers behind her head and drawn up her knees. She turned as Fletcher made his way to the back of the room. "Got any more of those pills?" she asked.

"You should take it easy with those," he said. "Don't take any more until we get you some real food."

"There's waves," she said. "Drew will want to surf. He'll want you to take pictures."

"I don't think he needs them now."

She said a strange thing to him then. "He needs you," she said.

Fletcher was not sure what to say, but then the girl saved him from it. "I know," she said. "But I think you should. It will mean something to him to have you there." She looked to the ceiling, leaving Fletcher to contemplate afresh the little tableau he had seen by the firelight, if, in fact, he had not dreamed it. But then, of course, one did not ask about such things. Not even Fletcher who, after all, had been made privy to more than he would ever have bargained for in setting out from Los Angeles in the company of Sonny Martin and Robbie Jones. He could not have guessed then the nature of what he would be asked to witness here, or the part he would take in it, for surely he had taken one. He was a player now and it seemed to him as if one more thing was about to be exacted. He listened to the distant muffled explosions of big waves. In the early light beyond the door, he could see Drew Harmon struggling into a wet suit.

"I'll be okay," she told him. She said this in response to a question he had yet to ask. "And anyway, it won't be for long."

"There isn't much film."

"See."

He was about to leave when she put a hand on his arm. "You asked me something once," she said. "Or maybe you didn't. I can't remember now, but then I guess it doesn't make any difference anyway."

"I have no idea what you're talking about," he said.

"That guy in the red long-johns, where you found me. You

wanted to know, I believe, what he was up to. I saw you looking. That was it. I saw you with that hose, trying to figure something out. Am I right?"

"Jesus," he said. "What a thing to remember."

"Am I right?" she asked.

"I suppose so."

He could feel her fingers, exerting a new pressure upon his arm. "It's in the trees," she said. "The money is in the trees. And I don't want you to forget it. Now can I have a couple of those pills?"

He gave them to her, then leaned forward to kiss her forehead.

"It won't be long," he said.

"I know," she said.

Drew was waiting for him on the grass. The wooden guns were there too. They rested on their decks, side by side. One was the board Harmon had ridden throughout the trip, the other was the one Fletcher had ridden in the little cove, on the evening of the second day. Harmon was suited up by now. He was holding the old Minolta and when Jack Fletcher walked up to him, he held it out for Fletcher to take.

"There's something I've been meaning to say to you, Doc," Drew said. "That movie of yours. Tits on a bull." He grinned as Fletcher took the camera. "Tool of your trade. The rest of it's bullshit."

Fletcher stood with the camera in his hands, the sun breaking above his back. It was clear to him that if he was to get pictures, he would have to do so as he had at the bay, from the deck of the board, and he looked at it now—ten feet of balsa and redwood, at rest in the rain-wet grass. He could not say that he was unafraid. He supposed that without the protection of the Devil's Hoof, the sea would be more turbulent here, the beaches more exposed. He had not been out in rough water since the drowning of the boy, and he had nearly drowned then himself. Drew seemed to pick up on what he was thinking. "You can shoot this place from the rocks, if you want to, Doc. 'Course you won't get much—"

Fletcher interrupted him. "How many wet suits you bring in that bag?"

"Should be two left. Yours and Robbie's."

Fletcher nodded. As Drew watched, he pulled one of the suits from the bag and set about dismantling it with a pocket knife.

Harmon watched him with great interest.

"Had this idea once," Fletcher told him, "a long time ago. Seems like now's as good a time as any to try it out." It was his intention to use the body of the suit like a big rubber band, to hold the camera to the deck of the board. It would save him from having to hold it with his chin, providing him with a better position from which to paddle.

When Harmon saw what he was up to, his face broke into a ragged grin. "And they told me you were all washed up," he said.

Fletcher slipped the piece of rubber onto the board, then slid the camera beneath it—a good, tight fit—and when he had done that he took off his clothes and struggled into a clammy wet suit and got to his feet to face Drew Harmon. He stuck the board beneath his arm, feeling its weight, the edge of its rail against the palm of his hand. "Fuck 'em," he said. "Let's go surfing."

The morning went before them, giving light to the sky. The air, washed by the rains, was filled with the scent of wet earth and the closeness of the sea.

"You know you can't always believe what she tells you," Drew said. He was not looking at Fletcher when he spoke and Fletcher did not answer. They continued, side by side, eyes fixed upon the sky at the edge of the bluffs.

"It's not exactly her fault. Men have not always been so good to her. She ever tell you about her old man?"

Fletcher started to say no, then checked himself. "She said something about being her father's girl," he said.

"Yeah, she thinks that. At least, I think that's what she thinks. It's not always easy to know. At any rate, the man spent his days in and out of the loony bin, as near as I can tell. He used to take Kendra to seances. She was a little kid, for Christ's sake. Even had her exorcised once. I asked her what that was like. She told me they got her bag of tricks." Drew shook his head as he walked. "She's funny," he said. "You've got to give her that."

"She's more than funny," Fletcher said.

Harmon seemed to give this some thought. At length, he nod-ded. "Yeah, she is," he said. "Anyway, when the old man wasn't in the nuthouse, or going to seances, he liked to chase women and gamble."

"So he wasn't all bad."

"He had his good points. He lost, of course, heavily. Eventually he got himself between a rock and a hard place. Apparently, it had come down to a race. Who would get to him first. The men in white jackets, or the knee breakers. So one night, he tells the wife he's going out to the barn to feed the horse. What he does is eat a shot-gun. When he doesn't come back, Kendra goes outside to look. She finds him in the barn. She was twelve at the time. The next one, her stepdad—I guess he was some kind of perv. The old lady could really pick them. I'd'a known that at the time, I would've offed the little weasel myself."

"How did you meet her?"

Drew did not respond right away. It was as if he held the time in question up to his mind's eye that he might examine it for a moment without comment. "I was doing some East Coast promo-tional stuff," he said finally. "I was looking for a boat. I'd heard about some surf that required one. Her stepfather had one to rent. I went to look at it. There she was. Tell you the truth, I think she just went out with me to piss off the old man."

They had come now to the end of the grass and Drew led them into a steep gorge filled with brush and a particular species of stunted pine, shaped in accordance with the wind, and the ocean lay visible before them, its ridged surface like a great piece of corru-gated blue metal laid flat at the foot of the cliffs. For a moment, both men paused to look at it.

"I guess I should ask you something," Drew said. "She told me about you two spending the night in some shed. Anything happen there I ought to know about?"

"She wanted me to hold her."

"Put your hand on her stomach. Here." He placed a hand on his own. Fletcher nodded.

Drew nodded as well. "You fall in love with her?" he asked.

Fletcher gave it some thought. "I suppose I did."

Harmon looked at him, then laughed. "I got to tell you, Doc. I always have admired your lack of judgment."

"Well," Fletcher said. "I suppose every man wants to be admired, as he gets on in life."

"Come on, Doc. I'm on your side. You must know Peters wanted to send someone else. You know why I made 'em send you, don't you?"

Fletcher supposed the answer would be forthcoming.

"Take a look around you, homes. Sonny's gone. Robbie's gone." Harmon laughed once more. There was nothing mean-spirited about it. It was just the way you laugh sometimes, when you see a thing for what it is. "Take a look at who's still here. These other pissants . . ." He looked toward the sea, dismissing them with a wave of the hand. "All they care about is the check."

"A check would be nice," Fletcher said.

Drew Harmon just looked at him. "Shit, Doc, you wouldn't know what to do with a check if you had one, and neither would I."

They went on after that, a final steep descent which was more of a climb than a hike. As they went along this part of the trail—if, in fact, one could call it by such a name—Fletcher noticed for the first time that Drew had strapped the diver's knife he had till now carried in a pack onto the calf of one leg. He had not seen Drew wear this article into the water before and could not imagine what use he had for it now, unless perhaps he intended to dive for his supper before returning to the beach. Fletcher came close to asking him about it, but they had come to a particularly treacherous part of the descent, and by the time they reached a flat rock overlooking a narrow sandy beach, his attention was focused on the sea below and he had forgotten about the knife.

It was a break of stark but not uncommon beauty, a shallow bay ringed by granite. Drew Harmon seemed to view it with great enthusiasm, proclaiming it the queen of the coast.

Fletcher saw only a horseshoe-shaped inlet, perhaps a mile across, half a mile deep, at whose outermost edge swell lines could be seen bending themselves across the point. In fact, they had been watching such lines for the last two legs of their descent, seductive undulations of the ocean's surface, dappled in sunlight, the product of a warmer clime. Seen from closer quarters, however, one might discover just what became of these lines as they found the reef and it was not, Fletcher believed, a pretty sight. He saw them now for what they were—cold and unforgiving, dull mounds of dark green water, as if the very cliffs had somehow made union with the sea and which offspring were then loosed, hissing and crashing, upon the glassy waters of the rocky inlet. Fletcher supposed he made a sound of some sort. He could not rightly say what it was. He was aware of the big man, smiling at his side.

"Thar she blows," Drew said. "It doesn't get much prettier."

Fletcher looked at the rocks and the waves that broke there. He did not reckon them any bigger than what they had seen at the river mouth. Perhaps not as big and if there was any doubt left in his mind as to the veracity of Kendra's story, the sight of the break before him served to dispel it. For if this was being presented to him as the end of their journey, it was clear to him that the journey had never been about the place. It had been about the past, or something in it, and would come to no end one could rightly call by that name.

The trail continued to the beach. As they passed along it, Drew offered instruction as to currents and line-ups, the position of rocks. They went out together, pushing through the shore break, angling across smoked glass as the outside sets caught the first rays of light, shimmering as they rose and stretched, wanting only someone to ride them to make them real.

They paddled side by side for a short distance, then separated, each finding the line-ups suitable to his purpose. The waves came on like two-story buildings making twenty knots. They hooked around the point, mirroring the granite walls, exploding upon the glassy flats.

Fletcher soon became engrossed in what he was about, the thrill of the hunt settling upon him once more, and, in fact, he could not say that he was sorry he had come. It was only the death of the boy he regretted, and he saw then how it would be. There would be recompense, and there would be work. The landscape itself suggested them and he turned his camera to the waves. He saw them framed by granite cliffs, their steel gray faces finding reflection upon the sea.

The sky broke to a pale blue as Fletcher watched Drew Harmon catch his first wave. He saw the man stroking down the face of mirrored wall, saw him jump to his feet in a single fluid motion set in contrast to the way Fletcher had seen him move on dry land. He sighted through his lens as the surfer drew out the kind of deep, carving bottom turn which had once been a signature move, and was still a thing of beauty, perfectly timed and executed. In fact, all of his moves were done with precision and power. There were no lip bashes or floaters, none of the maneuvers worked out to score points in surfing contests and even though these waves were a little big for such items one could see that such was not the man's style. It was too pure and too clean for the admittance of cheap theatrics and there was something about it which broke Fletcher's heart to see. It was a statement, a last will and testament written on the watery face of the world and there were none there to witness save for Fletcher himself and he was humbled in its presence for it was the thing itself.

Fletcher shot through the first big drop and turn. He stroked a few yards to his left, wanting a better position as the wave lined up on an inside bowl. He focused quickly as Drew set up for the section and it seemed to him a good sign, as if the two of them were in sync. He sighted through the lens and yet even as he began to shoot, he saw Drew Harmon fall. He went off his inside rail into the face of the wave and Fletcher thought it an odd miscue, both in place and in attitude, and he saw clearly that having thus fallen the surfer was sucked cleanly up the face and deposited over the falls. At which point a sharp cracking noise rang out, echoing across the water, caught between the walls of stone and as Fletcher heard it he knew what it was, without doubt, without confirmation. He knew what it was and he knew why Harmon had fallen. He had fallen because he had been shot.

42

Kendra was in the sweat lodge. She was going through the men's clothes when she found Drew's book. She had given up dancing. Those little pills the Doctor had given her were the ticket and she meant to have some more. And then she found the book. She laid it aside at first and went back to looking through the clothes. At last, she found what she was looking for in the pocket of Jack Fletcher's parka. Unhappily there were only three left. She took them for herself. She assumed there were more where those came from and though the Doctor might be mad when he found them gone, she was sure he would forgive her. He was a kind heart, she thought. He would know. When she had taken them, she picked up the book and sat with it at the doorway to the smoke-house, in the early light.

She could not say she was surprised by what she found, not in light of what had transpired. Nor could she say that she was not

moved. For it was all right there. She found it in his careful notations, in his descriptions of places and waves, in his listings of tides
and intervals, of boards ridden, of companions, when there were
companions to be had. It was all there, for someone with eyes to
see. For Drew had logged today's entry as well. And he had logged it
beforehand, in the hours before dawn.

He had camped, he said, with his wife and Jack Fletcher, an old
friend and photographer, in the cemetery north of Neah Heads.
The swell was a strong one, generated by a large winter storm showing intervals of twenty-five seconds. It had been preceded by a small
depression which had given them rain throughout the night but
which he expected gone by morning. He was pleased that he was
among friends, for he intended this as his last session. He regretted
that he would be unable to provide details afterward, for he
believed it would be an epic morning and he intended to ride as
many waves as possible. He was riding a new board on which he had
drawn in the tail and moved his fin and he was looking forward to
seeing how these changes might affect the handling characteristics
of his design in waves of some respectability. It was at this point that
Kendra Harmon heard the first shot.

From the smokehouse, she crossed the grass and came to the
trail. She reached the cliffs and looked down on the glassy water
and she could see the two surfers and she could see the other thing
as well, the dark shape which circled.

She heard a second shot and saw below her the short skinny
Indian, the boy with the rifle she had not considered much of a
threat. He had his back to her and before he could fire again, she
dug a stone out of the ground and threw it at him.

It hit him between the shoulder blades, and when he turned and
saw her on the trail above him, his face twisted and he stepped
backward toward the precipice. She picked up more rocks and went
down the trail throwing. It did not occur to her that she might be
shot. Some of the rocks missed. Some found their mark. The boy
ran. He was headed uphill now, in the direction of the cemetery
though by no discernable trail. He ran through the rocks and scrub,

stumbling as he ran. Kendra watched him. She saw him hit the grass and that was where Sheriff Blacklage found him as well.

Kendra could see both of them from where she stood. She saw the young man raise his rifle. She saw the sheriff draw his gun. She watched as both men fired and missed. The sheriff came on, the boy too, both firing and missing, and when they were close enough to hit one another with spit, she saw the sheriff come up alongside the boy's head with his .45, and she saw the boy crumple like a leaf in the wind.

The thought which occurred to her then was that she had seen him live when she should have seen him dead. She had cut his life-line and he was still alive, leaving her to conclude that perhaps it had not been her after all. Maybe it had all been dumb luck. Or maybe she had found what she came for. She had found the other pain and it was Drew's. At which point, she was stricken and turned to the sea. But she could not abide what she saw there. She swayed with the wind, dizzy with pills, with want of food. If she wanted to, she thought, she could just let herself go. The wind would take her. It would do with her what it would, and it was consequently with some degree of will that she determined it to be otherwise. Her life was on the land. The sea was behind her.

43

Fletcher saw Drew Harmon one more time. He saw him back on his board, paddling in a curiously broken motion. He saw something else as well, ahead of Drew. He saw two sea lions in a big hurry, their sleek heads breaking the surface of the water. The animals were traveling fast enough to generate small V-shaped wakes. Fletcher was looking at the wakes when something bumped his board, and though he had never felt the likes of it, he knew instinctively just what it was.

For a moment, he remained locked in place. The shark, drawn no doubt by the scent of blood, had come to check him out. Fletcher had two choices. Paddle or float. As he could not quite bring himself to put his arms in the water, he did the latter. A choice by default. He waited as some dim primordial intelligence circled unseen in the depths below, then watched, as Drew Harmon disappeared without a trace.

A set wave thundered on the bay. Drew reappeared, clinging to the deck of his board, man and board springing up from the depths like a cork loosed from the bottom of a bowl. White water made pink with blood arced in rainbird patterns before the sky. A dorsal fin appeared in the water between Fletcher and Drew. The dorsal was about two feet high. And then the shark rose. The great hump of his back appeared. Fletcher saw the water parting before it, white-capped ripples trailing in its wake. For a moment, the shark swam directly at him. Suddenly it turned, showing him a portion of jaw. A great, unblinking eye. It rolled toward him and then away, a blinding 180-degree turn. He saw the flash of a tail. He raised a forearm, caught the blow and was knocked from his board.

He thought it would take him then. He opened his eyes to an icy grayness, awaiting the strike. There was nothing. He floated to the surface. The wooden gun was floating nearby. He reached it with a stroke and pulled himself back onto the deck, still waiting to feel it, the death grip on a leg, the thing that would take him. The sea was empty. Nothing but sunlight on water. There were no dorsals. There was no sign of Drew Harmon, or of his board. It was as if it had never been.

He heard the explosion of a wave close at hand. He turned to find this play with the shark had left him dangerously close to the impact zone. He watched as a huge wave feathered and broke. A line of white water head-high rumbled toward him. There was no fighting it. No pushing under or through. He could let it roll him, or he could turn toward the beach in the hope of running with it, which was what he did. He shoved as much of the board as he could out in front of him, so as to keep the nose from the water, and clung to the rails well back of the midpoint.

The white water hit him in a explosion of light and cold. It pounded his back, driving his ribs into the board but propelling him forward with great speed, giving him to understand that he had been far enough out front, that he would ride it toward the beach.

He pulled himself forward on the board, fairly skimming over the water now, the rough stuff behind him, the beach drawing close and, in time, he could feel the white water loosen its grip. He could sprint paddle now, over the inside bar and into the trough which ran along the beach, just short of dry sand. In light of what had just transpired, it was no doubt the thing to do. The course of prudent behavior. He put the board up on one rail and rolled, allowing the white water to roll on past him. He righted himself and looked back toward the horizon and the place from which he had come.

There was still white water foaming around him. The sky was washed in light, filled with the mist generated by the power of the waves. Distant lines wrapped around the point and peeled toward the beaches below the cliffs. There was still no sight of Drew Harmon. No indication of anyone paddling toward the shore. Fletcher looked toward the cliffs but there was nothing there to see. He pulled the camera from its rubber pocket where, quite miraculously, it had remained, held to the deck of the board. He pointed toward the cliffs, scanning with the lens. Nothing there save brush and stone.

He had a decision to make then. He did not think he would see Drew Harmon again. But he could not be sure. He could not be sure the man was not out there, rolling the sets, looking for help. He could not be sure the shark was not out there either. Nor could he be sure whoever had fired on them was not still on the cliffs. He might be shot. Or he might be bitten. For that matter he might lose his board and drown. The trouble was, if he didn't look, he would always wonder. The boy on his conscience was enough, and, in the end, it was that image that drove him, the dark-haired boy in his red flannel shirt, alone on the face of the wave. He made one trip to the beach, to deposit the extra wet suit and camera, and having done this, he picked up the big balsa gun with the redwood stringers cut from the hearts of the ancient trees and paddled with it for all he was worth, pushing it through the shore break, then angling toward the waves and the distant reef and whatever else he might find.

He circled there for an hour, in the cold, rolling waves, pushing through the outside sets, then paddling back in. He called Drew's name but was never answered. There was no shark. And no more shots. The morning was still, and he was alone with the waves.

He was met on the bluffs by a portly Indian. The man sported military tans and aviator shades. He carried, Fletcher noticed, the gun and belt Drew had left in the sweat lodge. "There was nothing I could do," the man said. "The girl told me about the shark."

They went in silence across the grass. The cop did not mention the gun and neither did Fletcher. When they had come within sight of the sweat lodge, Fletcher broke into a run, but he found the room empty and the girl gone. He saw that she had been into his pills. The plastic vial lay empty on top of his parka. There was something else on the parka as well. Drew's black notebook. Clearly the girl had placed it there for him to find. For the moment, he left it where it lay and went outside.

He spent a long time there, walking, circling the land as he'd circled on the water below, a long time among those dead, with the waves pounding the rocks and the air filled with their spray, and he threw his voice upon the wind until he had no voice left to throw. The cop watched him from a distance, as if he were some curiosity, or something better left alone. Fletcher himself was reminded of the scripture Drew had cited. The madman among the tombs. He was that man, he thought, or would become so. And when his last calls had gone unanswered, on land as on sea, he went back into the sweat lodge and peeled off the wet suit. He dried and dressed, picked up the black book and left. The cop was waiting. "You ready?" he asked.

Fletcher nodded. He picked up the balsa-wood gun he had carried for so far along the beaches and the two men went in silence once more, coming in a short while to the stand of redwood where, much to Fletcher's amazement, a beat-up Jeep Wrangler with huge tires and full roll-cage sat just north of the trees.

"Couldn't get it through these things," the cop told him. At which point, Fletcher saw the boy handcuffed to the Jeep by way of the roll cage. He was a short, skinny Indian, with a stocking cap and two black eyes. No more than 120 pounds soaking wet. Fletcher asked if this was the man who had shot Drew Harmon, and the sheriff told him it was.

The plump cop who identified himself as Jerry Blacklage, Chief of the Tribal Police on the lower Klamath, drove Fletcher and the boy who had shot Drew Harmon and was apparently known as Bean Dip back along the trail Fletcher had hiked the previous day with Kendra Harmon. Fletcher would not have thought this even possible, but the cop managed it with a skill one would not have imagined from his appearance.

Upon reaching the northern trail head, Fletcher saw that the old Dodge was gone. He had never thought to look for the keys, and when he did so now, he found his pockets empty. He said nothing about it and the cop drove on, though once upon the logging road, the man made the observation that the girl must have taken the truck.

"I guess so," Fletcher said.

"I don't suppose you would know where?"

Fletcher said that he did not and they rode in silence after that, though from time to time, some sound could be heard coming from the boy in the back. It seemed to Fletcher the boy was crying but he did not care to look.

They reached Sweet Home late that afternoon. Blacklage drove directly to the tribal center. He pulled in next to Fletcher's van, which was parked at the rear of the building.

"You can sleep in it where it is, if you want to," Blacklage told him. "I got to do some paperwork on this one, then run him into town."

Fletcher nodded and got out. He set about untying the big balsa gun from the roll cage where they had carried it. "Thanks," he said. "I'll see about getting some tires in the morning."

"Other than that and the windows, the thing's okay. You're lucky," Blacklage told him.

Fletcher was not feeling particularly lucky, but he thanked him again. He put the board under his arm and carried it to his van. He was still there a short time later, sweeping the glass from the interior, when Chief Blacklage called to him. Fletcher looked up to see the man standing slightly above him, on the wooden deck which ringed the big A-framed building.

"I imagine this belongs to you," Blacklage said.

The chief was holding something out in front of him, and as he came down the steps, Fletcher could see it was the old Nikon in the orange housing. He did not immediately reach to take it, but stood for some time, staring at it with no small degree of wonder. "How . . ." he began, but the cop cut him short.

"I don't know," Blacklage said. "We went down to see the Zodiac. I found some kid running around on the beach with it. It must have washed up."

"I don't see how that could be."

The chief shrugged, as if he had little interest in how such a thing could be. It had and that was all there was. It only remained for Fletcher to claim what was his.

Fletcher took the housing. Some of the duct tape was frayed where he imagined it had tumbled over the rocks. When he looked inside, however, he saw that the camera and film was still in place.

"I wonder," he said, "if there is a phone I might use?"

Blacklage nodded. He led him into the tribal center, where, after only two calls, he was able to locate a lab in Eureka able to process his film. He thanked the chief, signed for his camera and vehicle and left. He passed the kid in the Jeep for the last time. He did so without looking, content in the belief he would never see the boy again and this, in fact, was the case.

He read Drew's final entry that night. It was the same entry Kendra had read earlier that day, as she'd searched for Fletcher's pills. He sat with the book on his lap for some time when he had finished, as the light failed, as the cold crept through the broken windows of the old van. At last, he wrapped himself in a sleeping bag and lay down, exhausted, ready to sleep, but he continued to think. He thought of the diver's knife Drew had worn strapped to his leg on the final morning. In light of the entry, its purpose seemed clear. The boy Bean Dip had only done what Drew himself would have done in time. He had called the shark. And Drew Harmon had gone out, still a legend, taken by a shark at a mysto spot of great secrecy, and no one would ever know about the girl with the crappy trailer, in a little California town with the unlikely name of Sweet

Home. And maybe, with luck, and with time, the girl he had married and brought to Sweet Home would remember him as he was and not for the thing he had become. In time, he would learn that Deputy Lemon had been found, somewhat the worse for wear, by one Art the Red Man Hancock, handcuffed to a tree near the campgrounds at Neah Heads, and this, Fletcher concluded, lent a certain credence to his theory. It was a fantasy bolstered as well by the simple tableau he'd witnessed in the old sweat lodge above the bluffs. Though, in the end, he supposed, it was really a matter of hope.

Fletcher spent the following night in the parking lot of the photo lab in Eureka where they had promised him the slides in twenty-four hours. He viewed them the next day, in the waiting room, holding them up to the overhead light to look through the loupe he carried in his gear. In time, his arms began to tire, his neck to cramp, but he could not quite bring himself to put them down.

The centerpiece was really something quite special, one of his best. A cover shot if ever he had seen one. It featured Robbie Jones in a doomed yet clearly heroic position, too high and too late on what had to be a thirty-foot face. The wave was bright and well-lit with the sky dark and ominous behind it, a truly rare shot, but powerful—as if lit in a studio. One could see the yellow rails of the Brewer gun and the red stripes of the surfer's wet suit reflected on the water. The wave itself looked immense in the dramatic lighting, already beginning to pitch, the face to go hollow, as if what lurked in the pit was nothing less than a hole in time. You stared at it long enough, you could feel the drop in the center of your chest, and Fletcher saw it for just what it was. Most likely, the largest cold-water wave ever ridden. The only verifiable shot of Heart Attacks, the premier mysto surf spot of the Pacific Northwest, in epic conditions, a rider up. The thing he had come for.

44

When the cop left Kendra at the cemetery, he had told her to wait, but Kendra had no intention of doing so. She had read Drew's entry. She had seen him taken. She supposed it would have been to his liking. She guessed the photographer was still down there. She supposed he would want to see her. She, on the other hand, felt herself done, at least for the present, with the company of men. As she went up through the grass, she passed the boy one more time. The cop had cuffed him, ankle to wrist. He was on his side in the grass, his back to her, and it had occurred to her that she could cut his lifeline big-time if she wanted to. In the end, she thought better of it. He would live or he would die. He was nothing to her.

On her way to the upper trail head, she passed a Jeep she took for the fat cop's. The sight spurred her on. For it was her intention to reach the truck before anyone else could get to her, which is what she did. She rested for a short time here, dizzy from her labors, seeking to catch her breath. When she had managed this, she jumped into the truck and drove away. She did so without looking back. She held to the ragged washboard road and came in time to a fork. One way bent southeast and she believed it to be the way she had come with Jack Fletcher. The other turned toward the north and this was the way she chose. She followed its torturous uphill path for perhaps an hour before the truck ran out of gas. When this happened, she got out and walked. She had no idea where she was going or why. She walked for some time before noticing she'd left the big sandals in the car, that her feet were becoming cut and dirty. When she looked back, however, the truck was already gone, lost around some curve. She elected to go on. She was more than half-looped on the photographer's pills. They were quite something. But then she had been the better part of two days without food. It was, she imagined, some combination thereof which accounted for her state of mind, for the fact that the road was insistent upon playing tricks beneath her feet, for the fickle nature of the sun.

In time, she heard something coming. She was still stumbling onward, barely, at this point, able to see. She supposed there was something one should do, some measure that ought to be taken. What was the photographer's line? The course of prudent behavior. On the other hand, she had come to think of this particular road as hers. There was the next step, and the one after, and that was all, and so she continued in this fashion until at the apex of some unnamed hill she came face-to-face with the thing itself.

It seemed to stand shimmering before her as might some distant object glimpsed in a desert landscape, the illusory progeny of heat and light. As she blinked the sweat from her eyes, it became clear to her that the thing was a house car of absurd proportions, tall and thin—a cereal box stood on one side and set to wheels—and that she and this object were alone, facing each other on a dirt logging road, waiting, it appeared, to see who might be the first to grant right of way.

Once more, she supposed, one ought to be afraid, but she had gotten beyond that. She stood her ground, wrapped in the pale winter light that filtered down among the trees. She seemed to have become engaged in a stand-off with the first Winnebago, reduced by time to little more than oxidation and rust.

Eventually, she became aware of a face peering down on her from behind a mud-streaked window, and she started when she saw it, for the face was long and thin, framed by graying hair. Her first impulse was to believe that she had proven too weak to cast a spell, that it had all come back on her in the person of William Longtree, risen from the rocks. At which time, the driver leaned from a side window and she saw that, in fact, the car was driven by a woman, and, for a moment, these two women regarded one another in the autumnal light, the one leaning from the window, the other positioned in the muddy road as if she were the wife of Lot, effigated in salt at the edge of the city.

"You don't look so good," the driver said at length.

Kendra put the back of her wrist to her head.

"Come on," the woman told her. "You can get in. It's okay."

Kendra moved for the first time after that. She went to a door on the side of the car and pulled it open. She did so without hesitation. She was done, she thought. The woman would aid her or feed her to the fish. Her fate had been cast.

The woman showed her to a narrow bed at the rear of the car. She covered her with a blanket. "You'll be okay," the woman told her. "I know what to do."

Kendra nodded. She watched as the woman returned to the wheel of the car. The woman was dressed like a man, in jeans and suspenders, a red bandanna about her neck. Kendra looked around her. She found herself surrounded by plaster hens and gaily painted teapots. These set side by side with taxidermied birds and quilted blankets of great intricacy. In one corner, there hung a coat made of monkey hair, and this was set upon a kind of wicker mannequin above whose featureless face there perched an elaborate red felt hat decorated with a huge emerald pin and about whose straw neck had been balanced a plastic samurai sword in a glittering plastic sheath.

She wondered at what these things might mean, and at where they were going, but she was too tired to discuss it. They were going somewhere and that was good enough. She rested in the belief that, in time, everything would be revealed.

•   •   •

When next Kendra opened her eyes, she saw that they had arrived in some town. The sky was blue and streaked with cloud. The air was hot and dry and she knew they were a long way from the coast. She could hear cars but she did not immediately sit up to look out the window. She was quite content to stay where she was, wrapped in the blanket. It was as if she belonged here, among these painted pots and stuffed birds. Everyone must have some niche in the world and it occurred to her that she had come, at last, to hers.

In time, however, the woman stopped the car. She turned in the seat and looked back at Kendra Harmon. "We're here," she said. "You made it."

Kendra righted herself on the narrow bed. "Where's here?" she asked.

"It's okay," the woman told her. "I know. I came here myself once."

"You're Tolowan," Kendra said.

The woman nodded.

"From the coast."

"You'll be okay."

The woman came and got her now. It was only when she tried to stand that she discovered how weak she was.

"That's a girl," the woman said.

Kendra leaned on her arm. They stepped outside and into the light.

There was a building before them. Concrete steps led toward a glass door upon which had been stenciled a name: Casa de Madre.

"This is a good place," the woman said. And they went up the steps and into the building.

45

A memorial service was held for Drew Harmon at the end of
that month. It was sparsely attended. Michael Peters drove up.
He had Robbie Jones with him. To Fletcher's lasting amazement, he
was pleased to see them. It meant that Drew would be laid to rest in
accordance with the tradition of his tribe.

There were no ceremonies on land. They rode in Michael
Peters's Grand Cherokee along the old logging road that ended at
the trail head above the cemetery. From there, they hiked out to the
cove where Drew had died. As no body had ever been recovered,
they took leis flown in from the islands and paddled with them out
onto the water of the bay.

There were four of them present that day. Jack Fletcher, Michael
Peters, Robbie Jones, and a local kid Drew had on occasion surfed
with at the cove near town. The men donned wet suits on the
beach, then paddled out to the spot where Drew was last seen. The
Devil's Hoof was to the south of them here, a barren outcropping of

stone extended into the sea—the westernmost tip of the western-most point of land the coast of California had to offer. Above them were the cliffs and the lonely grasslands where the Tolowans had come to bury their dead. Fletcher reckoned them at close to a half a mile out.

There was no swell to speak of that day though a wind chop moved the surface of the water and small whitecapped waves buffeted them as they joined hands in a small circle. Words were spoken. Hands were raised overhead, arms outstretched. They might have been the tribesmen of some lost people in performance of a ritual none could now name. The hands were parted, the leis cast upon the water. They watched as the flowers drifted upon the current, bobbing among the whitecaps until finally they were lost from sight. When it was done, they paddled in. They hiked with the aid of flashlights back along the trail to the road and, from there, they returned to town.

Fletcher showed them the slides that night. He and Michael Peters and Robbie Jones, seated in a booth at the local Denny's restaurant, for the two men intended to drive back without further delay.

Peters sat for some time in the Naugahyde booth, the loupe held to an overhead light. "Goddamn," he said. "I can't quit looking at it." Eventually, however, his arms got tired and he passed it to Robbie Jones. "That a cover shot or isn't it?"

Robbie raised the loupe, squinting at it for a long time, turning it to different angles. "Rad," he said after a good while. He passed it back to Peters, then looked at Jack Fletcher. "It's a rad shot," he said. "I didn't think you got it. But you did."

"O'Neil's gonna want this too," Peters said. "You know that. You may make some money on this one, Doc."

Fletcher shrugged.

Peters was silent for some time. "I don't suppose," he said at length, "you got anything of Drew Harmon, on that last day."

"There was nothing to get," Fletcher told them. "Nothing past the point. These were the biggest waves we found, right here."

"Heart Attacks?"

Fletcher looked at the slides. "Why not?" he said. He looked at Robbie Jones. The young man's hair had grown into a shaggy butch.

"Why not?" Robbie Jones said.

Peters looked at the two of them. He nodded and sighed, then picked up the loupe one more time, holding it to the light. "I gotta tell ya, Doc. I've been looking at surf shots a long time. And this is one of the best. They're going to be talking about this one for a long time." He lowered the slide then turned to Fletcher. "Why don't you ride back with us?" he asked.

"You go on," Fletcher told him.

The man just looked at him.

"I got something to do," Fletcher said.

"In Sweet Home?"

"Why not?"

Michael Peters looked around him. "You got to talk to O'Neil," he said.

"You talk to him."

Peters just shook his head. There were trucks and cars lining up in the parking lot and the restaurant was filling up with customers. Fletcher took them for the night crew from Scorpion Bay, for they seemed a drab and colorless lot, eager to wash away one more shift among the cold gray walls of stone, happy to sit now in the blood-red booths, some of them even old enough to trot out a story or two of how it had been in the old days, when there were still trees to fell and lumber to mill and fish to catch.

Peters was silent, considering his surroundings once more. At last he turned to Fletcher. "You're a strange one, Doc. You know that?"

"T'was always so."

Peters just laughed at him, then he grew serious. "Let me ask you something, Doc. There's this local kid they busted out there on the Heads. Did this guy shoot Harmon or didn't he? I can't get shit from that fat-assed police chief. What's it gonna be, Doc?"

"For the record?"

"We gotta print something."

Fletcher was some time in replying. He was aware of Robbie Jones watching him from across the booth. A truck rumbled past up on the interstate and it seemed to Fletcher as if the cold wind of its passing might be felt among the shadowed booths. There was a sudden chill upon his spine, a whisper that might have been the wind, or perhaps the voice of a hanged Indian, gone to his grave not knowing, or maybe that of a young, dark-eyed girl he would never know more of than a name. Or maybe, he thought, it was the two of them together, asking only that truth be told, and he was set upon by a momentary urge to oblige, followed by the rather hollow realization that he would not. In the end, it was for an old friend that he spoke, playing what he took to be his part in such things to the end. "A shark took him," he said at length. "In big surf, at a mysto secret spot in the heart of the red triangle. That's your story."

"Yours too?" Peters asked him.

Fletcher sat a moment longer in the booth, but already the chill had begun to fade, the voices to slink away, until there was only the hum of passing cars, the wind heard through an opening door.

Fletcher shrugged. "Mine too."

"Well," Peters said, "it's a good story."

When they had paid their bill, they walked outside. The night had cooled considerably and a wind could be felt blowing up from the ocean beyond the town.

"Let me set something straight right now," Peters said. They had come to the side of his Jeep. "I know you, Doc. I don't believe you didn't get pictures of that last session. And I think one of these days, you're going to want to sell 'em. When that day comes, I want you to remember who bankrolled this trip."

Fletcher smiled at him. "You know what the Indians called the big point out there where we said good-bye to Drew? Humaliwu. It means the place where legends die. How do you like that?"

Peters gave it a moment's thought. "That's too much," he said. Then he thought about it some more. "Besides, Drew didn't really die there. We were a ways north of that."

Fletcher shrugged.

Peters was still thinking. Fletcher could see the gears at work beneath that balding crown. "Sounds good, though, doesn't it?"

"You've got your picture," Fletcher said. "You've got your story. A good title is always nice."

Peters smiled. "Yes, it is," he said. "And you won't forget what I said about those pictures."

"The ones I didn't get."

"Yeah, those."

"I won't forget," Fletcher told him. The two men shook hands. After that, Fletcher shook hands with Robbie Jones. The kid looked like he was of a mind to say more, but seemed to be having a hard time getting it to come. But then words had never been the boy's strong suit.

"I'm glad you came," Fletcher told him. "I think Drew would have been glad too."

The kid looked at him. "You think so?" The idea seemed to please him.

"I do," Fletcher said.

Robbie nodded and got into the Jeep.

"You want a ride, at least?" Peters asked him. "Back to wherever it is you're staying?"

Fletcher declined. He saw them off. He saw them onto the interstate where their taillights joined the graveyard shift to Scorpion Bay, then turned and went on foot back into the town of Sweet Home.

Travis attended the funeral of Drew Harmon on crutches. The man, after all, had saved his life. He did not join in with the surfers or even ride out to the Heads in their Jeep, but went alone, by way of another logging road to a point further north of the trail used by the surfers, and came there to a high place which afforded him a partial view of both the cemetery and the bay at the foot of the cliffs. He was in no condition for hiking and he'd brought with him a powerful pair of binoculars with which he might watch at least part of what transpired below.

His father had been right. The holy man had been wrong. He would not participate in the Jump Dance. His leg prevented it. He had nearly lost the thing. The nurse, it seems, had done a poor job of cleaning it. No one had bothered to check it further at Sweet Home. He'd reached Eureka with a temperature of 104, been promptly packed in ice and rushed to surgery where a doctor scraped then pinned his bones. He had always fancied himself light on his feet and did not like to think about how things would have gone had the leg been lost.

He thought about it nonetheless. He thought about it as he stood in the wind and watched the gray ocean beyond the cliffs. In time, the surfers paddled into his view. He could not see them clearly enough to name them, but he knew Jack Fletcher to be among them. Travis found that he was jealous of the man. He'd had time with Kendra Harmon and she had not been heard from since. She had vanished was all, gone from the forests of Sweet Home.

He watched as the surfers joined hands, forming a small ragged circle in the cold gray water. He saw them cast what he knew to be flowers upon the water, though from the distance at which he watched he could not have identified them as such had not someone told him beforehand. After that, he saw them join hands and raise their arms over their heads. It was a primitive little scene, like something his ancestors might have done, had they boards to carry them past the surf line. And yet, the ritual only served to fuel his sense of futility and displacement.

The feelings had been quite strong of late. That he had been fooled by the Indians at Moke's still rankled, and with the capture of Bean Dip, he had learned of what had gone down with Kendra and he had cursed his ineptitude. He should have seen the Hupa from upriver for what he was. He should have taken steps. He'd gotten stoned instead and danced like a fool around a dead elk. When he had gone to warn the surfers, he had managed only to break his leg and strand himself on the rocks. If it had not been for Drew Harmon, he would have died there, which did not strike him as altogether inappropriate.

Travis watched as the surfers finished with their ceremony and paddled once more from his sight. He lowered his binoculars then, allowing them to hang from his neck. But he remained on the promontory at which his drive had ended. For the wind had held the fog at bay and the evening was clear, the darkening sky strewn with stars, and he stood beneath this immensity, propped upon his crutches as if he were no more than a sad scarecrow erected as an afterthought to some crop that had failed even before he was made.

A man should have something, he thought, some thread to the earth, lest he lose even the ground beneath his feet.

It was with this in mind that, in three weeks' time, Travis made the long trek upriver to the crossroads known as Soam's Bar, where a winding forest road took him deep into the woods and finally to a second road marked only by a cardboard sign nailed to a tree. The words "Jump Dance" had been written on the sign with a felt marker, and beneath these, an arrow pointed down the road which was steep and unpaved. Travis did not want to attempt it without four-wheel drive. He'd brought his son with him, and together, they loaded their packs and waited at the side of the road until an old Indian couple in an ancient Toyota Land Cruiser offered them a ride and so came in time to the camp of the Hupa.

The camps were divided according to family. Each clan leader, or fire builder, had his own camp. Travis's cousin, Frank, was one of the fire builders, and Travis and his son made camp there. The ritual was to last ten days. It was an arduous affair. The fire builders danced only after the sun went down. They danced barefoot around a fire in the woods some ways from the camps, and as the land was sacred, the people went barefoot as well, climbing a steep trail in the dead of night to watch the dancers.

After two days of sleeping on the ground and going barefoot in the woods, Travis was beginning to feel like one of the blood runners in Frank's story. He was covered with bites and rashes. His leg was killing him. He might have persevered but his son was worse off than he and begging to be gone, and so it was that on the fourth day, he threw in the towel and hitched a ride out of the encampment with a Hupa from Seattle who had gotten to the fires by way of a four-wheel-drive Range Rover with a wooden console and leather seats. Travis saw the whole thing as an admission of defeat.

The man with the Range Rover took them to their truck. From there, they drove to the nearest town where they showered and doused themselves with calamine lotion. Travis allowed his son to go first. He went next, and when he came out of the bathroom to dress, he found his son had turned on the television set. The boy was seated on the edge of the bed in his underwear, engrossed in a rerun of *The Munsters*.

The sight depressed him further. He had hoped to start something here. He had hoped to show something of the old ways and of the values which accompanied them to his son. But, in fact, he had known little about the dance himself and now here they were, holed up in a cheap motel room while Herman Munster cavorted on a miniature screen and cars whizzed past along the interstate.

Travis turned off the television, and, after dressing, they drove to town. They ordered burgers and fries and chocolate shakes. Travis watched as his son poured catsup on his french fries. They ate in near silence, surrounded by photographs of loggers and miners and other industrious sorts who had participated in the destruction of the very thing his people had come to celebrate, and still were, somewhere up the big river.

He was feeling quite low as they left the restaurant and walked out into the parking lot and the last light, and it was here he saw something which stopped him in his tracks.

What he saw was the photographer, Jack Fletcher. The man was dressed in jeans and hiking boots and a flannel shirt. His hair had grown long enough to wear in a ponytail. He was still driving the old Dodge van. Travis could see the tires were new, but the windows were still broken out of the back. When Travis called to him, he turned, then walked to meet him.

"What's the matter?" Travis asked him. "You lost?"

Fletcher smiled. He looked relatively well, Travis thought, although he was limping a bit, as if perhaps his back had stiffened up on him.

"I live here now," Fletcher told him.

"No way."

Fletcher nodded. "Not here exactly. Just north of the border. I'm on a river there."

A moment passed between them. In fact, Travis supposed, there was not really much to say.

"Funny I should see you here," Fletcher said. "I was in your office the other day. But the girl said you were out."

"Yeah," Travis said. "I was here." At which time, he thought to introduce his son. Fletcher shook the boy's hand, then looked at Travis once more.

"You remember that conversation we had once? You told me about the custom of making recompense . . ."

Travis remembered.

"I was wondering," Fletcher said, "if you knew much about David Little's family."

"That's why you were in the office?"

Fletcher nodded.

"What about them?"

"I guess I was wondering if you might know if there was something they needed. Something specific. A new boat. A car. Maybe there are other kids. Maybe they need something for school."

"I don't know. It's been a while since I've talked to them."

"But you could find out?"

Travis shrugged. "What is it? Your magazine come through with some money after all?"

"I don't have a magazine," Fletcher told him. "This would be strictly between me and them. But I would need a go-between. I can't just head out there and start asking around."

Travis looked at him a long moment. "A car?" he said. "A boat? Might run you into some money."

"I think we can work something out."

Travis nodded. He looked to the mountains. They were blue in the afternoon light. "You ever hear anything from Kendra Harmon?" he asked.

The other man was a moment in replying. "No," he said at length. "Have you?"

Travis shook his head.

"What I don't get is how she ever got away from those men. The Hupa was a bad one."

"I wouldn't know," Fletcher said. "I found her sitting on a little bridge on the floor of this valley."

"I know the place," Travis told him. "There was an old woman used to live there. She was suppose to be a healer. She could see things as well. If someone thought a *hee-dee* had put a curse on them, she was the kind of person they would go to. She could see if someone had put something on you."

"What's a *hee-dee?*" Fletcher asked him.

353

"A sorcerer. Something like that. My old man always called them *hee-dees*."

Fletcher nodded.

"The old lady died, maybe a year back. Last I heard, some cousin of hers was down there. Everybody figured he was growing weed. Blacklage was in there a week or two after you were. Said the old place had burned to the ground. There was no sign of anybody around. Only thing he could find to suggest someone had even been there after Rose Hudson was a new well pump. Guess you didn't see anything."

"Just Kendra."

Travis nodded. "Well pump would suggest the stories about the cousin may have been right. I mean you're gonna grow the shit, you got to water it."

"I suppose so," Fletcher said.

Travis looked hard at the man before him. The man looked back, an even gaze. A light wind was kicking down upon them now, out of the canyon and, at his side, he sensed his son, eager to be gone.

"So, how do you want me to get hold of you, I talk to the family?"

"I'll be in touch," Fletcher told him.

Travis nodded. The two men looked at one another again. At length, Travis held out his hand. Jack Fletcher took it, and Travis could feel the blisters on the other man's hand, not yet gone to calluses.

Travis got into his truck with his son. He watched as Jack Fletcher went up the steps and into the restaurant whose entrance was marked by a carved eight-foot statue of Big Foot, the beast.

"Who was that?" Jason asked him.

Travis continued to watch the restaurant. "Some guy," he said. And he looked at his son. "But I think he's okay."

His son nodded.

Travis felt himself smile. It seemed to him that he had not done so in some time. He started the truck and turned from the lot.

"You going to come back up here next year?" his son asked.

Travis was surprised by the question, but then his children were like that, he had found. He could not always tell what they were thinking and they often saw more than he thought they had. "You think we should?" he asked.

The boy looked thoughtfully out the window. "What did it mean," he asked, "when the fire builders held those baskets above their heads?"

"The basket is supposed to be the family. When the fire builder holds it above his head, that means he places the needs of the family above his own." Travis looked at his boy. "And then did you see what he did with it?"

The boy shook his head.

"He brought it down," Travis said. He made a motion with his own hand in the cab of the truck. He held it in front of his groin. "That was to show he placed the good of the family before his male drive."

"I don't get it," his son said.

"You will."

Travis felt somewhat pleased with himself, though, in fact, that was about all he knew of what they had seen. The rest of it was still a mystery to him.

"Will you dance?" his son asked him. "If we come back? If your leg is better?"

Travis looked across the hood toward the line of blue mountains. "I don't know," he said. "I might. I can buy enough bug spray."

The boy laughed. Travis laughed as well, for the fact of the matter was, he had been set upon by the sudden notion that indeed he would be back. He would persevere. He could not say with certainty where any of this would lead. Nor would he venture a guess as to whether or not the Jump Dance of the Hupa might have some function in the economy of the universe, as his cousin would no doubt assert. All he knew was that he would be back. He would take his place among the dancers.

47

Kendra Harmon spent some time with the women of Casa de Madre. For the Tolowan woman had brought her to a center for battered women in the town of Redding, some two hundred miles from the coast. It was not a bad call. And indeed, they were nice to her there, though she felt under no obligation to talk, as if she had taken some vow of silence unbeknownst even to herself.

She was seen by a doctor. The woman prescribed pills, which was to her liking, as the pills provided her with a place to hide. There were times when she thought of the Hupa, reliving what had transpired in the valley. The mystery was that the man who had taken her had saved her as well. He had killed the dogs, in rapid succession. A shot apiece, or so it had seemed. At which point, he had turned his attention to the men. The last thing she saw, before going into a full-on duck-and-cover routine, was the man in the T-shirt and boxer shorts. He was already going down—

a huge red stain blossoming across his shorts—but firing madly with the automatic weapon. She had felt the bullets in the air. When next she looked, however, everything was dead. Everything except her and the chicken, and she would never know about the Hupa, if he had really thought to save her, or simply reckoned his chances better at making a stand than at making a run, or how a man might act who believed his lifeline to have been cut. But then, she supposed, the actions of all men were beyond her. This went for Drew as well. In the end, she had offered him a life. Her offer had not been without its terms. She had offered herself, in Sweet Home, and all that that implied. He had turned her down. Sometimes, when she saw him now, it was on the beach at Hatteras, on the day of the contest. He was something else that day, fit and powerful. But when she had congratulated him on winning, he had only laughed and said it was a legends event. And when she had asked him what that meant, he had told her it was a contest for guys who used to be somebody.

Days passed. She could not have told you how many. On a particular afternoon, however, she felt moved to speak. She had been lying in bed. It was a position from which she was afforded a view of the small courtyard around which the rooms had been arranged. There were flowers there, a couple of dwarf orange trees come to blossom. She heard two women talking somewhere behind her.

One of the women was newly arrived. She had been badly beaten. She was speaking with another woman and they were talking about the men who had abused them.

Kendra listened for some time. At last, she rose from her bed and walked over to where they sat, on an old couch near a coffee table with magazines on it. The women looked up at her approach.

"I can tell you what to do," Kendra said.

The women looked at her. She might have been a ghost to their eyes, so pale and wan did she appear, a mere wisp of a thing in the winter light.

"You have to show them something," Kendra said. "You have to show them your magic is stronger than theirs."

At which point, she made a motion in the air, as if she were collecting something that she then folded and placed beneath her breast, her hands held now in the shape of a triangle, as if they were themselves that thing she had so collected. "They'll never find it here," she told them. And she smiled.

48

In the months that followed, Jack Fletcher's photograph appeared on the cover of Michael Peters's magazine. It appeared in several newspapers and in one New York publication as well, often in such places linked to the drowning of Drew Harmon, a big-wave legend who lost his life to a shark in huge surf at a remote spot in the Pacific Northwest, achieving with his passing a notoriety he had not enjoyed since his emergence as a young lion on the North Shore of Oahu.

O'Neil Wet Suits purchased rights, as Robbie Jones was one of their team riders, and the photograph was reprinted throughout the world. In time, you could find it on posters from California to Japan. Kids Jack Fletcher would never know hung it on their walls, and they knew the name of the spot and the name of the rider. Some even knew the name of the man who had taken the picture as well. But the name of Jack Fletcher appeared on no more mast-heads and his photographs were not seen in the surfing magazines, or any other, ever again. Nor did he, as Michael Peters had predicted he would, ever admit to having, or express an interest in selling any photographs of Drew Harmon on his last go out at a remote spot many a rumor held to have been the real Heart Attacks.

With the passing of time, Jack Fletcher himself became a more difficult man to find. Members of the surfing community would sometimes wonder what had become of him, and, in time, his name was often mentioned in connection with the likes of Drew Harmon. Because surfers loved their stories. Big waves and outlaws. Eccentrics who had managed somehow to beat the system, to stay in the life when others moved inland and paid taxes.

It was rumored that Jack Fletcher had stayed up north. It was said he bought land there, a choice piece with difficult access and a view to the sea. No one was quite sure where the money had come from. They figured the photograph probably made him some, but not that much.

As for Travis McCade, he never asked where the money came from, but then again, he never had to, though it did puzzle him as to how that particular crop had been grown up there in the little river valley, as neither he nor Blacklage could ever find any evidence that the land around the old sight had been in any way tilled or disturbed. It took some BIA agents and a bust upriver to show him the light.

"Damndest thing," Blacklage told Travis, for he was still in Sweet Home and he'd dropped by to talk about it. "The guy had filled these big burlap bags with sod and weed and hoisted 'em up into the branches of a bunch of scrub oak. Practically invisible."

Travis had given this some thought. "Kind of like that grove of oak up there by Rose Hudson's old place," he had said. And the two men had looked at each other, and laughed. And that was the end of it. And nothing was ever said about it again, either by Travis or by the Chief of the Tribal Police. For the important part was that Jack Fletcher was proving to be a man of his word—the Little family having, by that date, received in recompense for the accidental death of their son, a new Boston Whaler. In addition to which their daughter attended a beauty college in Eureka, eventually opening a salon on the lower Elwa, which, in fact, did quite well. The monies for these things had arrived in monthly installments. They were paid in cash, dropped on the first Monday of each month in an unmarked envelope at the Office for Indian Affairs in Sweet Home and passed on to the Little family by the office's director, Travis McCade.

Jack Fletcher's daughter remained in Huntington Beach, though in time the girl began to travel. By bus at first, later in her own car. Though sworn to secrecy with respect to the local surf crew, it was well known she would go north, and of these trips, she would say only that her father was able to show her wonderful things. For, in fact, he was able to take her to places like Witch's Rock, where one might camp amid the little stand of trees that grew there and, at certain times of the year, when the wind was from upriver, observe the stars as they plummeted into the icy Pacific. He took her to the ancient ceremonial grounds north of Neah Heads and to other even more remote places as well. He did these things without losing his way or without incident, as he had come to know the place like the back of his hand and was known himself to the locals. It was said by them that he had made recompense in accordance with the old ways, and they let him be, though some thought him a little strange as he was also known to walk the river alone at night.

Still, it seemed to his daughter that he was reasonably content there. He had his place and his trails, and come the winter, he would stalk the hills with his camera in a waterproof housing and he would shoot the waves.

He liked them hollow, empty and perfect. The few who saw them said they were like jewels. They said as well that he declined all offers to sell. They said his interest was with the waves and that he harbored little for those who rode them. They said too that many of the shots were taken in some remote place none could name—a great bay ringed by granite cliffs where a cloud break of indecent proportions broke upon an outside reef. They said a goodly number of these pictures had been shot from the water, and that having been so shot, gave evidence of a barrel big enough to build a house in and through which one might see cliffs capped by stands of old growth timber. But as to the whereabouts of this place, the artist remained quite mute, saying only that it was there for those who looked.

As for Fletcher himself, the waves were only a part of the thing that held him to the woods. For a woman with whom he had once become acquainted had expressed an interest in making her own living from these same woods and it was his hope that, in time, their steps might cross once more. It was his hope that these things were so ordered, though there was little foundation for this hope save hope itself. But then, he had come to the belief that all things were so ordered, from the steps a man took in time, to the tracks of a storm, the likes of which came with the season, exchanging their energies with that of a frigid and turbulent sea, and thereby raising waves as if they were themselves some variation on God's erring Wisdom and so able to labor their passion into matter.

NOTES

The paragraph on top of page 27 from Fletcher's *A Wave Hunter's Guide to the Golden State* is drawn from Mikol Moon's May 1993 *Surfing* article "Big Flat."

Kendra's description of the salt water purification ritual on page 63 is drawn from *The Spiritual Dance* by Miriam Simos (Starhawk).

Duane's description of a surfer getting bitten which appears at the bottom of page 175 is drawn from Michael Angeli's July 1992 *Esquire* article "Beach Culture."

Drew's description of the boards he found at the Bishop Museum which appears on page 180 is drawn from Sam George's October 1994 *Surfer* article "A Tribute to Tom Blake."

Kendra's mantra at the bottom of page 109 is drawn from Margot Adler's *Drawing Down the Moon*.

Drew's description of shark babies as predators from the bottom of page 214 to the top of page 215 is drawn from Elias J. Swift's October 1993 *Surfer* article "White Sharks *Can* Jump."

Kendra's *Spirita sancta* mantra which appears at the bottom of page 219 is drawn from Barbara Starrett's poem "I.D." from *Drawing Down the Moon* by Margot Adler.